SMILE PLEASE

Jonathan Keates is the author of a novel, *The Strangers' Gallery*, two collections of short stories, *Allegro Postillions* and *Soon to be a Major Motion Picture,* and acclaimed biographies of Handel, Purcell and Stendhal. He is a Fellow of the Royal Society of Literature and lives in London.

ALSO BY JONATHAN KEATES

Fiction

Allegro Postillions
The Strangers' Gallery
Soon to be a Major Motion Picture

Non-Fiction

Handel: The Man and His Music
Stendhal: A Biography
Purcell: A Biography
Tuscany
Umbria
Italian Journeys

Jonathan Keates

SMILE PLEASE

VINTAGE

Published by Vintage 2001

4 6 8 10 9 7 5

First published in Great Britain by
Chatto & Windus 2000

Vintage
Random House, 20 Vauxhall Bridge Road,
London SW1V 2SA

Random House Australia (Pty) Limited
20 Alfred Street, Milsons Point, Sydney
New South Wales 2061, Australia

Random House New Zealand Limited
18 Poland Road, Glenfield,
Auckland 10, New Zealand

Random House (Pty) Limited
Endulini, 5A Jubilee Road, Parktown 2193,
South Africa

The Random House Group Limited Reg. No. 954009
www.randomhouse.co.uk

A CIP catalogue record for this book
is available from the British Library

ISBN 0 09 928516 9

Papers used by Random House are natural, recyclable products made from wood grown in sustainable forests. The manufacturing processes conform to the environmental regulations of the country of origin

Printed and bound in Great Britain by
Bookcraft, Bath

To James Loader

I

BESIDE the bar stood the bald Byzantinist from County Down who had recommended him to read the poems of Romanus the Melode. They'd met at the Anvil over a year ago. Later Adam wondered whether anything more than mere curiosity had made him look up Romanus and his works during a desultory half-hour in the London Library spent dodging a cloudburst. There were no available translations, and since Greek was not even among the languages he claimed to speak, as opposed to those in which he was genuinely fluent, he had to take the Melode's claims to greatness as he found them.

Scholars couldn't agree on the exact century of the poet's birth. That the Byzantines had made him a saint seemed therefore like a compensation, as if they had known what problems, what crises of identity, must await Romanus twelve or thirteen hundred years after his death. Adam knew a little about Byzantine saints. You came across them tucked under church altars in Venice, loot from Constantinople or the islands, their incorrupt bodies, with mottled, corky flesh and talons for hands, got up in nylon doilies and cake frills, lying inside glass tanks with silver mountings stamped 'I H S', a sacred heart and a name in Latin. Furtively he'd pray to them and drop a few coins into the alms box because it was better to have them on the team than not.

Byzantium held no romance for Adam. It was the last place he'd ever have wanted to sail to, even across the most gong-tormented seas of his imagination. There was something implausible in other people's enthusiasm for it, a culture which had disappeared up its own arsehole for a thousand years until one day the Sultan of Turkey, with commendable impatience, stuck in a finger, pulled the whole thing out and dumped it on the scrapheap, so that scholars and modern Greeks might whinge for the rest of creation about what a wondrous thing had perished in flames and slaughter. Adam sometimes wished he had been there to light the odd fire or eviscerate the occasional logothete. He didn't communicate the heterodox views to the Melode's admirer from Newtonards. Touched with a residual snobbery, like every gay man he'd ever met, he narrowly stopped himself wondering aloud what the other guy had been doing dreaming amid the pages of Runciman and Obolensky when he might have been banging a lambeg in Drumcree, or asking for a verse of two of 'The Sash My Father Wore'.

Between sinking pints and talking about Romanus they'd done sex in the curtained alcove behind the bar. That was the thing about the Anvil, that the people you met there had lives and perspectives and opinions, and were not so totally off their faces that you couldn't snatch between you the occasional *kunstpause* to discuss early Antonioni or the Shostakovich cello sonata without feeling guilty that it wasn't something suitably post-ironic like Karen Carpenter or *Mommy Dearest* instead. Perhaps this was the real reason why the place had closed down. Arriving too late for the final thrash, when a thousand queens drank the cellar dry, Adam thought he detected a kind of triumph in the faces of those queuing hopefully along the pavement in the March evening. Their smiles proclaimed the successful defeat of rational discourse. No country for old men, this one. Crossly Adam turned for home, feeling suddenly preposterous in his blue combat pants and growing still more embarrassed when, on the tube, his zip kept sliding open under pressure from the belt drawn too tightly around a spreading *embonpoint*.

Tonight, somewhere in Bermondsey, he wouldn't go and talk to the Byzantinist. For one thing there was the conviction he was at no special pains to dislodge that men who show too much interest in you to start off with are the ones who most emphatically cold-shoulder you when you meet them somewhere else. Another more purely practical consideration was the noise from the sound-systems, too loud for either of them to have heard each other. Adam was concerned just at this moment, in any case, with getting hold of some popper to replace the bottle someone had prigged off him at the Holloway Road sauna during a clusterfuck in the steam-room. At a moment of regulatory hysteria during the death throes of the previous government, a ban had been clapped on amyl nitrate in the name of public safety, and thenceforward most of the stuff you got sold across the bar in clubs was little better than a placebo, a mixture of boot polish and vinegar. Since for Adam, however, peripatetic sex was mere vanilla without some sort of rush, the presence of the little sepia glass flask in the spanner pocket of his fatigues must always furnish a comforting sense of still unexplored possibilities. He knew, besides, that this place was one of the few in London to maintain supplies of the genuine article, as if it had been an Old Constantia or Brunello di Montalcino of unimagined maturity, and half-expected the barboy who took his money, a smooth-pated weasel with pierced eyebrows and scapular tattooing, to discourse knowledgeably on fermentation, bottling and bouquet.

With academic detachment he glanced at his watch. The fashion, which this evening he'd chosen to ignore, insisted on arrival after midnight, with an accompanying air of having somewhere better to go to afterwards. At the end of the corridor, its blotches of shadow nursing solitary drinkers slouched against the wall like the remains of some guard of honour drugged by conspirators, he could see the incoming punters unbracing themselves in front of the bored cloakroom attendant and settling the issue, by a process of tucking and buckling and the adoption of an appropriate facial rictus, of whom, for the next four or five hours they were going to be. In front of him, beyond a perforated screen of galvanized metal, spread the exiguous dance floor on which no one danced, except for the usual handful of airheads so up themselves as to have penetrated a dimension of narcissism even a club like this could scarcely accommodate. To either side lay areas of darkness within heavy curtains of tank camouflage netting, like giant bivouacs, in and out of which drifted questing files of the curious or purely predatory, expectantly lifting the edges of the web.

Adam had some time ago reached that dangerous threshold in the pursuit of recreational sex in which a plethora of opportunity starts thinning out sufficiently to allow the cynical intrusion of detached insights. He had begun to understand the exercise in which he and everybody else here was engaged as something poised uneasily between parody and critical apparatus. The standard text was already composed – had already been composed, rather – in order that they should each of them exist biologically. Yet all over London at this hour on a Saturday night, scores, hundreds, thousands of variants, alternative readings, annotations, glosses, exegeses and interpolations were being offered to it. Up against its terrible candour of insistent orthodoxy crowded those episodes of subversion, immense, clotted dramas of carnal engagement, veiled manoeuvres, killing performances and deathless impersonations being worked out along the route march of the night. Within a few hours the original, worn to exhaustion and irrelevance, was unscrambled into something like a palimpsest, across which could be scribbled the newest pastiches and translations, or, if there was space, those grander reworkings of passion and sensuality designed to end in love.

At thirty-five Adam was only marginally less certain of wanting a lover than he had been when aged twenty-one. An inevitable concomitant of his physical intensity during even the most casual encounter was that at some stage he should entertain an idea of the compliant partner – nearly always, to begin with, anonymous – as romantically inclined. He'd never acquired a means of shrugging off the question, insistently forming itself amid the earliest intensity of exploratory kisses, of whether this might after all be The One. To which, of course, were attached other, more obviously embarrassing questions as to what he wanted The One to be, and beyond these a question whose existence he was almost ashamed to acknowledge because its answer already seemed destined at a stroke to nullify the existence of love. For what irked Adam most, in his habitual state of self-accusation, was the simple idea that all the time, in these continuing surges of imagined possibility, the embrace he sought should be no more than that of his own shadow.

He'd begun to wonder lately whether the sheer mutuality in the engagement of lips and tongues, the very act of kissing, hadn't suddenly grown vulgar to a generation so inextricably glazed within the aspic of controlled self-absorption. Earlier that evening, soon enough after his arrival to make him suppose the episode a kind of dismal omen, a boy in a voile shirt with a dulled gaze under catatonic eyelids had pulled him into a corner and begun running hands over his chest and belly before imprecisely tilting a mean mouth towards the lower part of his face. When Adam, misinterpreting the gesture as one of mere clumsiness, started gorging on him in that way a malicious friend had once referred to as 'emergency services', the boy crossly pushed him off, not, it seemed, because of a breath soured by too much Beck's and Red Stripe, but through a flustered impatience with anything so entirely calculated to monopolize his attention.

Self-confidence withered after that. To Adam it seemed that all of a sudden none of those passing, in the ceaseless mooch and stalk among the camouflage netting or impacted knots of maleness in corners and passageways, actually looked at each other. Faces, their glum satiety enlivened only by an occasional hint of peevishness, echoed that of the boy in the voile shirt. At moments such as these, in order to fend off any more annihilating onrush of cynicism, Adam found himself strangely absorbed by a wish to know what each of them had been like as a child, at play or at school, when the whole point of this place, with its strenuous denial of perspective, its rhetoric of anonymity and disguise, was to efface the very notion of anything in their lives beyond the ruthless actualities of copping off.

Wearied by his own impassivity yet not specially eager to take his chances among the crowd, he perched himself on a ledge in a corner behind the dance floor, tucking his knees up under his chin and watching with renewed alertness the figures moving to and fro among the haphazard strobe splash. Occasionally he recognized some of them, card-indexed in that archival memory of tricks he both tormented and amused himself by revisiting. Others now and again recognized him and gave a little acknowledging grimace to show that they had done so in spite of their better judgement. It was typical of Adam that he should imagine of those who ignored him completely that they were just doing it to show off.

After a few minutes of this detached surveillance he was pardonably surprised when a tall man in green fatigues paused for a moment in drawing level, stripped off his vest, abstractedly wiped the back of his neck with it, then sat down on the broad step at Adam's feet. Leaning back on one arm, he sat looking upwards, his long, sharply drawn face charged with a doglike alertness which in this context seemed wholly incongruous. He could scarcely have been much older than twenty-five, but a sprinkling of grey around the temples conveyed, for whatever reason, implications of experience at odds with the candid innocence of his gaze. Seated thus, he reminded Adam of those figures fresco artists place *in contrapposto* at the edge of the compositions to lend a determining scale to the assembled scene. Those passing would need merely to see the shaded contours of bone and sinew in his back and shoulders to gain some just apprehension of the painter's skill in perching him on the edge of uncertainty.

Easier to think about him like this than to confront that unflinching stare, more especially when it relaxed into a smile. Not any old smile, what was more, an uncollected, all-inclusive, tab-induced grin or the icy smirk of self-absorption worn by so many who moved to and fro before them. Instead its strange, awkward, questing brilliance demanded something in return, beyond a mere acknowledgement that it shouldn't be seen either as casually instinctive or rehearsed before a mirror, in that crucial knock-'em-dead, hit-the-town moment when a six-pack appears at its most ingratiatingly contoured under the ribbed top and your bollocks feel snug inside a snowy pair of Lone Star or 2Xist. It was the smile which kept its object from falling out of the fresco on to the marble floor fifty feet below, which purposely ruined the *contrapposto* by slipping a protective arm around the shoulder even as a body began tumbling towards the ceiling edge, a smile in whose secure presumption of being irresistible lay not the least hint of vanity or arrogance. The horror it inspired in Adam pierced the marrow of his bones.

For a while he tried to shelter behind the rampart formed by gathering his knees under his chin. It occurred to him, in his mounting desperation, that if he stared back at the boy with a sufficient air of properly focused solemnity he might be let off the obligation to smile back, even briefly. The other must surely see that he was interested, but that he chose to show it by approaching from a distance, as it were, like the lope of a slow bowler, rather than in the same spirit of radiant, fearless immediacy. Yet even dodging it thus, half hidden, lurking behind his own knees, Adam felt afraid to look down into the play of light on the figure perched so expectantly beneath him, the patches of shadow across its contours shifting periodically as if the place itself were attempting to recommend to him the negligent beauty of this pose.

Again he blundered into the smile's way, less certain now than at first but still as infallibly devastating in its radiance.

Swerving to avoid it, he found his glance fixing instead on a guy in full leathers, sitting further along the ledge with the same air of fatigue and inappropriateness as he imagined himself to convey. This at least was something legitimately distracting, an excuse for not having to answer that intolerable stare with anything which seemed too obviously like an attempt to imitate it. For a miserable moment Adam held the leather guy, with his uncanonical mop of tousled black curls, his smudgy eyebrows and jutting blue chin, sternly in view. Then, in a fatal access of what-the-fuck bravado, Adam found himself simpering witlessly at the fresco extra, and knew in an instant he was to be sent hurtling out of the dome with not even a chequered pavement to break his fall.

Wearily the man got to his feet, hitched up his belt, and without so much as a shrug at Adam, turned nonchalantly in the direction of the sombre eyecatcher, whose leather blouson he began to unzip. There was no suggestion that either of them had seen each other before, but in the immediacy of their engagement Adam might not have been wrong in sensing a reproach directed squarely at him. Ordinarily he loved to be around when men kissed because of the feeling so often conveyed of something beyond mere appetite, of a clasp that momentarily held the partner from a vaguely implied perdition. Now he shrank from the sight of the pair entangled before him, from the way in which the strobe's capricious snatches suddenly enhanced the pearling of sweat across the young man's naked shoulders, from the other's exhilaration as he felt their warmth under his touch, but most of all from an inevitable glimpse, in profile now, of lips parted in a feral, triumphant smile.

Even had there been any further point in sticking around, he'd have wanted to quit the field as soon as possible. The

speakers' technoblast, a thickening reek of spilt beer, poppers
and sweat, and the onset of a certain resignation brought by
the hard hours to faces the thrill of the chase enlivened earlier,
were good enough excuses, supposing he needed them. In a
moment he had clambered to earth between the egg-bald
bouncers in their Schott jackets, and felt against his face the
night air's undiscriminating sweetness.

Briefly it seemed to Adam as if, like some escaping tunneller
in wartime, he'd surfaced at an altogether different spot from
the one intended. In front of him stretched the backs of a row
of slightly tilted brick cottages, each with its low-walled yard
and hints of watery electric glim behind thin curtains. A wedge
of moon hung above the taller housetops beyond, and from the
black church tower next to it a clock struck the half-hour. As
he moved further down the street, something of that purgative
clarity of apprehension which comes from the simple exercise
of breathing and moving in the open air after several hours'
clubbing recalled him at last to the fact of being adrift in
Bermondsey at half past two in the morning. Momentarily
forgetting the fresco extra and that all too dire glimpse of the
leather guy's hands kneading the warmth of those lean
shoulders, he felt a customary surge of delight at finding
himself alone thus in the gloom and vacancy. The bald expanse
of pavement, the hypothetical curve and bulk of walls and dim
indentations of a porch or a gateway with hints of a courtyard
beyond, gave him an oddly exhilarating sense of survival, as if
those who had wound up the clock in the tower or pressed the
switch of these anaemic lights behind the grimy net had
disappeared for ever, leaving him sole tenant of this emptiness,
not yet a ruin.

In the square ahead of him, the wind getting up to ruffle the
still leafless tops of the plane trees was the only thing which

troubled the silence, otherwise falling so densely as to make him think he owned it. Then he heard a window open, the noise of companionable voices and a rattling of cupboards and drawers from the kitchen. Dinner had ended this late and they were still laughing as he passed the house, a woman inspecting a glass with a tea towel thrown over one arm and somebody behind her stacking plates on a rack.

Adam's resilience ebbed. He wanted to be in there with them, unscrambling chaos before going to bed and feeling the comforting bunch of knees against the hollow of the back and an arm slumped over him in the nonchalant assumption of belonging. The sudden brightness and decorum glimpsed through the window, bringing this directionless access of envy, reminded him of a hymn they used to sing at his prep school, to a gorgeous dreamy tune by Parry which made his stomach turn over. There were some lines in it he remembered, perhaps just because they came at a point where the harmony achieved a peculiarly ingratiating resolution:

And let our ordered lives confess
The beauty of thy peace.

If I was in there, thought Adam, padding away across the square's ensuing emptiness, then looking back for a moment towards the lighted window, if I was in there with them stacking plates and settling the house to its interval of quiet, I'd forget the smile.

He remembered it on the night bus, with its atmosphere of almost palpable vulnerability among those around him on the upper deck, whether baffled by sleep or still desperately jubilant. In Clapham the air, chill and almost windless now, bludgeoned him into inexorable consciousness. Crossing the stretch of common beyond the Temperance fountain and the Polygon, he peered in the direction of the flats to see if a light was on. He needed, beyond anything, to rehearse the botched scenario of the smile with Theo, but all the windows were in darkness. He'd have to lie there till morning thinking about it, the *contrapposto*, the mealing of grey on either temple, the lacquer of sweat across neck and arms, the fingers kneading those glistening shoulders, and the leather man smiling because it was second nature in him to do so. 'Maybe I've got no second nature,' Adam thought as he let himself into the hallway and started to climb the stairs. 'But then maybe I never had a first.'

Theo always slept with his door ajar. Why wasn't said or, for whatever reason, asked. It enabled Adam, coming in after him, to catch his peculiar smell, mercifully inextinguishable even after endless applications of Loewe, Jil Sander or New West, a singular gamey musk like burnt wood, the dead ash of last night's fire left lying on the hearth. It was an earnest, especially tonight, of safety, but of a kind to which he couldn't give a name. Quietly he slipped into the kitchen and ran himself a glass of water from the tap. The message pad, open on the table, bore a scribble in Theo's starchy-looking copybook hand. 'I was Agatha five times on the Common,' it said, then, 'P.S. They called me back for Tuesday. Brilliant or what?' Under which Adam, at three twenty in the morning, felt entirely justified in writing the words, 'What, every time.'

II

❦

'DON'T treat me like this when I've made you breakfast.'

'You're meant to sympathize, not harp on benefits forgot.'

'And I always did worry about turning into Butterfly McQueen.'

'You're too much of a scruff. It's a sort of visual hypocrisy, taking hours in the bathroom with the exfoliants and the moisturizer, making sure your socks don't crinkle too heavily over the edges of the Fratelli Rossetti, and then, when there's nobody to preen at, just sloughing bits of yourself round the flat like a snake.'

'A green mamba.'

'I found a pair of your gym trunks under the sofa yesterday.'

'Oh, yeah, what did you do with them?'

'What the fuck do you think I did with them?'

'Cheap! What all this boils down to is that you weren't Agatha last night and I was. Well, doesn't it?'

Adam didn't answer, looking out instead across the littered

breakfast table at the cupola of the church, whitened yet further by the bland morning light. Ever since Theo had come to live here and their shared argot started almost at once to kick in, the phrase had established itself as a primary element. One or other of them had discovered it in *Mansfield Park*, where the disgruntled Julia, after parts are apportioned in the amateur theatricals, exclaims, 'And I am not to be Agatha.' Thereafter you were Agatha in some exuberant subterranean partouze at the Shoreditch Chariots, under the sycamores by the railway line across Tooting Common at two in the morning, or on your dominical knees in the backroom at the Fort. Conversely you were not Agatha at Pleasuredrome, when some peevish bambino from le Continong, newly disgorged from Eurostar, slapped you down for temerity in the steam-room, or when the titanium-framed boy sitting alone reading *The Spell*, opposite whom you'd carefully placed yourself when the train pulled in at Warren Street, sent his eyes devastatingly heavenwards, as if to say, 'For goodness' sake, try being original.'

Theo didn't raise his eyes, preferring to indicate his dissatisfaction with Adam by fixing him in a stare of liquid immensity, which after a while had its calculated effect. There was a way he had of waiting for you to stop pretending to yourself which disconcerted Adam as much as ever he valued it. In such moments you beheld his face in all its suddenly impassive boniness as nothing less than a carved mask through which he looked and breathed. After a while Adam succumbed to the calculated effect.

'Understand me, The. I just couldn't.'

'What?'

'Smile. It's all right for you, you're paid to do it, they taught it you at Webber Douglas along with all that shit about being a tree and empathizing and gender confusion. I never learned.

And as soon as I catch myself in the act I stop, because it seems so pathetically arch, this mimsy little thing with my mouth trying to stretch itself between my ears like a washing line. And always failing.'

'What would you have done if it hadn't felt like that, if you'd copped off with each other and he'd asked you to come back with him?' Theo crammed a forkful of egg and toast into his mouth, but before Adam could answer, went on, 'Mm, yeah, we know, don't we, because I've talked you through this one before. You'd have wrapped yourself round him like an octopus and then wondered why he backed off, and there'd have been another of those little tragedies you're so good at writing for yourself.'

'Yes, but why shouldn't I be able to walk into a bar and then just stand there radiating, with a you're-the-only-one-who-matters look beaming off my face? Do you think there's treatment for it, a smile therapist, some woman in a house in Crouch End or Kilburn with a dozen cats and a drawing-room full of shawls and cushions with little mirrors on them, smelling of patchouli and going on about auras and endorphins?'

Theo belched comfortably and, pushing his chair back, splayed out his long, bare legs.

'Dunno, do I? You're in a crisis, Ad. "Wanted – a rictus." Face up to it, be a man, it's what we pay you for.'

'Women can do it better. Smile, I mean.'

'Yes, but they're not serious about it like we are, it's just a girly thing. You'll never be a champion smiler, so knock it on the head, go up the Common tonight, get your rocks off and forget it.'

'As if I could!' muttered Adam, staring hard at the marmalade. 'Talk to me about something else, The, something not to do with sex. Tell me about being called back.'

'Thought you'd never ask. Nathan Lester phoned just after you went out. They really liked my stuff, and he wants me to go in on Tuesday and do a couple of scenes with some guys who are up for Achilles and Thersites, interaction, that kind of thing.'

'Aren't you a bit on the strapping side for Patroclus?'

'Look, he may be only a cheeky little bit of camp totty, but it's better than being a dealer in *The Bill* or that corny footballer I did in *Casualty*. The one with sickle-cell anaemia. And the Young Vic is class.'

Adam sniggered. 'Sounds more like Young Dick the way this show's going. I suppose Cressida is played by a woman? I don't understand why Lester specifically wants an Afro Patroclus.'

'Multiracial casting, innit? Troilus is this Parsee called Jamshid Dadabhoy, who they got off an end-of-year show at RADA.'

'A bit like catalogue shopping, if you ask me.'

'Well, I don't, so stop trying to trash it. Anyone'd think you weren't pleased.' The mask had faded and Theo's face was once again mobile, assailable, vivid with a need for reassurance.

'Sorry, The, I'm a selfish bastard. You knew that when you moved in.'

'Yes, but I can still have a go at making you unselfish. "I as your friend, not as your lodger speak."'

'Ho, ho, read the play, have we? Know everybody else's parts? You probably will by the time the run begins, given your track record where parts are concerned. What was it like on the Common last night?'

Theo's sudden access of insecurity had made Adam feel better, for whatever reason. Recently it had begun to seem as if after living with each other, even on the apparently formal basis of landlord and tenant whose paths might not necessarily cross more than perfunctorily during the course of the week, they'd developed a species of sensory equipment which, besides detecting moods and emotions, helped in some positive fashion to bring these into being. He got up and started clearing the table, the mere act of piling eggcups on saucers and glasses into mugs a measure, as it were, of newly acquired decisiveness. Theo, slouched against the wall, haphazardly monumental in his glistening, rangy near-nakedness, lit a narrative cigarette.

'Have you ever gone up there when there hasn't been a couple of black guys in hoods whispering to each other under a tree? They don't do anything, no sex, no dealing, don't even try to mug you like we're all meant to, they just fucking stand there or amble about for hours together nattering. They're around when you arrive and they're still hanging out somewhere when you're leaving.'

'You were the exception that proved the rule, I imagine.'

'There was a high dark content, yes, with me the only one offering outreach and input. I felt a bit exposed.'

'My heart bleeds.'

'And an Italian stole my poppers.'

'How did you know he was Italian?'

'Arse was as clean as a whistle for one thing. And they always smile. Oops!'

'Watch it.'

'They bloody do. You could tell them their mum and dad had gone down on the *Titanic* and they'd do the Perfect Pizza grin. You're such an English cherub, aren't you, Ads?'

'Naff off,' rejoined Adam half-heartedly, thinking how nice the touch of Theo's dry, leathery fingers felt as they sleeked the nap of blond fuzz across the back of his thigh.

'A little fat golden cherub on a map, flying through the air with a trumpet and a scroll. Be a love and put some music on.'

'Be an angel, you could have said,' Adam called back from the kitchen. 'Anyway you haven't finished telling me about your exploits as a predatory homosexual. Who else was there apart from the grinning wop? Point five on the Agatha scale, so I was led to believe.'

'I had the Australian with the pierced tits who wears those baggy cargo pants and takes about half a nano-second to shoot. Then there was a snogathon with someone called Graham, who wanted a home visit but that was only because he thought it was coming on to rain. Oooh wickeeed, what it is?'

'Diedrich Becker. And don't try dropping that name at parties, because nobody'll know whom you're talking about. Go on, I may as well hear the rest and experience ultimate humiliation.'

'Scene three, another part of the forest, with a guy who liked it plain or milk.'

'Did he say as much?'

'No, but I can always tell when massa prefers Sambo. Sometimes you think that for two pins they'd be forcing your mouth open for the auctioneer to make sure you had all your teeth and hadn't picked up a dose of worms on the voyage over. After that I blagged a cigarette off a boy in a Jigsaw suit and we gave each other a chaste J. Arthur by the football hut.'

'It was the suit that did it, presumably. Typical of you to spot a Jigsaw under the sallow glimmer of neon.'

'I didn't even have to turn him upside down to make sure. Last year's beige, three-button cuffs, no pocket flaps. Adsy, do you honestly think I'm too tall for Patroclus?'

'No,' Adam lied, 'and from what I recall he was meant to be the more butch of the two, Achilles having spent most of his formative years in drag. So go for it, as the laundress said. I'd offer to read the scenes with you, only Daisy's lunching me and I expect the rest of the afternoon will be devoted to baby worship. Basil Flecknoe's supposed to be turning up at some stage to provide a diversion.'

Theo winced. 'That's the scruff you told me about, isn't it, the one with holes in his socks. He sounds like the kind who gives straight men a bad name. And fancy anyone in the late nineties being called Basil!'

'He was born before *Fawlty Towers*. But the holes are still there. And they're probably the same socks, what's more.'

'Barf, sickbag, up comes breakfast.'

'He's an inspiration, pulling the way he does. A certain kind of woman likes a man who looks as if he's about to burst into tears any minute and moans about being unappreciated.'

'I thought you said he'd published four novels.'

'They're not the sort that parts the waters of the literary-critical Red Sea or makes the sun and moon stand still at the office of the *New York Review*. Some women like that kind of near-miss thing, it encourages their quaint view of men as basically clapped out and preposterous, and Basil plays up to it as yer never did. Actually I think he prefers being not quite a success. The Booker might be ashes in the mouth. Anyway I owe him, he's been touching up my Foundation prospectus.'

Theo silently shuddered, as if at the very notion of Basil in the act of touching up. Adam, rising from the table again, said, 'Will you be in when I get home?'

'You often ask me that, did you know?'

'I expect so.'

Theo said nothing.

'Well will you?'

'Aren't you going to ask me why I don't say the same thing to you?'

'No,' said Adam a shade crossly. 'I just wanted to find out.'

'I'm spending the evening at Guy's place,' Theo announced, breathing with noticeable deliberateness. 'Is that all you wanted to know?'

'Obviously not, but you're so bloody secretive about this one that it's getting seriously weird.'

For a moment the music, with its neat little tongue-and-groove overlaps between the instrumental lines, seemed to compensate for the sudden parching of spontaneity between the two men. Theo's eyes had narrowed and his lips puffed with irritation.

'Did I miss something when I moved in here, Adam?'

'What do you –'

'Seriously, was there a piece of paper I forgot to sign, something about having to give you precise details of anyone I happen to be seeing.'

'Oh, come on, The, I'm just curious, that's all. Blame me?'

Theo's stare travelled ruthlessly up and down Adam. 'As a matter of fact, I do. It suggests I can't be trusted.'

Fancying that Theo's reticence implied exactly the same of him, only somewhat more forcibly, Adam kept silent.

'I've told you everything I want to. If you had some imagination it might be possible to understand why I wasn't prepared to say any more.' Theo looked at the carpet between his feet, then muttered, 'For now, anyway.'

'Yeah, well, forget I ever mentioned it,' said Adam with a degree of resentment which took him by surprise. Moving into the hall and towards the bathroom, he called back at Theo, 'Try asking Guy about Diedrich Becker. I'm sure he's bound to have heard of him,' then, making certain the door was locked, he gave the mirror above the washbasin a ghastly grimace.

III

At Victoria, said the indicator board on the Stockwell northbound platform, there was person under a train. Except that wasn't exactly what it said, because nowadays the indicator boards on the London Underground are encouraged to refine their euphemisms, so up came the words, 'due to passenger action'. It could indeed have been an intransigent drunk exploiting his nuisance value or some prat setting off the alarm system for a dare, but cynicism born of experience encouraged a more drastic interpretation. Perhaps witnessing one of these platform suicides, as Adam assumed he was likely to in the fullness of time, must make him more tolerant of them, but for now they seemed merely arch and rhetorical in the amplitude of their selfishness. Marooned thus within the tube, he found himself occasionally taking stock of his friends and wondering which of them he had better advise in all seriousness not to make the attempt.

His irritation was heightened this afternoon by a residual

crossness with Theo, not allayed by some noisy and ostentatious stacking of dishes in the machine, followed by an effort at imposing order on the kitchen, already given a brisk semblance of neatness by Adam, which resulted in an effect of positive *embourgeoisement* disagreeable to the one and inauthentic to the other. It was so unlike Theo to atone in this fashion that the process only served to emphasize his wilful and infuriating concealment.

What, in any case, was there to hide? As far as Adam had so far been able to piece things together, Guy, the man Theo was currently seeing, worked as an investment banker in the city and was already in some sort of relationship involving a *mari complaisant* figure who appeared to spend most of his time looking after their converted oast house in the Weald. There was a flat in Bayswater, not far from the Porchester Baths, where on Sunday nights Theo had taken to going for champagne suppers followed – or preceded, it was never quite clear – by videos and sex. The point, apparently, was that neither of them was to be seen in public together, and that these evenings should be considered in the light of a reward for Theo's incuriosity, or his refusal at least to press the Affluent One for more information about himself than he proposed to give.

It was not unlike the story of Cupid and Psyche, with its implicit warning as to the danger of asking questions. Adam, meanwhile, was beginning to feel like one of the heroine's importunate sisters, but any guilt he might have experienced as to prying too deeply was easily assuaged by his sense of an inherent absurdity in the whole arrangement. There were, of course, even in this blatant metropolitan *fin de siècle*, people for whom reticence and concealment were essential to the pursuit of an affair or to sharpen its pleasures. Lying to everyone else and occasionally to one another formed a section of the particular textbook whose steps they were so careful to follow. That Theo, whose charm for Adam was predicated on his careless immediacy, should suddenly adopt this style, had started mildly to disturb him. The distance thus opening gave unexpected and disagreeable emphasis to the decade in age which already divided them. Even if Adam's concern was hardly parental, Theo's resentment, more frankly expressed that morning than ever before, seemed to cast him in the unwelcome role of an elderly fusspot.

There'd been other signs of this remoteness. Altruism played only a small part in the offer of a spare room, in return for half the bills, which Adam had made more than a year ago, after an encounter at the Two Brewers ended on a midnight's operatically noisy congress in the absurd matrimonial bed Daisy had talked him into buying from one of the shops along Northcote Road. About Theo's presence in the flat there was a spontaneity which kept on defying exasperation, to such an extent that Adam wondered how on earth, until his arrival, he could have existed in his own dimension of organized solitude. At first it seemed as if nothing beyond their sexuality bound them to each other, yet almost at once they'd clambered on to a ledge of firmly exclusive intimacy, whether in conversation or in the accurate guesses either was calculated to make as to moves and intentions.

An affair *tout court* was neither desired nor in any sense desirable. Each piqued himself on having thus passed beyond a responsibility for emotions which, pleasurable as they might be in connection with others, would simply have been cloying and burdensome in this case. Theo had, on the other hand, a tendency to use sex as a kind of small talk, a means of breaking the ice where more orthodox resources might fail, which Adam could never resist, even supposing he wanted to. Now and then, slouched across each other on the sofa with a roach and some cans, watching a crap video fished from Blockbuster because one or both of them fancied the cake, or coming back loose-ended from a duff Sunday at the Fort, or simply crossing in the corridor in the morning, they'd start. Or rather, Theo would start, jamming his lips against Adam's and dropping his huge lollipop tongue between them like a pelican feeding its young, while he tugged down whatever obstructed him from running an appreciative hand over an arse which, flatteringly, he always treated as if never having come across such a thing before in his life. If thereafter they bundled into bed, it was only because this was somewhat more comfortable than rough strife on the carpet, but the whole nature of these engagements was unpremeditated, a vague siphoning off of appetite, with energy substituting for passion and the specifics of desire conveniently lost beneath their combined versatility.

Adam had not been wrong, he now perceived, in sensing a recent decline in such attentions, due not to a sudden access of fastidious disgust on Theo's part, but to what looked increasingly like an amalgam of guilt and absent-mindedness. The former arose, no doubt, from a feeling that he ought to be reserving himself for champagne suppers in Bayswater with Guy the plutocrat, yet his expedition to the Common last night hardly supported a position of high moral scrupulousness.

That was where being absent-minded came in. How hateful it must become if Theo, for all his jumble of aspirations, his little bursts of perfectionism, his titanic self-absorption, ever genuinely got everything together and became something other than the creature of impulse he'd gone on being until now! The horror of the change preoccupied Adam as he mounted the escalator and passed gingerly through the ticket barriers at

Highbury & Islington. He'd always disliked the station, with its jerry-built booking hall, the foul stretch of yard behind the nondescript post office plonked down disobligingly at its entrance and the scatter of vaguely agricultural-looking slouchers outside the adjacent pub, like figures eternally left behind at the end of some long-varnished hiring fair from the days when hay was cut on Highbury Fields and cattle being driven to market browsed on the verges of Upper Street. As if to placate such ghosts, he gave a few coins to a beggar in a 'Buy yourself a drink, my good man' gesture, before zigzagging over the crossings into Canonbury.

Like most of the elements of Daisy's life, the house on the grander side of Alwyne Villas had required no effort on her part towards its acquisition. The opportune death of a childless aunt with an impulse towards keeping things in the family had dropped it into her lap some five or six years earlier, whereupon she abandoned her career as a dancer. Soon afterwards a sequence of elegantly chiselled male lodgers had begun to arrive, each of them on the verge of leaving in order to embark on some project of barely imaginable glamour involving a German choreographer, a video installation at a gallery in Antwerp, guaranteed apotheosis by various French festivals or an ongoing collaboration with Bob Wilson. The importance of these dancing parlour-boarders for Daisy lay as much in this transitoriness, denoting the house as an indispensable staging post *en route* to celebrity, as in the fact that none of them had ever threatened to be anything so perilously competitive as another woman.

Their emphatic masculinity, in a profession which the vulgarity of popular wisdom still associates with effeminacy, made Adam wonder, when Daisy first became pregnant, whether any of them were the father. There was a boy called Roger he'd always rather liked the look of, with green eyes and a lazy East Anglian accent, who looked as if he might have done the business niftily enough, and a strapping Israeli with nutcracker thighs who had served as a commando in the Lebanon and whom Adam always fancied catching sweatily in the act, but about them both Daisy kept an oracular silence, as indeed about all other possible candidates during the brief period when she still seemed poised to assign paternity.

Instead she'd surprised everyone by leaving for New York, almost as though antenatal classes and a caesarian at the Whittington were too desperately commonplace a resolution. Long ago Adam learned that you never asked Daisy how she got by. Her family, which included a Catholic mother and a baronet uncle in Hampshire, was of the sort which describes itself as having no money, a self-contradictory term which implies that you shouldn't expect any of its members to work honestly for their living on five days of most weeks in the year. One of her sisters, the one who lived in Italy, was said to be a painter, and we knew what that meant. Daisy, in fairness, had taken her career as a dancer rather more seriously, even going as far as to develop a talent for choreography. Having no money meant, however, that it was easier in the end to forsake doing for being and assume her present role as a sort of housemother to her fellow performers.

Their consistent physical graces were probably less important than the simple fact that none of them was a woman. Adam was aware that a female friend or two existed peripherally around Daisy, and that in certain unimportant respects she was close to her two sisters. Otherwise her general attitude to women was venomously competitive. On holiday with her in France he had watched in fascinated horror the expertise with which she marginalized or else blanked utterly those of her own sex who had the misfortune to be staying in the house, while simultaneously taking care to present herself as the sort of circumstantial casualty their husbands or lovers might be interested in protecting. Her skilful amalgam of the waif and the princess, someone on whom you could always depend for unpunctuality supported by the feeblest of excuses, and whose presence seemed invariably to bespeak an invisible retinue of servants (or 'staff' as she'd more smartly refer to them), belied the decisiveness of those manoeuvres with which she continued to adjust life to her advantage.

Thus when, with a good deal of complaint at the tiresomeness of it all, she had acknowledged her pregnancy, Adam at first interpreted this as a false turning, a sudden technical failure in the hitherto seamless mesh of calculation. Daisy as a mother was unimaginable, and whatever the consistency of her ruthlessness, hardly the kind of woman to enjoy browbeating and disobliging others with the pretexts and imperatives of maternity. When the baby she brought back from New York as recognizably her own turned out to be a girl, he was still more astonished, until he began to understand the nature of her designs for it. Named Edith, after a great-grandmother whose de László portrait, in an aura of tulle and attendant spaniels, hung rather too consequentially in the drawing-room at Alwyne Villas, the child was clearly intended for existence as another, not necessarily improved, version of Daisy, who, having done the baby thing, was disinclined to repeat the experience in case it should cramp Edith's style.

Too shocking, of course, to contemplate the possibility that the replica might turn out frumpish, plodding or insufferably high-minded. As she lay now, however, in the little nest Daisy had designed for her out of inherited swatches of Honiton and

Chantilly, there was no hint of any habitable dimension for her but that of self-conscious elegance.

'She's such a tart,' said Daisy approvingly. 'Pity it's wasted on you.'

'That's precisely why she does it,' retorted Adam, 'it's post-ironic, she's obviously a quick learner. Are you going to have her christened?'

'May as well. I suppose that means I'll have to start thinking about godparents.'

'Well, include me out,' said Basil, who, as the others ducked and craned in adoration over Edith, sat with his legs crooked over the arm of his chair, anxiously scanning the paper. 'I'm a heretic in every sense you care to name.'

'Poor Baz just hates the *baba-log*, don't you, darling?'

Basil ran a hand through his greasy mane. 'It's fear more than hate. Babies are so —'

'Time-consuming?' suggested Daisy.

'Selfish,' Adam volunteered, which made her frown.

'No, they're so . . . representative, that's the word I want. They're what might have happened to me if I hadn't been more careful. I've had several near misses like that. Cressida French, remember her? Did features for the *Telegraph*.'

As it happened they did not, and felt piqued in consequence. Basil's liaisons were a vitalizing agent of gossip, if only for their sheer haphazardness.

'Girls like that are always called Cressida,' said Adam, re-establishing control through a swift generalization.

'She's hardly a girl. And what do you mean by "like that"?'

'Or if it isn't Cressida, it's Cassandra or Jocasta. Their parents haven't quite the nerve to try Hypermnestra or Laodamia in the we're-far-too-posh-to-give-you-a-name-from-the-Bible-or-the-calendar stakes, but it'll come to that, mark my words. Andromache's the buzzname for the millennium.'

'So was that why Cressida didn't last, Baz, no futures in features?' asked Daisy. 'Because she wanted you to do a far, far better thing?'

'I was scheduled to help her start a literary dynasty, but we saw her off.'

'Who's we?'

'Betsy Kravitz rode to the rescue. Like a goddess on a machine, coming back from Kosovo with her CNN flackjacket in the nick of time and not hanging about afterwards like some of them do. Another week and I'd have been copped for good and all.'

Daisy guffawed, prodding the edge of the cradle with her toe. 'I think you'll find it doesn't work as fast as that, even with your strike rate. Count your blessings, Edie sweetheart, you're in a room with two men one of whom wouldn't be a dad if you paid him and the other says thanks but no thanks.' She turned again, with a comfortably imperious gesture, for all the world like some eighteenth-century salon hostess, to Basil, slumped across the chair in his eternal awkwardness, seeking to lose himself in the paper. 'It's such a waste,' she said, 'Cressida had the right idea. You could start a whole literary gene pool with some of those girls you pick up at book launches or whatever.'

'And have some brat who was better at it than me? Try Ad instead.'

'We never did, did we? I'm going to make myself some tea now Modom's had hers. It's PG Tips, by the way, motherhood transforms you into a complete scruff, but there's a biscuit or two.' She sailed out towards the kitchen, confidently leaving Adam to amuse Edith while Basil retreated more obviously into the review section. Given the fact that so many gay men feel competitive or resentful in the presence of babies, it was fortunate that Adam should experience a positively eccentric delight in their company. He liked the lacteal smell of their skin, the waxy indistinctness of their puffy knees and the way their moist little hands clung around his fingers like tendrils. Now he hunkered down on the carpet closer to Edith, feeling the warmth of her breathing against his face and laughing as her features perplexed themselves into a vast yawn followed almost at once by a volcanic sneeze. Out of the corner of his eye he glanced at Basil to see whether, with Daisy out of the room for a moment, he wouldn't after all unbend a little and deign however remotely to notice the child, restless now amid the spume of lace. It seemed odd that in the current rage for settling down and acquiring respectability via an attendant partner, Basil should so significantly have eschewed any enduring 'other'. Women hung upon him, worried themselves and each other about him, sought to make him stand upright, iron his shirts more than cursorily, remember to shave, put new laces in his shoes and replace jackets beyond recall by even the most imaginative of dry cleaning processes, yet in the end this resolute insistence on remaining unreclaimed had baffled even the most energetic. In his basement at the foot of grubby area steps in one of the streets off Theobald's Road, a flat which a friend had christened the Cave Of Spleen, he dwelt like Diogenes in his tub amid the defining elements of an intractably resistant solitariness, for ever at odds with an age so frightened as this one with whatever looks like leaving it alone.

Others besides Adam and Daisy had experienced this aura of dislocation, as if, touting books to and fro in a London Library carrier bag and dressing merely in order to clothe an otherwise inconvenient nakedness, Basil were some sort of irrelevant leftover from an age of hansoms and pea-soupers, a creature invented by Gissing or Wells.

'I'll tell you what you are,' Adam remembered someone saying to Basil at a party, the kind of person who makes a tiresome habit of dictating identity to others, 'you're a man of letters. That's what you are, Baz, you're a man of letters.' Basil's face, long and mournful like the back of a tablespoon, creased into an approximate smile.

'A man of letters and acquainted with grief,' he muttered, flummoxing the other completely, though Adam too had found it hard to imagine exactly what sort of grief was meant. Maybe it was true, though, about the man of letters.

Edith kicked and flailed more vigorously now as Adam grew desperately intent on amusing her. Suddenly someone came downstairs with a light, confident step, and he heard the front door open and shut. It was part of Daisy's careful avoidance of the bourgeois element in life that she never introduced her new lodgers. You glimpsed them through half-open doors, discovered them making coffee in the kitchen or, on one or two throat-lumping occasions, bumped into them towelled and glowing from their bath. Their autonomy amused Daisy the more because it maddened Adam, to the point that he'd started adding the words 'whom I'm never allowed to meet' whenever their names came up. Now indeed, as she swept back into the drawing room carrying a Japanese tray stacked with a little ziggurat of heterogeneous cups, he cried gleefully, 'And who was that you're not allowing us to meet?'

'Frankie. He's over from the States. I stayed with him for a bit in New York, remember? He answered the phone once or twice when you rang the night after Edie was born, and you said he was short with you. You didn't like his voice, or something. I told you he was coming.'

'What exactly bothered you about his voice?' asked Basil, rearranging himself into a tea-receiving position. It was exactly the sort of issue which interested him, but before Adam could answer, Daisy, who had deputed him to pour while she busied herself with Edith, starting by now to grow outrageous, said, 'He didn't like the way Frankie wasn't interested.'

Basil laughed savagely. 'How exactly is one expected to show interest, from the end of a transatlantic telephone, in somebody one hasn't met, and knowing Daisy as we do, probably hasn't heard of? "Golly-gee, so you're *the* Adam Killigrew, the one that works for the Ethel Chauncey Wooldridge Foundation and lives in Clapham, London, England? Oh really, homosexual? That's like gay or something? I guess I'm cool with that. I mean there's plenty of dudes in this town who —"'

'You're useless at being American,' cried Adam, 'and in any case I never said he wasn't interested, just that he sounded so chilly.'

'And Americans, of course, aren't supposed to be like that. Give me a biscuit. OK, I don't deserve one, but give it me anyway.'

Adam looked furtively at Daisy, the answering flicker of whose glance suggested that she too realized that something unconnected with either of them had got to Basil that afternoon. Hating discord among her friends largely because of its threatened demands for partisanship and sympathy, she hurriedly said, 'Anyway, he's around for the duration, Frankie, I mean. Brilliant for Edie, she adores him.'

Adam felt a spurt of envy. 'How can you tell at her age? And what's he doing — a sort of Stars and Stripes riposte to Louise Woodward?'

'He's a choreographer,' Daisy said icily. 'Francesco Damiani.'

'Frankie to his *cari amici* in the Mob,' muttered Basil.

'Actually his family's from Boston. I thought you knew about him, Ad.'

'He's a name, isn't he? They all are in this house, or else they're about to be.'

'Promise your mother you'll be a name, Edie darling,' Daisy said, determined not to be mocked.

'Or else,' said Adam. 'You still haven't answered my question about what the celebrated divo of dance is doing in Limeyland, apart from paying homage to the little princess.'

'Probably trashing it like they all do,' sneered Basil, 'complaining about the plumbing and the weather and the way everything doesn't happen as expected and the national penchant for obliquity.'

With careful deliberation Daisy bundled Edith into an aura of shawls and, ignoring Basil entirely, said to Adam, 'Come upstairs and help me change her before she has her kip.'

Obedient, Adam followed them up to the room at the back of the house now designated 'the nursery', as if it expected the appearance of maids in white caps with streamers under the supervision of a bombazined battleaxe with an honorific 'Mrs' before her name. It was not altogether clear how long Daisy would manage without an au pair, but the heart sank at the prospect. Better by far if the ballet boy of the moment could be persuaded to spend a *mauvais quart d'heure* among the Pampers and sterilizers than some hapless Kiwi boohooing in the attic because a few casual drops of Daisy's vitriol had fallen upon her for the crime of being female.

'What's the matter with Baz?' whispered Adam as soon as the door was shut.

'I didn't dare ask, you know what he's like. He was so gloomy and withdrawn over lunch, I mean what's the point?

He'll drop me now Modom's on the scene. The way he blanks her you'd think he was jealous.'

'Some men can't cope.'

'Most, in my experience. You're fairly exceptional like that. Has he talked to you about the novel?'

'No, that's another thing. Normally I get asked to the Cave of Spleen and he reads me bits and I have to be honest about it, which I hate. Novels are people's babies, aren't they, you've got to be nice, however embarrassingly unattractive they turn out to be.'

'Well, you've been tactful about this one so far,' said Daisy, beaming upon Edith as if looks were never likely to be an issue.

'You know what I mean. He was gutted by some of the notices for the last one, when it finally got any. Some of the papers took months and the *Telegraph* and the *Observer* didn't even bother. Perhaps that's why he's so desperate to wrap up this book.'

'Talking of wrapping, Adam sweetheart —'

'I don't believe this.'

'You were so good at it last time, she went out like a light.'

'A case of "You could always rely on Malcolm to know where to put the talcum." Oh all right, if I must.'

'And there's another favour I want to ask,' said Daisy shamelessly, as she followed him into the adjacent bathroom, where, comfortably perched, she could watch him at work on the baby, now settling into a congenial drowsiness. Adam, as he sponged and powdered and tucked, wondered whether there would ever come a time when the absence of scruple which characterized Daisy's dealing with her friends might begin to seem more than merely irritating. At present the consideration that she'd asked him round just for the sake of a seldom-exercised skill in changing nappies afforded a cynical comfort, so that he was not at all surprised at there being something else she was preparing to wheedle from him.

'I want you to come and watch Frankie next week.'

'Nothing if not straightforward, are you? What exactly am I to watch, the paragon of modern American choreography sending Edie off to bye-byes? Are we working towards a dance piece here?'

'Don't get fresh with me, as he'd say. You know perfectly well I mean rehearsals.'

'Is this a set-up, or just a sophisticated variation on asking me to dinner, which of course you'd rather die than do?'

'Oh, be like that then,' cried Daisy, on the edge of genuine exasperation. 'I just thought it'd be nice, that's all.'

Adam turned towards her, Edith fragrantly marmoreal in his arms. 'No you didn't,' he said softly. 'What are you hatching?'

Sullenly she accepted the child, then looked at him as if irked at having been found out. 'I thought the Foundation could help. It's the thing he's working on for Sadler's Wells, part of a triple bill. They need some more dosh.'

'But we only give to unknowns, and then later, when they're mega-celebs and get moody interviews in the listings mags, we programme them to say, "I couldn't have done it without the Ethel Chauncey Wooldridge grant." I'd hardly call Francesco Damiani a beginner.'

'It's the first big thing he's done here,' countered Daisy, rising from her perch with a sudden parade of preoccupation over the business of putting her daughter down to sleep.

'I suppose we should be grateful for his condescension.'

'Stop sounding like Baz, for Christ's sake. Snarling doesn't suit you. Anyway I don't see why it's a problem. The dancers are mostly unknowns even if Frankie isn't. And there's one you'd die for, a Greek.'

'I've had it up to here with Greeks,' said Adam, 'a lot of fucking tragedy queens with inferiority complexes growing out of them like humps. If it isn't the Turks and Melina's frigging Marrrbles, darrrleeng, then it's "We geeve you dhimokrasi, filosofi, dhramma, and what do you geeve us? Boolsheet!" Try tempting me with something else.'

'I've nothing left, have I?' Daisy said, growing resolutely winsome all of a sudden. 'He's really awfully cute.'

'Who, Frankie?'

'No, the Greek. "Cute" isn't a word I'd use to describe Frankie. Oh, come on, Ad, you've got money papering the walls in that wretched place. You told me so yourself. You can't always be handing it out to *Just Seventeen* Samanthas from Raynes Park who want to be Darcey Bussell.'

'I don't see why Gramercy Park deserves it more than Raynes Park, if you're going to be snobbish.'

She said nothing more, choosing instead to turn her back on him as if, apparently, to attend with greater care to Edith, now spark-out under the valanced canopy which had shadowed one of her mother's Scottish ancestors. By the time he'd slipped back downstairs to find Basil leeching the last tepid dribble of tea from the pot between cigarettes, Adam acknowledged to himself that his show of resistance was no less selfish than anything Daisy might have tried. What irked him wasn't the arm-twisting itself but the fact that she had embarked on it as soon as she saw how efficiently he'd dealt with Edith. Looking at Basil, glum and shapeless in his baggy sweater and rucked jeans, Adam felt a spurt of envy. There was nothing the other man had which Daisy could ever want to make use of. The thought made him decide it was time to leave.

'I'll come with you as far as the bus stop,' announced Basil. 'There's a chapter on the back burner in Rugby Street. And I've left the prospectus on the table over there. One split infinitive, a couple of misrelated participial phrases and far too many commas where there shouldn't be. Otherwise a perfect combination of blandness and mendacity. Pity you don't give funds to writers.'

'Adam doesn't give funds to anyone,' whispered Daisy, tiptoeing theatrically from stair to stair as they came out into the hall.

'I didn't say we wouldn't. In fact I can't remember categorically refusing to come and watch the egregious Damiani at work, let alone the shaggable Greek. I just wanted to make it harder for you.' Adam shrugged in resignation. 'You'd better tell me where and when.'

'It's up to Frankie,' Daisy said simply, having foreseen his surrender.

'I suppose that's one better than being down to him. Call me, like you never do.'

For a brief instant, walking towards Canonbury Lane, Basil was silent, not launching, as Adam felt he might easily have done, into a protest at the pointlessness of frittering away a Sunday afternoon as sideshows for Edith. Then, as if to explain his earlier access of moroseness, he said, 'You know I had a story rejected?' He made it sound as if London buzzed with the news.

'The bastards. Who was it?'

'The *London Review*, they've started publishing fiction.'

'What did they say?'

'Oh, they try to let you down gently. "It's not for us," which basically means it's crap. The funny thing is that I knew it must be when I finished it. Not total crap, but on the edge. I just didn't want to disappoint them.' Basil laughed. 'If you see what I mean.'

'And what do you feel about that?'

'You sound like some fucking psychotherapist. Like shit is the answer. Failing is so unprofessional. As for being seen to fail . . . Don't you ever let me catch you at it, Killigrew.'

'You won't, because I don't make things, so I'm scarcely in the big league when it comes to being a loser,' said Adam, hastily adding, as a recollection of last night's débâcle in Bermondsey arose to trouble him. 'All my disasters are little ones, bite-size chunks, nothing on a Gargantuan scale. Anyway, what was it about, the story?'

Basil winced visibly. 'Don't ask. One of these days I might tell you, it's something you'd probably understand. Have you noticed, by the way, how hopeless Daisy is about other people's failures?'

'It honestly never struck me.'

'She absolutely can't handle it. That's why I didn't tell her.'

Adam wasn't listening seriously. As they walked along the edge of the square, so cruelly bisected by that great trunk road which hurls the clattering trucks out of the plain of Shoreditch northwards into Holloway, his gaze had snagged itself on the presence of a man approaching from the direction of Upper Street. Never embarrassed by his automatic pilot of instinctive lustful appraisal, assisted by uncannily precise long-sightedness and a gift for reading others accurately according to the most trifling external features, he clocked the details as they came into focus. Total slaphead, faintly foreign-looking, not so tall as to make him feel self-conscious, collarless white shirt, and black jeans which even at a distance looked part of the décor, as opposed to having been flung on for decency's sake. Against the pavement's brownish grey and the sooty brick of the houses, the figure, as it came onwards, flourished a truculent assertiveness, as if these drab areas of colour were simply there to enforce its suggestions of brilliance and vitality.

His heart quickened, under cover of a tranquil pretence of agreement with Basil, returning obsessively to the themes of misunderstanding and rejection at the hands of the *London Review of Books*. Poised, supple, the man drew nearer. The face, taut-stretched and bony under its shaven crown, might have been that of a scholar or a priest – Romanus the Melode, thought Adam crazily – if it hadn't been for the unnerving coolness in the glance of its blue eyes. Catching the hunger in Adam's look, he broke into an indulgent, self-deprecating grin, as if there were really no help for them having to move in opposite directions. When Adam turned as they passed, he saw the other man look back and shrug in mock despair, standing on the pavement's edge by the crossing.

'You could always go back,' Adam heard Basil say, not without a hint of crossness. 'I can find my own way home. He looks as if he's waiting for you. Or expecting you to, which is rather different.'

Doesn't he though, mused Adam, walking backwards beside Basil into Upper Street so as to keep in the merest scrap of plain sight that image of the man standing, hands on hips, smiling after him, with the lorries thundering northwards at his back.

'I don't think so.'

IV

FUNNY how Theo always remembered at exactly the same place the moment when the two of them first met. He'd get out of the station at Queensway into the hum of evening pavement life in that most unEnglish of streets and begin threading his way among the lurid pools of light from the open shopfronts, the Arabic newsagents and video stores, the French bakers, the exotic greengrocers and sleepless coffee shops, with, around him, sad-eyed women in grey scarves and clackety slingbacks under the fall of their robes, and pairs of jowly, myopic men, ambling along on the backs of their heels twirling little strings of orange beads. Then, when he started to pass the long, glowing vitrines of Whiteley's the memory kicked in, with a clarity which, as succeeding months made its originating experience more remote, began to surprise him.

For one thing, it happened in another part of London altogether. Coming away from an audition at the National which over-confidence had caused him to fluff beyond hope of recall, he'd felt an access of that particular species of directionless randiness which prescribes sex with whoever as an immediate morale booster. Soon enough he fetched up in the sauna under the railway arches at Waterloo. Waiting for the door to be buzzed open, he turned as always to look up and down the alley. There was absolutely no need for embarrassment, yet in that instant he invariably felt a little frisson of anticipated shame at the unlikely prospect of someone, his parents maybe, with their air of slightly forlorn, reproachful propriety which nowadays it seemed his destiny to outrage, or his brother Aubrey, mobile nestling against one sleek jaw as if it had sprung up there like a cat, sweeping down upon him, accusing and inescapable.

Thus the surliness of the near-naked boy at the little window inside, who checked his name and gave him his key, seemed as welcoming in its familiarity as the thumping last-season club anthems contending from the speakers against the banging of sauna-cabin doors and the susurration of water from the showers. The commonplaces of refuge and certainty offered to him among the bins of crumpled towels, the sombre L-shaped locker avenues like the model for some brutalist housing estate, and the unsubtle gradations of shadow blocking the doorway beyond, gathered about him with the warmth of an embrace.

While undressing, he smelt himself. There were times when it made him feel comfortable, in the flat maybe after a night at Fist with Adam, for whom it was an established turn-on, but today the rankness of his crotch and armpits simply reminded him of a sudden access of fear at the audition, when they'd made him rethink a speech and he'd seemed to forget everything, not just what they were asking him to do but everything he ever learned at drama school, and stood there clumsy and gaping in front of them, hating his own apparent stupidity. He wanted to wash it off now, the memory of that half-engaged expression on the face of Dermot the director, with his peroxide shock-mop and love handles under the 'f.c.u.k.' T-shirt, and the look of ratty impatience in the eyes of the Polish girl assistant, and the sense, more repugnant to him than anything else in the world, of being entertained for a plonker. Angrily he peeled off his sticky socks, approximated modesty with a twist of towel and banged the locker door so hard as almost to dent it with his fist.

The showers here were not arranged, as at others places of the kind, within a separate room where it was possible, by means of a little assiduous soaping, to evoke the requisite air of enthusiasm for your fellow ablutionists. Instead, something which might have been practicality but looked more like inspired impudence had decreed that they should be ranked along either side of a dimly lit tunnel between the first sauna cabin and steam-room and those on either side of the ill-aired dark room beyond. Everything was thus on view to those who passed along the slippery tiled alley in between, though in compensation the pallid, peach-tinted glow of lights in the vaulted ceiling always appeared more flattering than cruel. The effect reminded Theo of a portrait he'd seen once in an exhibition, showing a nobleman in doublet and ruff against a suddenly luminous perspective of niched nude statues down a marble corridor.

That was how he first saw Guy, sumptuous and marmoreal in the tunnel's softened brightness, hands behind his head as the water dashed his shoulders and tumbled down the grooves and hollows of his heavy, over-emphatic body. To Theo, sitting there on the slatted bench in the dark, his cock thickening under the towel with which he'd muffled it, less from embarrassment than for the privilege of disappointing curious onlookers, it seemed as if the other man's laborious precision in soaping and shampooing himself from various flasks taken out of a spongebag on the tiles at his feet (he would somehow, wouldn't he, have disdained that generic blue liquid from the pump dispenser attached to the wall) was deliberately calculated, as though he had known what unruly tremors of desire were overtaking the watcher from the shadows.

'You knew I was there,' Theo had said to him afterwards, 'that was why you took your time,' but Guy denied it with the air of someone who always counts on being believed.

Perhaps it was the same delaying tactic which made him reject Theo's suggestion that the pair of them remove to one of the cabins upstairs, where on black gym mats behind slatted doors which irritatingly failed to shut properly, and to the accompaniment of periodic thunderings from the trains overhead, you could enjoy an unlimited intimacy without the tiresome adjunct of gropers and spoilers which a bathhouse always threatens. It felt oddly not disappointing to remove instead to the terrace of little tables under blue-shaded lamps on either side of the stairs and sit there while Guy talked and he mostly listened, acquiring at once, through this unorthodox manoeuvre, a sense of himself as something apart, too precious to be had on the spot and cast aside in the dire critical clarity of perception which follows sex. Of course it might have been sheer snobbery, reasoned Theo, which deterred Guy from seizing the chance of an instant consummation, but something in him, as he later acknowledged, had wanted such fastidiousness from the outset. In that florid, imperious face and half-mocking richness of voice lay a kind of promise, a barely imaginable sophistication of those things which, merely looked at under the shower, had prompted his initial longing.

The quality of this desire had neither altered nor lessened since that moment. Theo, always wanting to believe, found in Guy an abundant plausibility. The palpable substance of his shoulders and thighs, his thick-lipped, slightly scornful mouth, his plump cock bagged up as enticingly as a pudding inside its generously ruched foreskin, the volleys and cascades of his laughter, the splay of his thick-knuckled hands, the irrepressible bunching of his curls, overwhelmed any tendency Theo might have had towards doubting him. The sheer opulence of effects on display seemed as much a guarantee of integrity as the dismissive candour with which he spoke of his possessions or his friends.

What there were – or rather more eloquently, weren't – of the former, Theo had been allowed to see when Guy decided that the two of them should return to his flat in Porchester Terrace. It was Theo's first encounter with the kind of private space which uses carefully studied emptiness to articulate secure affluence. You read about these places in *Wallpaper*, but the actuality was more moving than he had expected. In its reductiveness he discovered the affirmation, if any were needed, of Guy's sincerity. The bare expanses of wall and uncarpeted floor, windows sealed only by the plainest of blinds, high white ceilings, tables as slabs of slate tenanted only by a chaste little sandwich of magazines and exhibition catalogues, nothing whatever in the way of ornament or intrusive plant life except a few pots, a gleaming laboratory kitchen used merely to contain the elements of a supper which was somehow always miraculously in place without Guy having to do more than arrange it to his satisfaction, all made it impossible for Theo's attention to be distracted from him as the one vivid, breathing object in a universe which assumed meaning purely through his presence.

'Have you always lived like this?' Theo said, almost hearing his heart pounding in the blank, reverberate immensity. Guy grinned, then snorted with laughter as if the question had been a child's.

'Don't ask about always because I won't tell you. Let's just make it now.'

Now was what they made it on the bed, like some enormous judo mat across which Guy flung and grappled Theo, periodically clenching him into immobility and staring quizzically down at the body under his hands as if temporarily puzzled with the task of smearing its blackness across the milky waste of sheet beneath in a way which should gratify his sense of arrangement and congruity. Even the way he fucked, jamming a palm over Theo's mouth to stop him crying out while using a free arm to thrust his legs back over his head, was a kind of peremptory answer which saw off doubts and demurrals. It felt as near to being raped as Theo had ever come, and however many the occasions on which they had repeated it afterwards, the recollection of that first time continued to thrill him deeply.

As Guy had said, there was to be no always. Every moment since, in that rich, ballooning emptiness, was a now between them. That was why Theo mustn't ask. With the extraordinary quickness of apprehension on which his fellow actors leaned so often in rehearsal, he'd guessed, before the night was half over, what Guy wanted in the way of patient incuriosity. They might tell each other things in the course of conversation, over supper on the grey stone slab in the kitchen, bundled together on the cream leather sofa while they giggled through a Cadinot video, or after fucking, as Guy's still-imprisoning weight lay across him and the slowly levelling rhythm of his breath stirred in the tiny tufts of hair inside Theo's ears, but etiquette – or whatever it was – decreed that neither should actively strive to find things out about the other.

Like that Theo learned to value reticence, because paradoxically it seemed like a form of trust. By degrees, in any case, enough emerged to create the shadow of a context, though at a point when, after four or five encounters between them, it no longer seemed necessary and Theo was almost beginning to feel he'd rather not know after all. There was a job, and a house in the country outside Canterbury where a lover lived who made pots and wouldn't come to London, but could be, as Guy put it, grown up about what he did in the city on his own. Something in Theo wanted to ask whether Guy had told the lover, whose name was Mark, about meeting him. It seemed like the kind of thing Guy would do, unafraid of the consequences because he made whatever consequences there were. Mark, like anyone else, presumably played by the rules down there in the oast house in a village called Chillingbourne.

So Theo learned what an oast house was, just as, on their other occasions together, he came to learn that Alvar Aalto was a designer – and not that sort of designer either – and what bresaola tasted like. Did Guy patronize him? Just a shade, or a tad as he would say. And did Theo mind it? Well, not specially, for the time being at any rate, if only because their relationship, which is what he soon liked to consider it, seemed based on the notion of Guy as his preceptor and because Guy himself seemed so readily flattered by Theo's responsiveness. Underneath the requisite layers of attitude and his own brand of innocent narcissism, what was more, there lay a humility in Theo that resisted nothing worth knowing or remembering.

It felt different from being with Adam, not just because of what he was beginning to feel about Guy, but because Adam never held anything back from him and expected the same kind of candour. In the conversations at Porchester Terrace he never mentioned Adam by name. It was always 'a friend' or 'the guy I share with' or 'my flatmate', and at first the avoidance had been merely a good-natured indication of his willingness to play to Guy's rules. Lately, however (the more so through Guy's complete lack of interest in this aspect of his life), Theo had begun perversely to savour the exclusion of Adam from their discourse as a token of something stronger between them, which should specifically depend on a deliberate erasure of anything beyond the immediacy their encounters created. This was why he'd given Guy his mobile number instead. The notion of Adam hearing and then commenting on the peculiar reverberations of that voice was hateful. He wasn't sure, indeed, if he particularly liked the idea of it regularly speaking to Mark the oast house potter.

Yet now a little shudder of retrospective embarrassment went through him at the memory of his sudden surliness that morning. The banal expedient of washing up the breakfast things instead of merely stacking them in the dishwasher had only made Adam more distant and offended, and it wasn't in any case as if Theo intended to tell him what he really wanted to know. There had to be a way of making him learn what Theo piqued himself on having grasped already: that with Guy, except in certain carefully delimited areas, you never asked, but might instead be told.

Hooped within Guy's arms, he gave another little shake.

'Feeling cold, tarbaby? Want me to put the heating up?'

'Not specially, thanks. It was something I remembered, that's all.'

'Don't remember, it's bad for you. People always remember the wrong things.' Guy's grip tightened somewhat as he crooked his thigh reassuringly over Theo's and nuzzled the back of his neck. 'It must have been before you met me.'

'Sort of.'

'Forget it, then. I'm not good at other people's anxiety.'

Theo turned his head just enough to be able to look quizzically at Guy. 'That sounds like a warning.'

'Could be. The answer's always to do something positive, that way it doesn't master you. Feelings are a bore when they take over.' As if playfully, he flopped backwards on to the bed, leaving Theo suddenly tenantless and unguarded. 'So get up and put on the Nina Simone I was playing earlier.'

It felt nice for the present, being told what to do, directed in the scene, as it were. Except that with directors you'd want to argue or give them your reading of a line, whereas Guy was different. Never before had Theo come across anyone who so completely assumed obedience, and the surprise temporarily disabled his more rebellious urges. So he got up now and padded over to the Marantz on its glass panel in the wall and clicked the disc into place, so that Guy could reach down to the zapper and press 'play'.

'Stay still, chocolate soldier, you look seriously munchy in those Armani's. Were they the ones I gave you last time?'

'Yeah, I thought you'd –'

'Good boy, too right I would. Hold it there, tarbaby.'

There was to be nothing, Theo realized, in one of those pulse-quickening instants of perception which desire induces, beyond Guy, superb and ineluctable in an almost nakedness, moving towards him across the bleached boards between little pools of shadow. This then was the point of the tabula rasa prepared by the flat's spaces and surfaces. Definition existed solely within the form which now approached, the sheen and contour of its muscularity allowing no other focus or credible rival as contender for his interest. The single fact the room contained was a present imperative in the rage of Theo's cock against its imprisoning mesh and in the touch, strangely cold, of Guy's fingers across the deep valley down his spine.

'What do you people do to keep your skins so soft? One of these days you must give me the secret.'

The music, knowing and worldweary, had begun to irk Theo in its studied refusal to let go.

'Have you ever –' he began.

'Have I ever what?' whispered Guy against Theo's parted lips.

'It doesn't matter.'

So he let Guy kiss him because, after all, that was better than discovering that he might indeed not have heard of Diedrich Becker.

V

SHE'D always hated couscous. She loathed its friable texture
and the way it so obviously tasted of nothing in particular, and
the miserably apologetic look it assumed in even the most
attractive dish or bowl. There was in addition the sinister
quality it seemed to possess of having things mixed up in it that
ought not to be there. You imagined suddenly chomping on a
hairslide or a toenail, or gulping down a pellet of navel fluff or
getting a hank of someone's old dental floss stuck between
your incisors. Above all, she associated it with the kind of life
marriage to Jeremy was supposed to have put an end to. On the
morning of their wedding some, at least, of her exhilaration
was attributable to the thought that she would never again have
to visit Kentish Town, a place where, on more than one dismal
occasion, they had tried to feed her couscous.

So she was shocked, as opposed to merely surprised, when
Veronica Mills suggested it at the meeting as an accompaniment
for the barbecue in aid of the bells. Tessa from the bookshop in

Pershore had got quite enthusiastic in support, and Serena's experience warned her that once Tessa got going she had to be sort of talked down like Samaritans with a potential suicide wobbling on a ledge. Thus Joanne's intervention with the idea of coronation chicken saved the day. Of course, it wasn't really suitable, and most people wouldn't want it as an alternative to chargrilled steaks, and in any case they were talking, weren't they, about things that went with rather than main meats, but at least it knocked couscous firmly on the head. Jeremy would have a fit when she told him on Thursday.

Serena was glad it was Thursday, rather than Friday, he was coming down. She'd grown increasingly to dislike the idea of him stuck in the grim weekend 6.20 from Paddington, with Oxford students dossing outside the loos and men in blue shirts telling their mobiles they'd just left Charlbury and would be in Evesham by eight o'clock. Travelling first, as of course he did, made him no less flustered, poor lamb, looking like a kind of crumpled god, she always thought, as he approached the car under the sporadic flare of the station lamps. She'd made things nice for him at the house, of course, taking his freshly ironed jogging pants and ribbed grey vest and putting them in a neat pile on a chair in his dressing room, checking that the mirrors were clean (he'd complained about that last time) and gouging the last little zigzags of clotted alluvial mud out of the soles of his wellingtons.

She never did this sort of thing in Holland Park. Carmen and Morgana managed that instead. Down here, on the other hand, it offered a kind of fulfilment, like a therapy in which the healing process is achieved through patient repetition. Thus it gave her a little vitalizing frisson whenever Jeremy started complaining about the draughts or the mess Gaga made on the lawn or the way other people's cars churned up the gravel and dropped bits all over it which he had to pick up. Besides the fact that he wasn't inherently a country person, something she'd understood ages ago and learned quickly to forgive – because forgiveness, Reverend Mother had taught them at school, was the ultimate luxury, wasn't it? – it meant that like most men he still needed taking care of, even at thirty-six. He could run the Ethel Chauncey Wooldridge Foundation like a clockwork battleship and still be a hopeless baby about getting a balsamic vinegar stain on his shirt.

He'd laugh, she knew, when she told him about Veronica Mills and the couscous. Alice, hearing about it now, for whatever reason, did not, sitting there staring over her cup as if the act of drinking tea had in some way become un-compromising as a result. Her face, Serena always thought, wasn't entirely modern in its moonlike roundness and the odd, slightly porcine tilt of its nose, the air of antiquity enhanced by the fringe of little curls she had worn for as long as they'd know each other. It reminded you of something peering down from a church roof or lying, serene and sightless, in alabaster on top of a tomb chest, next to some armour-plated husband. Except that Will was much too lanky to play the knight beside her and they hadn't got a dog to lie at their feet.

Sipping at last, Alice asked, 'Sib, do you enjoy that sort of thing? Meetings and minutes and people making points of order and putting each other down?'

'Well, you obviously don't.'

'I wasn't talking about me.'

Serena paused for a moment, more because it seemed appropriate than through any sudden onset of doubt.

'It's something one does in the country, isn't it?' she said. 'Going to meetings about church bells with people who want to eat couscous at a barbecue.'

Alice shrank from the notion of eating anything at a barbecue. The thought that she would almost certainly have to attend this one was bad enough.

'You don't spend as much time down here as me,' Serena went on, 'so you wouldn't –'

Alice laughed, indulgent of her patronizing. 'Not to save my life. Is this what you talk about in Holland Park when you and Jeremy are alone?'

'No, as it happens. Well, yes, sometimes. And we almost never are.'

'What?'

'Alone together in Holland Park. There are nearly always people to dinner, or else we're out at things. But when he's down here he thinks it's a total gas. I fancy he rather likes the idea of me doing that sort of thing, flower rota, polishing the brasses, WVS and whatever.'

And is that why you do it, Alice longed to ask but didn't, wiping down Captain the Hon. Reginald Stallard of the 2nd Battn. Worcestershire Regiment, killed in action at the battle of Spion Kop, with a lick or two of Brasso, or clattering in with the shepherd's pie and mashed swede to Mrs Amphlett who's ninety if she's a day, and putting smilax and madonna lilies in the green vases on those tall stands at either side of the rood screen, because Jeremy likes the idea? Instead she abruptly changed the subject.

'Adam's coming down the weekend after next.'

'Brilliant, we can play duets. Maybe Jeremy can give him a lift if he decides on the car. It's a bore Adam not driving.'

'I don't think it's a bore for him,' said Alice reprovingly.

'You're always so defensive of your cousin, aren't you? I only meant that he can't get about and look at churches and things unless somebody takes him.'

'He does pretty well. And it keeps him out of mischief.'

Serena gave an arch little laugh, as if detecting a hopeless naïveté in what Alice had just said.

'I expect he's got plenty of opportunity for getting into other kinds of mischief.'

'Such as?'

'You know what gay men are like. There are these clubs they go to, aren't there? And Clapham Common, Adam practically lives on it, I should think. It probably makes him rather sexy, with the right kind of man around. Jeremy and I are always spotting men for Adam. We went over to Bretforton in the summer to play tennis with Nick and Julia, and there was this boy stacking bales in the farmyard next door – sort of half-caste-looking with Afro hair and stripped to the waist – and Jeremy said, well, we both did, "That's one for Adam."'

Alice smiled wanly. 'I'm sure he'd be thrilled.'

'Are you? I don't know. They don't settle down, do they?'

'He shares with a friend.'

'Yes, but that's only a lodger. They aren't an item and Adam never talks about him, he's funny like that, living his life in separate compartments.'

'Can't you ever imagine doing that?'

'Obviously not,' said Serena a shade peevishly. 'It's always me, wherever I am. And I'm sure Jeremy's the same.'

Wincing slightly, Alice got up and feigned a preoccupied stare out of the window and along the lane towards the distant evidence of Will parking the car with laborious precision.

'Zoe's having a holiday homework crisis,' she said, 'and I've promised to help. They've dumped all this GCSE French on her. Drop by tomorrow, Will'd love to see you.' In a sudden guilty access of charity, she added, 'Let me know if there's anything I can do for the bells, won't you?'

Except standing around in a damp garden belonging to someone she hardly knew, with a glass of villainous wine and a congealing mutton chop. Bugger Jeremy! With a broomstick or the business end of a hock bottle for preference. Fuelled by the sudden rush of her annoyance, her pace quickened as soon as she had negotiated the path, generally made lethal to the unwary by Gaga's dark green turds, and got out into the lane. The shadow on the surrounding orchards seemed to have fallen with a curious abruptness that evening, like somewhere in southern Europe rather than central Worcestershire. From the fields towards the Pershore road she caught the barking of a fox, like somebody's louche, hysterical laughter. The silence otherwise, beyond the occasional hiss of traffic in the distance, was complete yet not threatening to her. She wondered why Serena, unafraid of darkness and solitude in the country, was always so frightened of this little bit of lane at night. You felt that for two pins she'd have put lamps in the hedgerows, as if to turn it into some suburban 'close' with planters full of nicotiana and geraniums and ramps for the disabled.

In the porch Alice paused for a moment before entering the house. She didn't want Will and the children to see she was cross, if only because having to explain it, even supposing that worth the trouble, would be impossible. And after it had stopped being impossible, there'd be some sort of residual embarrassment. Under the pall of shadow on the plum trees there was still the faintest snatch, after all, of daylight, and against it, among the little scatter of untended woodland on the edge of the big field bounded by the white iron paling of the park, she could make out the Hermitage, jaggedly convincing in the dusk, whereas during the daylight hours it looked like the amusing rococo fake it actually was. Better, presumably, to look like a fake than genuinely be one. Perhaps, on the other hand, the whole point was to do it properly or not at all. With the issue unresolved, Alice pushed open the front door.

The air of unbudging normality within the house did nothing to alter her mood. For a while, as pure occupational therapy, she sought to enmesh herself, like some classic co-dependent, in the toils of Zoe's French homework, before growing annoyed by the passivity with which her daughter sat there under the lamp, playing with the ends of her hair as she watched Alice frowning at the less reasonable demands of the textbook. It was exceedingly beautiful hair, and the thought that she had in part been responsible for the way in which its profligate ash-blonde sprays now tumbled around Zoe's neck began irritatingly to distract Alice from the pose of disinterested benevolence she'd adopted on sitting down.

It was too early to start making supper, and there was no Jack to do music practice with because earlier in the day Will had absent-mindedly allowed him to go to a party near Evesham with two of his friends from the village. Sooner or later the worries would kick in, about how he was going to get back and whether he'd remembered to take a key and what thoughtless contribution he might have made towards the demographic statistics of Worcestershire. Even at fifteen Jack, she had gathered from certain admiring asides, was a bit of a one. There was every sign, what was more, that he wasn't going to leave it at that.

She went into the dining-room and banked up the fire before settling down with the volume of somebody's diaries Daisy had given her as a birthday present. The whole business of present-giving with Daisy was a carefully orchestrated mixture of the haphazard and the condescending. Something always left you with the idea that the gift, whatever it might be, was fished off the shelf at the last moment, while she'd been running late or talking on the mobile, yet it was invariably given with that queenly air which, though probably inherited, might just as well have been among the things they taught her at ballet school. 'It is the Princess Aurora's birthday, and you are the beautiful Lilac Fairy who has come to bestow on her a rare and precious *cadeau*.'

The diaries were neither rare nor precious and the distance which, in earlier volumes, lent enchantment to the view had now sufficiently contracted for the writer's preoccupations to seem thoroughly commonplace and time-wasting. As honest with herself as she knew how to be, Alice scarcely doubted that in fifty years' time, as an old woman, she would be any more interesting than this, filling notebooks with little vignettes of Glyndebourne dinner intervals and holidays in southern Tuscany, or snobbish remarks about the way other people spent their money. She'd never felt inclined to keep a diary. Serena kept one, of that she was almost certain, with a lot in it, probably, about making jam.

She heard Will come downstairs as if to rescue her from the impacting triviality, not to speak of the feeling that she had merely picked up the book in order to avoid having to think about Serena. Without absolutely acknowledging his wife's presence in the room, he poured himself a whisky and flopped down opposite her, his long legs sticking out in a way which always reminded her of somebody trying to dismantle a tent.

'Aren't you having anything?' he asked, as Alice put the book aside thankfully.

'I got through three cups of tea at Sib's,' she said. 'I had to have something to do with my hands.'

'What would you have done otherwise?'

'Boxed her ears.'

Will snorted with glee. 'People don't do that nowadays, do

they? You only read about it in Victorian novels. But occasionally –'

'Not just occasionally. She gave me a bore-by-bore account of the parish appeal committee and why Jeremy likes to go jogging and how they'd got one of their ritzy architect friends to convert the stable into a . . . what was it she called it? A *foresteria*.'

'What the buggery?'

'Exactly. The gospel according to Jeremy, as revealed by Sib to an expectant world, tells us that it's a place they have in Italian villas for visitors to sleep in.'

'Which others might call a guest wing.'

'This one's definitely going to be a *foresteria*. Can't you imagine? "We're putting Dinah and Crispin in the *foresteria*." With an extra slice of polenta for breakfast, no doubt, if they make nice noises about the glass bricks.'

'Except it won't be, will it? They're so bloody authentic about everything, it'll be Prince of Wales heritage floorboards and tuckpointed bricks and original Ernest Gimson chairs from the antique shops over in Moreton. It'll be so in-keeping they'll need a resident innkeeper.'

Alice didn't laugh at his pun, despite her agreeably unfeminine fondness for them, but sat staring nervelessly into the fire.

'Was it that awful?' asked Will with a sidelong glance of compassion.

'I don't know why I bother. It's like visiting someone in an institution, it leaves me so depressed. You just know it's not real when you listen to her.'

'What is then?'

'Sorry?'

'Real. This is all Serena ever wanted, isn't it? A sort of middle age before she's altogether stopped being a girl.'

'She's not stupid. Before that hippy phase in Kentish Town

she got a university degree, and not at some Mickey Mouse ex-poly either. OK, it was medieval history, and that's often such a cop-out. Lots of people do it because they want to be nuns or mince around like something out of an illuminated missal. But Sib's got a brain.'

'Yeah, yeah, the last enchantments of the Middle Age that never wars, but you know what I mean. They're never going to make babies, are they? Just as well the kids were out of nappies by the time they got married. That house is the least childproof ever.'

'It gives me the creeps.'

'Don't exaggerate.'

Again Alice looked into the fire, grinning satanically as the piled logs spat glowing embers across the hearth.

'I'd like to trash it,' she said. 'We've got the spare keys, haven't we? We could go in there and spray-paint the walls like graffiti artists with our . . . whatever they're called, Jack told us the other night.'

'Tags, aren't they?'

'Yes, and after that we could rip up the matting, tip all the pot-pourri down the loo, cut holes in those expensive sheets Jeremy bought in Paris, and open everything on the larder shelves so that it rotted.'

Will rolled his eyes. 'Cor, you've got it bad! If she's happy –'

'You know she isn't. That's the first time I've heard you use a cliché in ages. Happiness is just something she makes for herself to please Jeremy, like needlepoint cushion covers.'

'I suppose it is a bit implausible wanting to please one's husband. I'm fonder than you are of old Jezebel, but people spent far too much time trying to keep him sweet. What does Serena say about the jogging?'

'Compulsive, apparently.'

'Bloody ridiculous in the country, coming on like a magazine cover in those vests. Who the hell's he trying to impress?'

Alice, looking at Will, a rumpled giraffe, whisky tumbler in hand, murmured contentedly, 'Not you, that's for sure. But probably not Serena either.'

She was glad when afterwards he offered to do the supper. Difficult to say exactly why, but the hour with Serena had been unsettling to a degree at which it seemed entirely appropriate for her husband to start treating her like an invalid. So Alice went upstairs and spread herself on the bed with the early TV news turned down to a comfortable mutter and a pile of magazines to leaf through if she felt like it. After a while she switched off the telly and listened to the noises in the house, the distant but steady thump of Zoe's music, the hum of the extractor in the kitchen, Will trying to shut the recalcitrant pantry door and the knocking in the pipes when he ran the hot water. Was this nothing more, she wondered, than the same kind of reassuring domesticity which coddled Serena and Jeremy? You couldn't imagine them, after all, on a housing estate, claiming benefit and living off pot noodles, but it was hardly more plausible to conceive of Serena dishing dollops of coronation chicken into plastic bowls for the church barbecue.

Restless again under the sheer weight of what she understood but hadn't been able to explain to Will, Alice got up, padded across the bedroom, opened the window and peered out into the dark. Warm and damp, the night seemed more autumnal than the harbinger of an early spring. Again she heard the fox's shrill, stertorous bark. Perhaps it could be persuaded to break into Gaga's pen and eat her, so that Jeremy, arriving on Thursday, would be met by a tearful Serena clutching a handful of bloodstained feathers. Well, it was an idea, wasn't it?

VI

You can't stop thinking about sex. You're selling the pass by admitting it, of course, in terms of the utterly hopeless position of men at the close of the twentieth century, bullied by women into accepting a dogmatic concept of themselves as moral and emotional paraplegics. What's more, you're playing into the hands of the family values brigade, who want everybody to believe that gay guys are hopelessly in thrall to an obsession with one another's dicks. Do you remember, during the late eighties, when, by a singular irony, the hooha over Clause 28 of the Local Government Act suddenly got people realizing how much of the unbought grace of life, the cheap defence of nations et cetera, was actually due to the pansies in their midst (who became thereafter an endangered species), how the phrase 'proselytizing homosexuals' passed current for a season? One had a bizarre image, didn't one, of faggots perched on soapboxes at street corners, punching their fists into well-thumbed copies of the *Spartacus Guide*, or marching up and down with billboards like that man in Oxford Circus who used to hand out leaflets warning that protein made you randy, and whose catalogue of its disastrous consequences ended with the oddly bathetic phrase 'and sitting'.

It's true, you think about it all the time (sex that is, rather than sitting, though you do rather too much of that as well, one way or the other). You think about it going to work on the Underground, when some half-awake boy in a shiny-kneed suit and scuffed, square-toed loafers is sitting opposite you trying to read *The Beach* as the equivalent of a cold bath and five-mile run, to douse the abusive thoughts he has of the girl invincibly ignoring him in the gangway of the Edgware-via-Charing Cross. You'd like to be the dark blue shirt that boy put on this morning, maybe not showering first, but just stumbling out of bed in his singlet and boxers (for alas, it is boxers he wears) after falling asleep again to Kiss FM on the radio alarm, the shirt that stays on him all day till he comes home some time around eight, numbed and zonked with work and carrying the take-out bag whose contents he'll microwave for supper, the dark blue shirt which knows the milky skin-scent in the hollows of his under-muscled back and chest, smooth, as most of them are these days, with, you like to imagine, large nipples, their rosettes a dark chocolatey purple like the underside of a mushroom.

Quite possibly he is stupid and vulgar, knowing nothing but the history of every goal scored by Chelsea since Gianluca Vialli, with the gap of good luck between his top teeth and that bald head you'd like to squeeze between your thighs, took over as manager. You don't care about this, but it might upset you more if it were true of the guy you stand next to on the Victoria Line to Oxford Circus. He is talking to an acquaintance met on the platform about things which don't interest you nearly as much as the tone of his voice, possessed of that throaty, caressing softness peculiar to those whose parents left the sunlight in Paphos or Lecce or Malaga to give life to them over a deli or a dry-cleaner's looking out on to damp-filmed pavements somewhere in Camden Town. The unmistakable London Mediterranean timbre, with which, by the time the train reaches Green Park, you've fallen hopelessly in love, enthralled likewise by the livid darkness of his mouth and solemn-looking brown eyes, their immense lashes like awnings over the shop windows of an afternoon street, and the sallow paleness of his forehead emphasized by an edging of coarse black curls. Not the shirt this time, says your lickerish fancy, as you try to avoid catching his glance lest it lifts the veil of your unhallowed imaginings. No, instead you'd like to be, wouldn't you, the pair of white briefs he has taken out of the drawer that morning, ripened by now with the sweat of his bollocks and drawn tight over the furry curves of his arse. 'Oh would I were a glove upon that hand!' By Oxford Circus, where, through a malign ordinance, you're forced to leave without him, you have reached the state of ecstatic lust in which a request to jump with him off the edge of the world must seem like a divine condescension.

Adam would never have wanted, even if he could, to forgo the pleasure of unsatisfied longing, to affect a celibate disdain for what lay in any case beyond his immediate reach, or to agree with those who maintained the merest acknowledgement of such imperatives to be pointless and demeaning. Yet there were moments when he found himself wondering if others dwelt quite so consistently in this universe of imperfectly scratched itches, mapping the sheets with the spillage of morning hard-ons from banal, preposterous reveries over what might have been, or all those needle-pinches of unspecified appetite prompted by turning the pages of a magazine or casually zapping the TV. Theo doubtless did the same, but then Theo was like another part of himself, *mein bess'res Ich*, with whom it seemed almost pointless to identify the problem, supposing it really were that. Was it different for straight men, like Basil, who sometimes seemed less inclined to want the straggle of women invariably surrounding him than to happen upon them in frank surprise, as if they'd been leaves or burrs snagged on his clothes?

There were times too when the sheer volume of memory grew burdensome. Once registered, images, instead of dutifully purging themselves, simply shuffled into the file, to be summoned up by the least twitch of association. Holidays abroad were particularly lethal in this respect. Adam had long ago stopped asking himself why exactly it was that he went on remembering a stocky boy in shades seen on a station platform at Menton, a thin, bald figure in vest and shorts perched reading on the parapet of a wall behind a white cathedral in the Apennines, or the coarse black hairs on a fisherman's neck which the breeze stirred in the taverna by the ruins on Delos. Tricks were almost as bad. In your nostrils years later was the smell of the carpet on which someone had fucked you in a top-floor flat up the scruffy end of Oxford Gardens. Or you shuddered still at how cold it was in that room in Mile End, where, out of sheer goodness of heart, you'd helped a pretty blond Lebanese called Sarkis to write a letter to his girlfriend in Australia assuring her of his undying love, before you both bundled into bed with your shirts to keep warm.

Thus the man at the Canonbury crossing last Sunday had already been folded into this process of nagging archival insistence. That insolent grin was not to be forgotten, purely because there had been no sequel allowed, no resultant disillusion, merely the abiding promise of him, neat and loose-limbed in the sunlight among the blotched trunks of the plane trees, perched like a confident acrobat on the edge of disaster. Adam should have taken Basil at his word and turned back. In any case he'd not been listening seriously enough to dis-entangle, from the plaintive litany of rejection, a genuine reason for his friend's access of gloom beyond a generic snub from an over-zealous editor. It ought to have felt like that night in the club in Bermondsey, only it didn't. There the smile had been conditional, a delusive handhold snapping under him as he fell. Instead came a sense, bizarre at these years of danger and ill-kept resolutions to go to the gym, that for a golden instant he was infinitely desirable.

Perhaps this, thought Adam, at his desk on the *piano nobile* of the Ethel Chauncey Wooldridge Foundation, was the real reason why people chose to spend most of their waking hours at work. It was entirely possible to believe that the paper-faced, slack-mouthed creatures he watched tumbling out of buses by the Polygon or being jolted off the up-escalator at Clapham Common at ten o'clock in the evening were all anaesthetizing a private obsession by staying so late at their law firms and merchant banks. One of these days he'd stay on after six at the Foundation, to see whether it made him feel more meritorious and offered the notional bromide to his horniness. As it was, even for a few hours, drudgery over begging letters and grant applications gave him the necessary relief from having to remember that gentian-blue glance, with its air, when he con-sidered it, of slightly glacial decisiveness, or the impression, swiftly but indelibly registered, of a disgusting perfection in the laundered pleats down the front of that collarless shirt.

The prospectus, as edited by Basil, provided an obvious refuge. Adam's heart sank, nevertheless, at the notion of his own neat little paragraphs, under 'Commonwealth Enterprise', 'Social Outreach', or 'Awards to Young Choreographers', getting swamped by the kind of splashy mission statement Jeremy was likely to clap on at the front. As for Ethel Chauncey Wooldridge herself, the Rhode Island widow whose Anglophilia had caused her to buy the moated grange near Tenterden where between the wars she had entertained Churchill, the Astors, Circe Londonderry and darling Herr Ribbentrop, before developing a social conscience to the infinite distress of her Stateside relatives and leaving everything to be enjoyed by 'the young people of Great Britain and her overseas possessions pursuing high endeavour in the arts and sciences', well, wasn't she going to look a bit shabby beside the latest portrait study of the chairman, benign yet ever so faintly Gilbert-and-George-posey in his Cerruti number against a cutting-edge vista of installations at a Goldsmiths' degree show?

That was him now on the stairs. Jeremy never simply arrived at the office as the others did, Adam and Celia the development executive and Liz the secretary. The performance, though it took place on at least three mornings in each of forty-odd weeks throughout the year, recalled a grand seigneur's return to his country estate. Following the bestowal of the coat and umbrella, there'd be a few minutes' noisy affability with Liz, including some well-placed condescension on the topics of her garden or her children, neither of them things for which Jeremy ordinarily gave a rap. The resonance would significantly alter as he wandered into Celia's domain. Celia, after all, had been a research fellow at Oxford, had worked at Chatham House and knew people who wrote 'Whither Europe?' articles for *Prospect*. She sometimes had the air of finding the Foundation much too frivolous, and therefore

Jeremy needed to moderate his patronizing with a pinch or two of cautious respect. After which it was Adam's turn for the kind of remarks which always made him wonder whether he shouldn't be stationed on the landing with wetted forelock and gleaming livery buttons, to say, 'Very good to have your lordship back with us once more.' For two pins he'd have done something like it – there was barely a year's difference in age between the pair of them – only Jeremy wasn't the kind you could tease with impunity.

'Had a bit of a run-in with the traffic warden on the square, didn't I?' he announced, as if answering the question Adam had not actually been going to put. 'Some bastard's practically parked on our bit of pavement, and I just asked, in the nicest possible way, whether they couldn't shift him, and the man bit my head off.'

'Goodness,' said Adam without conviction. Jeremy's idea of the nicest possible way was not everybody's.

'Only a brat, anyway.' He shot a sidelong glance at Adam. 'Looked rather your type, as Serena always says.'

'You could open up an escort agency if you get bored with the Foundation. The way the pair of you keep spotting likely lads for me, you wouldn't be short of a bob or two from anyone else.'

'It's Serena, not me. Most of hers are bits of Worcestershire rough with straw behind their ears.' He looked at the desk. 'What are you going to torment me with this morning? A Pre-Raphaelite angel with a peaked cap and estuarine vowels tearing a strip off me is bad enough for starters.'

Silently Adam shuffled him the file of applications and Jeremy, with a certain fretfulness, started to rifle through them.

'"Justine has been doing barre exercise", has she though? No thanks. Tiffany from Forest Hill. Hmmm. Wants a leg-up at Rose Bruford. Well, we just might. Duane from Leeds has sent a photo, very "Dance Theatre of Harlem" that, full marks for enterprise. A yes, I think, don't you? Sarah, can't spell "choreographer", but would like to be one. I'll have a long think about these. Oh, and talking of choreography, my sister-in-law's been on the phone.'

Jeremy always referred thus to Daisy, as if she'd been some necessary evil involved in marrying Serena. Their mutual dislike amused Adam by its obliquity. Less sophisticated people would simply either have avoided one another as far as they reasonably could, or else have declared an open hostility. Instead, important hours of their respective lives were devoted to putting up with each other in order not to seem as commonplace in their responses as everybody else. In an ideal world they'd have eloped together years ago.

'Presumably I'm supposed to know what she wants,' Adam said, more than slightly nettled at Daisy's manoeuvre.

'Apparently on Sunday you weren't enthusiastic enough.'

'If you'd been there on Sunday you could have done it better. Where were you?'

'What do you mean?'

'Just teasing,' said Adam. 'Doubtless it was something better than changing your infant niece's nappies. Or dy-purrz as we presumably have to call them, since Edie is American by birth.'

Jeremy gave a satisfied smile. 'Much better than that, yes. Anyway, she rang.'

'And the upshot is that you want me to go down to Clerkenwell and watch Francesco Damiani creating.'

'Well, I just thought . . .'

'It's not really us, is it? American whizzkid bored with Noo Yoyk and people who go around talking in that pathetic stuffy way about "Mister Balanchine" twenty years after the old boy's dead. So the whizzkid comes to Europe at some impossibly early age and gets himself a reputation in no time as a modernist show-off.'

'Isn't that a bit harsh, Adam?'

'I thought the whole point was that we didn't give to Americans. And we're in the business of making names rather than subsidizing them. The Arts Council's just pressed a five-figure envelope into that particular company's hands.'

'It's his first time in London,' said Jeremy weakly.

'My, my, so we all grovel at the favour done us! The god of the dance descends to Coldbath Fields or wherever the bloody studio happens to be. Cue orchestra, winch down the pasteboard clouds.'

Jeremy had turned to study himself in the amboyna-work mirror by the door. 'It'll be nice,' he said to the glass. 'Nice for our profile if we can hook on somewhere.' He brushed a little crinkly black hair off his lapel.

'I suppose if it's to get Daisy off your back then I'll go,' said Adam.

'Oh, come on, Ad, I didn't mean –'

'Yes you did. I told her I would anyway. When Daisy gets to write her autobiography it'll be called *Dancing Attendance* and it'll be a long list of everybody she's managed to get to do things for her. A bit of resistance is no bad thing now and again, don't you find?'

Jeremy wasn't listening. He had turned again to the mirror and stood gazing anxiously at something which seemed to displease him all of a sudden.

'Do you ever think –'

'About what?'

'Does it ever strike you that now and then you can look into a mirror and see somebody completely different?'

Not especially struck by the question's originality, Adam merely answered, 'No, I don't. Your image is reversed anyhow. Who did you want to see?'

'Well, me, of course.'

'You Jeremy? As opposed to anyone else you might be.'

Jeremy's face, with its sunbed tan and heavy parenthetical lines around the mouth, dissolved into a radiant grin, as if Adam had arrived already at a perception others must have taken ages to reach.

'It's just a thought. Ad?'

'Yes?'

'Do you think I need to lose weight?'

VII

THE studio wasn't in Coldbath Fields, but round the corner in that nowhere land of exclusive loft conversions above deep streets like crevasses, clinging to the edge of what had once been a little Italy full of revolutionaries and drawing masters, models and organ-grinders and pedlars of plaster images in the days of Mazzini and Garibaldi. It seemed entirely appropriate that a different species of vagrant Italian, albeit one whose status and prospects were more assured than any of these, should have fetched up here putting dancers in and out of attitudes, much as others had done when the theatres smelt of gas, orange peel and sweat, rather than of nothing at all as they do nowadays.

Adam was late, on purpose he had to admit. There was nothing he fancied less than watching a rehearsal involving people in shapeless clothes, whose movements discoursed a rhetoric which only became comprehensible in a context of lights and décor and a crowded auditorium. This emptiness made of mirrors and a bare floor was turned more chilly through the thumping of a tinny piano under the hands of the repetiteur, a boy in spectacles who did the job as a healthier, less legally hazardous alternative to busking on some more portable instrument in the tunnels of the Underground. Its reverberate noises had the unexpected effect of making the dancers, as they shuffled and squeaked across the room's steppe-like vacancy, seem still more unattractive than they looked already in an assortment of practice tights, leggings, headbands, comforters, floppy old harem pants and mangled vests. Adam had never bothered with learning to decode choreography sufficiently to be able to talk about it with anything which looked like authority. There were two reasons why he enjoyed dance, one of them as innocently idealistic as the other was brutally carnal. It enabled human beings to relinquish mortality and grow numinous for however brief an instant. And unless, as sometimes happened, their faces were irredeemably stupid, the men, especially when a seat in the front stalls allowed you to watch them sweating like horses, became elaborately flourished signatures of whatever was meant by the word desire. That was why he preferred modern dance. Classical ballet was the wrong kind of legs.

'Sweet of you to bother, darling' whispered Daisy satanically, under a sudden arpeggio gust from the piano. Adam stuck out his tongue at her.

'Beastly of you to phone Jezebel.'

'Thought you might wriggle out at the last moment.'

And you wanted to make it official?'

'That's the Greek over there, the tall one in the bandanna. He's called Paul. Quite scrummy, don't you reckon?'

As it happened, Adam did. There was a moody, pouting quality about the features which might have been off-putting

without the pencil lines of a double goatee *à la* George Michael
to give it the apposite Mephisthophelean finishing touch. To
archive for later, perhaps.

'I'm here to look at the dancing.'

'Don't be priggish.'

'Where's your friend?'

'They're all my friends. Well, most of them.'

'I mean genius Frankie from the West Village or wherever.'

'Down there, the one sitting with his back to us making
notes.'

Abruptly the music stopped. Seeming unmoved by the
choreographer's apparent lack of interest in what they had
been doing, the dancers scattered, relaxing into their routines
of casual exercise. With no obvious concern, the hunched
figure straightened, got up and moved towards the piano. Then
he turned, smiling vaguely and standing for a moment poised
like a tightrope walker, eternally ready to fall backwards yet
exultant in the supreme confidence of not doing so. He knew in
that instant who he was. Adam too had not forgotten.

No chance, after that, of concentrating on the rehearsal,
whenever it should resume. No room left for the slightest
interest in what its movement purported to design, some sort of
plot about a poet with a muse and multiple personalities,
according to Daisy's muttered commentary. The Greek, as
menacingly sultry in motion as in repose, became a mere
decorative flourish amid an ensemble which in any case acted
only as the background to furnish an occasion. There ought to
have been the sense, taken for granted, that Francesco,
deceptively slight-looking and small within that immensity, had
stepped into the midst of everything with a clear intent.
Frankly Adam could not have cared less for meaning, except
insofar as it stood in front of him, neat in a tight black vest,

hands on cargoed hips, shaven head thrown back, the one palpable element of definition and control. His own perpetual tendency to view life as a series of posed scenes, in which some invisible eye had carefully worked out the relationship between figures and objects so as to induce a continued air of intrigue, performance and deception, was the result of a deeper mistrust in his own validity amid a wider scheme of things. He seemed to himself to dwell for ever in a state of being only a moment or two away from discovering the hidden hand, the shadowy intruder stealing off so quickly after shuffling the latest contrivance into position. In this instant what had taken him by surprise was not so much the fact of recognizing Francesco as a feeling that he had caught the culprit red-handed in the business of putting everything together. Adam wasn't sure he quite liked that. It would have been better not to know. This was the first time he'd ever thought of innocence as a desirable condition.

Sublimely unacquainted with such a state, Daisy stood by him still, murmuring exegetically in the enduring assumption that it was the process which interested him rather than its divine manipulator. Had she guessed, or did she think the Greek was the beast in view? Certainly Adam wasn't going to tell her yet at any rate, though given the skill she had in clambering over even his most elaborate fences of secrecy, it would probably not be long before she found out. These was no harm, he realized, in her mistaking one kind of enthusiasm for another. The piquancy in their reversal of roles was irresistible. Now at last Adam was the opportunist, determined to exploit his advantage to the full.

Why then, when the rehearsal seemed about to end, did he suddenly feel like running away? For what must have been an hour Francesco had strikingly failed to acknowledge their presence as onlookers at the further end of the room, had not so much as glanced in their direction. Thus professionally concentrated he ought to have been admirable, whereas to Adam his behaviour was merely a kind of provocation, as though he knew they were both there — which of course he must — but was determined on absolute indifference. So, when at last he called, 'OK, break it there, you guys!' Adam made a little wincing movement of escape, which instantly flustered Daisy.

'What's the matter? Where are you going?'

'Off, like right now.'

'But you . . . Oh, Ad!'

'Your friend's not going to stick around?' Francesco was there behind him. Daisy's controlling hand grabbed his sleeve and hung on with ruthless indecorum.

'He's just a bit embarrassed, aren't you, Adam sweetheart? Come and meet Frankie. Frankie, this is Adam, Adam Killigrew.'

'Yeah, I know. Hey, Adam.'

As Adam sheepishly shook Francesco's hand, he was aware of Daisy's mild surprise.

'How did you know?' she asked.

'Because you said he'd come by.' Francesco beamed triumphantly. 'So I guessed this must be Adam. And it is. Bearing gifts from the Foundation?' He ran a mock-sedulous travel of regard up and down Adam's body. 'Somewhere in his pants maybe?' It was horrible, horrible because nothing in Francesco's blue eyes even hinted at recollection, and because of the cheap one-liner.

'I didn't know I was expected to provide handouts on the spot,' said Adam coldly. 'I suppose I could have brought tents and bandages and powdered soup as well.'

'You could, but you didn't,' returned Francesco, visibly nettled and executing a swift turn on the heel towards Daisy in best scornful-prince fashion. 'So where are we going, Sultana? I need some air.'

'Fear not, Cinderella. How about some food as well?'

'OK, food is cool right now. *Andiamo!*'

And, quite as if Adam had never existed, the pair linked arms and bounced away to the double doors like eager children, firing off a little volley of goodbyes to the departing dancers around them. It was the moment in which he should have run off and never seen either of them again, only that wasn't his style. Instead, like the dogged little terrier he knew himself to be, he went trotting after them downstairs and into the street. There was no use expecting help from Daisy, he realized, and she seemed disposed, in any case, to monopolize Francesco via the sort of dance-world gossip which should effectively exclude Adam from the conversation. It was managed thoughtlessly rather than with deliberate malice. When they sat down at one of the marble slabs in a restaurant at the top of the Farringdon Road and pointedly failed to consider the menu as anything more than a vulgar interruption, he resigned himself to the sickening awareness that this, for the next hour or so, was how things were going to be. The waiter hovered and the three of them irritably ordered, after which Adam, seizing any chance that remained, asked Francesco what exactly they'd been watching at the rehearsal studio, whereupon Daisy said, 'I tried to explain, but you weren't listening, were you?'

Francesco, a glint of crossness in his features, drew a breath wearily. 'There's a poet, Portuguese, Fernando Pessoa.'

'Yeah, I've read some of his stuff,' Adam blurted, as if that were of any account.

'And he was like these four totally different poets, all of them with something to say. And there was one who was like into the country, and fields and sheep and stuff, and then this other guy called Ricardo who was kind of a dandy and wrote these really neat little poems that were like – I don't know – classical or something. Oh yeah, and he started life as a woman, but he changed sex on the day he met the third poet, who was this totally weird dude named Alvaro, who did drugs and was like futuristic. It gets boring, I guess, if you don't know about Fernando Pessoa.'

Another flounce towards Daisy, as eloquently scornful as the first had been in the studio, seemed to imply that the real bore lay in having to talk to Adam, who writhed still more under the realization that his claim to have read Pessoa wasn't even acknowledged. Yet worse was the growing consciousness that Francesco, considered at close quarters across the lunch tale, a sort of no-man's land between their respective trenches, possessed a serpentine allure completely unsuspected in that afternoon epiphany at Canonbury, a glamour which his peevishness and impatience did nothing to dint. To the perverse attraction of that American gay voice, unmistakable as such in its timbre and cadence, was added the irrepressible discourse of his hands, moving as if behind some lighted screen where a shadow play was being performed. Even the way in which he enunciated certain words – 'Fernawndeau', 'woomin' – was cruelly entrancing to the victim, who now settled once more to the galling role of listener as the others traded reference and anecdote in their ostentatious you-can't-play interchange. From time to time Daisy, mischievously charitable, volunteered a scrap or two of explanation, but that only made things worse. When Francesco got a little restive at their order taking so long to arrive, with the implication that things were never like this in Manhattan, she seemed somehow to assign Adam the task of hurrying the waiters along, as though the choice of restaurant had been his in the first place.

He finished, of course, long before they did, and sat staring gloomily at the ruins on his plate, resolved, whenever the moment should present itself, to have things out with Daisy. Retributive sternness wasn't his forte, and experience warned him that it was unlikely to have any effect. She'd never, so far as he could recall, apologized to him for anything, preferring always to lay the blame elsewhere, unless he looked like being able to shoulder it himself. Once more he contemplated walking out, only to reflect that they might not even notice if he did. Distracted still by the grace and finish of line in the man sitting opposite him, by the porcelain blue of his eyes and by the comfortable way in which a smile kept settling itself between the lines framing his mouth, as the hands kept up their semaphore, Adam endured nervelessly until Daisy, just as pudding arrived, suddenly got to her feet, and murmuring, 'Please, don't wait for me,' disappeared downstairs.

For the briefest of moments Francesco looked significantly at Adam, turned to watch until Daisy's head was out of sight, then, seizing his arm across the table, half whispered, 'Hey, Adam, she doesn't know we saw each other already, right? Do you want to keep it that way for now?'

Utterly thrown by this manoeuvre, Adam could hardly speak. 'You mean you knew it was me?'

'What kind of dumb dancing nelly do you take me for? Why'nt you come back and talk to me anyway, instead of walking away with that friend of yours who looks like he could do with a valet service?' Francesco closed a hand over his. 'I watched till you were out of sight, you bastard.'

Disarmed by now, Adam burst out laughing. 'He may look

a total scruff, but he's a ferociously brilliant writer, and a friend of Daisy's, what's more.'

Francesco grinned, exultant in their suddenly realized complicity. 'Ferociously, yeah, that's neat, I like it, it's kind of Valley Girl. Instead of bodacious let's do ferocious. Ferocious is bodacious for the millennium. Keep watching for when she comes back.'

'We're all right so far,' Adam said. 'If you must know, he suggested I go after you.'

'Is he –'

'Basil is about as straight as the Greenwich meridian.'

Francesco's mouth fell open in exaggerated astonishment. 'Basil! Like in *The Bostonians?* Now that is truly ferocious. So why didn't you?'

'God, you don't give up easily.'

'Only when somebody bores me. Then it's *pour toujours.*'

'Because . . . because . . . This is completely third degree.' Don't come back, Daisy, not just yet.

'Because you imagined it might be . . . "inappropriate", isn't that the word? I love the way you guys say, when things are uncool, "That's not appropriate."'

'For a dumb dancing nelly you're surprisingly into words.'

'I was going to be an English major till I quit college and got into this shtik. You wouldn't think so from the ditzy way I talk, *n'est-ce pas?* They auditioned me for *Clueless* but I was too busy.' Francesco lowered his thick-lashed eyelids. It was the campest thing Adam had ever seen. 'I like to confuuuse peopaaall. Smokescreens, camou*flawge, mas*querade, transformayshin, I love all that stuff.' His voice had fallen to a gurgling Eartha Kitt baritone. Desperate to stay cool, Adam merely remarked, 'I've noticed,' then quickly added, 'she's coming. And we haven't touched our puddings.'

Francesco merely raised an admonitory finger to his lips, then, radiant, turned round to hail Daisy. 'Sultana, where've you been? We're getting withdrawal symptoms here.'

She surveyed the puddings. 'And you waited for me? Old-fashioned gallantry.'

'Yes, we shouldn't have.' The china-blue eyes took on a fiendish glint. 'We were ferociously hungry.' He paused to let the word sink in. 'Ferociously. But I guess we thought starting without you was kind of inappropriate.'

As Francesco's voice slid up to meet the end of the sentence Adam could scarcely forbear spluttering with laughter, but stifled it effectively enough by asking, 'By the way, what have you done with Edie?'

Daisy bridled somewhat. 'You make it sound as if I'd dumped her in a cupboard for the afternoon. She's in Holland Park keeping my sister company, which is hardly the same thing. Sib's better at it than I am, and as long as I collect before Jeremy gets back there won't be any blood on the carpet.' Brightly she turned to Francesco: 'Now where were we?'

'Oh, God, Professor Forsythe, Madame Tharp, stuff like that?'

This time, as they launched once again into their shoptalk, Adam's non-participation was that of the comfortable observer rather than the lurking groucher. Not by the merest facial twitch did Francesco indicate the shift he'd so successfully engineered in their degrees of knowingness, but from time to time Adam felt the deliberate pressure of a knee or an ankle against his own, designed to encourage a subversive enjoyment. When the bill arrived, he paid it with an almost exaggerated air of lordly munificence, as if it were the most natural thing in the world that the Ethel Chauncey Wooldridge Foundation should take care of the material needs of those to whom it wasn't necessarily going to dedicate a stiver in funding. Daisy smiled benignly as Adam picked up the tab. She had learned so well how to read him that he half wondered whether she guessed that the gesture meant something else altogether, a superstitious thanks offering for the presence of his fellow conspirator, saturnine, hands at rest now, and the hard calf of one leg pressed close to his under the table.

And the project, the very purpose of him being there at all? Not a word about it had been spoken, apart from Francesco's half-hearted explication as to Fernawndeau's alter ego turning into a woomin. That, of course, Adam reflected, would have been much too vulgarly straightforward as far as Daisy was concerned, while the demon choreographer, it was flattering to suppose, had his own reasons for wanting Adam to come back and watch some more. So he wasn't at all puzzled when, on the brash sunlit pavement outside, Francesco, buttoning his half-length leather against what was in the end not much of an afternoon chill, grew reptilian once more in the parade of leave-taking. A hand was extending and the lips were coyly pursed in the parody of regret.

'So good to meet you, Adam. Maybe you'll come by some time when I'm at Daisy's, I'd really like that.'

Adam knew how he was meant to play it. His stubby fingers touched Francesco's twitching fronds as if he were an Edwardian debutante getting ready to curtsey to royalty before passing down a palace presentation line. In the split second at which their eyes hooked on to each other's, he knew he'd got it right. This time, walking with Daisy towards her car, he was careful not to look back.

'Well?' she said as soon as they were out of earshot.

Adam had a calculated pause. 'Clever, certainly. Talented

maybe, one never honestly knows. They all seemed to think he was properly in control. I don't think I could ever –'

'Yes?' Her face was bright with anticipation.

'He isn't exactly Mister Likeable, is he? And you dropped me right in it with all that international ballet babble. Thanks for nothing.'

'You have to keep Frankie amused, otherwise he's on to the next thing, it's an occupational hazard with people like that. Were we horrendously boring?'

'Shitless-making. And don't say "poor you", because I know it's only pretence. Anyway I thought I was the point of the occasion, not him.'

'Well, you were, Ad darling, only –'

'Only you think he's more glam and you want to keep him sweet because that loft in Manhattan is sooo convenient.'

They got into the car, or rather, she got into the car and did the necessary fiddling with the inside door handle, which didn't work properly. Leaking and decrepit, its floors and seats cluttered with an occupational layer of old till receipts, theatre programmes, Edie's bonnets and wraps and a mangled, yellowing *A-Z*, it was the archetypal conveyance for People With No Money. Adam longed to burgle it one day, release the handbrake, trundle the wretched thing into the middle of Alwyne Villas and watch it skitter all the way down into Essex Road, where, with any luck, it would hit a passing truck and accomplish, probably not without a final arabesque of doomed elegance, its merited decomposition.

The idea of Daisy having thereafter to invest in a new car possessed him with a savage glee.

'Did you like the Greek?' she asked, as they lurched and hiccuped towards Holborn.

'On-the-spot shaggable but not for the anthology.'

'God, you're hard to please.'

'Not at all, I'd do it with a lamppost. But it'd still be just a lamppost at the end of it.'

'I don't think Frankie likes any of them much,' said Daisy. 'As dancers, I mean.'

'Too Briddish, I suppose. "We Americans know how to let it hang." Blahdiblah.'

'He thinks they're too good-looking. He's into odd shapes and saggy baggy oldies. He says they're more elastic.'

They fell silent for a moment. Adam felt suddenly exhilarated by what Daisy had told him. It seemed so much at odds with the notion formed, from the briefest acquaintance, of Frankie the perfectionist, in his gophered white pleats or muscle-hugging black top, growing crabby because the grub wasn't whisked up at the double, patiently ruthless in getting the dancers to be the things he wanted, complaining, rather as Basil had said he might, that England was a damp little place where nothing worked properly. Perhaps he only held physical beauty at arm's length for the sake of having something different to say. Or perhaps because his own version of it was enough to be going on with. Still, there was comfort in the sheer paradox implied, which Daisy, without knowing, had given Adam.

In New Oxford Street she pulled up sharply, close to the Centrepoint subway, and admonished him to let her know as soon as he could what the Foundation might come up with.

'And do you mind?' she asked, 'if I give Frankie your number? He might want to call you about it.'

Adam hoped his doubtful expression would offer her the requisite impetus of perverse encouragement.

'Yeah, well, maybe you can,' he said nonchalantly. 'Frankie might even make a bit more effort to explain the intellectualoid stuff about Pessoa's personality changes. I can't wait.'

Daisy laughed, comforted by his sarcasm. Then, as he jiggled the wretched door catch to get out, she remembered something else. 'Ad, what was the matter with Basil on Sunday? Did he say anything when you left?'

'It was over some story he sent to the *London Review* and they turned it down. Not their thing apparently.'

Looking away, she muttered, 'I thought that would happen. Maybe I . . . oh, it's not important, I'll tell you another time. Get him to show you the story and see what you think. Anyway, mustn't keep my sister waiting, or Edie for that matter. And you've got Jezebel to look after, who's the most impatient of the lot.' Leaning over to shut the door, she couldn't resist adding, 'You'll be kind to him, won't you?'

'Who, Jeremy? I'm much too nice already.'

'No, darling, I meant Frankie. He may act the tough cookie but he's probably quite vulnerable underneath. Likes to be appreciated, so be sweet. You can do it when you try.'

'Depends on whether I feel like trying. As I said, he's hardly a bundle of charm himself. But if you insist . . .'

Adam watched the rattletrap slew round into Charing Cross Road, as if to make absolutely certain that Daisy should be out of sight before the least hint of his exhilaration betrayed itself. Be kind to Frankie? How could he fail, unless Frankie himself didn't bother to call? Adam had lived long enough to know that to a certain species of man, in his experience more flourishing than endangered, the presentation of a telephone number means the very opposite of what the giver seeks to imply. There's something anti-erotic, a shot of bromide in the tea or a cold shower after a wank, in the presence of those names and numbers hastily scribbled on cigarette packets, torn-up lottery tickets, clubland flyers or the little cards on the bar saying 'Practise Safer Sex'. In a pitiless morning light the figures assume a suddenly baleful unattractiveness, and you grow fretful at details of the handwriting, details which the previous evening you'd have been only too happy to ignore. That dot over the capital I, those foofy little curlicues round a g or an m, are like members of a squad sent in to defuse an unexploded bomb. You don't immediately throw the thing away, but its presence, initially so reproachful, acts at length as a bizarre justification of your inertia.

So Frankie wouldn't ring. They'd meet again, if at all, under Daisy's surveillance, allowing him to indulge in that kind of roguish flirtation which Adam suspected was his stock-in-trade with everyone who hinted at the least susceptibility. Yet now, in the teeth of cynicism and experience, this kind of conclusion wasn't necessarily vouchsafed. Adam went down into the awkward, ochreous corridors of Tottenham Court Road station with a sense of truculent victory enhanced by recalling the businesslike deftness with which Frankie had stage-managed their lunchtime scenario. Picking his way along the platform, he muttered to himself the talismanic words, 'I like to confuuuse peopaalll', as if Frankie would spring in an instant, exotic as a genie, from the dark hollow of the tunnel.

VIII

HE'D got the part, hadn't he? OK, it was something of a forgone conclusion, given Nathan Lester's taste in off-white casting, but Theo was entitled to feel he'd earned it simply through the philosophic patience he was always able to muster at auditions. They'd gone over the same little scenes a hundred times, he and the Achilles, a laid-back ex-public school prop forward with lots of teeth when he grinned, and the ratty Scottish Thersites, whose beard looked suitably last-minute, in the approved just-got-out-of-bed-for-my-Oscar style. Theo had wondered whether, after all, Adam hadn't been right about him being too heavy for Patroclus. After a while, however, something quite natural had clicked into place about belonging to Achilles and being, in death, a motive for his contemptible vengeance. The instinct had nothing to do with the other actors, but derived, he saw later, from his times with Guy, a sense that there was nobody else he so wanted to trust in the taking care of him.

Except perhaps Adam, but that was always different. He'd never bothered to work out why, but it was. Though nearly a decade divided them, and there were moments when one or the other felt uneasily reminded of the fact, Theo now and then became possessed of this odd idea of the pair of them having been born together, hatched from the same mythic egg, the twin halves of some principle to which he couldn't give a name. Nothing in his life before, the orthodox sense of dutiful affection he retained towards his parents despite their seeming disappointment in him, the feeling that he ought to love his scornful, exacting brother Aubrey more than was actually the case, had prepared Theo for this peculiar closeness, which within so short a time had become as vital to him as bone marrow. Falling in love with Adam would have been impossible, because, however inexplicably, they'd been there already before they met each other. Beyond that lay the limitless embrace of another kind of intimacy altogether, protecting and apparently invincible, one which had waited for them to chance on each other 'foreknowing that the truth would fall out so'.

Theo wasn't sure he liked the possibility that its perspective might now be troubled by an emotional interloper like Guy. Lying outright wasn't what he wanted to do, but Adam's curiosity had lately shown disturbing signs of revolt, impatient at the scraps of information Theo judged adequate to satisfy it. He was Adam's secret, just as Adam was his. Early in their friendship they'd uncovered a mutual pleasure in a life of carefully sealed compartments, a sort of Castle Bluebeard in which you were allowed to roam freely, provided the locks were not tried and the handles of the doors were left unrattled. Except for clubbing or bathhouses, when it was always good to have someone to come giggling home with, they seldom went out together, and the edges of their respective worlds never impinged unless one of them brought back a trick who stayed over. The arrangement was doubtless eccentric, but so far it had worked brilliantly. To Theo, at least, it seemed as if each became more vivid for the other by virtue of the fact that experience was perpetually unshared, existing solely in the form of narrative, edited, heightened or suppressed according to the storyteller's mood that day. The effect, at first contrived deliberately, had grown indispensable, a challenge to forces of coincidence both were too intelligent to deride.

Perhaps because it came more naturally to him, Adam showed greater generosity than Theo in paying out the hanks of narrative. This didn't mean, on the other hand, that Theo should suddenly be required to compensate for this inequality by telling him everything about the liaison with Guy, even if its singular parameters of reticence and suppression, potent with what expressly wasn't communicated, seemed strangely in keeping with their shared orthodoxy. He was no more inclined to do so now that Adam had suddenly announced a willingness to fall in love and seemed to be wanting to tell him most of what had happened in the past two weeks to have brought this about.

They lay together on the sofa after supper, Adam cradled in Theo's arms according to custom. It was always good to have him bundled thus, plump and compact, to hold like a toy for safety while you smoked and watched telly or listened to the music one of you had chosen and he nuzzled your neck or cupped a hand over your packet. The idea of the cherub on the map had been spot on. They wondered why he hadn't thought of it before. That morning, naked and roseate from the bath, while he pottered in front of the airing cupboard looking for a shirt, Adam had seemed more abundantly angelic than ever, with his fuzz of tight ash-blond curls, his neat little bum, thick calves and stubby cock bouncing under the voluptuous curve of his belly. All he needed was a trumpet, a scroll and a pair of baroque wings. From a vision so appetizing Theo could have fancied the celestial proclamation of the millennium.

'So how many times have you been hanging around that rehearsal studio?' he murmured into Adam's ear.

'Five, so far.'

'Nothing like making it obvious, is there? And he still hasn't rung you?'

'Nope.'

'And if he doesn't ring, what'll you do? Hang on, forget I said that. What'll happen if he does?'

'Your guess is as good as mine, The.'

'Better. I'm getting prophetic, prophe'ic, yur, ju-ju in my genes. For starters he sounds like the sort who takes his time, so don't expect him to be pressing the redial for at least another week. Remember what the god says, "Whom best I love I cross, to make my gifts the more delayed delighted". Bet you can't tell me where that's from?'

'No I can't. How the fuck can you?'

'Patronizing little puffball, aren't we? Anyway, he's quite clearly a tart. What a mercy you haven't thought up a decent pretext for phoning him.'

'I'm trying to pace myself, just observing decorum, bastard thing that it is.'

Theo took a deep breath and, enfolding Adam more tightly, gave him a little understanding kiss on the forehead. 'Decorum, marshmallow, is what stops us from falling. If you genuinely want to be Agatha don't slag it off or you may do something stupid.'

'You seem to have decided I'm in love already. I never said that, did I?'

'Sure you're not? Sure you've thought of at least one other thing since you first saw him? Sure you've not spent every waking moment defining your existence in relation to a bald American sex god with blue eyes. Blue eyes! Banality, banalai'ee pure and simple!' Theo groaned, then shook with silent laughter. 'Ad, come on, be more original, your own eyes are blue enough.'

'Ish. And it's not the same blue, you haven't seen his, probably you won't anyway, they're like –'

Theo's hand clapped itself over his mouth before he could finish.

'I don't want to know, and you don't want to tell me, right?'

'Maybe,' said Adam, not sounding particularly convinced.

'And the thing to do first of all is lunch. The shagging comes later on. If you're really serious about pacing yourself, remember that.'

'Yeah, OK.'

For a while they lay silent together, as the music, so neatly imperturbable, lapped around them.

'I had this on the other night,' said Theo.

'Carlo Fontana?'

'Yes. When you were out at Substation and I was feeling knackered after that audition. There's a sort of sound it's good to be alone with in the evening.'

'You mean you and Mrs Fist and a substance or two for a spot of abuse. Well, it's perfect for that, it just makes you want to go on and on. By the way, did Guy know about Diedrich Becker, I never asked.'

'Neither did I.'

His laconic response, Theo realized, was as good as a provocation to Adam, looking intently up at him as if to seize the opportune moment. Yet the question he thought he was going to have to deflect didn't arrive. Instead Adam said quietly, 'You've changed.'

'Good.'

'Perhaps it is. I can't explain, it's just a feeling I've had lately about you being different.'

This was a new approach. Theo, instantly on guard, leaned back a little on his elbow as if better to free himself should things get suddenly uncomfortable. It irked him the more that Adam was so tenacious. Millennial cherubs weren't meant to behave like this.

'Does that frighten you, Adsy? Are you worried you'll lose me or something?'

'No, of course not,' Adam said quickly. Such an evident lie was curiously moving rather than tiresome.

'Maybe I wasn't whom you thought anyway.' There was a remoteness in his tone Theo was powerless to check. 'It's cool to talk about reinventing yourself, but that's what I've been doing all this time.'

'Yes, but –'

'Sometimes,' said Theo, 'I feel like that god in Greek mythology who became different things, a river or a horse or a tree or whatever, so as to stop people catching hold of him. Perhaps it's just being an actor, but I was like that before really. We've never talked about this, have we?'

Adam looked lost. All of a sudden Theo felt a not unpleasant sensation of age and experience, as if the gap in years between them had been reversed.

'What did you want me to be? A ditzy black disco queen with a big dick whom you brought home one night from the Two Brewers like a trophy? Does it give you a nice cachet at those dinner parties in Notting Hill, talking about "my black lodger"? Do they ask you how long it is?'

He heard himself now, possessed by a scorn and anger which came from nowhere in particular and for which, as a result, he took no responsibility. With inevitable awkwardness Adam sat up to face him, silent and confused.

'I wasn't that, Adam, ever. I hated all that shit, I still do. I'm not one of the brothers.'

'I never believed you were.'

'Talking with a Brixthton lithp through the gap in my front teeth, with a sister called Claudia and cousins named Junior and Jermayne, and saying "arks" instead of "ask" and waddling about in a cap and baggy bottoms with my toes pointing together and some crap rapper scratching on a Walkman. Is that all I'm fucking good for? The culture? Jesus!'

Adam said nothing, because, Theo realized, he would not let him.

'I'm upwardly mobile, Adam, do you know a gay man who isn't? Except the ones on top already and they're a bunch of tossers. And I'm a snob who likes classical music and people who can finish their sentences correctly. I wouldn't have come to live with you if I wasn't, sorry, weren't. So stop forcing me into a cliché.'

'I'm not –' Adam started feebly.

'We're only your commonplaces, aren't we, your substitutes for original thought. Every time the law stops me on sus for dealing, that's the idea that goes through my mind. First I was frightened, then I was angry, now I just feel get a life for fuck's sake, I'm not a walking excuse for your intellectual vulgarity. Because that's what I won't ever be, Adam, vulgar. I'll always become what you least expect, if that's what I have to do to stay ahead.'

Getting up majestically, as if there were nothing more to be said, Theo left the room with silent dignity, taking care not to catch his foot in the stretch of rucked carpet beneath the sofa. He was aware, once he'd shut the bedroom door, that his own last words to Adam had hovered on the edge of that very banality he purported to despise. With characteristic fastidiousness he wished he'd used some other phrase than the dire 'what I have to do to stay ahead'. It was the sort of language whose aid his brother Aubrey might have invoked, fresh from a successful day in court, as a none too oblique condemnation of him for not being a conspicuous achiever. He didn't mean it anyway, he'd wanted to say something else and that had come out instead. He'd wanted to say, 'Shut up needling me about Guy, stop trying to find out what it's doing to me, because I can't tell you, for the first time in my life words won't come.' As if that, in any case, were Adam's fault!

Wearily Theo started to undress, scattering his clothes across the floor as he'd done since a child as a revolt against the self-conscious neatness with which Aubrey, when they shared a bedroom, always folded everything before getting into his pyjamas. In the sitting-room the music, so abstractly impervious to his sudden gust of anger and Adam's breathless amazement at its onset, was abruptly turned off. Theo sat naked on the bed's edge for a moment, wishing that the room he had walked into was the white flat in Bayswater with Guy in it to ordain and dispose while he himself was charged with the simple obligation of being. What would Guy have done with Adam, whom plainly now he must never meet?

In one of the larger rooms at the National Gallery there was a picture Theo remembered, showing the family of the vanquished King Darius of Persia falling on their knees in an abject appeal for mercy from his conqueror, Alexander the Great. The scene, as imagined by the painter, took place before a vaguely realized backdrop of columns and balustrades over which a cast of ectoplasmic turbaned onlookers gazed with what seemed only casual interest at the momentous foreground episode. Initially Theo had been attracted to the painting merely by the handsomeness of its décor, the swagger of halberds and brightly coloured armour, the falls of ermine and brocade which clothed the kneeling women, the capering monkey placed, for a masterstroke by the artist, at a point in the composition which should render its presence, in such a meeting of grandeur with solemnity, absolutely indispensable. Then he'd learned of the work's graver intention, to celebrate the virtues of magnanimity, of subduing anger and revenge with a generous pity for the defeated. One detail in the story particularly appealed to him. At the Persians' approach Alexander had emerged from his tent alongside his lover Hephaestion, the taller of the two men. Thinking this was the King of Macedon, the women had flung themselves before him in an elaborate ritual of self-abasement known as the proskynesis. To their horrified remonstrance when it was pointed out by a bystander that they'd done homage to the wrong man, the King replied, pointing to Hephaestion, 'Do not be afraid, for this too is an Alexander.'

Soon after meeting Guy, Theo had gone back to look again at the picture, not because of any direct resemblance between him and the small, dark figure of Alexander in his crimson breastplate, but out of some deeper, more indirect apprehension of the context in which he palpably belonged. Theo had wanted to be the black-armoured Hephaestion, and he longed still more to be so now. 'He too is an Alexander.' Guy would have chosen magnanimity and forgiven Adam even without the least reciprocal gesture of apology.

Theo got up and went back into the sitting-room. Under a lamp whose wanness made his features look implausibly hollow, Adam sat reading, or pretending to read. The sight of him islanded and solitary in the surrounding wash of shadow made Theo want to take him in his arms again.

'I didn't mean you to think —' he began, then stopped, aware that magnanimity must choose its phrases carefully if it isn't to seem like an act of the most outrageous condescension.

Adam didn't look up. 'Maybe I'll see you in the morning,' he said. Or on second thoughts, he might have added, maybe not.

IX

~

'A PICNIC!' exclaimed Jeremy. 'You can't be serious.'

'Why ever not? The weather's perfect, unnaturally so if you ask me,' said Will.

'But the grass'll still be damp, and there'll be flies everywhere.'

'You've no sense of occasion, have you? There've got to be flies if you have a picnic, it's part of the scenario.'

'Where precisely were you thinking of having it?'

'The Hermitage, naturally. There's that big flat tree trunk where they chopped down the oak last year. And plenty of shade if the heat gets objectionable.'

'Why can't we just have it on tables in the garden?'

'Jezza, you don't have to come, you're free to stay and brood in the house, and we can watch your spectral form flitting to and fro behind closed windows.'

'I thought picnics were supposed to be things you do at the end of a long walk. Somebody always has to forget something, like a corkscrew or a tin opener. And generally there's a quarrel, and it rains a bit, and things are never quite as nice as you hoped. Disappointment, that's the essence of picnicking.'

'We're not going to be disappointed,' Will said firmly. 'I just liked the idea of the Hermitage, that's all. I'm sure that's what Lord Severnstoke did in the eighteenth century when he built it. Alfresco luncheons with Horace Walpole and Mrs Montagu and all those people who came sniffing around his ruins. We can't quite run to horn players and Negroes in livery handing the rout cakes and pouring iced champagne, but everything else should meet your exacting standards.'

Jeremy laughed, as if suddenly taken with the idea after all. 'Did Lord Severnstoke really have Negroes?' he asked.

'Four of them, it seems, bought as slaves in the West Indies. They were called Septimius, Valerian, Aurelius and Pertinax, though I expect those weren't there real names. Aurelius is buried in the churchyard at Defford. The tombstone calls him "An African born at St Kitts, the faithful servant for thirty years of the Earl of Severnstoke". Probably he hadn't much choice in the matter, poor sod. I don't know what happened to the others. There used to be little oval portraits of them all in the dining-room at the Court until the family sold up after the war.'

Alice sat listening, entranced by the deftness with which Will, via the manoeuvring of a typically good-humoured persistence, was managing to talk Jeremy into the idea. She would have liked to assure him that the children, in whose presence he always grew a little pompous and awkward, were not going to be there. Jack had remained in London on an unconvincing pretext of being able better to practise for his music exam, and a friend's mother was arriving tomorrow morning to take Zoe off to shop in Cheltenham. There was no need, however, to interrupt Will's good work, and in any case she knew by now what these interrogations of Jeremy's really meant. Even without Will's gift for making others feel wanted and indispensable to an occasion's success, he'd have come anyway, being more or less incapable of spending time in the country on his own. He couldn't be Jeremy without having someone to be Jeremy at. So tomorrow, in the shadow of the tall stuccoed Gothic expanse of ogival windows, niches and crenellations, he'd sit and fret and make condescending observations on Serena's picnic treats as if he were somehow responsible for having schooled her in the finer points of salmon mousse and pickled samphire. Serena meanwhile, wincing slightly but loving it hugely, would smile at him like the handmaid she so mysteriously delighted in being.

Now, as she played duets with Adam in the other room, the echo of her laughter as they hurried noisily towards the closing bars was without that nervous edge it generally carried in Jeremy's presence. Adam was always so good with her, better, thought Alice, than she sometimes deserved, given her continuing unease with gay men. He was almost certainly the only one among them who would be likely to accompany her to Easter communion, while the others addressed themselves to the complex business of finishing breakfast, or, if they were Basil, in the other spare bedroom, carried the remains of it upstairs to eat in bed with a cigarette and whatever bits of the paper he could snatch. And when they came back from church, Adam would doubtless be perfectly happy to help her feed Gaga and the bantams while she talked, at rather than to him, about the millennium plan for landscaping what was left of the village green and her ideas for signposting the footpaths. Serena ought to have been grateful for such unforced kindnesses, yet wasn't, for some reason Alice couldn't fathom. Adam was there, it seemed, merely to fill the periodic vacancies left by Jeremy, to play the classic role of a walker or an attendant eunuch, to whom Serena could be appropriately condescending. Such an attitude was the only thing she had in common with her sister Daisy, but whereas with her Adam appeared to give as good as he got, Serena drew from him instead a patient forbearance Alice continued to find puzzling.

She was glad he never seemed to want to stay at the other house, with its *mise en scène* of overwhelming orderliness in the manner of a place which was always expecting to be looked at. His loyalty to her and Will was not a cousin's instinctive clannishness. He liked, it was clear, the greater honesty imposed through a casual occupation by the children, scattering clothes and books among various rooms with territorial absent-mindedness, prodigally sleeping out the mornings and conducting their epic telephone lives behind doors eloquently slammed. Serena and Jeremy's might look less energetically inhabited by the pair of them, the more so because of its ample size, and was certainly a good deal quieter, but as Adam had once remarked, it was always as if, when you opened the doors into the hall, you'd find a posse of photographers and feature writers waiting to do a country-living spread for *World of Interiors*.

Perhaps with something of this kind in view, Serena insisted on bringing her camera to the picnic next day. The shots she took were always rather better than mere ill-aimed snaps, and Alice wondered why she never bothered to make more of her talent, given her evident knowledge of the hardware involved. She wasn't going to take more than a few pictures of them all, preferring instead to photograph the ruin from the opposite side to that on which they were preparing to set out lunch.

'I didn't realize you were so interested in the Hermitage,

Sib,' said Will as they picked their way along the edges of the first field.

'Probably I don't know as much about it as you,' Serena said a shade feverishly. 'I don't teach history after all.'

'It's only economic history, not the real stuff.'

'But I come here a lot when I'm on my own. There's a little place at the top of the turret where you can look across to Pirton. Sometimes you can see Worcester in the distance. Once I saw a poacher carrying off something he'd hidden under that pile of old railway sleepers on the edge of the wood. At least I think that's who it was.'

'What would have happened if he'd found you?' Basil asked.

'I'd have the advantage, wouldn't I?'

'Always nice to have the advantage,' murmured Jeremy, quite as if expecting nobody else to hear him. Having resigned himself to the inevitability of picnicking among nettles and cowpats on a day which was already growing uncommonly sultry for late April, he'd evidently determined on looking as photogenic as possible even if Serena wasn't going to take his picture. The studied simplicities of a lurid white T-shirt and loose green trousers did nothing to diminish his habitual air of wasteful profusion, by which Alice found herself so easily irritated. Quickening her pace, she moved on a little to join Adam, busy fiddling with the catch to a gate which seemed almost higher than he was.

'Do you think this was a good idea after all?' she whispered.

He looked at her in surprise. 'I don't see why not. Will's ideas usually are. And Sib's happy, that's the main thing. Don't ask me why, but it generally is.'

Leaving the gate open for the others, the pair of them walked quickly forward into the little coppice beyond which the ruin stood.

'I'll tell you what Jezebel looks like,' said Adam. 'It came to me just now.'

Alice giggled. 'You needn't, I already know. Catalogue shopping for bankers and lawyers, Johnnie Bowden's best!'

'I thought a shade more Hawkshead today. Maybe a touch of Racing Green, but the trainers are a mismatch, deliberate. Can't think who told him about duck-egg blue Pumas, not good with the trousers but definitely this year's mode. Fashion victim as you never did, our Jezza. How do you think Serena's looking?'

'The way she always does when they're down here together.'

'Mousy and adoring.'

'Yes, but don't believe all you see. It's just done to bamboozle.'

The stragglers caught up with them as they got out of the wood into the scrubby stretch of open field which surrounded the Hermitage. Its design made you think of a filmset. On the side furthest from them, crenellated walls pierced with narrow ogival windows and centring on a single turret containing a supremely narrow spiral staircase gave a successful impression of having grown out of the surrounding landscape, with its well-set hedgerows and heavy, consequential stands of oak and chestnut. Behind, of course, lay nothing but docks, thistles and tussocks of feggy grass where cows had recently been grazing. From here you saw that the façade, which, according to Horace Walpole, had 'the true rust of the Barons' Wars', was mere skilfully distressed stucco work against a core of brick. Only the broad platform below the turrets gave any impression that the place, as Will had said earlier to Jeremy, was meant for alfresco entertainment of whatever kind.

'Do you suppose this was where Lord Severnstoke brought his mistress?' said Basil, as they began spreading the picnic. 'What was she called? I can't remember.'

'Her name was Molly Hardacre,' said Will, 'and she

definitely wasn't the sort Mrs Montagu would have liked to meet. In fact I don't think anybody really knew she existed until they read the Third Earl's will.'

'How do you mean?'

'Molly never knew who he was either.'

'Don't be mysterious, Will,' said Serena crossly.

Jeremy laughed. 'Sibby hates mysteries. Except P. D. James and Inspector Morse, those are all right. Earls with girls, that's another matter.'

'Molly,' Will continued serenely, between getting a corkscrew out of one of the bags and opening the first bottle, 'was the daughter of a prosperous tailor in Kennington named Abram Hardacre, who had come to London from Tadcaster and been a sort of Hogarthian good apprentice. The Earl saw her from his carriage when returning from Dover after his second tour of Italy in 1764 and was so struck by her beauty that he made enquiries in the neighbourhood as to her character and fortunes and then decided to pay court to her.' Will paused for a moment to pop the cork, smiling at them as he did so, the big loose letterbox grin you couldn't not love.

'Well, go on!' cried Adam. 'Obviously you haven't got to the really interesting bit, this is just standard-issue upper-class infidelity.'

'Ad wants a bit of sleaze,' said Basil, 'a touch of the old Harlot's Progress and Fanny Hill.'

'It wasn't like that in the least,' Will resumed. 'In fact, it was almost pathetically respectable. The Earl came to visit Molly's father and asked if he might pay court to her. But not as himself, you understand. Every time he went to Kennington it was as Mr Dumaine, a Huguenot merchant of Spitalfields, recently widowed. It seems he told Molly he couldn't marry her, out of feelings of delicacy towards his late wife.'

'And the Countess, I suppose, was very much alive,' said Serena.

'Yes, and there were four children. Anyway, Molly and her father appeared to have accepted the arrangement, but to make everything decent it was decided that she and Mr Dumaine should retire to a farmhouse in Battersea, where they might live quietly as what purported to be a married couple. So they tonked along nicely together for the best part of a decade. Molly got used to her husband's frequent absences – on business, as it were – and so did the Countess, and neither of them suspected a thing. Then one evening, outside the Cocoa Tree in St James's, the Earl suffered a violent seizure, was carried home in a chair and died soon afterwards. And that was when Molly made her discovery, because the lawyer had to write and tell her that she was mistress of the farmhouse and ten thousand pounds, and that the money had been set aside to pay a dowry for their bastard daughter when she should be of marriageable age. And what do you think Molly did?'

'Blew the lot on designer frocks and turned the farmhouse into a brothel,' suggested Adam.

Will shook his head, triumphant in the assurance of having one more surprise left. 'She refused it, every penny. She wrote to the lawyer and said – this was her phrase – that as it had been dishonestly given, so it would be dishonestly got, and went home to her father. The daughter, who was called Caroline Augusta, married a schoolmaster in Putney and was apparently famous in the neighbourhood for her grand, ladylike airs.'

'I wonder what the Countess thought of it all,' said Serena.

'Maybe she never found out. The only people who seem to have known were the lawyer, Mr Pollock, who wrote a confidential memoir of the whole affair, which the Severnstokes got hold of in the 1930s from a descendant of his, and the black servant Aurelius, the one buried at Defford, whom the Earl took into his confidence early on, and who brought Molly the letter about the inheritance.'

'Bit of a rum go,' Basil said. 'Molly behaved like a trump, though. I'd have grabbed the money and run.'

'She's the one I feel sorry for, not the Countess,' said Alice.

'Why?' asked Serena sharply.

'Her happiness was based on lies, it's as simple as that. The Earl wanted to have his cake and eat it, the way lots of men do, and she could have accepted that. But why did he have to pretend? Why couldn't he be who he was?'

'Perhaps because he was someone different,' said Basil. 'Most of us don't know who we are anyway a lot of the time. That sounds naff and portentous, but you know what I mean.'

'I don't, but never mind.'

'He must have enjoyed being Mr Dumaine the Huguenot merchant of Spitalfields, putting on a bit of a French accent, wearing black, maybe an old-fashioned wig as well. And think what a thrill it must have been, as the Earl in the House of Lords or at the opera or a levée at the palace, thinking, "in a few hours I'll be a different person altogether, with different words and values and feelings, and nobody will ever know".'

'I'm not sure it was how people thought in the eighteenth century. Anyway it'd be impossible today.'

'Not necessarily,' said Will, 'all sorts of people lead parallel lives.'

'I still feel he oughtn't to have lied to Molly like that.'

Jeremy refilled his glass. 'I'm hungry,' he said. 'Let's start, for Christ's sake.'

He wouldn't come for a walk with them after lunch, pre-ferring instead to sit and smoke with Basil while Serena began taking her photographs. Alice was glad that Baz for once had not brought the reigning Sultana of the moment with him. The children were admittedly both old enough now to be discreet rather than sit on the stairs spluttering with laughter at the various earth-moving noises from the bedroom. It wasn't the bonking for England she minded so much as having to feel sorry for the woman in tow. They were always the same sort, with slightly distracted-looking hair and approximate make-up, working in publishing or on the arts page of a Sunday paper, who looked as though they had woken up that morning as the drugged victims of a white slaver to find themselves in Basil's bed and were still in the process of getting used to the novelty. Alice longed to tell them, never maliciously but out of sheer solicitude, not to bother. What looked like buccaneering spontaneity in him would turn out to be no more than ordinary male selfishness and negligence, and when they started to cling or grow proprietary he'd simply shrug and let them fall. There'd been one woman, she recalled, who looked like knowing this, a bobbish American journalist called Betsy, skilful in contriving to be absent just when Basil might have started to find her an annoyance and always dramatic in her unheralded reappearance from places like Chechnya or Yemen, where she had managed once again to outsmart death. Betsy had the knack on such occasions, what was more, of seeing off whatever competition happened to be around. Alice was careful never to mention her to Basil in case of frightening him off. The notion that he, as well as death, might in the end be outmanoeuvred by Betsy was altogether too piquant.

'Baz never comes for walks, have you noticed?' said Adam, as they got out of earshot.

'Being in the country is a sort of penance for him, I imagine,' Will said. 'Whereas Sib believes in every minute of it.'

'Oughtn't she to?'

'The belief is more important than anything else,' said Alice. 'Tell me why she's always so bloody patronizing to you, Ad. And don't come over all coy and say you hadn't noticed.'

'Because she can't patronize Jeremy, I imagine.'

'Or doesn't care to,' Will said. 'Much more sexy being the dust under his chariot wheels. God knows why, but it is, for her. Maybe she thinks you're a bad influence on him, that the pair of you go clubbing when her back's turned.'

'Jeremy's far too image-conscious to be a clubber. He's got premature gravitas and I'm turning into a senile raver. Thirty-five is like Methuselah for a gay man. Sometimes when you're dancing at four in the morning you get the feeling you're She out of Rider Haggard and you'll turn into some hideous monkey and become a heap of dust under the eyes of the horrified onlookers, all buffed up to the last detail and aghast at the thought of becoming old like you.'

'They will,' said Alice encouragingly.

'No they won't, they'll keep on lying about their age. Gays learn dishonesty from their mother's knee. It's why they're so creative.'

'Spare us the Wildean patter, Ad, the sun's cooking my brain!' cried Will. 'All the brittle epigrammatic lobes'll have turned into pork scratchings pretty soon.'

They walked on a little in silence, with the conversational cooing of woodpigeons in the trees around them and, in the distance, a cuckoo going off suddenly as if at the nonchalant throwing of a switch. Then Adam said, 'Dishonesty, that's what Sib's afraid of. She thinks I ought to be louche and dangerous down here, cruising the farm lads and cottaging in public toilets. It must be awfully disappointing to her that I like to sit and read and go to bed early. Alone.'

Alice laughed inwardly at the notion of Serena being afraid of dishonesty. 'She resents your freedom. Some of us get very edgy in the presence of the great unmarried.'

'It'd be just the same if he was here with a partner,' Will pointed out.

'Pigs will fly when that happens,' said Adam.

'I rather thought I saw one flapping over your head when you showed up yesterday,' Alice said. 'There's a look I remember you to have.'

'You were four when I was born and don't I bloody know it. Did you really think –'

'No harm in guessing.'

He didn't respond and she wasn't going to press him on the point, but there'd been something she was quick to catch when he got off the train, an alertness to matters which wouldn't ordinarily have excited more in him than a measure of polite interest, an instant disposal to be engaged and entertained, asking Zoe the right questions about a half-term trip to Spain and listening to Will's jeremiads about university funding. She knew where all this was coming from. Behind it lay that paradoxical mixture of tumultuous gratitude at the fortunate upshot of circumstance with something extremely like atone-ment, a propitiation of whatever might threaten to obliterate promised happiness. Was he then in love? Perhaps he didn't know, but to Alice's practised eye that was how it looked. Sooner or later he'd tell her, because it was less dangerous than confiding in another man, and because from childhood she'd always kept his secrets. And if he didn't tell her, then she could ask Daisy. Daisy now would be invaluable.

As they walked back along the edge of the park, past the lake which seemed to become weedier and more forlorn with each year's passing and the prim-looking Georgian shoebox of a church, whose key someone kept in the village but everybody else had forgotten exactly where, they came up against the Hermitage as the third Lord Severnstoke must have wanted them to see it, gaunt and elegantly astounding against the softness of trees in their earliest leaf. In front of it, to one side, sat Basil, propped up against a couple of cushions, reading the paper and smoking what, at a conservative estimate, must have been the day's eleventh or twelfth cigarette. In the scenic embrasure formed by the central turret and the false bay window under tall crockets at the other end Serena stood with her camera, her thin body tensed by an unaccustomed air of genuine competence, engaged in photographing – well, not the building after all, but Jeremy, leaning against the bare grey stucco in the grateful light of mid-afternoon.

The others came up silently across the field, unwilling to disturb them until Serena had obviously finished. She gave a single impatient glance, then turned again intently to the matter in hand. To Alice he did not look the same as when they had left him an hour before. It was as if he had changed for the part, as though at the back of the ruin, on the stone platform, they might find his sloughed skin lying ready for him to step into again should he choose. He stood barefoot with one knee crooked up, shoulders against the wall, his heavy-lidded eyes almost shut, his lips slightly parted, a cigarette dangling from one hand. The effect, heightened by the fall of shadow against his face, was unutterably low-life. Alice looked for a moment in Adam's direction to see if he noticed it too, but he was making knowing grimaces at Basil, slumped behind his paper. A little breeze got up, tickling her shoulders and making her shiver. No you wouldn't, you honestly wouldn't have known it for Jeremy.

X

꩜

'I LEFT the story in London. Sorry about that,' said Basil, 'but it goes something like this.'

They sat, he and Adam, on the brick-paved terrace at the back of the house, with a smoke and the bottle of Highland Park Will had generously, if also somewhat resignedly, decided they should be allowed to enjoy between them while he beavered in the study over a conference paper. Alice, deliberately remote, had retreated upstairs with a book, and the only noise from within was Zoe's irregular 'mmm', 'right', 'yeah', punctuating a friend's apparently interminable phone monologue.

Far from dissipating with the onset of darkness, the day's collected warmth seemed to have sunk into the walls. The air of the garden hung thick and unstirring, with a heaviness like summer's. Considered purely as weather for the time of year, it made Adam, always responsive to the potential of the pathetic fallacy, deeply suspicious. 'Taint natural, so it aint.

Experienced, however, as something in which to sit and chat softly with Basil on an Easter evening, it was almost seductively congenial.

'About five years ago I went out to dinner with Daisy at the Boulevard in Notting Hill Gate.'

'That's the place which closed down, on the left past the Coronet and Pizza Express. It was only there a short time, but they had some munchy waiters in skinny tops.'

'No doubt. Anyway, we'd been to a film, and Daisy suggested there for afterwards rather than the Malabar round the corner where we'd always gone, because the last time there'd been a woman with a peculiarly aggravating laugh, the sort which gets the whole restaurant wanting to chuck her out into the road.

'I'd never had the hots for Daisy. You'll say you don't believe me, but so what? Even when we were younger she had an oddly anaphrodisiac quality about her, a sort of come-on-you-can't-be-serious manner which was calculatedly off-putting. There wasn't anything she ever seemed to need. But that evening she got to me just by being the mock princess she essentially is. The way she walked in ahead of me and did these little turns to left and right, as though she knew everyone sitting at the other tables and they were all going to applaud. And then giving her coat to some faggoty Australian as if it was ermine and she'd just staggered in from her own coronation. That stretched paleness of hers, with the swept-back hair which normally looks just like any ex-ballerina doing the Dame Margot number, and the slightly accusatory expression she always has, as if, being a man, you can never quite do things right – I don't know, it got to me somehow, I hadn't felt like that with her before.

'She had something to tell me, but when Daisy has

something to tell you it's never delivered straight off, it's got to come wrapped up inside something else, and the wrapping is very often as interesting as the present, occasionally more so. She asked me a few half-hearted questions about *Last Enchantments* – I was working on that at the time, do you remember? – and we ordered, and then she started off about this party she'd just been to with Tommy Diamond. Who, by the way, isn't Edie's father. Remind me to tell you how I know. Anyway, this was in the days when she still thought Tommy was going to be a name to conjure with and she was always repeating the clever things he said. And that evening, for whatever reason – well, I make up a reason in my version, but I can't remember how it really came about according to her – he'd told Daisy a story.

'It was about a poem by some Greek writer in the early nineteenth century from the Ionian Islands. They were a British colony at the time – people still play cricket there, did you know? In this poem an English soldier goes down to the beach and peels off for a dip. He swims out a bit and an enormous shark suddenly attacks him out of nowhere. The shark starts tearing into him. You have to realize, Ad, that at this point I did a double take and wondered what on earth Daisy was doing telling me all this. It was so totally removed from anything you'd ever associate with her emphatic urbanness.

'She was leaning towards me now across the table. Her voice was really low and thrilling. I got hard from just listening to it. "And in the poem," she said, "at that point, what do you think the poet says? No, what do you think?" Christ, I didn't know, did I? "He says – and it's really amazing, Baz, this bit – he says, 'And in that moment, as the young man's blood mingled with the sea, he lost all fear. For an instant he knew who he was.' Isn't that fantastic? Don't you love it, Baz? I was mesmerized when Tommy told me. I mean, the idea of knowing who you are when it's too late to do anything about it!"

'I forbore to point out that even when armed with such knowledge the soldier might not have wanted to do anything about it. And then Daisy, I don't mind telling you, really surpassed herself as far as surprises were concerned.'

Basil paused, as if invoking the silence of the garden around them as an assistant to effect. Pouring himself another slug of whisky, Adam said, 'So? Go on.'

'You remember she had that friend she used to go on about, a dancer, Bulgarian I think, called Stanko?'

'We were never allowed to meet him. Or at least I wasn't, she thought we might get too chummy. What about him?'

'Daisy repeated the phrase from the poem, this time so quietly it was almost a whisper. "For in that moment he knew who he was." Then, looking over my shoulder at some point in the middle distance, she murmured, "Stanko, I wonder if that's what Stanko felt when they told him he'd tested positive."'

'It's what he died of,' Adam said. 'She never talked about it at the time even to me, and I'd have been the obvious person. He just sort of dropped out of her conversation after being there so often. Then from one or two things she said I put two and two together. But why were you so surprised?'

'Actually I wasn't,' rejoined Basil. 'Not at her, but at me.' He took a deep breath, then fell quiet again. His fingers beat a little tattoo of desperation on the weathered garden table. 'Because of what I felt, you see, when she said that. I could have shown a decent regret, or put a hand on hers, the sort of thing you're meant to do. Maybe that was what I did without knowing. But it wasn't what I felt inside, underneath, whatever.'

'So what was it? You haven't got to tell me, but I'll be awfully miffed if you don't.'

Basil stared at Adam for a moment with something almost like hostility. The ravaged public-school angel look, the straight man's unruly handsomeness, seemed suddenly crumpled and shapeless.

'I never met the guy, did I? What would we have said to each other if I had? Dancers are mostly pig-ignorant. So why was it all so powerful? The sensation—.' He stopped once more. Whatever it was had clearly been easier to write about than to voice. 'It was a kind of joy, Ad, a deep, visceral exultation, a pleasure like nothing I've ever felt before. That doesn't mean I want to experience it again. He was dying, this Stanko, a good deal faster than the rest of us. There are these combination therapies people live on now, aren't there? But the way Daisy described it, he was finished already, washed up, poor bastard. And what I had was this weird sense – groundless, horrible – of triumphing in my own immortality, as if I'd somehow beaten him in a contest of survival. After that I couldn't eat, couldn't look at Daisy again. I thought she must have guessed what it was.'

'She didn't say anything to me,' said Adam, sitting back in his chair and surveying Basil as though unconvinced, yet also with a certain envy. His own risk must always be the greater, but so far he had never surprised himself with a delight as grotesque as this one, or known anybody else who had. He remembered Frankie's comment about the English penchant for referring to everything of the kind as 'inappropriate' and smiled. 'So what did you do?' he asked. 'Go on the wagon? Take the sex pledge? The thought of you resolutely not putting it about for England is fairly staggering.'

'I went up to the Cobden and got totally caned. It was quite a cold evening, I remember, and when I came out into the street and walked along to Ladbroke Grove to get a cab I sort of sobered up, though I was still so smashed I had to stand for a bit with my hand pressed up against a wall. There was a big moon, and I recall thinking the house opposite was swaying in front of it and ready to fall flat on to the street. Then I remembered the story Daisy told me about the soldier and the shark. And then the memory of the feeling came back. "As the young man's blood mingled with the sea, he lost all fear. For in that moment he knew who he was." But I hadn't lost all fear, had I? I was just shit scared, that's all.'

'Sorry, Baz.'

'What for?'

'Don't know, I just am. The story's probably better the way you've told it now than as something tarted up for a paper. I'll read it if you want to give it me, but I'd rather have heard it like this.'

'Did Daisy say anything to you about it? I showed it to her, you know. I fancy she didn't care for it much. Probably the way I made her look. And the fact that I mentioned her breasts.'

'They're quite nice, I'm told,' said Adam absurdly, and Basil's snigger dissipated the miasmal seriousness which had hung around in the wake of his story.

'Did Jezebel go back to London this afternoon?' he asked.

'Apparently it's the only time the architects have got free who are doing this loft in Hoxton for the Foundation. They're off to Dresden to design a museum.'

'Bit rough on old Sib. You'd think he could manage Easter weekend without itching for the metro-glitz.'

'He was quite sweet with her last night, did you notice? Even went out and fed Gaga, which is greater-love-hath-no-man. And he came to church this morning, against everybody's expectations.'

'You're joking!'

'Mm-mm. The suit was far too top-of-the-range, and the pair of them turned parish communion into something more like an *OK!* wedding, but Sib was over the moon. Must be that photo shoot yesterday. The way to Jezza's heart is an Olympus. Anyway she said she was going to friends tonight over at Eckington or somewhere, so she's hardly a golf widow. Is that the phone?'

A window opened and Zoe's head appeared above them, dark against the lamplight. 'Adam, it's for you.'

'Me? Who the hell . . .? Nobody knows I'm here.'

'It's somebody with an American voice. Take it on the other line.'

Almost tripping on the steps, Adam charged into the house and took care to shut the drawing-room door before he scooped up the receiver.

'Hey, this is your personalized pager. *Madame a foutu le camp ce soir*, but she said to bleep you in the primeval wilderness so that's what I'm doing, Huckleberry? How many logs did you split today?'

'We don't split logs, we do it with hairs instead.'

'Pardon me?'

'Are you seriously alone, Frankie?'

'I don't believe I gave permission to call me Frankie. Application has to be made through my secretary, a strict Presbyterian from Poughkeepsie with a chignon, and all letters must be in triplicate. Which sounds like a place in New England, *n'est-ce pas?* Triplicate, Connecticut, hey, I like that. And yes I am, seriously, totally solo. For now.'

'I don't like "for now".'

'Neither do I? What shall we pretend we're talking about? The economics of dance, the disparate identities of Fernando Pessoa? You choose, you're so good at these things. Don't ask me how I know, because I don't, I'm just guessing. Guessing is so much better than guesting, don't you agree?'

Adam didn't want to answer, preferring instead to let the gurgling voice trickle over him like melted butterscotch. Patter as unselfconsciously camp as this wasn't something you got much of in England and was probably rare enough in America, so it mystified him as to where someone as young as Frankie could have grasped and perfected the style. Quite possibly he was on some stuff which might seem to lend reason to a pointlessness whose sublimity made Adam scarcely able to breathe.

'Daisy says you have a goose. Called Gaga.' Gaw*gaw*.

'It isn't my goose.'

'We're not talking legal niceties here, Addy. So when am I getting the golden egg?'

When I get laid, Adam thought but studiously didn't say. 'For lunch next week, I imagine.'

'Everything else is passé, but lunch is so next week.'

'Wednesday?'

'Happening. Maybe even conceptual. Millennial is a possibility. Hey, that's my pumpkin coach I hear, the rats are squeaking. Call me. And if she asks, the guy's name was Fernando, but I guess you know that already.'

'Where are you –'

There was only the lugubrious wail of the receiver unhooked. Evidently, like an Asperger's syndrome child, Frankie didn't do answers to straight questions. How about gay questions? Adam thought of himself as not especially adept at banter. It was a thing people did in dismal TV comedy shows where poofs identify themselves by allusions to Judy Garland and the Eurovision Song Contest. If there was one thing which made Adam shudder it was the notion of having to pretend you enjoyed the Eurovision Song Contest, even on a post-ironic level. He remembered, purely because he could not forget it, a terrible evening in a house near Willesden Junction with a tarty Dutch guy met in some long-since defunct club, who lived with a prissy Welsh boy, an intrusive spaniel and several rather unhappy-looking pieces of deco furniture. Adam had sat there simpering miserably through the impacted kitscherama, listening to the others rocking with laughter at successive entries, while he came closer, by rapid degrees, to that state of consciousness which manages to persuade you, in such situations, that your authentic self has been left somewhere ungetatable but at least miles from the immediate horrors of circumjacent actuality. One of the pleasures of being thirty-five was not being twenty-three and having to feign enthusiasm for the sake of acceptance.

Frankie, one could safely assume, had never heard of the Eurovision Song Contest. Why, anyway, was he phoning now, having so conspicuously failed to do so earlier? Adam was too cynical to believe in this as anything beyond a momentary diversion, yet found himself growing unreasonably irked by the idea of the pumpkin coach. Frankie had patently never had to be Cinderella, that bit was preposterous. But who was the driver? Not Daisy, evidently, and probably male in any case. It was better not to dwell on the likelihood of where they might be going.

By the time Adam prepared for bed, Frankie's rogue call had sorted itself pleasantly enough into the desirable culminating vignette of a not altogether disappointing weekend. Serena and Jeremy had more or less behaved themselves, Basil was surprisingly quiescent, and Will's and Alice's was the island it invariably proved, on to which Adam felt as if he'd scrambled like the last survivor from a shipwreck. Outside, the owls were hooting in the park. Their kee-wik kee-wik kee-wik made him glad not to be in London, given over to fidgets about where Frankie had gone clubbing and trying not to betray his unease to Theo. Who in any case wouldn't be there to conceal anything from, busied instead with getting sophisticated in Bayswater amid libations of Heidsieck paid for by Guy's buoyant billions from Morgan Stanley.

Snuggling down under the sheets, Adam didn't read, but lay there, his head against the propped-up pillow, idly stroking his cock to hardness as he thought of the soldier in Baz's story slipping down on to the Corfiote beach, where the olives grew so thickly that at each lifting of the breeze a little black shower of them pattered on to the rocks and the sand and their dead leaves littered the foreshore. Of course, the squaddie boy, his tunic unbuckled and the rest of his uniform sloughed around him, would be untanned, a livid white except for the fell of hair on breast and belly like ivy matting a wall. For a moment he'd stand there savouring, a bit guiltily perhaps, the alien contact of sunlight with his infrequent nakedness, stretching maybe and yawning like a cat, before running down into the warm sea to encounter death. 'For in that moment . . .' Not a bad end, all things considered. You'd have liked to be the shark, wouldn't you? Easier, on the whole. Except that the wretched creature's eyes, for no reason you could think of, were a brilliant china blue.

XI

IT'D be nice to know. Nice to stand back from the experience and consider exactly what it is I think I'm falling in love with. It's meant to be instinctive, natural, spontaneous, uncontrollable, all these things which are supposed to validate our experience and give us the right to speak of it with some authority. Detachment isn't considered merely as counter-productive, but as something completely inauthentic, a sort of vulgar emotional faux-pas, the equivalent of eating peas with your knife or using expressions like 'toilet', 'foxhunting' and 'afternoon tea'. If you're swimming, drown, baby. There's an uncouthness almost to the point of being gross in trying to get distance and perspective on an affair, paddling about at your ease in the midst of an agreeable ebb and flow of aspects, reservations and insights while others are thrashing around for their lives.

Yet I don't believe I'm particularly odd for wanting to find out, especially if the process involved renders the whole thing more convincing. You run the inevitable risk of the opposite happening, of the entire peeling off and unzipping business leaving you with nothing but a certain self-disgust which your inherent good nature makes it impossible for you to share with the person you thought, until that moment, was your lover. I'm not into pretending, however. Not that I make an outright fetish of honesty — never, by the way, give any credence to people who keep telling you how much they respect honesty — just that it's difficult for me to avoid confession or at least acknowledgement. At any rate to myself.

Acting's different. No honestly, though you don't believe me. As Patroclus, for instance, I can be somebody intrinsically I'm not — or at least I don't think I am — somebody who's just a chancer a lot of the time, like the bit when he teases the Greek generals by seizing his opportunity with Cressida and shows them in the process what a little slapper she is. I didn't think he amounted to much, frankly, until Nathan the director talked me through the part and made it seem as if the whole play depended on it. Shakespeare gives you your moment, doesn't he, when Patroclus admits his responsibility, as love object, for having seduced Achilles from his true role as hero:

> Sweet, rouse yourself; and the weak, wanton Cupid
> Shall from your neck unloose his amorous fold,
> And like a dewdrop from the lion's mane
> Be shook to air.

That's all I am in the end, a fucking dewdrop, a little Greek tart in a cheeky loincloth, but Achilles doesn't shake me from his mane. Instead I become a reason for almost everything which happens in the closing scenes of the play. My death ordains the mood, enabling my lover to act like the selfish, cowardly shit he's always been underneath all that posey heroic stuff.

Let's imagine Patroclus among the Grecian tents allowing himself an interval of seriousness, dropping the disco-bunny persona in favour of something more reflective, and asking himself why exactly he was in love with Achilles. In those days it would have been easier to cast about for an answer. Somewhere out there he could have found an oracle to consult, a mad old woman in a dark sanctuary who might have told him – well, not the truth perhaps, but an approximation of it, a form of words which enabled him to gauge the peculiar reality of the emotion and perhaps even to confront the possibility that Achilles was less important than the thing itself, with all its baggage of ardour and obsession, suspicion, misgivings and utter wilful absurdity.

All of which, considered Theo, I don't yet feel, but think I'm probably about to. He'd have liked to talk of it with Adam, only that was impossible without telling him more about Guy than he dared. Their shared reticence by now had acquired the firmness of a pact he was too honourable to violate. Yet tonight he just wanted to go home and climb into Adam's bed and whisper everything to him as though he were indeed the oracular giver of answers and authentications. Or else he wanted to stay here with Guy till morning, as at other times he'd done, and fall into rehearsal still pleasantly sore from his last fuck and with the smell carefully not washed off on the excuse of scarcely having time for more than a dry polish before bundling out into the daylight.

It was a different smell, Guy's, from the one he ordinarily enjoyed, that compounded essence brought away on you from bouts of clubbing or the Common, made up of sweat, tobacco, beer and an acrid, salty reminiscence of greedy kissing. It was the kind of exhalation you'd expect Guy to have, opulent and allusive, reminding Theo of those idiotic marketing descriptions of this or that fragrance which always made him laugh out loud when he read them in style mags or the poncey little booklets accompanying the atomizer packaging. 'Woody notes of cinnamon and benjoin are joined by subtler hints of vetiver and a counterpoint of ylang-ylang.' He couldn't exactly have put his finger on the ylang-ylang, which sounded like the name of a medieval monkey, but the generic lavishness was there, one of those strange invisible perfumes emanating from the incorrupt bodies of saints, a sort of inevitable consequence of what Guy palpably was, both within and without his clothes, so that Theo, feasting on him, took great breaths of it, as though such a thing had been necessary to life.

'Like this, choccy?'

'Yeah,' murmured Theo drowsily, ready, in this moment, to like more or less anything without too much discrimination as regards its precise identity.

'I mean the champagne.'

He twisted his head round to look at the label and read 'Ruinart'.

Guy laughed. 'It sounds nice like that.'

'How should I have said it?'

'Doesn't matter, big boy, I'll settle for your pronunciation any time, it's more fun. Ruinart, perhaps we ought to sell it as a concept. Are you fond of ruins, choccy-pie?'

'I don't know many,' admitted Theo, somewhat mystified by the question.

'Keep it that way. You and dead buildings are all wrong for each other. I was thinking how good you looked just now when you came back from the bathroom. As if you belonged in this flat, you know? Like I'd chosen you to be here, like I could put you anywhere in this space and you'd be a part of it.'

'An accessory?'

'No, tarbaby, an essential, an absolute must have to make it all work properly. Don't know why I didn't see it before, you're bloody perfect. It's like I made you up to go in here, and now everything fits.' Guy burst into incredulous laughter. 'I'm a fucking genius, they ought to give me a prize at Central Saint Martin's or wherever.'

Theo felt the tiniest frisson of unease, he didn't know why. Or at least that was what he told himself. The words, as seemed increasingly to happen nowadays, had vanished which would tell him what the feeling really was, and it passed almost as soon as it began. Yet Guy must have noticed something, for he ran a hand across Theo's face, whispering, 'Everything all right, *mousse au chocolat*?'

'Yes, thanks.'

'You're always such a good-mannered boy, aren't you? I really like that. And you gave me a nice time this evening.'

'That makes me feel cheap.'

Guy laughed again, his reverberate, bellowing guffaw, the sound, Theo chose to think, of someone who had never needed to show deference or humility.

'Darling, I didn't know you cost anything to start with. And I'm certainly not selling you on, even at auction. Like I said, you're too fucking decorative to be disposable.'

'Does that mean . . . ?' Theo halted. Every moment was potentially inappropriate, so there was no harm in trying now.

'What?'

'Well, can I stay the night?'

'Please, I thought I heard you add.' The smile, unwavering till then, abruptly transformed itself into a pout. 'And no you can't, this time. I've got work to do for a meeting tomorrow morning, and I'd much rather be missing you than have you lying there waiting to be fucked. You'd make me feel guilty. Guilt's so totally pointless, don't you find?'

No, thought Theo. 'Yeah, I suppose so.'

'Anyway we agreed, didn't we? So don't get iffy. Have some more Ruinart instead, that always helps.'

Remorseful and obedient, Theo did as he was bidden. The dryness of the champagne burned his mouth as if he had swallowed acid. His body, tensed till then with expectancy, electric almost under Guy's touch, grew suddenly nerveless, and he turned his face away into the pillow so as to conceal the gloom which overwhelmed him. Inert he lay there, hearing the snap of the rubber, suffering, without any accustomed joy, the coldness of the lube against his arse and the weight of the other man hunkered over him, pinioning his arms against the attempt he wouldn't in any case have made to free himself. He might have believed it meant as a consolation if he weren't certain that Guy had never in his entire life stooped to console anybody. For the first time it didn't feel like rape, was without the least hint of abusive exhilaration. He was just being fobbed off and hated himself for not being angry enough at having allowed it to happen.

'Aren't you going to come?' murmured Guy into his ear.

'Not just now,' said Theo, aware that it sounded as if he thought there'd be anything like later.

'Be like that.'

He was, for some minutes at least. He heard Guy get up, go into the bathroom and turn on the shower. For a single preposterous moment the thought came to him that he might simply lie there prone and unresponsive, refusing altogether to do what was expected of him, ruining everything in an ecstasy of disobedience. Then, with a sigh, he hauled himself to his feet and went to join Guy in the shower. Often, as a kind of playful coda to a more serious engagement, they'd do it again, with much deft soaping of each other and kisses under the deluge of water, and Theo (always Theo, never Guy) on his knees, laughing and spluttering as he tried to duck the torrents coursing down the valley of Guy's back. It was their own shower scene, consciously staged, an intentional parody of which might have taken place that first time in the sauna if they'd chosen — of if Guy had chosen — to remain there.

As it was, Guy, towelling himself among the mirrors, seemed quite irritatingly contained within his autonomy. He was impatient now, apparently, to be at work, something about which Theo had never even bothered to be curious, since the details of how others got money both mystified and bored him, and an investment banker was merely something he was glad not to be. Disconsolate, feeling the heaviness of his bones and the redundant musculature which packed them, he went through the motions of showering. Guy padded back into the bedroom and stood, not necessarily having gauged the effect beforehand, where he could be seen pulling a pair of jeans and a T-shirt from the wardrobe space behind its frosted perspex panel. Thus preoccupied, he wasn't, in this instant, any more conspicuously beautiful than always, yet Theo felt within himself a sudden wrenching spasm of longing, made sharper by his residual guilt over the sullenness with which he'd given himself to Guy. Soon, soon, he'd find a way of expressing what he already knew, and that great canopy of reticence they'd stretched so carefully over them would be dismantled and packed away, never to be needed again. Armed now with this wise patience, Theo began to dress himself, not unaware that one man is always more attractive to another while putting on his clothes than when taking them off.

Guy must have thought so, for after standing there restless, rocking up and down on the balls of his feet, he came behind him, hung for a moment with his arms dropping down over Theo's shoulders and began nuzzling his neck.

'We don't like it when you have to go,' he said, 'me and the flat. We get lonely, we lose all our meaning.'

I don't have to go, thought Theo. Maybe after all you're only trying to hurt me. If so, then perhaps you're the lover I took you for, because isn't that what lovers do? In a moment he had turned, and abruptly taking Guy's face between his hands, kissed it with infinite sweetness. The gesture, revolutionary for being so decisive, was startling to Guy.

'Was that in aid of something special?' he asked, with what sounded almost like distaste.

'Yes,' was all Theo said, as if Guy ought to have known. Picking up his jacket, he slipped out on to the stairs.

In the square the night was warm and dampish. On the opposite side Theo paused to look up at the flat's high windows, with their blinds, as always, so closely drawn and occasionally the very vaguest shadow made by the figure of Guy moving to and fro behind them. If, as he knew was often supposed, houses absorbed emotions as fabrics take this or that colour from a dye, then the place was marked for ever by some of the intensest physical excitement he had ever known. His earlier resignation had turned readily enough into the kind of contentment which comes of knowing how to wait. After all, it had not been such a bad day. He'd gone to Southwark Cathedral with his parents and prayed for Adam out of instinct and Guy out of need, and a woman in front of him named Connie had clasped his hands in both of hers at the peace and told him afterwards what a nice strong voice he had in the hymns. His mother, as they walked along towards Tower Bridge, had asked him, as she always did, when he was coming home again, as if living away from Southwark was merely a species of temporary aberration, along with his homosexuality, for both of which he was certain her prayers that morning had requested the favour of a cure. At lunch in his brother's loft above Spice Dock he had not – for a wonder – been lectured by Aubrey or patronized by Nadine, Aubrey's girlfriend, probably because Aubrey the previous week had landed a fraud case from under the nose of a rival who happened to be a fellow member of the Society of Black Lawyers. So the pair of them were prepared to be amused, in a condescending sort of way at least, by his account of Nathan Lester's antics at the *Troilus* rehearsals. His father delighted them all, what's more, by a tale of an island in the Grenadines called Cariacou, where the people had a custom known as 'speeching', which involved on-the-spot competitive recitals of passages from *Julius Caesar*. For once he'd not gone home to Clapham feeling borne down by the family's hints as to his unregenerate lack of respectability, or by the statutory question as to whether or not he'd found himself a girlfriend.

Not such a very bad day then. Theo still stood in the humid shadow, not yet wanting absolutely to remove himself from the spot whence he could continue to look at the house, or altogether hoping that Guy would raise the blind and, silhouetted against the light within the room, summon him to return, but wanting, in a moment of delicious regret, to imagine it were possible. Then he realized that someone was sitting in a car parked just beside him who might wonder what exactly he was doing watching so intently from the darkness. Reluctantly then, he began to walk away in the vague direction of Craven Hill. As he reached the corner of the square he heard a door bang shut and, turning his head, saw Guy come out on to the pavement, get into his own car, start the engine and at some speed drive off. Observing the other car slew out almost immediately into the road, Theo hurried away, fearing, for whatever reason, lest it might slow down as it passed him. The last thing he'd have wanted just now was anybody to speak to him.

XII

~

'YOU'VE got to sit on the desk.'

'My skirt's far too long for that.'

'But it's what women are supposed to do when they come into a man's office. It used to be just a bit flirty, but nowadays it's meant to be empowering.'

'I don't see how parking one's bum on a desk can possibly make one more powerful.'

'It says, "I'm a woman and I don't give a fuck."'

'What happens if we make an alteration to one of the verbs?'

'Nothing, because women aren't allowed to admit to needing sex from men. You're always meant to be looking in another direction while you're doing it.'

'Which, of course, you never do.'

'Does that mean "you, men" or "you, Adam"? In either case the answer's sometimes but not always. You meet – that's to say, one meets – these guys in the backroom at some underwear night who do that sort of thing, pulling your tits or squeezing your packet while they're looking over your shoulder. Brass, I call it, sheer unexampled brass!'

'I don't want to hear about it,' said Daisy in her sister's voice, making Adam laugh because it was wickedly alike.

'Why does Sib hate it when anyone talks about sex? I don't mean sex *qua* sex, *quaquaqua*, but just anything that suggests you might even be preparing to mention it.'

'It's got something to do with Algerians in Kentish Town,' Daisy said with purposeful vagueness. 'In her pre-Jezebel phase. But don't tell her I said so.'

'I'm hardly likely to, am I?'

'You might, you're horribly indiscreet sometimes.'

'Comes of knowing you, sweetheart. Anyway, to what do I owe the refusal to perch cutely on my desk? We gave Frankie a cheque with several noughts on it. And I've seen all I want to of Pessoa's myriad forms.'

'Hasn't he thanked you?'

'We only sent it yesterday, and not to him personally anyway.'

'We haven't seen each other for about three days, he's ferociously busy. That's a word he's got hold of recently, everything's ferocious all of a sudden.'

Adam stared down at his papers, then said, 'But it was not of Francesco she came to speak. Or am I wrong?'

'Something which concerns you both, as it happens.' Daisy tossed the rust-coloured pashmina back over one shoulder for the sake of significant punctuation. The day was less actually cold than merely not warm, but the *frileuse* reflex of the professional dancer had stayed with her as much as the habit of standing in an assortment of 'positions' or that of gathering her hair into an austerely practical arrangement which might allow her to go on as Odette-Odile should the guest principal artist fracture a metatarsal.

'I should have asked you this ages ago, Ad, only I didn't know how interested you were. But you're so adorable with Edie, it seemed the natural thing.'

He knew what was coming. When he looked down at his papers this time it was with a kind of grateful embarrassment that she should after all have seen fit to ask him, though he knew he would have been piqued beyond endurance if someone else had been named as godfather instead. The gesture was of the kind she always seemed capable of making at the last moment, just when he felt himself lulled into the securest cynicism regarding her, a renewal of everything which had bound them together since, at a party in Oxford years before, they'd sought out the nearest comfortable scrap of carpet on which to sit and exclude everyone else for the evening.

'God, you're so cheesy with that smile!' Daisy laughed. 'You don't do it often enough.'

'Some people think I don't do it at all.'

'It's only a christening, Ad.'

'Does it matter that I'm a Prot?'

'So's Alice, and she said yes last night. I sort of seduced Father Costello at Our Lady of Victories because officially you're both damned to hellfire for ever as heretics. And even Sib's deserted the Faith for your lot. But Frankie's more or less the real thing.'

'Frankie?'

'Don't sound so sceptical. He may behave as if he's out to lunch most of the time, but he and Edie carry on like ancient friends.'

'Bet they do. So when do we all converge before the Miraculous Weeping Madonna?'

'I've fixed it for the middle of next month. And my sister has graciously agreed to host the recep, I fixed that as well. Pity Jez isn't here because I'd worked out how I was going to get him to pay for the champagne.'

'I should like to have seen that. You've got it so fine-tuned, the pair of you, it's a real double act.'

Daisy, twitching her shawl, stared out into the square. 'I don't exactly hate him, you know. He's just never known where I'm coming from. He thinks I'm a layabout.'

'Women can't be layabouts, it's a man thing. But I suppose in comparison with him you are. Well, for that matter I am, anybody is, he's so restless. This morning he came in for half an hour, did his e-mail, glanced at the post, told Celia her hair looked Japanese – not meant as a compliment – and then bombed off in the BMW to the Whitechapel to look at some conceptual buckets. Anyway you'll get your champagne, he's feeling very generous these days. He didn't even want to know the details of the Pessoa piece. Was Frankie pleased? Oh, of course, you haven't seen him.'

'Not for dust. He goes clubbing in the small hours and seems to thrive on it.'

Adam stifled a spurt of annoyance sufficiently to ask with studied unconcern, 'Has he found someone nice to fritter away the non-choreographic hours with?'

Smiling, she turned from the window. 'I'd soon know if he had, wouldn't I? He tells me everything, just like you.'

'Then he's more of a fool than I took him for.'

'Frankie doesn't know what stupid means. You must have found that out from watching him in rehearsal. Don't be misled by the camp riffs, they're just a front to hide the pussycat within. Try and be nice to him at the christening, won't you?'

'Only if he's nice to me. Which isn't necessarily guaranteed. It really is sweet of you to count me in. I'll make it worth Edie's while, I promise.'

'You don't exactly have to put your name to a bankers' draft at the font, my love. And Alice isn't short of a bob or two. Talking of which, I've got to go and buy myself some shoes, otherwise you could have stood me lunch. This bit of London's like a filmset in the spring, you're lucky working here. Tweak Jezza's perm for me.'

Adam was glad he'd not absolutely had to lie to Daisy and that once again it only involved a certain negligible economy with the truth. Her complacent assumption that Frankie must keep nothing hidden merely sharpened the pleasure of his own concealments. He liked to hear her talk about 'fixing' the christening and the party afterwards, let alone her plan for blagging champagne off Jeremy. *Au fond* she was, wasn't she, a fixer, a buccaneer, a freebooter, like one of those women who screwed fur coats and Mediterranean cruises out of doting millionaires in the twenties or got driven round the Riviera after the war by King Farouk in an open-topped Bentley. Fixers need foxing now and then, thought Adam, and it seemed harmless enough to be bamboozling Daisy over the precise nature of his connection with her house guest.

Knightsbridge was where she'd be buying shoes, so there was no danger of her stumbling across him lunching *à deux* with Frankie behind Charing Cross Road, yet the vaguest hint of a possibility that she might do so served to lend a more intriguing air of clandestine assignation to their rendezvous. Growing bored with sifting through clutches of CVs and elaborately constructed begging letters, Adam shuffled everything into an appearance of order and slipped downstairs, anxious to avoid meeting Celia on the way, given as she had been lately to a sort of censorious attendance-clocking for him and Jeremy.

Daisy was right, the quarter, in the slick, ingratiating April sunlight had a distinct air of the movie backdrop, something a little 1950-ish, with Googie Withers or Sylvia Syms in an A-line skirt, lantern-jawed spivs in trilbies and the odd Austin Princess or Riley Pathfinder pushing its way consequentially up Charlotte Street. A happiness not entirely related to notions of Frankie awaiting him a mere few blocks away began to take hold of Adam, and for once the feeling didn't seem to carry with it the usual shadowings of attendant nemesis, shame and embarrassment. Everything, the dusty little trees, the broad, uneven pavements, the unexpectedness of small, singular shops, the simple virtue of the zone as an expression of everything that wasn't Oxford Circus, seemed suddenly imbued with a promise the more gratifying for its vagueness, perhaps only, after all, a generic sense of release and fulfilment carried on the air like pollen by the approaching season.

They always got his name wrong when he booked as Maschera. Nobody save a handful of the super-literate could spell Killigrew correctly in any case. Once, to Adam's intense delight, a boy at a sauna in New Cross enquired his name as they stood post-orgasmically 'together clinging' under the rachitic shower, disconcerted him still further by asking 'Adam what?', and on being told, adding a knowing, 'Oh yeah, like the guy who wrote *The Parson's Wedding*.' They'd swapped numbers but left each other unrung. He couldn't remember the boy's name. Hardly considering it worth even pretending to a descent, he had never read *The Parson's Wedding*. Neither, he was prepared to bet, had the waiters at Maschera, who must be the ditziest in London, but that was no reason to get Killigrew wrong. Especially as he knew the name of the restaurant was stressed on the first syllable, Maskra, not M'sharer, let alone Mascara, which seemed altogether more appropriate.

It was precisely that aspect which had prompted him to select the place for their meeting. The air of self-mockery, not merely in the *mise en scène* and cast of regulars, but in details like the wording of the menu, printed in an almost invisible sans serif, and the wine list's careful avoidance of all but a few European labels in favour of their smarter colonial equivalents, was exactly calculated, by his reckoning, to appeal to that peculiar species of alertness with which Frankie seemed programmed to monitor every detail of a conscious existence. Adam mustn't arrive too early. He'd made that mistake too often before, yet still needed to remind himself on this occasion that a delaying tactic must always score better than sitting with grimly reproachful punctuality in wait for the Desired One to do a hi-have-you-been-here-long number. Dawdling purposefully among the shops in Goodge Street sharpened his appetite, however – not for lunch, which the nausea born of emotional panic would almost certainly prevent him from eating, but for the man with whom he'd contrived at last to be alone for the first time.

He pushed open the door with something like incredulity, which the maître d' in his dark blue Hugo Boss must have noticed, since the cynicism of his smile betrayed more than a simple recognition.

'Mr Killigrew? Your guests are here already.'

'I don't think . . .'

The waiter deputed to show him to the table might have been a prison warder jangling keys on a giant loop. Adam heard their footsteps thump in amplified echo on the blond parquet, and there was something so much like mockery in the exhilarated rhubarbing of the lunch mob on either side that he wanted to put his hands against his ears and start to wail and scream. Instead he sat down, a nerveless victim, to hear Frankie say, 'You have to insist Paul drinks at least half a bottle of wine. And I don't mean first-base stuff like Chardonnay or Chablis, we're talking *la rouge baiser* here, something with a kick, so he can't ruin himself in rehearsal like he just did today, but be a good old-fashioned lush for twenty-four hours.' He turned, archly maternal, to where Paul sat slumped, scowling under the black smears of his Greek eyebrows. 'That's the official prescription, darling, and you know I'm not wrong about these things.'

Paul said nothing. He had not even specially bothered himself with acknowledging Adam's arrival.

'We're going to have the beef teriyaki with plum chutney, doesn't that hit the spot? And I guess you're going to do something English and perverse and start with coffee and a lavender custard maybe? Hey, who is this Lavender Custard I hear so much about? They say Condé Nast are poaching her for American *Vogue*. That's one *poached* Lavender Custard.'

Just now, thought Adam, just now I'd like to take something blunt and heavy, the glass ashtray perhaps, or the cooling bucket beside the next table, and bring it down on your beautiful shaven skull. I'd wait for a minute or two to relish the pleasure of watching your blood trickle across the floor while the egregious Paul snatched this opportunity to stop smouldering, and sank beside your lifeless body in the pose they taught him at dance academy, the one which means 'a faithful friend mourns the departed hero'. OK, so maybe they don't teach that, but it's the sort of thing he'd just about do. Then, laughing satanically, I'd walk, with slow Olympian equipoise, out of the restaurant between serried ranks of applauding punters, to where the police were waiting, not to arrest me for wilful homicide but to give me the public's thanks for having rid society of a serial tosser. In my dreams, thought Adam.

'I think I'll do it the right way round,' he simpered.

'We were just at Martin's,' said Frankie.

'Who's Martin?'

'You never met Martin Oakes? He styles the big couture shows. Like big big *big*. So we're all looking at vests for Paul.'

Adam, in the interests of his own survival, and because a doctor had warned him that being plumpish he was at greater risk of heart trouble, found himself taking several deep breaths.

'Has it got to be a special kind of vest? I suppose Diesel or somewhere like that would have done.' Venomously he grinned in Paul's direction. 'Or if you were looking for something a bit cheaper, Gap do them in nice little packs of three.'

Paul glowered back at him. You could see the coarse black hair beginning in the V of his shirt. Theo would have clocked the label at once. He wanted Theo there, like an angel with a sword to hew the others in pieces.

'Frankie's talking about waistcoats,' muttered Paul.

'Yes, I know that,' said Adam, buggered if he was going to admit to having forgotten that 'vest' in American is something you button under a jacket. 'I was only playing.'

'Adam likes to play.' Frankie's glance was lurid with mischief. 'Adam is what we call amusing. We like amusing people.'

'I thought confusing was more your line. Amusing people is what you do for a living, so it must get a bit samey after a while.' For the crucial instant his eyes locked defiantly with Frankie's. The mouth quivered ever so slightly, enough to betray uncertainty. Seizing his advantage as soon as the waiter had gone, Adam brightly asked, 'So was it tiring, Paul?'

'What?'

'Trying on vests with Martin?'

'We had to get it right,' Frankie said, like a manager fencing awkward questions for some bozo in a boyband. 'Paul's a perfectionist.'

'Do I need to know that?' Before the other man could respond, Adam went on, 'You're awfully fond of telling us what we are, aren't you? Anyway, Paul, you didn't answer my question, the one about being tired. Were you?'

'I am now.' Paul looked murderous, his perfect bones shadowed by the blood-feud hostility of some abandoned village in the wilds of Epirus or the Mani. Bingo, thought Adam.

'Yes, I know, it's a bitch, isn't it? Getting things right, I mean. Perfection sucks, basically. I'd rather be blemished and totally fucked up, with only one eye when the popular prejudice runs in favour of two, or a wooden leg or a pair of false gnashers, anything so long as I wasn't perfect. Actually I'll settle for being short and fat. What do you think, Paul? You look like the sort of person who knows about these things?'

The charge in the air across the table was at precisely the level he'd intended. In this moment Adam felt like a mad professor twiddling knobs and watching, exultant, as the indicator began seesawing out of control and rainbow-coloured fumes started to hiss from under panels and keyboards. Paul gave a little tea-tasting noise and shook his head in sheer uncomprehending crossness. Frankie's countenance meanwhile had begun to cloud with the earliest signs of serious unease. Attempting to rally, he said softly, 'We can't help it maybe.'

'Who's we?'

'Us,' Frankie answered grimly. 'It's the way we're trained. Everything has to be beautiful.'

Like you, thought Adam, with your smile-brackets and

grapeskin lips and strong neck and shoulders like newel posts and intolerable grace in every sodding bend and turn of your body.

'It hasn't got to be,' he said. 'That's where we go wrong. Once, when I was at college and went Inter-railing in Europe, we got to this place in Germany, I don't know how, called Langenburg. Just a village with a castle on top. And next to the castle there's a church, with all these tombs of the grand family. And one of the tombs has a big oval portrait of a man in a wig, with a fluffy lace collar and bits of armour. And he's looking at you full of pride and contempt, handsome, you'd do it with him, but he'd spurn you afterwards, a face which says, "You have nothing I want for more than five minutes", confident, powerful. And across the whole portrait the artist, whoever he was, had painted a great jagged line, a fissure opening in the smooth surface of the painting, as if there was an earthquake or something.'

'Sounds like one hell of a big cliché,' said Frankie.

'So maybe it is, clichés aren't altogether ineffective at times. I remember that picture because it stopped me believing in the value of perfection. And because it made me see that what's wrong with us, the great jagged flaw running across every assumption we make, is that we put beauty and the desire for it and the possession of it above everything else.'

Frankie's mouth pursed impatiently. 'I was talking about dancers, Adam.'

'Well, I wasn't, was I? I was talking about the friends of Dorothy. Which used to be the same thing.' He put his hands on the table with a decisiveness which surprised him. 'Stuff this for a game of soldiers,' he said. 'I'm off. See you around, Francesco.'

Not quite an Olympian equipoise, not quite the lunchers

dividing in best 'all the ranks of Tuscany could scarce forbear to cheer' fashion, but head erect, carriage firm, pretty damned good all things considered. 'Leaving us, Mr Killigrew?' said the maître d'.

'Got to go,' said Adam cheerily, as if it were the most natural thing in the world to fling out with your first course untouched on the plate beside a forlorn half-glass of Coonawarra. Had anybody stood in his way, rage must have blinded him enough to strike them to the floor. Even the coat-check girl looked ready to drop a curtsey as he passed.

Once outside, Adam paused for a moment to consider what exactly he intended to do next. Then, as he turned, still aimless, to walk vaguely in the direction of Bloomsbury, a clench on his arm sent him spinning backwards, and there stood Frankie, ferocious in earnest this time and not inclined to let him go.

'So what's eating you, sweet British asshole?'

'I thought we had an appointment,' said Adam rather tremulously, yet finding the surprise not altogether unpleasant.

'Don't get British with me. Who said you make the rules?'

'I did. Rule number one, dump your Greek statues in the museum just up the road. Ever so convenient, don't you know?'

'Fuck you!'

Keep it there, it's nice, thought Adam. 'What's really pissing you off, Frankie? That I didn't laugh at your joke about the lavender custard? I'd like to see a giant vat of it with your big knobbly dancer's feet sticking out of the top. That's a joke, but of course you do the jokes, we have to remember.'

In a kind of soundless snarl, Frankie's lips tightened with rage, but as he made to shake him once again, Adam struggled free and starting back a pace or two he hurled a defiant: 'Get back in there, Winsome Torment wants his pudding! Those thighs need building up for Pessoa. And you're the one who's paying, remember?'

'Asshole!'

At the top of the street some triumphant impulse made Adam turn round. To his amazement, Frankie still stood where they had faced each other, his fists clenched, his cropped head thrown forward, burly, menacing and suddenly unexotic.

Good, thought Adam. Let's go home.

The stomach-churning fury and dismay at what he saw as Frankie's treachery in bringing Paul with him had evaporated, along with any more specific doubt as to whether the prompting behind it were mere caprice or else a prescient strategy for self-protection. What mattered to Adam was not the débâcle in the restaurant, or indeed the embarrassing re-collection of his own portentousness in bringing that about, but what had happened afterward, the touch of Frankie on him, the anger and sense of affront he'd succeeded in raising, the fact that Frankie should have done anything so resonantly uncool as to pursue him into the street with an intent little short of murderous. They had known each other barely three weeks, yet however crudely and, Adam must admit, without meaning to do so, he had shaken Frankie's maddening composure and felt in the process bizarrely desirable, as if the quivering hand shaking him against the wall were there for another purpose entirely. In that instant Adam, armed with victorious opportunism, might have snatched at Frankie's mouth and gashed a kiss across it. Perhaps the fact that he'd done nothing so vulgar was what Frankie meant by 'getting British'.

By the time he crossed the grass triangle by the Polygon Adam felt the usual urge to tell Theo, holding nothing back. It would go some way towards atoning for his behaviour the previous week. From the safe distance of Worcestershire he had made up his mind not to mention Guy again or to hint at any further curiosity regarding him. After a fashion, mysterious as it was to Adam, Theo appeared happy. To probe the sources of such happiness seemed calculated to destroy the peculiar equilibrium sustaining the pair of them.

His best intentions were disappointed. Theo was at rehearsal, he should have remembered, and when he got back the whole ragged immediacy of what Adam wanted to tell him would have sorted itself into something more discreet, a set of edited highlights which by then in any case might be less interesting to either of them. It irked him now that the only trace of Theo's presence was a sort of *Marie Celeste* scatter of fragmentary human indicators, two or three crinkled cigarette butts in the ashtray, a sheet torn from a notepad on which the words 'scurril' and 'livelong' were doodled several times above the phrase 'thy topless deputation', and a vinyl disc of the *Trauer-Ode* which with his customary obsessiveness he had lately been playing almost every day, whistling snatches of 'Lass, Fürstin, lass noch einem strahl' through his teeth as he pottered in the bathroom.

Theo would have known the answer, if only Adam were able just now to formulate a precise question, or rather the one question he was increasingly reluctant to ask himself. Doubtless he'd blown it with Frankie and, to make matters worse, Daisy would have been told and the flimsy fabric of their deception of her torn down, so that even now the pair of them must be cackling at his crass assumption of moral rectitude as he waddled down the restaurant's parqueted gangway. What after all did he want, more than that coarse sense of notching up a trophy whereby one man pursuing another reduces him to the level of a stuffed pike in a glass case over the fireplace in a pub? What fun a taxidermist would have had with those florid purple lips, the squared-off temples, that nose with its pencilled tip and the geometry of those sharp jaws and cheekbones, let alone with the business of finding the right enamel to reproduce the particular shade of blue in the eyes, which Theo had so thoughtfully prevented Adam from describing in such terms as 'cornflower' or 'aquamarine'.

There's a kind of face, isn't there, which you recognize at once as homosexual, in the same way that when you're standing behind a man on the up-escalator you know he's gay from the way his jeans dent so snugly into the crack of his arse. If pushed to describe it in detail, Adam could never have singled out any determinant feature. It has nothing to do, as he knew, with the obvious signifiers, hairs, beards, earrings or even that lascivious mobility in the eyes which is supposed to indicate a degree of ever-present lust unknown to straight males, celebrated for their respectful continence and ascetic preoccupation with things not of this world.

Adam thought now of this face as it became Frankie's, and was cynically not surprised at finding himself unperturbed, after all, by what had happened that afternoon. At any rate lunch between the pair of them was no longer an immediate option, happening or millennial. He had guessed why Paul had to be there, with his fuzzy neck, treacle-toffee eyes and general air of overblown gigolo handsomeness: to provide Frankie with the means of making a gesture of deliberate insolence for the sake of heading off Adam's own less sophisticated manoeuvres towards a greater intimacy. Then he remembered what he'd said about rejecting beauty and blenched somewhat at the memory. It had sounded like Nancy Reagan inviting decent Americans to 'just say no' to drugs. He'd meant perhaps half of it. As for the rest, well, Frankie right now, all the irritating effulgence of him, was starting to make Adam feel hopelessly insincere.

XIII

SOONER or later they'd have to get Gaga a mate, or people would start to talk. If you lived in the country, Serena reasoned with herself, it had to be in such a way that nobody could point an accusatory finger at you as an ignorant townie, the sort of person against whom the more aggressive and patronizing articles in *Field* and *Country Life* seemed nowadays to be directed, the kind who wanted the right to roam and gave money to the sabs in the hunting season even if they didn't actually join them in staking out the field gates, laying false scents and trying to head off the pack so as to give Charlie Reynolds an extra minute or two's advantage. To this end, when preparations for the Countryside March were on foot, she had made all the right noises, but carefully contrived to remain in London on the designated weekend, privately judging the whole thing to be as ostentatious a morsel of humbug as the legislation it was intended to overthrow.

Nevertheless she felt a shade embarrassed at having yielded

to mere sentimental impulse in adopting Gaga as the lone survivor of a gosling gaggle crushed, along with its mother, by an earth mover clearing space for a new silo on the edge of a nearby farm. Kathy, whose husband Rob drove vans for a galvanized window firm outside Evesham and who came in to see to the house while Serena and Jeremy were away, had started making remarks about Gaga looking ever so lonely at feeding time and about how it wasn't natural, was it really, to leave them on their own when they got big like that and had all their feathers and everything. It was true that the goose had grown immensely attached to Serena and that the various manuals she consulted, with their warnings about the danger of bumblefoot and gapes and advice as to what measures to adopt in cases of coccidiosis, each emphasized the birds' essential sociability. Something, however, made her perversely reluctant as yet to do what she knew ought to be done and drive over to Fladbury where, so Kathy and Rob had taken the trouble to find out, a beautiful English Emden gander could be acquired at a very reasonable price to make the perfect consort. She loved instead the insane cackling Gaga set up each time she arrived after a few days in London. There was something wonderful about stepping out on late spring mornings like these, with her feet making trails in the heavy white dewfall across the lawn as she went to open the pen, calling, 'Gaga, brekkies!' and the big white bird, bosomy and stately as some Edwardian contralto, came out to meet her and thereafter to follow her around the garden.

For some reason Gaga had taken to Adam too, maybe because he was so unthreatening. There were times when Serena wondered whether she ought not to busy herself more over finding a mate for him besides. It was pointless Alice trying to assure her that he must be happy as he was and that life without a regular partner was something he had either got used to or else embraced from the onset with an active enthusiasm. Alice, in Serena's view, tended to stumble too easily over her own sophistications, whereas she herself was so often right through simple instinct. Only once had such a prompting let her down, but that was a long time ago when essentially she was someone else altogether.

As she'd said to Alice, it couldn't be much of a life for him, hanging around in a disco till three in the morning or picking up men in dark places whom you didn't know from — she'd been going to say 'didn't know from Adam' until she realized how silly that sounded. And he was so good around women, especially with somebody like her, going shopping in Cheltenham, having a giggle in front of the TV or reading her the more cretinous bits out of the lifestyle mags, you couldn't believe he'd never fancy them occasionally, just a bit. There were lots of women who'd kill for him. Not that he looked anything special, being a bit too rolypoly and chubby cheeked, but that gave him a sort of boyish charm you couldn't resist and those tight, crinkly blond curls were made for someone to run her hands through. And he was so sweet-natured and patient and clever and always seemed to know just what you were feeling before you even got there yourself.

Serena's conviction that this was what Adam needed had been strengthened by reading an article in the weekend edition of the *Daily Telegraph* which claimed that hundreds of men who merely supposed themselves to be gay were sub-consciously longing for the chance to be straight, and that 'ex-homosex', as one of them put it, would be the flavour of the approaching era. She was not blind enough to reality to imagine that the next decade would indeed witness quite such a wholesale sloughing of one sexual identity in favour of another, but gay was a fashion, wasn't it, like shiitake mushrooms or Prada handbags, and men were hopeless pushovers when it came to suggestion. Apart from anything else, they liked, as a rule, to get married. It enhanced that sense of experience which was pleasing to them to possess, and the appearance of children, even if it was a bore having to take responsibility for their upbringing, at any rate proved to a man that he could do the job in hand satisfactorily.

Marriage, for Serena, held a mysterious inevitability. Imagination was always something of an effort if it involved trying to place yourself in any situation other than those to which you were fully accustomed, and she couldn't now conceive of an existence for herself as an unmarried woman. Her sister Daisy's choice, insouciantly to return from a protracted stay in New York sporting a daughter who might have been found under the proverbial gooseberry bush for all trace of communication as to the father's identity, seemed comprehensible only because it was Daisy who made it. The same spirit of imperious contrariness with which she had sailed through childhood and adolescence evidently guided her rejection of orthodox parenthood as something far too vulgarly predictable for her to be bothered with.

Not without a certain smugness, Serena felt that she herself could have predicted Daisy's response long before it was so publicly enunciated. There'd been a scene, she recalled, at the convent when Daisy was fifteen and Reverend Mother had been telling a select group of girls – chosen, it now seemed to Serena, on the basis of their social connections rather than their prospective fecundity – that it was their duty to marry and bring children into the world to be baptized in the Faith, and that their destiny as Catholic women was that of wives and mothers. With singular coolness Daisy, looking Reverend Mother in the eye (something you were not supposed to do unless she suspected you of having told a lie) said, 'Yes, but you're not married, are you?' and then, with a confidence perfectly breathtaking, adding, 'You're not even a mother – a real mother, I mean. How can you tell us what we ought to do with our lives?'

Two of the burlier sisters present had hustled her from the room, and Reverend Mother, shaking her head and smiling grimly in an 'ah, youth! youth!' fashion, had benignly exploited the situation by suggesting that some among the group of girls would choose instead to devote their lives to God, that the marriages they would make must be to Christ and his Church, and that the example of womanhood before them was the greatest of all, His Immaculate Mother herself.

It was ironic then that Daisy should have held on to her Catholicism – at least to its more silver-fork, social cachet aspects – while Serena had to all intents renounced hers in favour of the Church of England in all its dire unsmartness. For as things had since turned out, it was she who had taken Reverend Mother's injunctions most deeply to heart, and after a year or two of aimless unhappiness in her early twenties, an episode blanked easily from her recollection by embarrassment as much as distaste, she had met Jeremy beside a swimming pool in Italy. Beyond his obvious sheen of glamour and the fact, which Daisy (who disliked him at once) was quick to divine, that he was unostentatiously rich, something incomplete about him appealed to Serena's protectiveness. There was – or at least there seemed to be – an innocence like her own, a naïveté belying all his accumulated sophistication, which she found herself wanting to shield against Daisy's abundant scorn and the knowingness of her other sister Isobel, whose role in the business was that of a lipsmacking go-between.

Nothing of significance had occurred since to alter this initial impression. It amused her to watch him try, with varying degrees of success, to persuade others that he must always know more than they did about the world's internal mechanisms. Doubtless this explained his decision to forsake contract law, at which he was apparently the suavest of adepts, for the directorship of a charitable trust giving money to artistic enterprises deemed either too risky or too unfashionable by the Arts Council and the Heritage Lottery Fund. It wasn't that a barrister's chambers looked, in the end, too much like hard work, simply that at the helm of the Wooldridge Foundation he could be everywhere at once, his perennial restlessness gratified by a vague yet continued sense of others' breathless expectation, so that his arrivals should seem like those of some Renaissance archangel, radiant and desired.

Serena hadn't reproached him, even silently, for appearing rather relieved than otherwise on learning that she was unable to conceive. She'd realized almost at once that as a father Jeremy would have been hopeless. The personal triumphs and individual attractiveness of his children he could have enjoyed, but on the ugly and unpromising he'd simply have turned his back. Thus childish himself, with such potential for unreason, Jeremy grew the dearer to her. She could never have told him how much she loved the peculiar boyishness that experience, because it had dealt kindly with him almost to the point of spoiling, had done nothing to coarsen. Occasionally, when he was sulky and cross or desperately in search of something he'd lost, Serena felt the surge of an inexpressible joy, as if she were the wise, patient governess of a prince who had yet to learn the full reach of his best intentions. In such moments she acknowledged, not without an agreeable sense of her superiority to Daisy for being unable to do so, that Reverend Mother had probably been right, after her fashion, as to the nature of an ultimate fulfilment.

It was time to go and feed Gaga, but first she wanted to take the prints out of the darkroom and look at them in a decent light. There was no shortage of it in the house. For the past two or three years it had seemed that spring, as formerly remembered, was no longer an option and that the seasonal cycle was henceforth to entail an abrupt shift, somewhere around the beginning of May, from a grey, chilly fag-end of winter to the full, torrid summer with nothing in between. The sudden warmth with which this Easter surprised them had lingered on, so that the new leafage in the garden seemed less forlornly persistent than in previous years.

Late afternoon and early evening she loved best of all. As a child she'd believed – and her sisters had teased her about it – that she looked different at night, and that if she stood long enough in front of the mirror she could watch her long, serious face change its aspect, perhaps even its shape, to a point at which she might at last acknowledge it as something she could be satisfied with. The feeling hadn't altogether vanished in adulthood. At times like this, with the day's garishness starting to shade off, she became in some sense less afraid of herself, and mirrors, as she passed them, grew less like traps. Glad she'd come down from London early again, she heard the house breathing contentedly around her its intimate discourse of creaks and rustlings. On Friday, when Jeremy arrived, they'd have a look again at the ideas he'd jotted down for the *foresteria*. 'We'll call it that just to wind people up,' he'd laughed, the end of his beautiful nose wrinkling in that funny way it always did when anything specially amused him. 'It's what they had in Venetian villas. Do you remember we saw one when we went to look at those frescoes outside Vicenza? The ones with the blackamoors on the ceiling.' She remembered the blackamoors. They weren't on the ceiling, but in the corners of the room, big, glistening, muscly figures in ebony, almost naked with red glass eyes and ivory teeth, carrying gilt candlesticks topped by bunches of spiny leaves. Jeremy had told her the name of the carver, Andrea something, it began with B and sounded like Bristol but she'd forgotten.

In the darkroom the prints hung pegged to the line. She should have worked on them that weekend before they all left on the Monday, so that at least they could have had a giggle at themselves in the contacts, those few shots she'd taken at the end, casual snaps really, when they'd come back from the walk and Baz had got through most of the Saturday paper. There was a neat one of Will, looking more like a stick insect than ever, towering over Adam and shaking a finger at him while Alice stood smiling indulgently at them. Another one, which would make them hoot when they saw it, showed Baz going through the picnic basket in search of a corkscrew, just like some old tramp fossicking about in a litter bin.

She took the prints off the line and carried them carefully back in through the kitchen and upstairs to the room at the end of the house where she liked to sit and watch telly in the summer and thought of as her study because she kept maps and guidebooks and parish council minutes there, along with stacks of old magazines and a pile of violin music she hadn't seriously looked at since she moved to Kentish Town. Her violin itself lay on the table, coffined securely inside its case. One day she'd get round to some solid practice again, but only when she found a decent accompanist. Adam was just a fudger really, all right to thump through piano duets with, but fairly useless when it came to something serious like the Brahms A Major or even the best of the Mozarts. That was another thing about gay men, she found. As a rule they had dismally short concentration spans.

There was a wonderful smell filling the room, where the afternoon sun had warmed the bowls of Italian pot-pourri on the windowsill. Serena spread the prints on the table and looked out for a moment across the garden, which had once been an orchard and still retained two or three old pear trees, now in white spray, whence the fruit had been gathered to make perry. Mrs Crittall in the almshouse cottages could remember drinking it when she was a little girl after the First World War, cloudy stuff, made your head spin after a few sips, nicer than cider though. In the distance, beyond the feathery woodlands of Severnstoke Court, the sudden, surprising line of the Malverns, their pinkish-grey crags scarred with darker patches of gorse and bracken, stacked itself ineluctably against the landscape. Serena, looking down again at the prints, realized she would have done better to go on staring out of the window.

For the memory of him that afternoon was as something so radically different from whatever these images now disclosed in remorseless daylight that it seemed as if the camera itself had betrayed her or at least as if someone creeping into the darkroom had substituted another film for her own. She'd known what she wanted, something to tease him a little for his birthday which was coming up soon, a parody of some 'country casuals' spread in a magazine, exactly the kind of thing he loathed because, as he said, the men in it looked like a lot of dumbo investment bankers. She'd been going to ask Jack, already a wiz at computer graphics, whether they couldn't between the pair of them do a mock catalogue with the best pictures and some faux text as accompaniment.

Mesmerized by the very fact of her inability to recognize her husband, Serena sat staring at the photographs, somehow aware, despite her numbness, that she had been responsible for taking them. The figure astride the fallen tree in front of the Hermitage, asprawl across the battered steps, crouched in the window or lurking under the tower, was no more Jeremy to her than one of Lord Severnstoke's negroes in the story Will had told them that afternoon about Molly Hardacre and the farmhouse in Battersea. Something then had found him out, but in a way which excited rather than discomfited him, so that in successive shots he appeared to be revelling in his autonomy, stepping beyond the limits prescribed by the lens into a private domain. His gaze at her now was one of collusion, as though, behind the camera, she had grasped something he would otherwise have been too impatient to explain. Even though there had been others present, she felt him purely alone there, and the resilience in his solitude began to make her afraid. With an impulse of something like loathing, Serena gathered up the prints, and as she did so, felt herself start at a sudden noise outside the window. Nothing more, she realized at once, than poor Gaga announcing it was time for supper.

XIV

THEO could only laugh when Adam told him.

'She's got you to babysit? In Islington? I hope you make her pay your tube fare.'

'It's unbelievable. And I didn't even have the presence of mind to pretend I was going out tonight. I suppose you are.'

'There's Fist at Imperial Gardens. I'd have asked you, only I thought . . .'

Adam didn't pause to wonder what exactly Theo thought, preferring instead to consider the bizarre quality of the lives governed by a choice between sitting quietly for several hours in the company of a baby girl and prowling a discreetly illuminated labyrinth among men dressed in an assortment of straps and chains, in pursuit of various kinds of sexual opportunity.

'How are the rehearsals?' he asked, blandly changing the subject, then almost at once cried: 'Oh, God, The, I never thought, when's the first night?'

'We've got previews in a week, and Nathan still hasn't got

the fucking battle scene sorted. He wants Achilles to carry me on to the stage, and then I've got to lie there for the rest of the play. Thersites has to kick me and Pandarus has not to trip over me when he's doing the epilogue about the galled goose of Winchester. I mean, do I want this or do I want this?'

'Is he nice?'

'Who?'

'The Achilles.'

'You mean like tasty?'

'Yeah.'

'He drives all the way to Ealing on Saturdays to play rugby. Has a French girlfriend called Marie-Jo who works for a TV production company. Reads *GQ* and Nick Hornby and hangs out at the Jazz Café. But yeah, I'd like to lick the sweat off the hollows of his thighs after he made a touchdown. And he's comfy with that.'

'You told him!'

Theo sighed under the burden of his wisdom. 'Little Adipose, some straight men – just a teeny fraction, OK – are completely happy with being straight. So people like us aren't a threat, right? So now and then they're curious to know about how we do things. Like anthropologists, yeah? You don't become part of the tribe, get the fetishes, cut off the fingers, do the dances, learn the magic – unless you're like that wacky American you gave me the book about, who ate human flesh with all those Indians fucking each other up the Amazon, as opposed to anything else up which they might have fucked one another. Instead you just watch and laugh occasionally because it's so totally different from anything you'd ever want to do yourself. That's what being straight means, incidentally. The opposite of being gay.'

'Did you ever want to be . . .?'

'Something other than a screaming sister? Yeah, but only

because it seemed the easier option, which is bollocks either way you look at it.' Sighing again, Theo gave Adam a squeeze. 'Wish you weren't going babysitting, Adiposity. Wish you were coming to Fisticuffs with me.'

'You're going on your own.'

'Mm.'

'What does . . . ?' Adam checked himself sharply, but Theo was quick to answer.

'Guy doesn't mind. We don't talk about it.' He laughed ruefully. 'There's a lot of things we don't talk about, actually. As I expect you must have gathered.'

Rather to Adam's surprise, this was said without any hint of menace, almost as if in self-criticism, but he was sensible enough not to pursue the proffered advantage.

'Anyway there's nobody else I'd rather go with,' added Theo, devastatingly ambiguous. So why go at all, thought Adam. 'Still, at least it's not babysitting. Don't you introduce me to that Daisy of yours, she'll have me tying my head up in a madras bandanna and singing "Don't you cry, my little piccaninny".'

'Daisy,' said Adam, 'is a shade more subtle than that.'

But only just. Her wheedling techniques, he must remember to point out, were growing banal with overuse, and her invocation of his role as a prospective godfather seemed the cheesiest thing he ever heard. It was typical of him that he should have consented through sheer idle goodwill and a general fondness for Edie, when the alternative was razzling with Theo down Camberwell New Road at two in the morning. 'The grenadier on duty goes in search of beer and beauty.' Not this one, though. There was something inherently knackering about having to keep alert for gurgles on the baby-com. And by the time he got home (no, Daisy wouldn't stand him a cab) he'd only want to hit bed.

By the most indirect means at his disposal, Adam had taken care to establish that Frankie would be absent throughout, 'closeted', as Daisy post-ironically put it, somewhere near King's Cross with the lighting and set designers, and since she'd ungrudgingly agreed to be home by half past ten, there was no likelihood that their paths would cross, unless in some fluke rerun of that earliest meeting in Canonbury Square. It was now more than three weeks since the lavender custard fiasco, and though Daisy had twice invited him to rehearsals of what was now being advertised as *A Keeper of Flocks* – a title whose susceptibility to ribald adaptation could scarcely have escaped Frankie – Adam had managed to field a cast-iron excuse for absence on each occasion. After burning his fingers thus, through his usual mix of ardour and complacency, he was determined to maintain a suitable distance until the King of the Confusers should have left for Paris in July. Sullenly he acknowledged to himself that their abortive encounter at Maschera, with all its superstructure of lubricious fantasies about Francesco in the sack and wild, glistening-eyed declarations of mutual commitment, was in essence no better than any of those other little sentimental failures whereby he'd grown to comfort himself that he was useless as a lover, while wanting at least to recall how it felt to be in love. Wryly he remembered now the grizzle-templed boy under the strobes in Bermondsey. Theo, for all his youthful tendency to facile moralizing, had been right: if Adam had smiled back, it must only have been the prologue to another tragedy. Yet he wondered why, by this time, he didn't know himself rather better.

An ingratiating lick of daylight still hung over Highbury Corner as he emerged from the station. Adam loved the sense, in this season, of London stretching, yawning and unbuckling itself for summer, of the casual enchantments of those he passed heightened now by the sudden softness of the air, the smell of new leaves and, at one point, like a benediction, a waft of cut grass from the earliest garden mowing of the year. By the time he reached Alwyne Villas he was almost prepared to enjoy himself that evening with Edie, however fractious she should turn out to be.

Daisy whisked him into the drawing-room as soon as he arrived, fluttering and solicitous as he expected her to be.

'She's down like a lead weight, bless her. A matter of waking the dead, I think you'll find. You are an A1 sweetie-pie, gold medal with bar and crossed palms, Ad. I'd light candles for you but I can't remember just now who the patron saint of babysitters is. Saint Nicholas, probably. Or is it Saint Zita? No, she's the one who looks after charladies.'

'Yes, well, I don't think it'll quite come to that. Is . . .?'

She made a little moue of mock sympathy. 'I did ring round, I promise, but Rowan next door didn't want to do it because she's got a geography project to finish or something, and Helena was in the middle of a fully-orchestrated domestic crisis, and it's their au pair's night off.' Daisy paused to exhale, with a 'gratefully' perceptible in brackets after her name in the margin. 'At any rate, darling Ad, there's you. And as I said, I won't be back late. It was only that old Robin Bartlett phoned out of the blue and said would I go to this international rich white trash bash, and he's been so lonely since his wife died, and he was a friend of Pa's . . . God, it's fucking seven bloody thirty! Anyway there's heaps of cold supper put out, and you've got my mobile number in case. I'll give you the Jennifer's Diary bit when I get back, and if you've been very good, I'll tell you just how many rhinestones the Margravine of Schwarzwalder Kirschtorte had in her tiara. Bye! Think of it as your first good work as a godfather, time off in Purgatory, plenary indulgences, bye!'

Adam heard her clatter down the steps, get into the car and drive off. He felt grateful for the consequent silence, and it wasn't after all so disagreeable to be ensconced for three hours in a house whose style Basil had once categorized, whether correctly or not, as '*Country Life* edited by Bruce Chatwin'. This was the way in which People With No Money lived, with small mounds of catalogues, magazines and art books on low tables, a lot of rather battered but distinguished-looking furniture, clearly inherited rather than acquired, and indifferent Victorian watercolour sketches of ugly aunts in weepers and puffy-faced, whiskery men wearing checked waistcoats. Daisy's natural eye had varied this in certain details; a drawing, a photograph, odd stones, shells and pieces of wood gathered up from successive holidays, stacks of crime novels whose urgently cracked spines somehow enhanced the prevailing air of habitation, and grey wooden shutters retained in preference to more operatic-looking curtains with the appropriate loops and valances. Edith's presence would do nothing to ruin the overall effect. As a social signifier she would be perfect. Daisy at any rate would see to it that she was.

For a moment Adam sat down on one of the sofas and started leafing through a magazine. Other people's furniture always seemed more comfortable to him, and besides, there was now that pleasant let's-play-house sensation brought about simply by being somewhere you don't belong but are awarded the freedom of for a limited season. Kicking off his trainers, he settled himself more comfortably against a couple of cushions and began to read an article about a garden in Ireland, wondering as he did so whether after all he'd really miss going to Fist with Theo, and if, among the muscle-Marys in rubber thongs waiting to cop off on the balcony at Imperial Gardens Camberwell, there weren't one or two who, against the grain, didn't hanker after an interlude like this one, with its cheaply acquired aura of anchorite virtue. Then from the kitchen came the sound of a cough.

That at least was what Adam supposed it must be. The notion of somebody breaking into the house at this early hour was patently ridiculous, but these days you never knew. For a moment he remained on the sofa, as much from a hope that he might have been mistaken as from a natural reluctance to do anything which should seem too plainly confrontational. No instrument lay to hand with which to crack the intruder's skull, though the knobbly bit of Barbara Hepworth on the table next to the fireplace might come in handy as a last resort. He would simply have to be the ballsy little number he knew he wasn't. Another cough, louder and more abrupt, forced Adam to decide whether or not he was merely going to sit there quaking until the burglar entered the room. The thought that whoever it was might prefer to go upstairs first of all determined the issue. He himself could be considered as fair game for assault: Edie, asleep in her lace-bedecked cradle, was emphatically not to be disturbed.

Getting up, he walked delicately as King Agag towards the half-open kitchen door at the end of the hall and, heart in his mouth, pushed it back.

'Hey, asshole,' said Frankie, responsible for the cough.

'I was going to murder you,' Adam announced with impressive coolness. 'To be more precise, I was preparing to beat our your brains with a distinguished item of twentieth-century British art. We've got some, in case you hadn't heard. You'd have gone to kingdom come with the accolade of having been the first person, so far as is known, to fall a victim to *Recumbent Form: 1947.*'

Frankie sat at the table with a beer and a cigarette between his fingers. In the pool of lamplight and wearing a slightly dingy white singlet, a shadow of day-old beard on his face, his shoulders nacreous with the faintest sweat, he looked like something out of a *film noir*, a bald version of Farley Granger or Robert Michum, sulky yet vulnerable. The effect was un-utterably sexy, yet by now Adam was wary enough not to suspect at once that this might just be a carefully-sprung trap.

'So why'nt you do it?'

'What?'

'Murder me?'

Adam sat down, took Frankie's beer bottle and swigged it empty. 'Firstly, because I left Barbara Hepworth in the other room. Secondly, because it'd have made you too glamorous. Your glamour's the most sickening thing about you.'

'Because you want it?'

In spite of himself Adam laughed. 'Yes, I can't deny that.'

They had a little pause, in which the quietness of the house seized its chance to fall more thickly around them. He could hear the touch of Frankie's lips dragging on the cigarette.

'Do you want to tell me about it?' Frankie asked at length.

'Not specially. It's that feeling you have . . . well, quite possibly you don't have it, I don't know.'

'Sure you do, Adam, everybody knows what they feel. And then they lie to protect themselves, like you just did.'

'Yeah, maybe. That's what your ballet — sorry, your dance piece — is about, no?'

'Call it a ballet, I'm not picky like some people. It's not, actually. Fernando Pessoa was no liar. OK, he invented himself several different ways, but that's not lying.'

'So what is?'

Frankie yawned and stretched, exposing thick black tufts of armpit hair like marram grass in the dunes.

'Something negative, sterile, the kind of story you tell to save yourself when you could be telling it to entertain other people.' Then, with a neat twist of his body, he leaned forward across the table. 'So entertain me, astonish me, *Jean, étonne moi.*'

Adam drew his chair away a little. 'You don't deserve it. Anyway you're supposed to be somewhere in Lloyd Baker land, on the windswept slopes off the Pentonville Road, not bamboozling me with abstractions.'

Frankie laughed. 'Yeah, you wish!'

'So why aren't you?'

'Because I knew it was what you were expecting. And as you say in London, "I simply couldn't be awrsed." So I said to them "Hey, guys, this is Frankie and I simply cawn't be awrsed."'

'Which Paul taught you.'

'Adam, are you still mad at me?'

Adam got up, went to the fridge, took out two more beers and opened them. As he set one on the table in front of Frankie, he felt himself mildly apprehensive in case by accident he should touch him. Sitting down again, he said, 'It's mostly myself I'm cross with. I ought to have guessed that was what you'd do.'

Frankie looked surly all of a sudden. 'You don't fucking know me, kid.'

'I'm older than you, so stop calling me kid. In any case I was being generic. I mean, what you did that afternoon was something lots of people do. Not necessarily on purpose if it comes to that. There's a sort of sixth sense they have that you're looking forward to spending time with them, so they spoil everything by asking somebody else, who probably won't enjoy the occasion precisely for knowing that's why they've been invited. As the gooseberry, the duenna, the earthing device, the novocaine, whatever.'

'You think I was scared?' Frankie gave a little snort of incredulity. 'Of you?'

'I concede that I'm not especially frightening,' said Adam quietly. 'About as terrifying as a marshmallow, I suppose. Do Americans eat marshmallows, by the way? Anyway I meant it was the situation which unnerved you. Paul came along as your minder because you couldn't handle it.'

'That's crazy. Paul came because I asked him. We had this really heavy morning with Kevin and Simone doing the transmogrification – that's the bit where Alvaro turns into a woman – and then we had to go to Covent Garden with Dusty to look at the vests Martin had found.'

'The prosopopoeia is making my head spin. I'll need footnotes.'

Frankie banged to table jubilantly. 'Ooh-kay! Now I know you're still mad at me!'

'How the fuck?'

'Because you use words like prosopopoeia. You think ha-ha, stupid Yank, cawn't tell his awrse from his elbow, won't understand a word of more than one syllable, let's diss the bastard with Greek.'

'You'd know all about Greeks. Anyway, what does it mean?'

Frankie's dark lips curled in a smirk like the decoration on a frieze. 'Not what you think, honey. You got everything sooo wrong! Prosopopoeia is a rhetorical device for introducing an imaginary person into a speech. And you thought it meant like a list of names or something?'

'But it's . . .'

'Yesss! Gotcha, asshole! Surrender, Lord Cornwallis! Know how I know?'

'Surprise me. *Étonne moi.*'

'OK, Sergei. The first ballet I ever choreographed, six,

maybe seven years back, was called *Flowers of Rhetoric*, shit a mile high but they're still doing it in Berlin. And there's a kind of like a wacky pas de deux called "Prosopoeia", where the boy conjures the girl into existence, blahblahblah.'

For a moment they fell silent again, then caught each other's eye and burst into cathartic guffaws. Frankie stretched a hand across the table to clench Adam's.

'Peace?'

'Yes, peace. But you were even crosser than I was, weren't you?'

'Later,' Frankie said, and to Adam's infinite astonishment, he leaned across the table as if to kiss him, when from upstairs there came a sudden inopportune squalling. 'Damn it! You'd have thought she'd know when not to interrupt.'

He sprang up and Adam followed, fretful at being balked off anything so immediately precious as the touch of that glistening mouth. Edie lay, pink and peevish, in her lacy nest. It was only a little burst of attention-seeking wakefulness which they might have done better to ignore, but Frankie was on his knees now beside her, crooning tenderness and mock reproach.

'Mommy's been failing in her duty, yes she has. Mommy should have taught you about gentlemen who want to be left alone together. Ladies don't cut in like that, do they? Not this little lady. Because Mommy knows lots of gentlemen who like being left alone together, yes she does, she does, she does.'

'Only maybe she did it on purpose,' muttered Adam.

'Who, Edie? Did you, little sourpuss? Did you want to spoil it for me? Jealous little sourpuss wants to keep Frankie all for herself. Hey! Look how quickly she went off again, like magic, I'm a magician, I wave my wand and little ladies go off to sleep. Talking of wands, how's yours tonight?' still kneeling, Frankie threw a lubricious glance towards Adam's crotch.

'Quiescent,' laughed Adam.

Frankie got up. 'Did you know there's an English ballet called *Adam Zero*? One of those old birth-to-death numbers they used to do. It bombed after the first night, the principal flunked a *jetée* and had to be hospitalized.' Grinning wolfishly he dimmed the light. 'Weren't we going to add some digits to that zero?'

Via the gloom thus induced, his body took on a sudden exotic alienness, as if he had ambled out a shadowed nowhere into whatever faint luminescence remained to define him. Expertly he drew the still unkissed Adam, nervelessly responsive, into his embrace. Frankie's mouth tasted of beer and tobacco and his chin was sandpaper rough. The curves of his arse felt hard to the scoop, hard as the ridges of muscle up his spine, their furrow scored by Adam's fingertips.

'We should have done this on the sidewalk outside that big fancy restaurant,' Frankie whispered. 'You were so cute I wanted to rape you.'

'Except it wouldn't have been rape,' said Adam.

'Pardon me?'

'Because I'd have had to refuse.'

'And you're just a girl who can't say no, right? "Ravish me, violate me, abuse me!" Oh my God, I know your secret!' Frankie cackled.

'Shh, you'll wake Edie.'

'Correction, *we'll* wake Edie.'

But she'd regained that enviable infant serenity best expressed by the throwing back of little fat arms on either side of the pillow and the barely audible clack of rhythmic breathing. Frankie snatched Adam again into a kiss, greedier and more urgent this time, as if he knew the precise limit to their enjoyment and it had nothing to do with Daisy's inevitable return. For Adam the edge of pleasure was made yet more keen by this sense of imminent ending. With anyone else his initial incredulity would have given way almost at once to doubt and suspicion. Now, while Frankie's spidery, shadow-puppet hands clasped his head to gentle it into more perfect focus for the pair to gorge on one another, Adam was still confounded with wondering why any of this should be happening at all, puzzled at the quality of existence being suddenly determined by the rawest feeling of sensual achievement in having got where he was without any obvious prelude. Frankie cupped his hand between Adam's legs.

'And lo! in a matter of minutes the zero becomes a millennium. Not one but two thousand years of human history lie in this woodiest of woodies. A dragon somewhere in there maybe? You can't have a millennium without a dragon. Or a woody.'

Something in Adam instantly didn't want this. Imperatives were one thing, surrender to them on Frankie's terms was a different matter. Feeling him push his hand away while it sought to unfasten the studs, Frankie, as if grasping the situation forthwith, muttered, 'Uhuh, if we can't have the dragon, let's try this old Yankee eagle,' and insouciantly tugged his cock out of its imprisoning fly. 'Eh, *guapo, chupame*! It'll make you less nervous maybe.'

Adam rather supposed the contrary. Overcome with a sense of awkwardness and absurdity, he backed away towards the door, as Frankie, cock still blatant and peremptory, moved towards him, mystified. That they had to speak in whispers, sexy until that moment, became all of a sudden ridiculous.

'What're you . . . I don't understand.'

'I can't. It's not that I don't want to. I just can't.'

Frankie looked at Adam in amazement. Spontaneity was what

made him so attractive, whereas he seemed to think the easiest way to appear utterly devastating was to be as meretricious as possible. Yes, thought Adam, this is how I want to kiss you, standing there with your shoulders twitching, the sweat making your bald head gleam, and your dick sticking out of your trousers – nice as dicks go, but just now totally fatuous and malapropos. So instead he winced from the proffered embrace.

'Is it Edie?'

'Yes,' Adam lied eagerly.

'You mean it's inappropriate?'

'No, I . . . Oh, Jesus, yes, it seems so completely wrong. We're meant to be shielding her from harm, not giving her the home video version of *The Joy of Gay Sex*. What if it's the first thing she remembers?'

'Adam, she's a little baby.'

'Some people have amazing memories. Compton Mackenzie could remember being in his pram.'

'Who the fuck was Compton Mackenzie?'

'A best-selling author whom nobody reads. He was . . .'

The grotesquerie of the situation hit home. Adam started to splutter with silent laughter, made worse by the spectacle of Frankie, no longer quite as rampant, sullenly adjusting himself.

'You're crazy, you know that?'

'I'd rather be crazy than pervy like you. Next time we do this I'll sell tickets.'

'Who says you're having a next time?'

Before Adam could return a suitable answer, there was a click from downstairs, the front door opened and they heard Daisy's voice call softly:

'Where is everybody, for goodness' sake?'

'Shit!' whispered Frankie, flinging himself down beside the cradle once more. 'Make believe she woke up.'

'You're not supposed to be here,' said Adam theatrically, as Daisy tiptoed into the room. She gave a perfunctory glance at Edie, as though to confirm all was as it should be, then motioned them back downstairs.

'Robin double-booked, he's getting so absent-minded. Someone called Leonie Hindlip whom he was doing hush-hush at Bletchley with during the war was there, and apparently she expected to go, so I'm afraid I can't tell you what Stephanie of Monaco said to the Crown Princess of Yugoslavia, but you can read all about it in *Hello!* or there'll be one of those ghastly polaroid spreads in the Friday *Standard*, where you get to see everybody's zits and grog-blossoms.'

She looked around her at the kitchen, at the empty beer bottles and Frankie's cigarette stubs in the ashtray. 'You haven't had supper yet,' she concluded with some satisfaction. For a moment it crossed Adam's mind that Frankie had been lying, and that the idea of placing him there at the table as a surprise had been Daisy's all along. Then he reflected that she couldn't have known about their spat at Maschera, any more than she must have suspected their crim.con. tongue-fest in the presence of her slumbering child. Frankie still looked a tad cross at not being Agatha, and Adam was cool with that.

'We got talking,' he said.

'So I see. What did you talk about? Something useful, I hope?'

'Compton Mackenzie,' answered Frankie without batting an eyelid.

'Ask a silly question.'

'We thought it was appropriate, didn't we, Adam?' Adam's eyes narrowed. 'And Edie seemed pleased.'

XV

SHE hadn't been altogether displeased, if it came to that, by the attention lavished on her at the christening. The impression already formed by those closest to Daisy of her daughter as being in some sense brought up from the outset to be conscious of an audience was scarcely belied by Edie's behaviour during the ceremony. Where other babies might have been expected to howl and kick at the merest splash of baptismal water she preserved an astounding serenity, as if the rite itself were merely what was due to her. In the lugubrious church somewhere on the edge of Westbourne Park at which her mother, only living in Islington by accident of inheritance, had decided the service should take place, she became a cynosure not just for being the reason why they were all present in any case, but because instinct had seemed to tell her that nothing else there could possibly be interesting enough to distract their attention. The Blessed Virgin, blue-mantled and downcast-eyed within her little emplacement of candles, and the gaunt crucified Christ above the altar were suddenly little better than sideshows. Even the cheerful, bespectacled Glaswegian priest appeared somewhat cowed under Edie's ruthless scene-stealing, in her flounced layers of cambric and point de Venise. There'd been a moment which made them all laugh, when she'd stretched out an imperious arm towards him, as though grasping an invisible sceptre and expecting him to perform some well-rehearsed act of homage.

'I know Catholics think it's important to save little souls from hell,' said Will to Alice as they all began drifting off down the aisle after signing the register, 'but do you think this one was worth bothering about?'

'I thought you were fond of Edie.'

'Fondness has nothing to do with it. People were fond of Lucrezia Borgia, for goodness' sake. I'm going to give up teaching and start a magazine called *Babes With Attitude*.'

'Someone's probably patented that already.' Alice glanced quickly over her shoulder. 'Do you think Sib's OK with it all?'

'Why on earth not? She's had enough time to get used to Daisy flaunting Edie about as the hereditary Grand Duchess. And Daisy gets tired of being spiteful to her sisters after a while, it's too much emotional hard work.'

'I just fancied she looked a bit glum,' persisted Alice.

'Being in London always does that to Serena. You're meant to notice these things, not me.'

'I do, only . . .'

'You never see her looking sorry for herself like that in the country. And she's worrying about that bloody goose again.'

Alice, looking round again to notice the others catching up with them, thought it inopportune to share her impression that Gaga was merely an excuse for those other more complex feelings which seven years of marriage to Jeremy had now started uncomfortably to refine. There were times when Will's prevailing sense of being at ease with himself brought about a curious and one might almost have supposed deliberate dulling of perception.

Though the day outside was cold, they waited now in the porch while Serena acted as official photographer, shuffling them into their various groupings with that instantly assumed bossiness which was almost the only family trait she and Daisy seemed to share. Her other sister Isobel, uprooted for the occasion from life as a painter in Italy, had clearly renounced this long ago in favour of being able to laugh at the pair of them for keeping the tradition going with such earnestness.

'Move in,' Serena was saying to Jeremy, 'closer to Zoe. And Baz, don't stare at the ground. If you can't bear to look at Edie, at least face the camera. And Adam . . .'

'Yes?'

'For God's sake smile. No, *smile*! *Please*!'

'What if I can't?'

'Everybody can if they stop thinking about it.'

'Adam is spontaneous,' said Frankie, whose 's's today seemed more than usually sibilant. 'He abhors the artificial. Adam is *l'homme au naturel*.'

'There now, you've been categorized,' Jeremy whispered in Adam's ear, 'and all for not smiling.'

'Jealous, Jezza?'

'I try to resist categories. Generally I'm successful.'

'Snob.'

'Can we get on with this please?' came Frankie's voice, plaintive and tinged with the note of peevishness Adam had caught in rehearsal, which basically meant 'hurry up or else you'll know about it from me'. He was starting increasingly to give the impression that occasions like this were more than his time was worth. Being a godfather was fine as long as he could be selective about times and people, but the relevant rites, with their impacted heterosexual presence and the demands they made on reserves of charm and civility he deemed too precious to waste, were an exorbitant price to pay for his condescension. It only made matters worse when, Serena having snapped her last, they all began to argue about who should go in whose car to Holland Park and the champagne which Jeremy, only so as not to be shamed for failing to do so, had provided after several heavy hints from Daisy. Finally, just as Frankie was starting pettishly to suggest that it might be better if he just went on to the street and hailed a cab, Alice, sensing what the trouble was, swept him off with her, Will and an assurance that they'd probably arrive in Addison Crescent before any of the others.

'Billecart-Salmon,' muttered Basil to Daisy, as the two maids, clucking occasionally to each other in Tagalog, plied their glasses. 'Given the décor, you'd think Ruinart would have been more appropriate.'

'Shh, you're not allowed to diss *le patron*, that's my job. Anyway there's a truce today, or hadn't you noticed?'

'I still think a solitary picture in a room which looks like an igloo designed by Albert Speer is carrying statement too far. And it isn't even a painting to speak of, just a lot of coal sacks stuck on a board.'

'It's a Kounelis. Baz, you're so *traditional!* Alice, my love, you were marvellous throughout.'

'You make it sound as if I'd done *Giselle* or something. But yes, now you come to mention it, I was rather good. So was everyone.'

No we weren't, thought Serena, catching this last remark. Or at least I wasn't. I had a weird feeling throughout the service, standing there at the font and signing the register afterwards in the sacristy, that I was too tall. It felt as if I could see into everyone just by looking down at them, and frankly that wasn't what I wanted at all. I'm not into revelations, especially not recently, I had enough of those in Kentish Town. At the convent they taught us it was better on the whole not to know things by finding them out, but to wait until somebody told you officially. Anyhow I'm not sure, in this case, what it is I know, or what to do if it turns out to be something important. In the sense, that's to say, of being disagreeably significant, like dropping Edie would have been when Daisy gave her me to hold. One of the nuns, Sister Mary Attracta, used to talk to us about anger, and she was fond of quoting a verse from one of the psalms where the captive Jews ask for vengeance against the Babylonians and say, 'Happy shall he be that taketh and dasheth thy little ones against the stones.' I used to feel something tug at me inside every time she quoted that, as if I believed I was capable to doing something similar, just flinging down a child and watching its head break open like a piece of fruit and standing there not caring if it was actually dead. I thought of that today when Daisy gave me her, in a sort of pass-the-parcel fashion like any old bundle, because at that moment I didn't want her in my arms. When I took her from Daisy I somehow couldn't feel the substance of Edie's body under all those christening robes, and we had a kind of lurch, with Daisy laughing and going 'Oops, hang on, Sibby!' so that I genuinely thought I was going to drop her and hear the sound of her head cracking against the chequered marble. But I didn't, just this once.

She could see Jeremy plainly now, at the other end of the room, talking to Zoe. Odd how quickly Alice and Will's children seemed to grow. At fifteen Zoe had acquired a profile and the self-assurance to go with it, so much so that Serena felt she ought to have been jealous of them standing thus close to one another, briefly wondered why she wasn't then, dismissed the answer as if batting away some tiresome insect. I don't want to know, she thought, not now. She'd told him when he bought it that the black Armani with concealed buttons didn't go with his hair. It made him look like somebody else.

'Your daughter's been breaking the law,' Jeremy said to Will.

'Impossible, she's never broken anything in her life. Except a dinner plate, and even that was supposed to have come to pieces in her hands before it hit the kitchen floor. Women always have excuses, Jezza, you must know that.'

'I was telling him about this pub we went to in Kilburn with Sidonie and the girls in the play.'

'Trust you to know somebody called Sidonie. I hope you're not going to become a laddette and get pie-eyed and embarrassing on pints of Stella and talk about Man U's prospects in the Premier League or whatever it is they do. What was this pub called? I suppose I ought to know, in case we have to come and drag you out legless before the police arrive to haul you off to the cells for a hosing-down.'

Zoe fixed her father with a pitiless stare. 'It's called the Black Boy, and Jeremy asked me whether we'd met any real black boys there, and I said the people were mostly like Irish or something, and there was this notice by the bar telling you it was Kilburn's oldest pub and it was named after King Charles II, because he was like really dark and people used to call him the Black Boy.'

'Have you noticed,' asked Jeremy, smiling saturninely, 'how the young nowadays always go up at the end of their sentences, whereas older people come down? It's an American thing, isn't it?'

'I thought it was those Australian soaps,' said Will, '*Neighbours*, *Home and Away*, you know the sort, Zoe and Jack used to watch them at a formative age.'

'Isn't now a formative age?' asked Zoe disarmingly.

'If you visit Irish pubs in Kilburn with friends called Sidonie, yes it is. Anyway I'm allowed to talk about "the young" but Jeremy isn't.'

'Why not?'

'Because he's maddeningly ageless, and I'm at least ten years older.'

'And he goes to a gym.'

'How do you know that?' demanded Jeremy with a sharpness which surprised them both.

'Sibby told me ages ago. Can I have some more champagne?'

'As long as you promise not to advertise that I go to a gym.'

'Can't think why you're so bashful.'

'Zozo, you're hopeless, you haven't an ounce of your mother's discretion,' cried Will, as if rather pleased that was the case. 'Come and embarrass somebody else before we put a blanket over your head and pretend you don't belong to us.'

Will's good intentions were not necessarily gratifying to Jeremy, who found something piquant in Zoe's nascent yet still rather absent-minded glamour, and saw their conversation as the sole refuge from the boredom which threatened to overwhelm him. It had been a moment of weakness offering to give the party here in the first place. He should have told Daisy in the most urbane manner possible to get lost, only of course he hadn't. To his aid now came a well-exercised habit of reviewing his own motives, not through any special impulse of guilt or remorse so much as for the sake of deciding whether they satisfied a sense of what he was worth. Why had he let all these people into his house and served them his second-favourite brand of champagne, together with what the senders of invitations in London had started to refer to as 'serious canapés' – you had to pronounce that first word exaggeratedly as 'saahrious', hadn't you? To humour Serena no doubt. Jeremy had other ways of humouring her and had long ago stopped studying his impulse to do so. To please Daisy? Children bored him, though he was as adept as anyone else at pretending, in opportune moments, that they didn't. He'd be profoundly uninterested in Edie until she turned into something like Zoe and developed that sombre self-absorption which a girl with any sort of claim to beauty acquires following the necessary period of mortification in the shape of puppy fat and peevishness. As Basil once said, if Edie threatened to be anything other than attractive, Daisy would certainly have dumped her on somebody's doorstep and run off.

No, Jeremy had given in, he acknowledged, on no worthier pretext than that of spiting his sister-in-law's expectations. She had wanted him to make an excuse, perhaps even to detect him in the act of lying, but he only lied to people he found genuinely interesting or glamorous. Or in Serena's case so as to protect her, because it would be too tiresome if she ever got hurt that way. He and Daisy detested each other, it had long ago been made clear to them both, not through unresolved differences but out of an irreconcilable similarity, so maybe it wasn't so disgraceful after all to be giving the party. She'd know, wouldn't she, that he wanted to give a deliberate jolt to one of her favourite assumptions, and in some curious zigzag fashion she must have been disappointed that he hadn't contrived to do so.

He had never understood why Adam liked her so much, but then Adam was far too unselectively nice about everybody. He could see him over there by the armchair, laughing with Isobel as the pair of them squatted on either side of Edie, who had apparently refused to go to sleep as long as the party was in evidence. It was obvious to Jeremy what the matter was. For days now Adam, while at the Foundation, had seemed strangely unfocused and blunted at the edges, like a singer at an opera rehearsal mugging the part to save his voice. They'd gone to have a look at a theatre project in Kennington about which Jeremy felt a legitimate excitement, but it had become embarrassingly clear, as the young directors made their earnest presentations, that Adam simply couldn't concentrate for more than a few minutes on what they sought to expound. During the drive back, passing between the pale yellow Georgian terraces lining the road towards the Elephant, Jeremy, to break an increasingly oppressive silence, remarked, 'Bet this was where Molly Hardacre lived.'

'Who?'

'Molly Hardacre, you know, the girl in the story Will told us at Easter when we had that picnic at the ruin. The one Lord Severnstoke kept as a mistress and the Negro called Aurelius brought the message to.'

'Oh yes, I'd forgotten,' said Adam, patently uninterested. 'Yes, quite probably.'

Probably Alice, with her lethal gift for establishing the truth of a situation without ever having to put it into anything more direct than a hint or an allusion, would already know whether Jeremy's hunch were justified or not. He'd have to frame the question with suitable obliquity. You couldn't nonchalantly ask 'Is Adam in love?' and expect a direct answer, any more than you could have done by quizzing Adam himself. Certain things he kept private. It was all right enquiring after his parents in Shropshire or his sister in Japan, but on subjects like the flat in a Clapham mansion block, to which nobody had been invited since he moved there three years ago, there was only an obstinate opacity. Perhaps this after all was what Jeremy most found in him to respect. Adam's character, with its all-purpose amiability and easily adjustable sense of humour, presented nothing out of the ordinary. What appealed instead was the notion of a life certain of whose compartments were resolutely alienated from those who might most obviously expect to be allowed a share in them. Just now Jeremy felt he had never understood so well Adam's determination to keep the arrangement firmly as it was.

He glanced at his watch. Alice, having seen that glance on other occasions, decided she knew what it meant, but she wasn't quite yet going to gather up Will and the children and whisk them home to Hammersmith for tea and a gleeful post-mortem on the whole jamboree. There were things that needed her attention here, Jeremy himself being one of them. She wanted, what was more, to indulge her infrequent privilege, that of a short unsanctioned tour of the house while the others remained downstairs. It was only four or five times in the year, after all, that she ever set foot across the threshold, and there was always something fresh to be clocked which it might be pleasanter to see without either Jeremy's suavity or Serena's fussing. A party like this one offered easier opportunities for slipping into the gallery or the garden than those allowed by a dinner, where people might start thinking you'd been detained by a seizure in the loo. So now, after ensuring everybody was suitably distracted, Alice stepped out into the hallway, pausing only to simper good-naturedly at a maid coming up from the kitchen with a plateful of miniature samosas before darting upstairs.

The house was of course far too big for Serena and Jeremy,

especially since there were never going to be any children, and there wasn't even the excuse of something like an infirm mother-in-law, an American cousin over for the year or a lodger playing the part of Mr Gatsby's parlour-boarder to justify the squandering immensity of it all. Serena had never openly articulated her feelings on the subject to Alice, but it seemed impossible that she should actually like being in such a place for longer than might be necessary to keep Jeremy happy. You might as well live in a bus garage or an out-of-town shopping mall. It reminded Alice, as she wandered down the corridor pushing open the bedroom doors and taking stock of the way in which everything held such an unnerving air of preparedness, of palaces in pre-Revolutionary Russia whose myriad servants were kept in a perpetual state of expectation lest the Dowager Empress or some minor Grand Duke among sundry Kyrils and Konstantins, having suddenly motored up the driveway *nebst begleitung* complete with lapdogs and an English governess for darling little Sofotchka, should fancy stopping the night.

You could moralize from such profligacy, armed with your wisdom after the event, but it seemed vulgar to do so here. There was no likelihood of a revolution, not yet at least. The rhythm of their lives, however much Alice found herself longing for something to upset it, was at any rate consistent in its unease. She had told herself now and again that Serena enjoyed occasional troughs of unhappiness (this, apparently, being what Will believed) with which to offset the laboriously engineered *urbs-in-rure* pastoral she had contrived for herself down in Worcestershire. Wasn't morality, for Catholics, a sort of bazaar where you could always count on getting something in exchange, whereas Protestants hadn't any assurance of that kind? And Serena, however much she might wallow in the quiz nights and barbecues and altar flowers and brass polishing, had never entirely let go of the gleaming baggage labelled 'Rome' in favour of the dingier, more self-effacing portmanteau of Anglicanism. Yet imagine earning days off in Purgatory for being miserable in Holland Park!

There was a new pot on the table at the end of the corridor, next to the Lucie Rie which had looked so gauche and in need of a mate since Jeremy had put it here last year. Alice knew this one for a Michael Cardew, the sort she used in lectures to first-year students, and remembered the suddenly ardent focus of Jeremy's attention when – when? God, ages ago now – she'd told him about Cardew's visits to Africa and the curious fashion whereby the Nigerian bush had become for him a secret country of the heart. She ran her palm over the glaze, which had taken warmth from the later appearance of afternoon sun, a surface rough like an animal's hide. Then, lifting the vase altogether, she heard something rattle inside and pulled out a set of keys on a ring. For an instant she looked at them carefully, wondering less at who had dropped them into the pot than why they were there in the first place. Not evidently the keys to the house itself, which Jeremy had recently boasted of having turned into a kind of W14 Fort Knox with a state-of-the-art system designed to baffle the insurance company, let alone burglars. Neither did they belong to the cottage, since Alice and Will possessed a spare set, which she'd used on several occasions, not always officially. She stood for a moment in the slanted bar of sunlight, tranquil in consideration, before putting the keys into her bag. She wouldn't go downstairs just yet. There was another thing she wanted to have a look at.

Or at least thought she did, until the sound of a voice from behind one of the bedroom doors froze her in her tracks.

Whoever it was might have witnessed the removal of the keys – or at any rate Alice's failure to replace them – but as she was swiftly cobbling together an excuse she realized that the other person was talking to someone on the phone. Curious, she moved closer, noticing that the door was merely pushed to rather than fully shut, and wondering why Frankie, whose tone after a few hours' acquaintance was unmistakable, should have chosen this degree of remoteness from the others when he might simply have retreated into one of the cavernous spaces downstairs.

'Trade?' she heard him say, 'Yeah, and before that we can do – what's that place we went to under those arches, like it was Piranesi on acid? – yeah, Crash. No, I'm not, totally free, *il Francesco liberato*. But can't you hear my chains rattle right now? No, of course not, he's downstairs making love to a baby, that's what you do in this fucking screwed-up little country, an elaborate variety of child abuse. Yeah, I said "you", I know you're Greek, treasure, but not Greek Greek *Greek*. And they've asked me . . .' Alice inched a little closer to the door as Frankie's voice grew thrillingly conspiratorial, 'they've asked me down to the country, can you imagine? *Le sacré weekend anglais?* God, you're one jealous queen, how the fuck do I know if he's coming too? Anyhow it isn't till like the end of next week. Sure there's time. And we need some distance from the blessed Fernando. Or maybe you do, a little perspective maybe. Hey, I've got to go back and play Prince Charming to the impacted straights in the salon. Jesus, the preppiness you could cut with a knife! Yeah, you too. OK, like a quarter after, *chez toi?* You too, sugar. *Ciao, bello!*'

Temptingly as its prospect unfolded, the evening would need some nifty balancing, but then balance of one kind or another was second nature to Frankie. Adam must be fobbed off with a suitable excuse, after a dinner at Daisy's during which care would be taken to give him sufficiently flattering attention. Frankie would be at pains to suggest that tomorrow's schedule, with class and rehearsal and a business meeting at the theatre, was particularly punishing, and that no sooner had Adam left than he was going straight to bed. The hint would almost certainly be taken, because Adam was of that uniquely British type whose guilty susceptibility to such nudges had a morbid self-consciousness built into it. Like the way people here said 'sorry' all the time. You didn't necessarily want them to mean it absolutely. The word's intrinsic value was continually cheapened by the realization that they were saying it in order to absolve themselves, as opposed to feeling any regret for the inconvenience they might have caused you. Thus Adam would get up and leave so as to obviate any likelihood of being remembered by the other two as the guy who stuck around, a Sheridan Whiteside *de ses jours*.

Not that Frankie honestly gave a fuck, save insofar as other people's motives continued to interest him and it was something to laugh about with Daisy. Like today, for instance, with all that standing around waiting in the church and the priest having to go back to the car for his eyeglasses and one of Daisy's sisters popping in a contact lens in the darkest part of the aisle and those frigging photographs which the other sister, the one with the white face and scary green eyes like Morticia Addams, just wouldn't give up on till she got everything right. Frankie was all for perfectionism, but *non esageriamo*, per-*lease*! He couldn't decide which bugged him more, the hetero-sexuality itself or the peculiar degree of indecisiveness which seemed integral to it, the more so for being British. Longingly he remembered his immaculate apartment in a tiny uptown block and his gay friends with their impeccably calibrated amalgam of unexaggerated glamour and selectiveness, and raged the more at the various failures of decorum he'd witnessed today, at the sheer inelegance of a life which chose not to incorporate such a carefully pondered faculty of discrimination.

Adam, as he'd been quick to perceive, uneasily straddled both worlds. Without ever needing to visit it, Frankie could imagine his flat (he hated that word) somewhere south of the river, a place where he and Paul went clubbing but which he had never knowingly seen in daylight. It was a domain, most probably, of compromise and expediency, in which the paramount orderliness of an existence like his own, raised as he had been in a family which made an art form out of ironing and table-setting, was always aimed at and never achieved. Maybe this was what Adam hoped must rub off on him if he hung around long enough, that shimmer, that phosphorescence Frankie knew himself to possess and which, provided it were only for a season, he was ready to let others enjoy. Only he doubted whether Adam knew the secret of enjoyment without attendant anticipations of misery.

He was cutesy, wasn't he, in a kind of baggy Bill T. Jones company way, and bright and ironic, a feature Frankie, accustomed to lead with the jokes, resented while simultaneously respecting it. But not anybody to stage the big number with, to gnaw the pillow with impatience at having missed or sit waiting for their voice at the end of the phone and then finish up in the shit because you just had to call instead and afterwards got frightened in case he backed off. You didn't miss Adam after he'd gone, but you were more grateful than otherwise that while you had work to do he was around, *disponible*, apparently without a life of his own he wouldn't eagerly cut into for your sake. You'd always rather they didn't do that, it made you too responsible, laid you open to their accusations, yet even this attempt at spreading the blame (which you were careful never properly to assume) was a type of unconscious flattery.

For this very reason Trade with Adam in tow would have been unbearable, a disaster. The whole point of going there was the deliberate absence of dimension, the sense the place afforded of a single plane, a sort of flat earth where gravitational pull didn't exist, on and off which people tumbled for a few hours in forms they had devised so as effectively to discount the realities of before and after. Frankie didn't think Adam would understand this, or that if he knew it he definitely didn't want to. Instead he'd stand around at the bars or on the edge of the dance floor, doing the one thing you were never supposed to do which was waiting for it all to end.

With Paul it was different. Guys like him weren't made for conversation, however much they talked. There was a quality Frankie liked to identify as physical intellect, which kicked in sometimes with a kind of dancer who in every other respect was sophomoric, inarticulate, not necessarily even interested enough for his head to be filled with someone else's curiosity and alertness, but instinctive, almost weirdly so, in grasping any sort of discourse involving steps and gestures. Paul, who only spoke Greek because programmed to do so within his family, would never have known the difference between prosopopoeia and prosopography. No doubt there were those at Trade and Crash and Queer Nation who did, though the thing was not to admit it. God-given ignorance like this was useful right now, and it might just be that Adam, able to understand everything else, could start to appreciate why Frankie chose to nurture it.

Or maybe not, what the hell? He sauntered slowly along the

landing, slipping the mobile into his pocket, his earlier discontents lifting amid a radiant awareness of how much at this moment he was able to control. They'd started now to trail *A Keeper of Flocks* with interviews, in which he trod an expert line between wacky and portentous, and soon the listings magazines would be heralding it as a must-see. In a month or so he'd leave for Paris with Paul in tow because he needed him for Fernando, at least till Frankfurt when Stefan would become available again. He'd leave the problem of what to do with Paul on hold. Maybe Daisy would have some ideas, she was useful like that. In the hall stood Adam, looking up. Frankie descended smiling at the idea of him there, chubby and adoring at the bottom of the stairs.

XVI

FROM the Pillow-Bites Of Should'avegone Longago.

Things You Hate About Saunas:

Yourself for going there in the first place. People who sit in the steam-room staring at the floor. Everybody who doesn't notice you or – still worse – pretends they don't. Professional gropers, mostly because they remind you of what you'll be like by the time you're their age. Anyone of any description who insists on walking about in the common parts without wearing his towel. Narcissi of various kinds unknown to Linnaeus but all too familiar in a world predicated upon auto-eroticism, whose deliberately distracting presence while soaping themselves under the douches or executing a three-point dive into the plunge pool has an instantly damping effect on the atmosphere of opportunity and gratification which places of this kind are expected to induce. Boys who take ages in the showers poking about from time to time like analytical chemists among the contents of little drawstring spongebags, the things handed out to club-class passengers on long-haul flights, for the next phial of enchanted unguent whose merest application to the body's more arcane flukes and grooves will ensure a *summa cum laude* in the Winsome Torment championships. Spoilers, the type who assume they have a right to join in simply because you and somebody else have got a thing going and there isn't necessarily a door to lock them out. People who ostentatiously Don't Do It, like that man who has visited a certain bathhouse in west London for the past twenty years solely for the purpose of showing off a perfectly cinched waist and a pair of buttocks worthy of a National Hunt thoroughbred. Pairs of giggling Brazilians or gossipy Italians, loudly scornful Parisians, podgy Arabs wearing bathing costumes under their towels, and – the inevitable concomitant of afternoons at the baths – myopic, mop-haired Oriental dwarfs. Men who get conversational in the sauna, like it was dahn the old Poplar Bahvs or Yawk 'all Beffnal Green, and, most embarrassing of all, any sort of prolonged verbal intercourse in the backroom. The staff, never more pleasant to you than is absolutely necessary and invariably rude if they happen to be nice-looking. Yourself yet again, for perpetually hanging about longer than is decent to the amour propre because your inherent sexaholic sluttishness fancies one last bout, preferably in the company of the drop-dead gorgeous number with Ralph Lauren round the band of the snowy briefs he steps out of just as you contemplate leaving.

Actually Theo had thought of it for some time, but this evening a kind of boneless inaction overpowered him almost from the moment of setting foot in the place. That certainty of being desired, which on earlier occasions made him relaxed and selective about those with whom he might care to enjoy himself, had now got translated into the dire condition of absolute passivity, accepting the grossest, most ineptly offered attentions as if secured by an anaesthetic. Without even the reassurance of surprise or disbelief he didn't feel so much as watch himself being licked and tweaked and stroked and sucked, receiving kisses as though his open mouth were merely another vacuum abhorred by nature. For a period of two hours he moved through the automated sequence of steam-room, backroom, sauna, showers, chill-out space, jacuzzi, cabins and corridors in an unbroken vagueness which, from the half-closed state of his deep-lidded eyes, might have been mistaken for narcolepsy. People drew him into embraces, flung themselves on his neck or steadied him against the wall so as the better to kneel and take in their mouths a hard-on which seemed strangely to have arrived without the customary assistance from fancy or excited anticipation. Meanwhile, even if making no positive reciprocal gesture beyond instinctively caressing the heads of those crouching at their devotions, he pushed none of them away. He'd approached this level of inertia before, yet never had he appeared so profoundly dead to himself as now.

The same peculiar quality of absence continued to brood over Theo as he started for home. Usually what made you leave these places was either the saving grace of some impending engagement, dinner, drinks, a movie, now and then the high-risk activity of going back with somebody you'd met there, or else a feeling of satiety induced by the sheer repetitiveness within the continuing quest of gratification, like Lysimachus in the brothel, 'How now! How a dozen of virginities?', so that you groaned inwardly at the prospect of another plump dick or a neatly crafted arse water-dashed from the shower. Today, however, the impulse towards towelling and scrambling back into his clothes was simply something existential, happening for its own sake, with none of the coquetry ordinarily accompanying the process and designed to make those arriving curse your heartlessness as you bagged up your assets and pulled your T-shirt down tightly enough to emphasize the definition over which you'd laboured through the previous autumn and winter.

At present Theo didn't care who failed to notice. Creeping down into Waterloo Underground, with its imperishable smell of sick in the passageways, he boarded the incoming train forsaking his usual survey of the advancing carriages to see what might sauce the journey with a hint or two of imagined possibility or be worth pulling should they disembark at Clapham Common. Somebody had left a *Hot Tickets* on the adjacent seat, but he didn't feel like reading anything right now. In a week or two, he knew, there'd be a crisp little bite in the Theatre section about Nathan Lester's fresh take on the play, an interview with Maxine, the Cressida, who'd say something defensive about women as victims in a world where men made the rules, and maybe a rehearsal shot of the battle, with Tom as Achilles, his face a rictus of agony as he tried not to drop his burden, that burden which now sat slumped in the train's white glare, hearing, without his usual irritation, the gurgling female voice like that of some charm-school starlet in an Ealing comedy, announcing 'This station is Kennington'. Even when it declared 'This station is Oval' he was not tempted, as generally, to mutter something about having always supposed it to be rectangular.

Picking his way mournfully along the narrow parapet that formed the Clapham Common platform, Theo scaled the stairs, an exhausted mountaineer, to let the escalator carry him up towards what remained of daylight. If he felt anything at all now it was a wish that Adam be there when he got home, profound only because of the way the dusk of a May evening beset him with sudden tremors of loneliness and vulnerability. Of course Adam wasn't in. The pad on the kitchen table bore nothing by way of explanation. Theo went into his room and lay down for a moment on the bed, staring at the ceiling. Normally when you came back from a razzle you'd put some music on, something purgative like Bruhns or Frescobaldi, have a smoke and savour lickerish recollections of those you'd fucked, their smell perhaps still on you, remembering their styles of kissing, the touch of their hands and the tantalizing hints, involuntarily released, of emotions about to be shared. At present, however, Theo's memory was blank, clinging to nothing from the past few hours, not because he specifically wanted to reject the experience entirely, but for the sake of something else he was unprepared as yet to acknowledge.

He got up and went to open a drawer in the little desk by the bookcase. Taking out an envelope, he gingerly pulled from it a photograph which he laid on the bureau flap, and sat looking concentratedly at it, chin perched on the backs of his fists. The picture was a large black-and-white print showing Guy standing against a wall, a cigarette dangling from one hand. He was staring slightly downwards and his mouth bore the merest traces of a smile. It was the first such token Theo had ever received from him. There'd always been presents – shirts, underwear, pairs of socks, cuff links, aftershave, CDs – but this inevitably held more significance than any of them. He turned it over to read the pencilled inscription on the back, 'To my chocolate soldier, my tarbaby, my darkest secret, from your chocaholic pale companion and niftiest be-Guy-ler – geddit?', then flipped it back again to gaze on the image once again, as though his absorption might draw some hidden charge from its glistening surface. For a long moment Theo sat thus, then, as if ultimately disheartened by not finding what he was looking for, he put the photograph back into its envelope and, sighing, shut it away in the drawer as Adam entered the flat.

Theo stayed there for a moment with the door closed, not knowing, if he opened it, what on earth he would find to say. The little squalls gusting between them of late had died down. Adam seemed to have given up his annoying manoeuvres towards prising more out of Theo about Guy, and besides, his own private preoccupations looked likely to dull the edge of his curiosity. For whatever reason they had seen less of each other during the past fortnight than before. Theo, remembering his crossness when a month or so back Adam had innocently enquired whether he'd be around that Sunday evening when he returned from Islington, felt correspondingly guilty at his present recognition of the same wish. The sound of Adam now moving to and fro between the kitchen and the bathroom muttering to himself because he thought he was alone became all of a sudden unbearable. Going to the door, Theo stepped out into the hall and softly called his name. Adam, when he appeared, made no attempt at concealing the dejection beneath his immediate surprise.

'Why didn't you leave the light on?' he asked.

'It wasn't quite dark when I came in.'

Adam's gaze held Theo's accusingly. 'I could have been here for hours and not known.'

'So could I, if it comes to that.'

'You'd have heard me.'

'If I was listening. Where've you been?'

'At the Cave of Spleen. Basil's, I mean. He needed cheering up. He wants a book launch and his publishers won't give him one. And he's worried that it won't get reviewed. And he's between women, or maybe not even between. It's difficult nowadays being an unattached straight, especially if you aren't broody. They can't get their rocks off every night like we can.'

'I envy him,' said Theo sombrely. 'Right now do you know what I'd like to be?'

'Probably the same as I'd like to be. Not Agatha, that's for sure.'

'Only if she entered an enclosed order, became one of the Poor Clares or whatever they were called. I could fancy being a hermit, that's what, one of those people you see in old Italian pictures kneeling among jagged rocks, with a skull and rosary beads and a crucifix, and fir trees in the background, wearing a brown robe.'

'You'd look hideous in brown,' muttered Adam, 'it's one colour which does nothing for you.'

'OK, black on black then, it doesn't matter. And whenever anyone came near my cave I'd ring a little bell at them and start saying my prayers.'

They both stood in silence for a while. Adam toed the carpet with his foot. 'I hope you'd pray for me,' he said at length.

'Yeah, I expect,' said Theo, staring at the floor. Then, going towards Adam, he took him in his arms and held him there, less for affection than for his own safety. In the same sort of impulse Adam's arms came round him and the two of them stood clinging thus, while through the open window came the sounds of the suburban evening, ordinarily so companionable at this time of year when everything carried more clearly on the air, but now just a heartless emphasis of that isolation each felt and could not yet declare. Thinking, for no good reason, that he must be the stronger, Theo took Adam's face between his hands and kissed him on the forehead.

'That bad?' he enquired, or suggested rather.

'Once when I was little,' said Adam, 'a little boy in

Haslemere, and it was my first day at school . . . and you know you're meant to be like wildly excited and can't wait to be off and keen as mustard with your satchel and your new uniform and that? Well, I started crying. I mean, it was only round the corner, for Christ's sake, and I'd be home in the afternoon. Anyway my dad was brilliant. He sat me down and told me about when he was a kid and went to boarding school in the Midlands. He used to go on the train, and for some reason it was always one of those crawling ones which stops for no obvious reason just outside a station and you think it's going to be stuck for ever. And he'd sit looking out of the carriage window into people's back gardens and watch them doing kind of gardeny things like tying up the raspberry canes and setting out the cloches and mulching the blackcurrant bushes. And he'd see people pottering about inside the house changing beds, laying the kitchen table, stuff like that. He said it was the most horrible thing about the journey. Because he'd think "How can it go on? How can they be so totally callous and indifferent and not know anything abut me and how miserable I'm feeling?" He wanted normal life to be suspended, at least until the train moved again. I don't think I quite understood him, but at least it stopped me crying.'

'Come into the sitting-room and let's shut the windows and have some music,' said Theo, 'so we won't know it's there. Whatever it is.'

'It's always there, you know that. Every bloody moment of my waking life.'

'Do you want it to go away?'

'There are times . . . Do you really want music just now?'

'Maybe not, I don't know. It'd have to be something completely neutral, preferably without words and with nothing like a tune in it. I'm not strong enough for other people's emotions tonight. Except yours, I mean. They don't feel like other people's.'

'Yeah, well, I try not to be commonplace.'

That wasn't what Theo meant at all, but he didn't bother correcting Adam. They went into the sitting-room and Adam flopped down at once on the sofa, his head in the cushions.

'Do you want me to skin up?' Theo asked. 'I was going to anyway.'

So he did, and they sat quietly for a while, the windows still left open because each was afraid to shut out the traffic's anodyne murmur below. The sense of that persistent ordinariness of which Adam had just spoken came, after all, like the promise of an eventual rescue, should either of them need it.

'Was it . . .' Adam began at last, speaking quietly and effortlly. 'Was it straight away, when you first met him? Did you think "this is it", like we're always doing when somebody's nice to us?'

'I don't know that he was particularly nice to me,' whispered Theo. 'I thought he was at the time, but I'm not sure now. And no, it wasn't then. You're supposed to remember exactly when, aren't you? "It flashed upon Emma with the swiftness of an arrow" blahblah. Only I can't. Can you?'

'Nope. Well, yes, maybe. Or perhaps it's just that I realized after a bit that I'd stopped fantasizing about what we were going to do together. I don't mean sex, we haven't had any apart from a kiss. Isn't it weird? Perhaps I'm frightened that if we do I'll stop wanting him.'

Theo laughed grimly. 'It doesn't work like that. You get to desire them more, and they know it.'

'Frankie's known from the start. I'm talking as if it had gone on for months, aren't I, only it hasn't. But that's how it feels.'

Adam's voice subsided into a mournful echo. 'Months upon months. With absolutely bugger all to show for it. I'd rather be you, The, any day.'

'Fuck off.'

'Seriously I would. At least you get to spend time alone with your mystery man in Bayswater. If you tot it up, from the night you first started seeing each other – somewhere around the end of February, wasn't it? – you'll have had the equivalent of several weeks non-stop together out of all those evenings. Maybe not exactly, but you know what I mean.'

'He's not a mystery man,' said Theo, 'it's only the way we like to do it, that's all.'

'Yes, well, I don't believe you.'

'Why?'

Adam paused for a moment, surprised both at his temerity and at Theo's apparent calm in the face of his scepticism. 'I just don't believe you aren't always wanting to do the same sort of things with Guy as I find myself wanting to do with Frankie.'

'You said earlier that you'd stopped fantasizing about him.'

'I didn't mean . . . I meant . . .' Theo was gazing down at him, devouring and inexorable. 'I meant that he'd become real for me, that's all. I wasn't translating him into somebody else. Anyway, don't you? Don't you want to be everywhere with Guy as your lover and notice the hunger in people's faces because they didn't get to him first? To be one of those couples who sit in the corner of a restaurant totally cocooned in one another's adoration and don't even so much as flicker an eye at the waiter, even if he turns out to be the most jaw-droppingly shaggable beast in the whole city? And be seen at plays and concerts talking to each other in the interval in that sort of holy hush, as if there was darkness all around and the only light was from the rows of candles lit in front of you, as if you were the patron saints of sodomy?'

'Like those two soldiers that church is dedicated to in Istanbul? Yeah, that'd be nice.'

'Maybe Romanus the Melode wrote a poem about them.'

'If I knew who he was.'

'Somebody told me once, but I've forgotten. It was just before I saw Frankie.'

'That's an excuse?'

'Excuses are all we've got left, the pair of us. When the iceberg struck we came on deck in our pyjamas, remember? "There's your beautiful nightdress *gorne*." What shall we do, The?'

'Think and die. Only just at present I hate thinking. That's why being in rehearsals is cool.'

'Because it takes your mind off him. You're lucky, there's nothing like that for me. I thought work was going to be the painkiller, but it's not. As soon as we get submissions from a new dance outfit or some kid sends a CV asking for a bursary so he can be the new Nureyev, Rudi Redux, I'm poised to phone him. Frankie I mean, not the kid. But I don't, because it looks seriously naff.'

'You'd do better with the kid.'

'Is that why you go out? Because Guy's not cool with you calling?'

Theo was silent. Again Adam braced himself for a rebuff which surprised him by not arriving. 'You're wrong about them knowing how much they hurt us,' he said. 'In some sense that suggests they care about who we are, whereas I don't believe Frankie honestly gives a shit. He might in the end — whatever the end may be — but not now.' There was another silence between them. Predictably, Theo hadn't answered

Adam's question; yet, as if to forestall another which might follow in its wake, he said, 'It's not that I want Guy to make a confession. Or at least I did once, but I've abandoned the idea.' He paused again, mired in wretchedness. 'Their silence isn't what hurts most. It's when they won't let you speak, the hand over the mouth, the scissors against the tongue, that's what makes you squirm in agony.'

'I'm jealous of you.'

'Jesus, Ad, why?'

'Because in some way you're where I want to be. Once I saw this wildlife documentary about the Arctic, and there was a polar bear floating along on a block of ice. And in the distance you could see another bear standing on a different bit of ice, only, because of the currents or something, it was going in another direction. That's what we're like, only your ice block's going faster than mine.'

'To hit nowhere maybe.'

'With Frankie I haven't even got that. Just a load of emotions I can't get rid of, supposing I wanted to. Shall I tell you what I really want?'

'What?' Theo's voice was as flat and unenthusiastic as it had been from the outset, but that didn't deter Adam now.

'When you come back from holiday, and you've done baggage reclaim and you go through the blue channel and the doors slide apart . . .'

'Yeah?'

'And out there in the airport lounge there are all those figures waiting round the rail, drivers with names written in big smudgy capital letters, and tour guides and lots of people dancing up and down expecting someone they know to come through, as if whoever it was had descended to earth off a cloud like some fucking goddess in a Jacobean masque. And there's lots of squeezy, huggy, kissy-kissy stuff going on.

'But you, you just go forward, you and your trolley, with the duty-free bag and an umbrella and suitcase wobbling, alone to the Heathrow Express lift and those horrid shiny tunnels, the sort of thing people run through in movie dream sequences. There isn't even a chauffeur with "Mr Killigrew" held up on a piece of paper.

'Just once I'd like there to be somebody smiling at me out of the crowd, who'll hold me for a moment and ask me how my flight was, and when we get to the car park – for of course there'll be a car – and the case is stowed in the boot, he'll take me in his arms again and kiss me slowly, slowly, because in that moment nothing in life seems urgent any longer. Corny, yeah, but it's not much to ask.'

XVII

WONDERFUL. No, he was, wasn't he, and Daisy was frankly astounded. Getting him asked down for the weekend had, to start with at any rate, been her idea of a joke. The pair of them would have something to laugh at, and, more significantly, it was a means of trouncing Jeremy for the cavalier way in which, invoking the excuse of a postponed meeting (on a Sunday, for goodness' sake?) he'd left the remains of the christening party to be managed by Serena. Her sister's loyalty to him always irritated her, but that afternoon, to do Sibby credit, it was modified by signs of unmistakable restlessness. All things considered, Daisy had been glad not to accept the offer of a spare room at Holland Park for the night. The thought of babysitting for two, rather than the statutory one (who'd honestly, bless her, been a star) was more than reasonable flesh and blood, adult and vaccinated as the Italians say, could have put up with.

She was rather glad than otherwise, however, that her

original plan of flinging Frankie, as the quintessential metropolitan jackanapes, into the ordered calm of south Worcestershire and watching what happened was simply not working. For one thing he hadn't been nearly discontented enough at foregoing London pleasures in favour of early dinners and bed at half past ten. Alice, already interested in him as a character type, had been further intrigued by his conscious attempts at disappointing their expectations. When they went church-crawling he'd charmed the socks off Will via several perspicacious remarks on the Elizabethan triptych at Besford and by his sterling efforts at keeping a straight face in front of the Baroque monument at Strensham whose effigy of a dying husband in the arms of a distraught wife looks for all the world like a habitual drunkard being turfed out into the gutter for the last time. He had captivated Zoe, not just by his pantherine agility on the tennis court but through his grace in losing to her when he might so obviously have won. Even Jack, normally so grudging and laconic in offering opinions on others, looked as if he might eventually be brought to declare that Frankie was a great bloke with potential for being a diamond geezer. Daisy had her reservations on this last point, yet she was touched by Frankie's attentiveness to Gaga, who made them all laugh by taking a shine to him in return and following him raucously up and down the garden.

'At first,' she said to Alice, as she watched her making salads for lunch, 'I thought it was just to ingratiate himself with Serena. You know how guests do, it's instinctive in most people, isn't it? But of course I should have realized how much he understood, and that actually it was empathy rather than striving to please.'

'He's got our numbers, hasn't he?' said Alice. 'All of them, I should say. Or most. But he's really awfully cute. If I didn't think the country bored you both rigid and this wasn't just an anthropological excursion for him, I'd have asked you down ages ago instead of leaving it to Sib. When did you say he was off to Paris?'

'Next month. The ballet's part of a triple bill at the Wells, and then it gets detachable and he's going to restage it in September on Le Continong. Nobody does anything in August, as you know, so he'll probably just doss about on a beach somewhere.'

Alice's eyes met Daisy's. 'And not come back to London,' she added rather than enquired. 'Does Adam know about this?'

'I expect Frankie's told him. Why do you ask?'

'I just wondered, that's all.'

'You never just wonder, Al.' Daisy laughed sardonically. 'You've always answered the questions in your head first of all.'

'So what question do you imagine I've already answered?'

'I don't know, you tell me. The one about Adam, for starters.'

'I thought you might fill in the details. You've been seeing both of them more than I have.'

'You make it sound as if I'd been availing myself of their personal services.'

'I should have thought . . .' Alice remained still for a moment before returning ostentatiously to the business of stirring the vinaigrette. Her silence had the desired effect on Daisy.

'Oh, for goodness' sake get to the point, Al!'

'Well, is he or isn't he?'

'Is who?'

'Adam. In love with Frankie.'

Daisy snorted. 'I very much doubt it. For one thing the

whole business would be such a waste of time. And I don't mean just because Frankie's terminally besotted with himself. I know it doesn't show, that's the point, not all serial egoists are total bastards – unlike somebody not a million miles from us. But Frankie isn't really interested in anyone else except insofar as they're useful to him or feed him ideas.'

'Is that why you have him around?'

Daisy's eyes narrowed. 'Sorry?'

'I meant, because he's not likely to give you any grief. You don't have to worry about people like that, they look after themselves. Whereas if it was someone like Adam you'd be fretting all the time.'

Daisy sat quietly staring at the Aga, as though vatic insights lay concealed beneath its gleaming hob covers. 'When did you first notice?' she said at last. 'Come to think of it, why the fuck haven't I noticed?'

'It was only that I was reminded of certain things,' said Alice. 'Do you remember that lover he had a year or two ago, the one Basil used to call "the Professional Boyf"?'

'His name was Ben. They're always called Ben, that sort. Or else Alex. And they sit and simper in corners, and get miffed if the Beloved isn't paying them enough attention, and never have anything to say for themselves in a million years, even though you go out of your way to ask them interested questions. And they look completely anonymous, in that sort of standard-issue gay style, with a little bit of hair sticking up in front and moisturizer on their face and a necklace and a huggy T-shirt so that you can see they've been to the gym. And in the end they just go, like that, poof – as it were – and we'd never remember they were there at all. One of Frankie's dancers has got a prof. boyf., called Alex, wouldn't you guess? You long to tell him not to bother.'

'For a time Adam was besotted with Ben, wasn't he? And the same sort of thing's happening again. He can't concentrate for more than a nano-second on what anybody says. You get the sense of him humping this great big bag of emotions around but not wanting to open it for fear of being embarrassed.' Always so neat in her *modus operandi*, Alice began putting everything back on the shelves and slotting bowls and saucers into the dishwasher. 'I imagine Frankie's well aware of what's happening,' she said, not altogether satisfied that Daisy was sufficiently concerned for Adam's feelings.

'Frankie can always handle these things,' said Daisy. 'In any case he'll be off with the raggle-taggle-gypsies-oh, and he isn't the sort who writes letters.'

'Whereas Adam is. Sometimes they're voluminous. Paris is a mere three hours by train, incidentally.'

'Shit,' muttered Daisy. 'Shit, shit, shiitake mushrooms.'

'Why exactly?'

'Because it's so fucking inopportune.' She turned on Alice a malevolent stare, as if the whole thing was somehow her fault. 'I wish you'd never told me. There are times when I want to be Sib and shut the door on anything which looks too much like sophistication. Pour me a Scotch, there's a sweetheart.'

Alice thought it politic to do as she was bidden, tipping a generous slug into the glass on the assumption that Daisy would thereby grow more amenable. 'I fancy you'd probably better not mention any of this to Adam,' she said, 'I don't want him to imagine I was stirring. Anyhow it'll just make him feel more vulnerable to think of us all gossiping.'

'Don't worry, I shan't breathe a word. The last thing I want is him sobbing on my bosom. I hate it when men sob anyway, especially gay men. I'm absolutely not good at that sort of thing. Thank God Edie's not a boy. I'll just have to try and keep them apart.'

'Adam and Frankie? Do you think that's wise?'

'Anything to save trouble, darling.'

'I should have thought it would lead to more. And think how mortified Adam would be if he found out you were doing that. Honestly, I thought you'd be more pleased.'

Daisy looked mystified. 'For Adam, do you mean?'

'Why ever not?' Alice was equally puzzled. 'One of your best friends – so we're always led to believe – gets the hots for another. Who doesn't exactly discourage him, from what I can see . . .'

'Oh, for Christ's sake, it's only flirtation on automatic pilot. Frankie's an Olympic champion when it comes to being a tart, you've seen that all through this weekend. I can't imagine why Adam bothers with the serious stuff. They only met each other three months ago.'

'You've obviously forgotten what it's like.'

'Perhaps, yeah, I suppose so. I'd better go and see if Zoe's all right with Edie. She's such a trump, your daughter, they ought to erect a statue.' As she got up, Daisy noticed a photograph in a clip-frame on the wall. 'Is that one of Sib's? Awfully good, looks like an eighteenth-century portrait.'

Alice laughed. 'She probably meant it to be, unconsciously. We were all picnicking at the ruin. Will was telling us that story he told Frankie last night, about Lord Severnstoke's mistress and being different people in different places.'

'I like the way Baz is sitting at the end with his head in the paper. It looks as if she's put him there to balance the composition.'

'That may have been the idea. It was almost the only one she kept. She gave the other prints to Jeremy. She said she didn't want them, and she wouldn't show them to us.'

'My sister Serena is seriously weird at times,' murmured Daisy, still peering at the photograph. 'You know she goes and sits on top of that tower. She says it makes her feel like the saint who spent his life on a pillar in Syria. Still, if it makes her happy . . .'

Alice shuddered.

During lunch, under the arbour because it was hot enough to be worth risking the odd insect plopping into the salad, Alice found herself in the bizarre situation of watching Daisy observing Adam trying to engage Frankie's attention. There was no point in attempting to distract Daisy from what so patently absorbed her. Any move in that direction would have seemed obvious to the point of coarseness. Alice felt guilty now for having raised the subject at all if it meant that life was suddenly to be made difficult for Adam purely because he'd become the temporary prisoner of an infatuation. There was something sweet, wasn't there, in the defencelessness of his eyes and in the painful ineptitude with which he kept trying to deploy his feeble smile as a means of hanging on to Frankie on the other side of the table, who so maddeningly wouldn't be clutched at like this and kept darting to and fro among the various dishes and bottles and being industriously brittle in response to anybody's most trifling remark. She was grateful therefore when Jeremy, apropos of nothing and in the most matter-of-fact way, exclaimed, 'Bugger.'

'What?' said Serena.

'Or who?' whispered Frankie, which made both the children giggle. Jeremy appeared not to see the joke.

'Nothing. Just some post at the office I meant to pick up before I left.'

'Adam brought it down on Friday,' announced Serena, 'but it didn't look very important so I left it in the study.'

'And forgot to tell me.'

'I'm sorry.'

'I suppose I'm not to be the judge of whether my correspondence is important or not,' said Jeremy pettishly. Serena, as it happened, did not look especially penitent. 'Adam, you might have said.'

'I didn't think.'

'You never do these days.'

There was a little embarrassed silence. On other occasions Serena, apparently used to coping with Jeremy's spurts of pettishness, might have offered more wine or changed the subject. Now she sat there staring at her plate with Delphic reticence.

'Adam is busy pondering the secrets of the universe,' said Frankie, 'the alpha and omega, the Logos and the mighty om.'

Adam squirmed with pleasure. It was all Alice could do not to tell him to stop it immediately. 'You do talk such bollocks, Frankie,' he said in such a tone of desperate adoration as made her want to scream.

'I could go on for ever,' rejoined Frankie satanically, 'only this ferocious heat is drying up my powers of invention.'

'Thank God,' said Jeremy, knocking over his chair as he got up from the table and flung off into the garden. Will drew a breath and whistled softly through his teeth. Frankie simply muttered, 'My, oh my.' Serena, however, who could have been expected to run after him in an attempt to defuse the situation, stayed where she was, listening, sibylline, as he banged the garden gate and they heard the sound of his retreating footsteps crunching the newly laid gravel in the lane. Zoe and Jack looked at one another and corpsed.

'Did anyone see that film *The Madness of King George*?'

Jack asked. 'Because Sib's got to be like Queen Charlotte when the King goes ballistic after dinner and say "It vas somesing he ate."'

'Only it wasn't,' said Daisy ruthlessly, 'because your mother and I made lunch.'

'And you left out the belladonna?' cried Frankie. 'Tut, tut, thoughtless princess, when we picked it at midnight so carefully.'

'I bet you didn't make lunch anyway,' Adam said. 'You just sat there and let Al do it all.'

'We had things to talk about, didn't we, Al? Anyhow, where were you when needed?'

'He was teaching Frankie how to pronounce "Malvern",' said Zoe. 'Frankie said it looked like somewhere in Italy, all along the side of the hills like that, and then he started imitating Adam going "Mawlv'n". Only he did it like "Mooawlvin" and we just cracked up he was so funny. And he told us there was this old movie about a hotel, and the star . . .'

'Ginger Rogers.' Frankie sat there beaming. 'You mean you never saw it? She's cast as a Broadway diva called Irene Malvern, Eye-reen Mall-vurn. Only over here you'd say it like Ahreenee Mooawlvin and lose that platinum blonde effect. Talking of divas . . .' Will shook his head knowingly, as if to indicate that they were unlikely to see Jeremy for the rest of the day.

'I made a pavlova,' was all Serena said.

The heat gagged and bound them for the whole afternoon. There'd been talk of driving down to Tewkesbury, which Adam was all for, only enthusiasm regarding anything which looked too much like movement seemed to have been siphoned off into a general torpor and a subliminal spirit of mutiny at Jeremy's fretfulness, which expressed itself in doing nothing at all for several hours. Even at the pool hardly anyone swam, preferring instead either to stand in the shallow end occasionally dipping up to their necks, or else to lie sprawled on cushions along the grass borders with bits of the paper they hadn't read. Snatches of talk drifted among them like pollen or dandelion seeds, between the long arcs of a silence filled by the scratching of Jack's Walkman and odd ineffectual stirrings of the air which lightly flapped the leaves of the big sycamore overhanging the fence.

Adam glanced around him, at Alice dozing on the lounger like an effigy, at Daisy, her straw hat tilted forward, reading an orange Penguin fished out of the bookcase by the downstairs loo, and looking quintessentially 1950s South-of-France with her tortoiseshell shades and mulberry nails, at Zoe earnestly making notes from her revision tape for next week's exam, and Jack, who seemed to be inheriting both his father's stick-boned gawkiness and his relaxed amiability in the face of every crisis. Each of them possessed a curious but not necessarily alarming quality of remoteness, which seemed to Adam to disprove the idea that an amorous obsession enhances your sensibilities, like something sold to you in a club at four in the morning. Love, as he felt it now, was more like the needle they stick into your wrist as you lie powerless on the pre-op trolley. Everything unconnected with the dominant passion was carried out in a state poised somewhere between polite condescension and that total loss of muscle tone which certain tropical diseases are rumoured to induce. Either you did things because others expected them of you and it would seem callous to disappoint them, or else you operated according to instinct, your limbs or your tongue moving regardless of any more refined controlling nuances you might apply. It was as if, out of sight of Frankie, Adam had forgotten who he was.

The weekend seemed, as a result, to have lasted ages, but though he wasn't necessarily happy, there was no particular urge for it to be rounded off tomorrow by Daisy driving them back to London in her infernal machine. He would be no nearer than he had been on Friday to telling Frankie what he felt or knowing if Frankie, under his camouflage of self-awareness, had anything to offer in return. What unnerved Adam was not the business of finding the moment, which must in any case depend on judging Frankie's moods and pre-occupations, but the possibility that he himself might after all feel more comfortable with whatever was left unsaid. Perhaps he had been wrong to try and encourage Theo, however obliquely, to break the truth to Guy. Better, maybe, to live within the protecting shadow of the unexpressed, as Jeremy and Serena had always seemed to do. His own bizarre act of continence in refusing Frankie's offer of instant sex the other night in Alwyne Villas, when he'd scarcely ever known himself to turn down anybody's else's, now appeared positively heroic. It hadn't been because of Edie's innocence that he'd declined it. Too much value, he privately maintained, was set on a child's not being acquainted with the intimacies of adulthood, and it was unlikely that in old age Edie would record her earliest memory as that of an American choreographer unzipped and erect in her nursery one evening in the early summer of 1999. Adam, by the same token, nevertheless felt privileged to doubt most of what Daisy had said earlier as to Frankie's sincere adoration of her daughter. The immodesty wasn't so much inappropriate – a concept flattering to his banal ideas about English reticence versus American unembarrassment – as merely lacking in consideration for Edie's privacy.

They hadn't, besides, done what Frankie suggested, so the point was academic. It was Sunday afternoon now, a time when, had he been in London and felt an unspecified impulse towards lewdness coming on, Adam might have chosen from among a dozen different opportunities for staunching lust. Near Surrey Quays, for example, there was a pub whose Doré-like gloom, even on the gaudiest days of the year, guaranteed the requisite sense of transgression and impersonality, let alone enough shadow to blur those bodily imperfections on which homosexuals waste so much preposterous grief. Further west along the river lay a gym where, amid the jets and vapours, you could find a sequence of blond-eyelashed games captains who went home to achieving, Nicola Horlick-style wives in Wandsworth or Battersea after furnishing you with those agonized, if-we-must moments of opportunity whose accept-ance, on one or both knees, is said to indicate low self-esteem but which no genuine connoisseur will turn away.

This was the kind of thing Theo sought out in order to forget, for an hour or two, about what still needed saying to Guy. Coming home on Tuesday night Adam had guessed that was what he'd been doing, but they said nothing about it. The experience had somehow not registered as worthy of particularizing from a retrospect either of triumph or of rueful amusement. For his own part Adam had begun to feel an almost hermit-like remoteness from recreational sex as an unwavering imperative in the course of his waking life, let alone as something meshed within the fabric of his dreams. The memory of the kisses Frankie had given him, of their voracious, tyrannical indulgence, of the warmth of his face and the smell of sweat on the shaved sides of his dark head and that acrid intimation of *menus plaisirs* in the taste of cigarettes on his tongue, still wet with the beer swigged in Daisy's kitchen, was something that needed to remain indelible, as if part of a leisurely ritual still expecting significant completion.

Tonight, at any rate, would hardly be propitious. Frankie had spent so much time, over the last two days, being quite laboriously agreeable to everybody that it was unlikely that he'd choose to relax the mode until the weekend were over. Mournfully Adam watched him now as he clambered out of the pool and sprawled for a moment on the big flagstones along its edge. He watched the runnels and droplets coursing down the hollows of his chest and flattening the black hair on his thighs, the sudden alien pallor of his mouth, ordinarily so dark, the gatherings of muscle above his hips and the way the line of his cock glistened against the wet bathing slip which held it. The commonplace burden of wanting to possess another man's beauty, not for desire as much as for envy, lay on Adam, delicious in its grim heaviness. At this moment he found he didn't specially mind the realization that Frankie had hardly spoken a word to him all weekend.

'Adam, where's Sib?' Daisy's voice, presumptuously intrusive, caught him off guard.

'How on earth should I know?'

'She went off ages ago to feed Gaga,' said Zoe, as though in a deliberate effort to deflect attention from him. 'And Dad went with her to see Jeremy.'

'Will does the peacekeeping force as usual,' laughed Daisy. 'It's not fair on him, we ought to try harder.'

'You don't believe that,' said Jack without turning round.

'Don't be pert.'

'In the States we say "don't be fresh",' murmured Frankie, lying on his back across the grass now, the palpable curve of his packet pointed irritatingly in Adam's direction.

'Except over here it means something different,' said Daisy, 'or used to.'

'Which is?'

'Can't you guess? It's what boys used to do with girls at parties in the sixties, when I was just born and you were nowhere.'

'I'd rather be anywhere, treasure, it's more *branché* right now.' Still not looking up, Frankie called over to the other side of the pool, 'Hey, Adam, where are you this season, nowhere or anywhere?' But before Adam could answer, there came the sound of a car being driven up the lane at a speed it wasn't hard for any of them to interpret as the product of intense annoyance.

'Well, I call that very sensible of Jeremy,' Alice said, surprising everyone by speaking so alertly from her tombchest pose, 'driving off to do his laps of honour round Bredon before supper so that he can get it all out of his system, whatever it is.'

'How do you know?' asked Zoe.

'I don't know, sweetie, I was just guessing. He takes the car to places like Brockeridge or the path below Eckington Weir and does the serious marathon stuff. We saw him when we were walking on the common last year, don't you remember?'

'Oh yeah, in that vest and those blue lycra trunks. Actually, for someone that old, he's quite hunky.'

'He's thirty-seven, Zozo, which is only two years more than me,' Daisy said, 'so watch it.'

'He'll probably collapse from dehydration in this weather,' said Jack, 'and we'll have to send out bloodhounds to look for him, or St Bernards with little bottles round their necks full of Evian. And he'll be brought back on a stretcher and there'll be a touching scene with Sib, and Gaga will lay them both an egg for breakfast.'

'That's the one thing she's in no position to do,' said Daisy, 'unless there's an *in vitro* arrangement for geese.'

'Sib said something about getting a gander.'

Abruptly Frankie sat up. 'Pardon me, but did I miss something just then?' he asked with a certain asperity. 'I mean when we were eating lunch and he left like it was the worst thing anyone ever did to him? It was only a lousy bunch of mail, for Christ's sakes. He made it seem like it was all our fault.'

'I'd forgotten how much you hate feeling guilty,' said Daisy.

'So? You do too.'

'Anyway, we weren't responsible, were we? And here's Will with the text of the peace agreement.'

As it happened he had brought nothing of the kind, sheepishly announcing instead that Jeremy had gone back to London. From around the pool came something in the nature of 'a dismal universal hiss'.

'May we know why?' Alice asked.

'Well, it could have been the letters,' said Will, 'but somehow I don't think it was just that. According to Sib he didn't even bother to open them.' He fell silent, with the air of somebody expecting by this means to be invited to go on.

'And?' Frankie said obligingly, his face suffused with enjoyment of the unfolding situation.

Will shrugged, as if it were beneath his dignity to supply the detail they craved. 'He'd thought of going for a run . . .' Alice nodded smugly at Zoe. 'And he'd changed into a vest and shorts.'

'What kind of shorts?' said Jack.

'Oh, God, you're such a circumstantial boy, I don't know, short shorts, white and clingy to show off his legs. Anyway, it was my fault.'

'Do tell. We're simply agog,' gurgled Franked. 'I'd forgotten I knew that word till now.'

'Will, you have five minutes,' said Adam, 'in which to explain how Jezebel's white and clingy shorts were your fault.'

'I thought I'd try and suss out what the trouble really was. Funnily enough, I don't think it had anything specifically to with Sib. It was something more . . . I'm not sure . . . interior. So I suggested that before he went on his jog we should go and have a look at how the *foresteria* was coming along.'

'They've hung on to that poncey name,' said Daisy. 'It's only an outhouse turned into guest rooms.'

'Actually, I wasn't interested, it was just an excuse to get him on his own, without the sense of Sib hovering about in the background looking mysterious. So we went into the garden, and you know where there's a bit of lawn by Gaga's pen, above the pond? Well, as we were crossing it, Jezebel went arse over tit, just like that, and almost slipped into the water.' Will paused again, his face a mask of mock horror. 'And when he got up, his bum was bright green.'

'The gooseshit!' exclaimed Jack, cackling. 'Oh my God, why weren't we there?'

'It could be a fashion statement,' Frankie suggested, 'distress your shorts with goosepoo. Of course you kept a discreet silence.'

'I'm afraid I thought it was hilarious, so he told me to fuck off and did his second flounce of the day. And in as long as it took for him to change and gather up whatever was needed he was off, as an aunt of mine used to say, like a fart in a colander.'

The children continued to thump the grass and rock with laughter. Daisy and Alice remained triumphantly sibylline, while Frankie stared up at Will as if in search of more detail. It was Adam, however, who asked at length, 'Did he tell Serena where he was going?'

'Didn't utter a word. Normally when he goes back early she gets rather low. She always looks as if she's waiting for him to tell her that he loves the country after all, and that he wouldn't mind running the bouncy castle at the fête or touting for signatures against the gravel extraction. But this time she didn't. She came and stood in the hall, where he could see her, and watched him drive off.' Will sat down as though having richly deserved it. 'Someone else'll have to make tea, I'm too emotionally drained. Serena doesn't want the four of you there any more. Or to put it less baldly, it's probably better if Daisy goes and gets your things and you shake down here for tonight.'

'Are you sure there's room?' asked Daisy, for form's sake rather than through any undue concern at her sister's sudden inhospitable craving for solitude. 'We're such fusspots about personal space.'

'I don't care where I sleep,' said Adam untruthfully. The chance, as it now appeared, to share a bedroom or even a bed with Frankie had jolted him into an unusual attentiveness.

'Probably on the folding bed in the playroom,' Zoe said, 'with a wonky leg so you wake up in the middle of the night doing yoga positions.'

'Fine by me,' Frankie said, demonstrating it by flipping both legs whorishly into the air so that you could see the taut contour of his calf muscles.

'I think not,' said Daisy firmly. 'The end room for you. Al's made it so nice, and it's gorgeous in the morning when you wake up and the balsam poplar smell comes through the window.' She got up. 'I'm going down to Sib's. As the man said, I may be some time.'

She did not return until just before supper. Her face seemed drained of its vivacity and she had nothing constructive to tell them about Serena. Indeed the fact that her sister had behaved in a way which confounded all expectations seemed to have contributed to Daisy's exhaustion, the kind which easily arises from having done almost nothing the entire day. Apparently Serena maintained that she had known Jeremy would return to London that evening and was not at all surprised by his behaviour. Rather as Will had suggested earlier, she seemed cheerful, amused and, in the most amiable way possible, unwilling to share any more of her time with them until tomorrow morning, when she'd come up for breakfast. Tonight she was going to do the flower rota, ring round to check if Tessa from the bookshop had distributed envelopes for the appeal, maybe play the piano and then go to bed early with a Rosamunde Pilcher. She didn't even tell Daisy that they'd have to understand. Feeling faintly queasy and irritated at being made so *de trop*, Daisy had crossly allowed her to bring Adam and Frankie's bags, with Edie's impedimenta, down to the car, while deciding that she herself, the heat remaining so stickily God-awful, would kill perplexity for the rest of the evening with a headache and a temazepam.

There was little else to be said. Under the circumstances Serena's desire to be alone seemed entirely acceptable, since most of them were used by now to her being there for long periods without Jeremy. Besides, it was nicer to be at Alice and Will's, where you could leave things lying about with no sense that in so doing you had violated some universal governing principle of order, and where an ideal of consummate perfection, if they sought it at all, wasn't to be expressed in rose bowls, neatly ranked kitchen storage jars or cushions which miraculously never lost their plumpness. The only one who seemed slightly disappointed at the evening's enforced migration was Frankie. He had not been as pleased as Daisy hoped with the end room, but at least, she reflected as she went to bed early after refusing almost everything at supper, he and Adam were sleeping at opposite ends of the house.

Nobody appeared much inclined to stay up late that evening. It was as if what had seemed little more than a trifling demonstration of childish pique on Jeremy's part had become something on the scale of a sudden death in the family and that Serena was being treated with the respect due to a grieving widow. After supper a decent quietness fell upon the augmented population. Zoe and Jack, with their enviable adolescent capacity for self-effacement, simply disappeared. Even when later it sounded as if one or other of them might be getting ready for bed the process was carried out with none of the usual thumping up and down stairs and banging of doors which had always unsettled Adam's bachelor selfishness on earlier visits. While listening to Frankie playing Donizetti duets with Alice he sat pretending to talk to Will and longing to be asked to join them. The fact that he wasn't seemed somehow to encapsulate the atmosphere of non-achievement with which the whole weekend was fraught. He reminded himself of one of those people you read about in descriptions of old battles, who drove out with opera glasses and a picnic basket to watch as the opposing armies went about their business, but whose presence, even allowing for the more theatrical dimensions of war, the combatants barely acknowledge. His own patient endurance, in such a context of apparent detachment and remoteness, had a comforting heroism about it. There was something too energetic in Frankie's strategy of evasion for Adam not to suppose that it concealed truths he was reluctant to admit, a stronger dimension of feeling he'd determined shouldn't take him by surprise. So they'd wait, the pair of them, and circle one another until the archetypal good minute arrived.

The *alla polacca* caracoled to its triumphant close and Alice and Frankie came back into the sitting-room. 'There's a word they taught me in Berlin,' he said, '*Prunk*, it means like really stylish, eat-your-heart-out ostentatious, and Adam, your cousin Alice has *prunk* in spades.'

'I was just showing off,' said Alice, 'you can't not in that sort of music.'

'Is it possible to have understated *prunk*?' asked Will plaintively.

'You only want to get in on the act.'

'Well, that's the English kind, I guess.' Frankie yawned, a touch too elaborately Adam thought. 'I'm going to hit bed, guys. Daisy and I leave early tomorrow.' He blew a kiss to Alice. 'Darling, you were fabulous, we're a great double act, the Prunksters, how do you like that? Something to dream about, *sogni d'oro a tutti*!'

They watched him up the stairs, then Adam said, 'Maybe I'll go to bed as well. Perhaps I'll even go to sleep. Have I got *prunk*, do you think?'

'Your shorts certainly have,' said Alice, 'and they're nicer than Jeremy's.'

'And you haven't got a bright green bottom,' added Will.

For a while, after shutting the door of the playroom, Adam sat on the folding bed, under which Zoe, having made it up for him, had thoughtfully placed a brick to stop the leg slipping back in the night. Sounds of the house sinking into its final stages of repose gradually faded out around him. He heard the loo flush upstairs and the stertorous hiss of water in the pipes as the bathroom taps were turned on. Alice called something to Will, then shut the bedroom door, and Adam caught the distant, not unpleasantly conspiratorial ripple of their shared laughter. Thinking he might not, after all, sleep much tonight, he looked along the bookcase, always preferring to read what he could find in other people's houses to anything packed in his overnight bag. From the eclectic jostle in the shelves he pulled out the memoirs of some veteran bar-propper at the Colony Club, a volume of *The Saturday Book* and an *Eagle Annual* for 1954. He couldn't cope with fiction tonight. The moral stamina required was simply not within his reach. Prising his trainers off, he padded to the window and peered out. The air in the garden was thick and viscous. On it rose the scent of something – stocks? nicotiana? – which carried a slightly mocking intimation of other kinds of sensual experience, those he had resigned himself to not enjoying, for a while at any rate. Then, as Adam stared vaguely across the empty lawn beyond, the unmistakable graces of Frankie, holding a cigarette, suddenly defined themselves from the edge of the moonlight.

'You're meant to be in bed,' whispered Adam, though almost beyond utterance. For answer, Frankie came, sure as a cat, across the grass in his drawstring trousers and sleeveless top with 'Peckham' printed on it, murmuring something which became

> '"Mon destin fut digne d'envie,
> Et pour avoir un sort si beau
> Plus d'un aurait donné sa vie,
> Car sur ton sein j'ai mon tombeau"

Only we'll have to do it in reverse, I'm not in my Nijinsky mode tonight and you're too small for Karsavina. I didn't mean small like that.'

'Couldn't you sleep?'

'It's kind of Nathaniel Hawthorne, but I don't fancy being

Esther Dudley or the White Old Maid just yet. Why'nt you join me in a cigarette and drive away the moths?'

'I'll have to climb on a chair. Maybe the window isn't big enough anyway.'

'Quit making excuses, do it instead, there's a world out here.'

Adam turned for a moment to put something in his pocket, then, clearing a mug of dried flowers from the window ledge, scrambled up off the chair and managed somehow to thrust himself forward through the window into the taut clasp of outspread arms. Disappointed not to be kept there, he was thrilled nevertheless at finding himself thus clandestinely alone with Frankie for the first time since their arrival. He didn't want a cigarette but felt he ought to take what was offered, for the sake of sheer gratitude at the moment's singular advantage. There came the quick sharp spurt of the lighter. For a while they stood together in silence on the lawn. Bending down, Adam ran the flat of his hand across the grass and held it up glistening wet in the moonlight.

'Another hot day tomorrow.'

'This place really freaks me out,' said Frankie. 'I don't mean like here, your cousin's house, I mean being in the country.'

'Why especially?'

'Because in a place like this you have to concentrate longer. There's nothing to distract you, to invite you to think ahead, so that you don't have to spend so much time in the now. Or more than you need.'

'This isn't really being in the country,' said Adam. 'People like us are just playing at it. We'll always have London to go back to.'

'So why don't you stay there?'

'Why don't you stay in America? English people don't

believe in towns, they mess them about it in a sort of resentful way, simply for being the things they are, and then try to get out of them as often as they can. Has it really been that unnerving?'

Frankie laughed softly. 'No, but I reckon I've had enough for the present.'

'And does that mean . . .' Adam paused, eager to give his question the precise shading, lest Frankie should misunderstand its intention. 'And does that mean you won't come here again?'

'I can't answer that. I don't know. Most of the time when you make decisions it's stupid.' His voice, like Adam's, had dropped to a careful whisper, losing, in the process, its camp rasp of habitual knowingness. Perhaps Daisy had been correct after all when she suggested that the perpetual clowning concealed a certain vulnerability. 'I'm right about certain things, steps, music, lighting maybe. Everything else is just one experience coming after another.'

For the first time Adam felt unafraid of him, purely through knowing, in that moment, what they had to do. It was as if the two had changed places and the desire rendering him so nerveless earlier was now imbuing him with a power lost to Frankie. He finished his cigarette.

'Let me show you something beautiful,' he said, 'so that you won't think this weekend's been a total waste of time, when you could have been making hay with Fernando Pessoa and his four identities. And we can talk properly instead of having to whisper like this.'

'OK, lead me wherever, it's like I'm blind right now, I don't know why. I'm thinking about Fernando all the time, by the way. When that jerk got out from the table today I had a few new ideas. How can she stay with a guy like that?'

They went out into the lane, Adam being careful to shut the gate as quietly as possible, and walked on some little way in silence down the track, until he judged they had got sufficiently out of earshot of anybody in the cottage who might be awake. Then he said: 'Serena loves Jeremy. Or at least did when she married him. She had a sort of hippy phase in the late eighties, living with a Moroccan in Kentish Town. She doesn't talk about it and neither does Daisy really. Something happened which meant she couldn't have children . . .'

'Which is why he married her, the bastard.'

'Is that Daisy's idea or yours?'

'Mine, but it figures, *n'est ce pas?* The guy is such an asshole.'

'You only hate Jeremy because you couldn't impress him and he didn't laugh at your jokes.'

Frankie stopped walking and spun round. 'How can you . . .'

'You mean how dare I? It's true, isn't it? You hate people who don't notice you.'

He laughed ruefully. 'Yeah, I guess so. But with him it's worse than that, a kind of embarrassment, like he recognized himself in me. Or he thought I knew who he was.'

'And you did. Or thought you did.'

'Yeah.' Frankie was unusually laconic. As if to supply what he hadn't chosen to articulate, an owl hooted from the trees to the left of them and another answered further off.

'So what did you think?' persisted Adam.

For an instant Frankie didn't answer. Then slowly he said, 'Jeremy is just pretending, the way hundreds of other married guys are. He's the type you don't want on the team, not in a million years.'

'I suppose it depends on which team,' said Adam. 'Maybe you could work him into *A Keeper of Flocks*. Actually, sometimes I think he might do better as a woman. These days we probably all would.'

'I'll take a rain check on gender reassignment.' Frankie gave Adam's arse a comfortable squeeze. 'And so should you, sugar. That was what turned me on to dance when I was a kid, one beautiful man's ass after another, all in tights and so hard you could play squash games off of them. A woman's butt is like some fucking eggplant. Stay with the males, Adam.'

'I'll give it some thought. Meanwhile . . .'

It was not just the richness of moonlight which seemed to define the Hermitage but the quiet in the landscape itself. Now the owls had fallen silent again the only noise was of an occasional distant car along the Pershore road and, still more remote, an unvarying low murmur from the motorway beyond. Otherwise nothing stirred among the leaves or in the air, still sultry and slow to give up the day's gathering of heat. Frankie looked around him, suddenly reanimated, as it were, by the ruin's glistening theatricality.

'God, Blanche Dubois and Mr Poe, Mr Edgar Allan Poe, never dreamed of this between them!' He slipped an arm round Adam's shoulder and pulled him closer. 'Or you just made this up.'

'Don't you recognize it from yesterday?'

'Maybe. It's different somehow, nothing's the same tonight.'

Almost nonchalantly, via some afterthought as it were, Frankie drew Adam into his embrace, yet held him there as though the intention behind such a movement had always been meant to seem less playful than before. Whatever happened earlier, then, had been a mere rehearsal. One of those variations on chronology that lovers plot for themselves, a sense of refashioning conventional days, months or even years into an epoch before which you only pretended to exist or even never existed at all, started for Adam in this instant. Nothing here could more astound him than the completeness of accomplishment. As the blood knocked in his skull and he felt Frankie's tongue bickering against his own, tasted the rim of salt along his upper lip and drank in his gusts of breath, Adam hung on to whatever remained of pure incredulity. Faith was a matter of not believing too absolutely in the fact of consummation.

'These stones,' whispered Frankie, 'can't you feel how hot they are?' Still holding on to Adam he peered around him. 'Do you think we might . . .' He shrugged as if the rest were an indiscretion, better imagined than spoken of.

'What exactly?'

'Well, don't you have like forest rangers or something?'

Adam laughed. 'There was a gamekeeper when the last Lord Severnstoke lived here, but that was yonks ago. Maybe there's the odd pheasant in the woods which the poachers haven't got, but they don't come here much. Nobody does.'

'Promise?'

'Not cross my heart. We'd be safer up the tower only I haven't got the key. Just trust me.'

'My life in your hands, kid.'

'And everything else tonight,' said Adam triumphantly.

With a slight shake of the head, as if what he now prepared to do was against his better judgement, Frankie kicked away his sandals, undid the drawstring of his trousers, then, sighing, peeled off the top which said 'Peckham' and standing perfectly naked in the moonlight began to stroke his cock.

'I thought dancers had this fetish about keeping warm,' said Adam, stepping deftly out of his shorts. 'It looks as if you're going to fuck me, so I brought this just in case, for the better prevention of scandals.'

'Hold on, I didn't finish my vampire act, Anne Rice is developing the screenplay, didn't they tell you?'

'That's more like.'

'Like what?'

'Like I remember you,' Adam murmured, believing still less as he smoothed exultant hands over Frankie's shoulders and down against the small of his back.

'Great, I got a past, the one I always wanted.'

'Liar.'

'It's beautiful.'

'Whatever.'

'No, it beautiful, your ass. Like it got lost on the way to the Zwinger Palace. Or maybe the Collège de France. Baroque, somehow.'

'B'roak, somehow. Do you hear angels playing a trio sonata?'

'I figured more a nun doing Charpentier lessons, real high. And maybe a battle scene. And some banditti hiding out in the rocks. Lots of alexandrines, that's for sure, and a confidante called Céphise or Phénice who says "Madame" to fill up the line, so that inside the dome there's this deep echo. And a big, big overture with a fugue that goes on for a hundred pages.'

From up here everything was audible, down to the scuffing of Adam's trainers on the flat stones of the platform – why hadn't he taken them off? – and the little delighted exhalations coming from Frankie as he sensed the line of a finger drawn lightly across his skin. She leaned forward slightly, nervous lest some of the mortar be dislodged by her hand clutching the sill of the arrow slit, to get a better view. If she'd climbed up through the hatch on to the top of the turret they might have caught sight of her peering over the battlement, which would have been, well, embarrassing frankly, and she'd had enough of being embarrassed to last her a lifetime. It was better like this, even if she couldn't see quite all of what was happening without craning her neck round and perhaps scraping her blouse against the wall, which they'd almost certainly hear.

She couldn't be quite sure what it was. Not altogether beautiful, though Frankie's elegance, cowing her into a respectful silence when, clothed, he appeared at the christening or even padding along the poolside in his bathing slip this afternoon, appeared to equal advantage in the context of a moon-blanched nakedness. Adam, on the other hand, looked faintly idiotic with his vest and shorts off, flabby, slightly bewildered, as if needing Frankie to tell him what to do. His penis, sticking out like that from under his stomach, recalled one of those attachments on to which you fit a hose at the side of a garden shed. Ever so slightly sickening perhaps, but more because she wasn't permitted to move from where she sat until the pair of them had gone than from answering the demands of a recently alarmed curiosity. It was tiresome, when she'd wanted to watch the owls, to have to wait for the two men to finish off the business satisfactorily and then maybe hang about with cigarettes. She longed to lean out of the embrasure and tell them to hurry up and get on with it.

Instead, Adam, as far as she could see, was kneeling down now in front of Frankie, whose hand abstractedly ruffled his curls and whose voice had sunk to a throaty, monosyllabic growl. Serena felt a spurt of compassion for Adam at his devotions thus, remembering what he'd brought with him on Friday without knowing how grateful she'd be. That wasn't really what had made Jeremy angry. He couldn't have known after all, could he? It was just an accumulation of things, one after the other, topped by what she'd detected as being a perfectly monumental jealousy of Frankie, especially in those clothes he wore at breakfast. Though if she'd been Jeremy, she'd have concentrated her anger more obviously on Adam for not giving him the post directly, instead of passing it to her. That little burst of crossness this afternoon wasn't as much as an error like this deserved, even when made unconsciously.

Adam got up again. Frankie stood at the platform's edge, gross and truculent, hands on hips. 'Where is it?' he asked.

'In my shorts pocket. There's lube as well.'

'You brought the whole picnic basket? Resourceful it is we are!'

Adam tensed himself, with contented gracelessness, against the coping of the balustrade. Serena watched Frankie, having impatiently tugged on the rubber, withdraw a glistening finger from Adam and pull steady against his plump haunches before thrusting home. Bizarre essentially, that was what it was, rather than simply repellent. Her own physical discomfort, as she crouched in the angle formed by a bend in the stair, made her wonder why on earth bending forward like that, purely for the sake of penetration, should be conducive to pleasure. What Adam was prepared to put up with increasingly surprised her.

For Frankie, of course, it was just the ticket. In the moonlight his nakedness had by now lost any touch of its former refinement. At work, his thighs and shoulders glistening, he looked as coarse as a butcher. Incautiously, Serena leaned a little further out of the arrow slit, and in that instant he turned his head. For a second his face froze in amazement, then broke into a broad, complicit grin. Without relaxing the piston movement and still glancing in her direction, he raised a finger to his lips.

XVIII

EVERY time they did it in rehearsal Theo corpsed. It ought to have been second nature to him — third or fourth if it came to that, fiftieth, hundred thousandth — to go into a passionate clinch with another guy, but when it came to kissing Tom as Achilles he just couldn't hack it. For Tom, of course, this wasn't a problem. As Theo had formerly tried to make clear to Adam, an infinitesimally small proportion of straight men have no particular difficulties over who they are when it comes to sex, and Tom happened, whether fortunately or not, to belong to so rare a subspecies. Besides which, he was one of those actors who got everything right without needing particularly to work out why, and then buggered off to the pub. At drama school they'd probably taught him about getting into character by sitting in the dressing-room being ostentatiously antisocial, sulking on a staircase or standing in the wings with his back turned just before going on. Tom had clearly bunked that section of the course. He played patience, read the paper, spoke urgently on the mobile to his girlfriend, anything rather than be Achilles without an audience expecting of him. So kissing Theo, which the director had determined should happen on at least four different occasions during the show, was simply something he did because it was there to be undertaken. His mates in the five-a-side probably joshed him a bit about snogging a bloke, though Theo considered it unlikely that any of them could actually have been arsed to come and sit through a play which wasn't just Shakespeare, someone you did for school exams with revision notes, but one of the knottiest, a play which probably wasn't even acted in its own time, 'never stal'd with the Stage, never clapper-clawed with the palmes of the vulger'. *Art* or *Closer* they might just manage, but *Troilus and Cressida*?

Only at the last dress rehearsal was Theo able, through sheer force of circumstance, to get it right, possibly because Tom, patient to a fault, was starting to show signs of twitching at his umpteenth spluttering 'Sorry!' They'd gone through the scenes without a hitch, and to make it easier Tom's girlfriend had given them each a little yellow box of liquorice cachous labelled 'Lajaunie, *pharmacien*, Toulouse', one of two of which they were meant to pop in when a snog was coming on.

Tonight, however, was different, not just for being the first preview but because Guy was out in front. You could see him plainly, in his suit and tie, the periodic light changes catching the opulent moulding of his face, the mouth slightly open in something which looked like a smile yet wasn't necessarily, scratching the underside of his chin occasionally with a corner of his programme. When Theo caught Tom in his arms tonight, what must have looked to the audience like a fervent professional conviction was meant as a signal to Guy alone. He wanted to show him that he knew how it should go, as if he doubted Guy quite believed in the thing itself, kissing, except in terms of a footnote to sex, a casual reward like giving chocolate drops to a dog or an apple to a pony. It was meant not as a spur to jealousy – as though Guy, incapable, apparently, of self-doubt, could in any case have been made seriously uneasy by Tom – but as something more in the way of a demonstration, whose blatant intensity might move him to be less wary of whatever was mutual and levelling in the act through its very openness. Afterwards they'd drive back to Bayswater and kiss for the first time under a new dispensation, and Guy would maybe acknowledge that until this instant he hadn't understood. Since he'd undoubtedly feel the need to do better than his lover at what he now proposed to teach him by example, that bond of noble emulation would fix itself between them which Theo had craved from the outset.

By the same token he hadn't wanted his parents to see the show. Aubrey and Nadine said they might if there was an evening free, which meant that they'd wait for the notice in the *Guardian* or the little row of smiley masks in the *Evening Standard* chart before deigning to appear. Once again his mother was pressing him to move back home, a place nice boys didn't leave until they got married. Having so far betrayed her expectations by failing even to produce a fiancée and compromising himself still further in his obstinate devotion to acting as a serious profession, Theo had forfeited his last rag of respectability through becoming a lodger in somebody else's flat. She had long ago given up any attempt to prise out of him such information as he made up his mind not to give. There was no point, after all, in explaining quite how he had met Adam or the circumstances in which they lived together. She was as impenitently curious as most mothers are about their children's lives, and he had learned early the value of obstinate reticence as opposed to the sloppy vulgarity of lying. His father, more patient and philosophical, said nothing, though Theo guessed that he was merely waiting for an end to what seemed like the caprices of a delayed adolescence.

Prone against the stagecloth stretched tight across the floor, Theo was glad that so far they hadn't shown more than a polite generic interest in his present engagement. It must have been tiresome, whether in advance or over dinner afterwards, to have to expound the kissing and nuzzling with Achilles, let alone his present blood-stippled nakedness, undefended except by a leather jockstrap. In any case, what the audience saw at this point, amid the alarums and excursions, with the smoke hoses pumping fit to burst and much electronic clangour over the sound system, was not much more than his buttocks and thighs, glistening under the heat of the lights but patently superfluous, whatever Nathan the director might say, to the sequences of rage, betrayal and anti-heroics being played out around or sometimes across them. Perhaps this was all they'd noticed about him, ignoring entirely his delivery of

'Omission to do what is necessary
Seals a commission to a blank of danger'

Or the pertness with which he seized his advantage with Cressida in the scene where she was presented to the Greeks.

It was Nathan who insisted Theo took the curtain call thus, still blood-covered and glistening, an object the more desired for being so spectacularly unobtainable. Only Guy, waiting now in the car, could have him tonight, and Theo, confident that all had gone well, was in a mood to dictate the terms of his possession. Walking out into the bar he found Tom and Marie-Jo.

'You made me jealous,' she said with cheerful cynicism.

'I didn't mean to,' said Theo. 'Was it that convincing?'

Tom stared at him, his heterosexual eyes full of something like amazement. 'You've got to agree you were different to-night.'

'Yes, maybe.'

'More than perhaps. When I carried you on in the battle, you were light as a feather. It was the first time I didn't have to worry about doing my back in. I thought you'd fly away, it was just so weird.'

'I don't understand, honestly,' said Theo.

'Think about it. If it doesn't happen tomorrow and we're back to Linford Christie as a sack of potatoes, then I'll seriously want to know why.'

How the fuck, thought Theo, could it have been like that, unless by some obscure transference to Tom of his feelings about the character? This would amuse Guy, who sat waiting for him in the car with the door open even though the night was a touch cold and the windscreen was silvered with drizzle.

'Couldn't take my eyes of it,' he said. 'It was like one those tartuffo ice creams they give you for pudding in little Italian restaurants. I wanted to be up there astride.' Theo shut the door and turned to kiss him, but Guy raised a warning finger. 'Ah-ah, not here, we'll get arrested. Besides, it's good for you not to have everything you want at once.'

'Perhaps I want something different tonight,' Theo said, not necessarily cross at finding himself baffled thus. 'Apart from training your opera glasses on my bum, did you manage to enjoy the rest of the show?'

'Apart from that, Mrs Lincoln . . .? The Cressida's a total bimbo, which rather spoils the idea of her as a victim for being so intelligent. And someone ought to teach that curry-palace

Troilus what to do with his voice. Don't they give diction lessons at drama school these days? You were exemplary in that respect, by the way, not just a nice big tartuffo, no indeed.'

'I had some help,' said Theo, thinking of several sessions with Adam telling him at least to sound as if he meant it.

'Clever little chocs. That Ajax is nice, he's blacker than you and he's got even bigger thighs.'

Clearly the level of discourse was not going to get much more exalted. Theo would have liked Guy to be properly critical, to make comparisons and talk about production values, but the mood tonight was one of slightly callous light-heartedness, a determination at all costs not to grow too serious, which seemed less like an instinct than a conscious warning. It was as if Guy knew what Theo was preparing to do, as if that disembodied weightlessness which so mystified Tom had communicated itself for instant decoding as a signal of Theo's intentions. The feelings which had buoyed him up through the performance now defined themselves as a kind of fear that his chance to speak would be thwarted by Guy's deliberate strategy, suspicious as he must by now have become of his lover's capacity to embarrass him simply by being in love.

'Where are we going?' asked Theo, as Guy started the car.

'Where do you imagine?' said Guy in surprise.

'I thought we could go to a restaurant first, to celebrate.' Theo heard the words fall flat even as he spoke them.

'That's not quite what I had in mind.' Guy's tone was coolly determined. 'We're going home to Bayswater and a lobster salad, and you know what they say about shellfish, little coco pop.' He put a consoling hand on Theo's leg. 'I want it to be just us.' Then, sensing a lingering disappointment, he added:

'You can stay the night if you like, I don't have to go to work tomorrow.'

Calculated as it was, the offer had the anticipated effect. For a time they drove on in silence, Theo far too excited to speak, as though half the effort he'd supposed it necessary to make tonight were suddenly set aside in the sheer unexpectedness of Guy's proposal. Even imagining he were capable of sleep, things would be different between them in the morning, with the cloud of reticence dissolved, rewarding his own tough willingness to believe. Out of what he now prepared to tell Guy – which in any case seemed so laughably simple all of a sudden that he wondered why on earth he had never acknowledged it openly before – sex and sleep would flow seamlessly. Crowning both would come that incomparable sensation of waking to the warmth and grateful heaviness of someone who, a mere few hours ago, had not known himself for a lover and needed telling. A mad notion of speaking now, as they coasted up Park Lane and round Marble Arch, with Guy for the time being not quite in control, if only for having simultaneously to master the car, seized Theo so that he began, 'There's something . . .'

'Keep it, tarbaby, we're almost there. Things are so much easier over dinner, don't you find?'

Theo took a deep breath. 'It's the first time we've ever been in a car together,' he said. Guy didn't answer. His smile, as he peered at the wet road in front of him, had enough tyrannical self-possession in it to beat back, for the moment, Theo's newly gained resolve.

The lights were on in the flat, displaying a prodigality which Theo, accustomed to Adam's chivvying about unnecessary expense on electricity, had always been inclined to admire as a further example, if any were needed, of Guy's nonchalant lavishness. Perhaps after all it was not so bad that they'd come back like this, with supper only a matter of setting plates, slicing the ciabatta, shaving Parmesan over the rocket and putting the wine in the cooler, things Guy always insisted on doing himself, not through any particular wish to assume the role of waiter or cook but because he wasn't convinced Theo knew how to do them properly. That would change after tonight, of course, along with certain other things which Theo's passivity had so far been happy to accept as part of a general dispensation.

'I'm a bit disgusting,' he said, 'do you mind if I shower?'

Shutting the fridge, Guy turned and looked him up and down. 'I've got something for you afterwards.' He smiled, yet more confidently saturnine. 'A present for my starry young choco-warrior.'

Theo surprised himself by shivering slightly.

'What's the matter, are you cold? We don't want you catching a chill. We'd have to nurse you and we don't like that, we get cross and we've got a truly beastly bedside manner. Turn up the heat in the douche and use one of those nice bathsheets to rub yourself down. Maybe I'll come and do it for you.'

Theo felt better under the shower, soaping himself carefully with one of the battery of scented gels lined up along the shelf. Their marshalling thus, a toy guard of honour primed to salute, reminded him of how much, after all, he hated being in control. There was something undeniably seductive in the present arrangement whereby he was not expected to make anything in the way of a decision and the merest suggestion was seen as a potential flag of revolt. He could not be absolutely certain that when he'd spoken the necessary words this freedom, which essentially wasn't anything of the kind, wouldn't fall away and he should find himself bound instead to something like a responsibility, as weighty and complex as any he had ever tried to avoid earlier. Yet this very same power of choosing, as though quite without expecting it he held Guy's fate within his grasp, made him the more relaxed. Towelling himself dry with the immense white bathsheet, he draped it around him in a certain consciousness of décor, aware of the effect he must have and of his body, thus adorned, as an overwhelming instrument of persuasion.

Guy could scarcely be, and indeed wasn't, unmoved. 'Next time we'll make sure there's a turban, darling, and a scimitar! You've just got to sit at table like that, even if you die of a fever in the process, so we can write "He was drop-dead gorgeous" on your tombstone.'

With majestic humility Theo did as he was bidden.

'We're not having champagne tonight,' Guy announced, as if Theo had expressly demanded it. 'Lobster tastes nicer with Sancerre.' He filled their glasses, then, struck with a sudden idea, cried, 'We haven't drunk a toast for ages, have we?'

'What do you propose?' asked Theo in his quietest register, with an air of somebody biding his time.

'We'll drink to me. I know we ought to be pledging you, coco pop, and wishing your show would run as long as the fucking *Mousetrap*, but that's so banal, anybody can tip that one in your direction over a pint in a pub. No, we'll drink to me for buying this flat and putting all this stuff in it . . .'

'There's hardly anything,' Theo said, 'apart from the pots and the sculpture and those pictures of you like the one I've got and that casting photo of me.'

'Choccy-babe, I was being ironic. Never mind, there's another reason altogether for raising a glass. I mean choosing you as the *pièce de résistance* or whatever. Do you know, when they laid out landscape gardens in the eighteenth century, they used to put temples or mock ruins, like a castle or a tower, on the high ground as eye-catchers. And that's what you are, darling, you're the great big scumptious chocolate eye-catcher in my pleasure grounds. And I'm a creative genius, just like I told you. So here's to me! And nobody else, except possibly you.'

Silently Theo clinked his glass against Guy's as the room became filled with an atmosphere of self-congratulation which threatened to become positively suffocating. How ironic, besides, was Guy being? Evidently he was quite sincere when he asked, 'Aren't you going to eat your rocket? The oil's the very best. I got it from my . . .' Laughing nervously, he checked himself.

'Sorry?'

'Just a place I know near Arezzo.' His features recovered themselves into a winsome grin. 'Do you think I'm a dreadful show-off? Be honest.'

'Sometimes.'

'God!' Guy put his hands up to his mouth, mock-modest.

'It's why I love you to bits,' said Theo without the least hint of calculation, amazed forthwith as the words slipped from his mouth.

'Yeah, well, we'll forget you said that. Eat up, sombre secret, and we can binge on the lobster.'

'Who's we exactly?'

'I see, melt-in-the-mouth but also a bit iffy tonight.' Guy breathed deeply and turned his grey eyes to the ceiling.

'Well, it isn't me, is it?' persisted Theo. 'I don't want to forget. I might not even want the lobster. Or the rocket if it comes to that.'

'You can watch me eat it then.'

Fearful of starting to lose his advantage, Theo said

impatiently, 'I can't forget what I told you just now, because it's true.'

His mouth defensively crammed with rocket stalks, Guy managed somehow to rejoin, 'Truth doesn't guarantee that you'll remember something.'

'In your experience, is it the other way round?' Theo was aware of sounding a shade spiteful, which wouldn't do at all.

'Let it go, I should, whatever it is.'

'You fucking know what it is!' hissed Theo. 'You've known all along, it's happened exactly as you wanted. How can you expect me not to tell you?'

'There are plenty of other things we don't tell each other,' said Guy with an air of weary self-control. 'It would be colossally boring if we did. I know caring and sharing is what people do these days – maybe I'm getting old, but spare me the pre-millennial touchy-feely bit. Every affair makes its own rhetoric, you must be aware of that.'

Theo, equally in search of decisiveness, stared hard at the purplish slate of the table top. 'I was taught rhetoric was all about utterance,' he muttered.

'Ours isn't, that's the distinction, I thought you understood. A touch paradoxical, I admit, but special, not to say unique.' Guy's face brightened artificially, as if he were coaxing a stubborn child. 'Just imagine, choco-warrior, all over London at this moment men are fucking with each other. Most straight people would probably rather they weren't, because it sickens them to contemplate a chap with his todger up another chap's bum, but there's nothing to be done, is there, it's what we're into, our consuming passion. The thing is . . .' He spread his hands wide as if what he was about to say must be too obvious for explanation. 'Can't you see? Knowing everything about each other, the sheer blinding triviality of it all, great dreary lumps of detail about jobs and parents and who else you've had sex with, why should it matter? You know you don't believe in that.'

Theo was silent for a moment. 'The fact is I do rather. You've never wanted to know what I believe. Our relationship . . .'

'Spare us, for God's sake!' Guy groaned. '"Relationship" is so Diana!'

'Affair then,' said Theo meekly, then, gulping as if constricted by something swallowed whole and threatening instant suffocation, went on, 'I thought I didn't mind, I actually quite enjoyed it at first, or at least imagined I was getting to like it, the way we never go out, we never do a film or a concert or eat restaurant meals or go to exhibitions together. Yes, I know this sounds cheap, but this place really did become like something we'd invented, as though it could disappear at the snap of a finger and then be brought back on a Sunday evening, the most God-awful boring time in the week, with you there on the sofa as I come into the room, with the light across the muscles in your shoulders and that look in your eyes as if you'd been there since last time waiting for me to walk back in.'

Guy looked pleased at this, but said nothing, as though waiting patiently for Theo to finish.

'You think it's what I want,' said Theo, 'but it isn't, even if we do it so many times that I become incapable of imagining any other way of being with you. And sometimes this is what it feels like, though we've only known each other six months. I could add the exact number of days, probably even hours and minutes if I thought about it, only that's the sort of thing you'd hate. Pretty amazing, isn't it, that I can talk about the sort of thing you'd hate after just six months, but it's like . . .' Reckless now, his nostrils tickled, as it were, by the fume from burning boats, Theo exclaimed: 'I've got it! I know what all this reminds me of! I read about this painter called Haydon, in Victorian times, who wanted to do these really massive pictures of big historical scenes from Roman history and Napoleon's battles or whatever. But he couldn't afford a big enough studio, so he had to paint very close up to the canvas and got all his proportions and perspective wrong as a result. That's what it's like with you. I can't get the distance.'

As Theo drew breath, he noticed the expression of astonishment on Guy's face and guessed at once what had caused it. Not the significance of the words themselves, which a foregone conclusion decreed would be quickly brushed aside, but the plain fact of Theo's ability to articulate emotion, this was what had surprised him. For different reasons it had been a trifle staggering to Theo, yet even stranger was the realization that Guy should not have supposed him capable of such eloquence.

'I thought that was what you didn't want,' said Guy eventually.

'What?'

'Distance.'

'You know what I mean. A prospect, a context, something to put you against.'

Guy got up from the table to clear their plates for the next course. 'Well, you can't fucking have it unless I choose.' Disappearing for a moment into the kitchen area, he put his head back round the partition to announce: 'Oh, and by the way, you don't love me.'

'I . . .'

'It's an infatuation, coco pop darling, pure and simple. If you really loved me, you'd know not to talk about it.'

'Is that so Diana too?' asked Theo bitterly.

'Perhaps. It's just so messy, like something people leave

lying about, a sort of litter word which has to be picked up and dealt with.'

'And if I can't?'

Guy, spooning out the mayonnaise, put his head round once more. 'Don't threaten me, that's not nice.'

'Neither are you tonight,' said Theo, standing up decisively, yet careful at the same time that the towel shouldn't fall off him as he did so. 'In fact, you're so unbelievably antagonistic I almost don't recognize you. But the bit I do I love to distraction. I always wanted to use that phrase and now I have. A bit of distraction's good now and then, don't you find? And I know exactly what you're going to say in reply, so don't even bother.'

There was a suitable silence from the other side. Such a ducking beneath the parapet, as it were, simply emboldened Theo the more. Easier to talk to a white wall than to somebody who had made up his mind not to believe you at any cost.

'Everything I do is defined by you, as if you stood behind a camera filming my life. I wake to you, your image complicates my dreams, I choose and decide and reject in the hope I'll deserve your good opinion for the way I do all of them.' The fridge door banged, which made Theo wince in spite of himself. 'So don't have the nerve, the fucking brass neck, to tell me what my feelings are, OK?'

'I've already told you more about yourself than you deserved,' said Guy, emerging with two plates on which the food was disposed with such masterly consideration for colour and texture that one might have imagined it prepared to illustrate a recipe book. The effect was lost on Theo, who suddenly wasn't there.

Guy found him in the bedroom, hastily tugging on his clothes.

'I don't believe you're doing this!'

'You've always had a problem with believing anything,' said Theo, conscious of generalizing extravagantly.

'And what about my feelings?'

'"And I? May I say nothing?" Two years' hard labour to contemplate your abominable crime. Don't bother to see me out, you never do anyway.'

Guy flinched murderously, but Theo, whatever his earlier willing submissions, knew himself in this instant as physically the stronger. Striding grimly to the door, he turned only to say: 'Haydon committed suicide, by the way, but I'm not going to top myself for you,' then flung down the stairs and out into the square, as if the dark beyond were a gulf into which he could purge himself by leaping.

Only when he'd got a little way along Porchester Gardens, with the drifting fringes of rain against his face, did the sense of a vulgar selfishness begin to kick in. He'd not even wanted to hear what Guy might have to offer in his own defence, for fear, he now acknowledged, of being told that he wasn't to be loved in return. A moment ago his own defiance, the delivery of passion wrapped up in a resolve that it should not be flung back at him as something merely illusory, had seemed wonderful, the kind of heroic act of sentimental engagement to which his fancy had always clung. Nothing could be gained now from going back to lay a penitent head on Guy's shoulder, as if in admission that, after all, he'd mistaken the simple glamour of erotic attachment for emotional truth. He was alone as he hadn't wanted to be, defenceless in self-reproach, and seized on a sudden with the most enormous, griping sensation of hunger. He could have done with that lobster salad.

XIX

SOME hours earlier Adam had sat down to write Frankie a letter. Or at any rate to think about the kind of letter it would be appropriate for him to write when finally he had sorted his ideas on the subject into a suitably connected argument. Its subject was Frankie's intentions, or, rather his infuriatingly Delphic concealment of them – supposing, indeed, that there were any, which Adam now and then found himself beginning to doubt. Besides being easier under the circumstances, a letter would allow Frankie the opportunity to consider, whereas a direct interrogation, however much Adam felt inclined to make it, must look merely ruthless and desperate.

The night in the ruin seemed to have gained him nothing. After sex, and the momentary sensation of achievement induced by the instant concurrence of act and desire, they had stood about agreeably for a while on the platform, feeling moonlight warm against the skin and not caring to get dressed in a hurry. Adam was surprised not to experience the truth so often proved that in the immediate aftermath of consummation men loathe the partners on whom, only minutes earlier, they lavished caresses. With a condescension allowable in someone who looked, in that instant, as though he were about to assume a pose in one of the vacant niches along the ruin's curtain wall, Frankie had remained casually affectionate, not disinclined to receive a kiss or to clasp Adam's head against his shoulder. There'd been a certain inspiring degree of reluctance in the way he put on his clothes at last. The lingering embrace given Adam at the window when they got back to the house was like an earnest of something better to arrive in the morning. The pair of them, as it then seemed, went to their separate beds without satiety, but touched by a pleasing sensation of having completed something too long deferred.

Yet in the morning Frankie, who'd evidently slept better than Adam, showed no obvious wish to remember. The knowing glances Adam contrived to give him over breakfast went unreturned and the pretext of packing his bag amid elaborate protestations to Alice about not leaving his room in a mess because he was a real neatness freak, and he'd just have to fold the sheets because it was like, you know, that kind of corny Freudian thing, offered a clear deterrent to any clandestine exchange of last-minute intimacy. So they bundled into Daisy's rattletrap and Adam sank morosely into the back seat, resigned to a pretence of dozing while she drove them back to London in the approximate fashion of People With No Money, as if keeping an eye on the road ahead were far too common an exercise to be taken seriously.

In the week which followed, Adam, whatever the collaborative promptings of lust and impatience, had to respect Frankie's renewed involvement in the culminating rehearsals. A tentative offer of dinner in Clerkenwell was brushed aside, as if Adam really ought to have known better, and two phone calls to Alwyne Villas were fielded by Daisy with an expertise born of countless other such interventions designed to protect her guests from unsympathetic intruders on their creative concentration. It was possible, of course, that Frankie might not have been concentrating to the exclusion of absolutely everybody else, and that even a single-mindedness such as his needed occasional remission (with help, no doubt, from Paul, who didn't strike Adam as one for an early night and a book). The notion of him, on the other hand, as someone able to tune into an obsessive absorption at will was attractive enough to make Daisy's role as self-appointed minder, a handmaid to the muse, seem positively admirable. Added to which, it was what Adam just at present wanted to believe. Used as he was by now to an idea of Frankie's life as a sequence of neatly poised calculations, he understood their sudden remoteness from one another not as the result of a deliberate neglect, but in terms of the careful husbanding of resources. Once *A Keeper of Flocks* had received its première, the choreographer, with suitably Olympian self-assurance, might turn once again to the business so vigorously undertaken that evening in the Hermitage. Adam, with a pardonable complacency, felt he hadn't after all been wrong when administering the rebuff in Edie's nursery. In the implied sense of aptness as to time and place lay a professionalism Frankie couldn't but respect. If this present marginalizing was by way of being a riposte, then he must take it as a singular compliment.

A letter now would be ideal. Frankie's insistent awareness of irony would take it at once as a stratagem of laborious obliquity which suited his view of Adam as somehow incurably British, spectacularly out of touch with his own emotions and thus more likely to use the epistolary medium as a comfortable surrogate. The gesture's sheer quaintness and ineptitude might serve as recommendations of its sincerity. What was more, Adam had always piqued himself on his skill as a letter-writer, relishing the whole business of tone, vocabulary and gradations of self-consciousness. It wasn't simply a matter of telling Frankie what he wanted him to hear, but of saying it in a way he himself would appreciate if he were Frankie. Quite what needed to be said was another matter, but at least he could put a sheet of paper in front of him, drop a cartridge into the Waterman and see what came out.

It augured badly that for a start he had run out of writing paper. Sheets off the printer bank were inadequate if he was bent on trying to impress, even though Frankie, seemingly lacking in consumer snobbery, couldn't honestly have given a toss. It was too late to go down to the shops at Clapham Junction in search of some sort of 'bond' or 'wove' which should lend Adam's endeavours the appropriate air of high seriousness. He heard the swifts screaming above the chestnut trees along the edge of the Common at the reluctant approach of evening. Theo, surely, would have some paper. Nice, slightly queeny paper on which, no doubt, he wrote letters to Guy in those old-fashioned copperplate flourishes of his. They didn't often trespass on one another's domains, but this was in the nature of an emergency. Adam got up and went into Theo's bedroom.

The wood-ash smell was there as always, and the floor was strewn reassuringly with socks, a Hawaiian shirt and a pair of Punto Blanco, which Adam instinctively picked up and sniffed as though to summon Theo like a genie. There was the carton of a Marenzio disc beside the microsystem. One stage gloomier, presumably, than the *Trauer-Ode* he'd been bashing away at last month. Adam had offered to go to the first preview tonight, but Theo had told him to wait until after press night when things had settled down. Let it run for ever and make him a star, thought Adam as he dropped the briefs back carefully on to the carpet and went to open the bureau.

In the first drawer lay what looked as if it might be a cuttings book, placed amid bundles of letters, programmes and files. In the next were computer discs, piles of postcards and a nondescript mess of papers, including ticket stubs, restaurant bills and the baggage control tags from various air journeys. It was when he opened the third drawer that Adam whispered 'Shit!' and for quite some time after having done so sat perfectly still. The swifts went on screaming outside. A police siren whooped and skirled on the road. Eventually, still shaking, he managed to pull himself together sufficiently to go to his own room and pick up the telephone.

'Are you busy, Baz? Can I come over?'

'Like when?'

'Like now.'

'It's not going to be another evening having to listen you moaning on about that slaphead choreographer, is it? I'm not in the mood for another fytte of the Ballad of the Bald Ballerino, thanks. That precious little Goody Two-shoes publicity girl at Haphazard told me today that I can have a launch if I provide my own plonk. I mean, should I do it like Seneca and invite all my friends to watch me slit my wrists in a hot bath or what?'

'Promise I won't say a word about Frankie,' said Adam, 'but Baz, I've got to see you. Now, this instant. Go out to the Indian place and find us some takeaway, nothing special, biriani with mango chutney, raita and two poppadoms each. And maybe a nan. I'll bring the bottles, we'll want more than one.'

'You're being mysterious, I like that, it sounds promising. It'll make up for little Mrs Twiggywinkle at Haphazard. I suppose you couldn't leave me with a clue to ponder while I'm sitting among the flock wallpaper and *filmi-git*?'

'No, I couldn't. Oh, and by the way, make sure your order's mild, no vindaloo or Madras or whatever, because this one'll blow your skull to pieces, unclose the fucking fontanelle, I swear!'

The train north was a crawler, dawdling in and out of Stockwell, stopping for a suspended eternity on the perpetually empty platform at Oval, and shutting down at Kennington while the guard, a gawky boy with blond dreadlocks tied in a bunch, reading Irving Welsh between stops, gossiped to a fat man in an orange jacket about whether Henman deserved to win. Journeys like this one made you want to behave like some peevish *milordo* on the Grand Tour, leaning from the carriage window to bawl out the postilions, screaming for fresh horses or promising a purse of gold pieces if they reached Radicofani by nightfall. Meanwhile, the train sat there, absorbing refugees from the City platform with a sort of Ellis Island give-me-your-poor world-weariness, but showing no special determination to budge. Basil by now would have plumped himself down beside an ashtray in the lugubrious, always nearly empty Peacock Delights Tandoori House. Adam wondered whether they shouldn't have ordered the complete works, dhal, parathas, aloo gobi and some of those sticky pink things with silver on top for pudding. Given what was uppermost in his mind, on the other hand, they might not even feel like the merest crunch of a poppadom.

Extruded finally from the ill-built awkwardness of Russell Square station, he dropped along damp pavements towards Rugby Street. The Cave of Spleen occupied the basement of one of those sensibly proportioned early Georgian buildings which Adam in another life, the life in which he was taller and thinner and younger, with buffed pecs and possibly No Money, had earmarked for himself, along with several hundred other such London houses between Earls Court and Shoreditch in one direction and Camden Town and Kennington in the other. As occupied by Basil the flat recalled nothing so well as those sets of rooms in an Oxford college where dons give tutorials and now and then seduce their pupils, taking care to shift old copies of PMLA or *Past and Present* from the bed before getting down to the business in hand. The dust was as authentic to the general occupational layer as the smell of cigarettes, and the lurching ziggurats of books gave the requisite impression of not quite allowing the ceilings to collapse.

Basil had got as far as spreading out the various takeaway elements on a table by the time Adam arrived. A couple of cloudy-looking wine glasses were placed ready, but Adam fancied a double shot of Talisker was probably more in order just now.

'Water, not ice, they say it's stronger, don't they?'

'Could be. "You do look, my son, in a moved sort." I believe I'm going to enjoy this.'

'I'm not sure "enjoy" is the right word. Give me a decent slug of the creature, and oh yes, maybe a fag, why not? Then you'll be able to see my hand trembling, a very aspen leaf.'

Basil handed the whisky, then slung a leg over the chair arm in an attitude of preparedness. Adam, meanwhile, began slowly to open the envelope he had been carrying with much delicacy all the way from Clapham and handed its contents to Basil, saying quietly, 'Have a look at this.'

After a moment Basil, nodding in recognition, said, 'Yes, I remember, that ridiculously sweaty afternoon we picnicked in the folly and Will told us the story about Molly Hardacre and Lord Severnstoke pretending to be Mister Average. One of Sib's pics, isn't it? Rather good actually. You know what John Huston said about Marilyn Monroe, "the camera loved her", well, it's a bit like that here with Jezebel. She's made him look sort of subversive, I wouldn't have recognized him at first if I'd not been there.' He glanced up at Adam. 'And?'

'Turn over and read what's written on the back.'

Basil did so. 'You'll have to explain the pun. "Be-Guy-ler", sounds a bit feeble. And who the buggery is "my chocolate soldier, my tarbaby"? It's in Jezza's handwriting anyway. Where did you get this, Ad?'

'I'm glad you recognize the writing,' said Adam. 'A bit of corroborative detail always comes in handy. I snitched it, didn't I? Off my lodger, when I was looking for some writing paper in his desk.'

'Which he doesn't keep locked, stupid prat. I'd forgotten you had a lodger, you're so secretive.'

'Not as much as Jeremy, it seems.'

For a minute or two Basil turned the photograph to and fro in his hands. 'You can see it, of course. Or at any rate I can, if I'm getting Jezza's message correctly. I'm surprised you of all people hadn't noticed. I thought you lot could spot each other in the twinkling of an eye.'

Ruefully Adam remembered what Frankie had said about not wanting Jeremy on the team. 'There's a kind of straight man who comes on as if he weren't. It's a sort of wannabe thing, they call them "strays" in America.'

'Perhaps Jezebel's a "gate" by the same token,' snorted Basil. 'Only it's not as simple as that. Jesus, what a dish of pork and greens, eh?'

'And you get the bit about the chocolate soldier.'

Basil nodded. 'I once called him a dinge-queen for a joke, when he was going on about Tricky and Puff Daddy and how their bodies were iconic for the millennium, and he almost gave me a haymaker, said I was implying he was racist. How does . . . what's his name, your lodger?'

'Theo Lestrange. He's an actor.'

'How does he take to being called "tarbaby"? Well, presumably that answers itself, since this is clearly in the "most precious treasures" category. But you still haven't glossed "be-Guy-ler".'

For answer Adam flung himself against the tutorial sofa and pounded the arm with his fists, sneezing at the resultant dust cloud.

'That's the bit that makes my toes curl up! Jezza met Theo in a sauna, apparently. Places like that are hoaching with married men, fishing for trouts in a peculiar river before going home to their wives in Raynes Park or Norwood or wherever. And he came on that he was an investment banker and lived in Kent with a partner – male, which I suppose adds a certain verisimilitude to an otherwise bald and unconvincing narrative – but kept this *garconnière* in Bayswater in which to pleasure his *garçons*. And he calls himself Guy.'

'Which you could say had a certain zigzag honesty about it. One better than calling yourself Bloke or Chap or Type or Geezer.'

'This is serious, Baz.'

'More than you realize,' said Basil with a certain asperity.

'Meaning?'

'You've violated Theo's trust for a start.'

'Hang on, I . . .' '

'And not just by purloining the photo.'

'He's performing tonight. I'll get home before he does.'

'Not just by purloining the photo,' Basil resumed inexorably, 'but by telling me. Do I want to hear this? I know I'm the only unmarried heterosexual man left in London, but precisely for that reason I don't greatly relish the prospect of watching somebody else's marital fantasy melt into air.'

'Jeremy wouldn't let it.'

'I was thinking of Serena. Let's have supper, by the way, shame to let it go cold for the sake of moral imperatives.'

They sat down and began dishing dollops of curry and rice on to the plates, Adam feeling both chastened and slightly irritated at Basil's sober, authoritative assessment but unable to deny convincingly its intrinsic justice.

'Do you think she knows?' he said. 'It's a thing women deny a lot of the time, to themselves most of all. Having bisexual husbands, I mean.'

'Bisexuality, it seems to me, is the ultimate narcissism,' said Basil, with an impatiently epigrammatic wave of his fork. 'It just means "Everybody's dying for me to fuck them." I thought of putting one of them in a novel, but I don't think I had Jeremy in mind, he'd have been much too obvious.' He stuck a wedge of nan in his mouth. 'Isn't now, of course. Any more than Serena. She married him as a deliberate compromise and look where it's got her. You're wrong about women not knowing, incidentally. She does, I'm sure. Jeremy always tonks off to London early when they're in the country, they spend lots of time apart from each other, it's like Queen Alexandra and Edward VII. She's meant to have looked at the King turning rigid on his deathbed, all twenty stone of him, and said, loud enough for Mrs Keppel to hear, "He was my naughty little man but he always came back to me". Probably just our old chum Ben Trovato, by the way, but I'm sure that's how Serena sees it, and I don't want to spoil it for her.'

'How could you exactly? You're Daisy's friend more than hers.'

'I'm not breathing a word of this to Daisy. Can't you imagine how she'd love it? Alice too if it comes to that, though knowing her she'll have guessed already. I've always suspected Alice of keeping a diary and this is exactly the sort of thing they'll find in it after we're all dead.' Basil swigged his wine glumly before announcing, 'I know what Serena feels.'

'Novelist's empathy exercise.'

'I don't mean that. You know how she always jibs at any of us getting too precise about the bedding department. Generally it's boring and prudish and says more about her than us, but over matters like this I can't help feeling a certain sympathy.'

'I thought you'd enjoy it,' admitted Adam weakly. 'Sorry you think it's so vulgar and sordid.'

'Your words, not mine.'

'That's how you seem to see it.'

Basil's glance was bleak with contempt. 'Jezza lording it over a swarthy paramour is neither here not there. I assume he does the lording, he always has to be Number One. And most men lie to their wives, or so the Sunday papers tell us. No, "I will tell you what, Fanny", the essential banality is as follows.' He wiped his mouth on the piece of kitchen roll which had done duty as a napkin, but before he could draw breath and start again, Adam said:

'Jeremy lying to Theo.'

'That's the one. Quite possibly Theo feels happy with something like that, I don't know . . .'

'He'd hate it if he found out.'

'Will he? If you don't tell him?'

'Hey, I'm not responsible for all this!' cried Adam. 'Why do straights always stake out the moral high ground?'

'You may not be responsible for it, but you are within it,' Basil insisted. 'Are you going to tell him?'

Adam paused, pursing his lips in the effort of making a decision which presented itself as one of uncomfortable gravity and feeling ruefully that he should have weighed everything with greater care before sprinting towards the Underground, the photograph in its envelope so triumphantly brandished in anticipation of a stunning *coup de théâtre* in the Cave of Spleen. Accusingly he stared at the greasy remnants of his biriani, as if they'd delayed unconscionably over vouchsafing some oracular answer.

'Not yet,' he said, as honestly as he knew how.

Basil's answering 'Hmm' was doubtful. 'The whole performance is bound to come apart in the end, I suppose. It's amazing they've got this far. Surely your lodger isn't that incurious and acquiescent.'

'He gets nice stuff in return.'

'You betcha. Do they do drugs, do you happen to know? It's the sort of thing Jezza would like to try, he's such an old wannabe. Oh, Ad, why couldn't you have taken him in hand? Nice spot of clubbing at some of those Stygian vaults you go to, a magic capsule or two, a blow job off a peripatetic sex god, and that would have set him up for a week or so until the itch started over again. But this . . . I don't know, a flat in Bayswater and the whole accompanying scenario, I mean honestly! Or dishonestly. "Guy"! It's too blush-making.'

'I can't get over how protective you sound.'

Basil had begun picking abstractedly at the leftover curry and rice. 'There's something wretched about people who have to bend circumstance to their will, a kind of fear that unless they do they'll find out something hideous about themselves. It's a strategy of evasion. You don't need it, neither do I. I'm a minor literary figure of the last years of the twentieth century, who's never had a decent American publisher or been asked to contribute to the *New York Review* or had agents busting a gut to get him a six-figure sum or cut a deal with Channel Four, let alone Hollywood. My books came and go with all the *éclat* of distant railway trucks being shunted into a siding, and I can't even console myself with posthumous fame. There are times, yeah, when it gets to me and I wonder whether I oughtn't to go and be the person under a train who fucks up the tube line when you're trying to get somewhere in a serious spurt . . .'

'Better not be.'

'I won't, simply because of knowing that's how it is. But what does Jezebel know? How does he imagine himself? Does Theo get more "nice stuff", as you blandly put it, for encouraging him in the belief that he's actually been Guy all the time, and that Jeremy, cosmetically married and dragging Sib off to parties with the Culture Secretary and notching up photo opportunities for the Miss Otis Regrets Foundation, and turning a farmhouse in Worcestershire into a Nigel Coates rip-off, is actually an ignis fatuus, a djinn, an afreet, a gytrash? Therapy's meant to do the trick, only I fancy it wouldn't in his case.'

'He'd do better to have it out with Sib.'

'That's not his style. "Joy's soul lies in the doing." The pleasure's in playing away, like kids making tree houses.'

Basil picked up the photograph again and scanned it closely, as if looking for something he'd missed earlier. Then silently he handed it back to Adam, who said slyly, 'She's made him quite sexy, hasn't she?'

'Oh, for Christ's sake, Ad!'

'Well, that's what you meant about Marilyn Monroe. You're right, Sib knows more than she cracks on. You can almost tell what he was thinking about.'

'Not her, that's for sure.'

'No,' muttered Adam, suddenly troubled at the idea of Jeremy enjoying from Theo what he himself until so recently had taken for granted. 'Poor old Jezzbags!' he exclaimed, magnanimously pulling himself together. 'What do you imagine he and Sib have got planned for the millennium?'

XX

DAISY liked to dawdle over breakfast. One of the more tiresome aspects of her schooldays was the speed with which the nuns at the Sacred Heart insisted that you bolted your cereal and toast before bundling dyspeptically into chapel. She'd complained about it to her mother, who pointed out with some truth that since most of the sisters came from poor families in Ireland there probably hadn't been things like porridge and kedgeree for them to take time over in the mornings and that they would have been lucky to get bread and butter. Daisy did not pursue the matter, but made up her mind, with a resolution worthy of Scarlett O'Hara, that as soon as she left school she would never allow herself to be hurried at breakfast again.

In this respect Edie was a distinct plus. Lacking the crude intensity of most babies when it came to food, she seemed to spend much of her time inspecting, as opposed to immediately consuming, what was put in front of her. In this, as in other senses, she became a companion in enjoyment rather than a hindrance to it. Daisy had no intention of spoiling her — brats are boring and their brattishness makes you look parentally incompetent — yet she was determined that her daughter should learn to share the more harmlessly sophisticated of her own pleasures as soon as possible. The noxious ones, such as they were, must arrive in due time. It was enough that Edie wasn't a boy. There was something to make Daisy catch her breath in gratitude at not having to bring up a son, burdening her in adulthood with irksome accusations of irresponsibility and probably turning out gay into the bargain. The thought of having to be a sympathetic mother to a homosexual boy made her shudder at the vulgarity of it all. There'd be, wouldn't there, one of those features on the lifestyle pages where caring mum is shown with her arm slipped round an elfin adolescent sporting an earring and fatigues and the pair of them talk about being each other's best friend. In a comparatively brief life Daisy had been the best friend of around a dozen gay men, but the last thing she would ever have wanted was to have given birth to any of them.

Except possibly Frankie, perhaps because he was the one who least obviously wanted mothering. There was an abundant tribal matrix in New York and Boston, with sisters called things like Donatella and Annunziata who periodically married dull realtors and eye surgeons, and occasionally he would pay the dues of family piety by eating tortellini at an uncle's restaurant. Since his childhood had been generally a fortunate one and there was no suggestion that either of his parents had been less than sensible or affectionate, he placed no demands in front of Daisy apart from those based on the type of mutual loyalty which survives even the most cynical assaults made upon it. He had never expected her to listen indulgently to narratives of love unreciprocated or of the perfidy of some boyfriend who only a week or so earlier had been a paragon of graceful constancy. Indeed, she wondered whether Frankie had ever been seriously in love. The effortless completeness of his detachment satisfactorily explained everything there was to like or admire in him, and Daisy found it odd that other men should ardently pursue the chance of emotional involvement when a relaxed distance like his was so easy to achieve.

Not that he didn't play around. It should have been obvious to her from the start, only somehow it wasn't, that casting Paul Vassilakis as the most dashing of Fernando Pessoa's four selves hadn't simply been prompted by assurances as to the brilliance of his technique. For one thing he was far more glamorous in outline than Frankie's usual leads, chosen as these were on a deliberately subversive basis of facial angularity and the kind of leanness which, unless skilfully used by a choreographer, looks decidedly inelegant. For another Paul had a reputation as a thoroughgoing old-fashioned low-life queer in an era when most male dancers are looking at marriage, a terraced house and babies to follow. She'd mentioned this latter point to Frankie, supposing he hadn't divined it already, without thought as to its potential allure for him. Daisy's guiding principle in life was that people should be kept happy in order to prevent them from growing tedious later on. The actual business of contriving happiness in the first place was often more than she could be bothered with, but she had developed something of a gift for sustaining the flow of pleasure through a careful attention to apparently minor details. Frankie, bored, impatient, congenitally restless, needed entertaining, and Daisy viewed with saturnine contentment the enthusiasm with which he embraced Paul's unimproving formula of clubbing and debauchery as the natural conclusions to a day of intensive class and rehearsal. Observing her house rule of no overnight visitors, Frankie had managed to end up, on various occasions, at Paul's flat in Camden Town, where the pretext of not coming home to disturb her and Edie in the small hours was mutually satisfying to both men.

Like most dancers, Paul had no conversation worth speaking of, and this, according to Daisy's design for the summer, was where Adam came in. His role, as she quickly taught herself to perceive it, was that of engaging Frankie in those areas not directly connected with the pelvic thrust in its various permutations. Sex was to be accommodated only as something accidental, a favour it was up to Frankie to grant rather than Adam to expect. Frankie's tastes in this area were catholic, so far as Daisy knew. Here, also, Paul had seemed almost too conventionally attractive. It wasn't wholly impossible to imagine someone as fubsy and undergrown as Adam, who reminded her of illustrations in the Enid Blyton stories she'd devoured as a child, engaging Frankie's perverse attentions for an hour or so. Adam must feel suitably flattered, and it would give him a name to drop later on. Gays, mega-snobs that they were, liked that sort of thing. It was the equivalent of people in her grandparents' generation decorating the gunroom with the stuffed heads of kudu and hartebeest they'd shot on safari in Tanganyika or Nyasaland. She wasn't sure what sort of animal Frankie would answer to. A cross between a monkey and a cheetah most probably. Whatever nonsuch creatures he was, Adam had no business to be falling in love with him.

Daisy dropped the letter distastefully on the table, next to the butter and a half-emptied coffee cup.

Amused by her reaction, Frankie threw his head back, saying, '*Chacun à son goût*, darling.'

'It's not my *goût*. I wish I could have stood over him and told him what to write.'

'My, my, *la musa ispiratrice*, if only we'd known. It's not a role you ever danced before.' The cerulean gaze transfixed her. 'What would you have told him, precious?'

'Not to use ten words where one would do. Not to downgrade himself, because Americans don't understand about modesty and what it really means . . .'

'It's a variation of arrogance. I've lived long enough in Europe to know that.'

'But if he really is? Modest, that is, rather than arrogant.'

'What the fuck use is modesty? Dance is about showing off.'

Daisy laughed. 'Adam couldn't dance for toffee apples.'

'Then I'm not interested. Only it's kind of nice, I guess, this little English guy who gets the hots for me. As Willy Loman said, "Attention must be paid." I read this poem once about a girl dancing, and the last line goes "The floor lay paved with broken hearts". Fantastic or what? That's how it's got to be, guys fighting duels and shooting themselves, swallowing arsenic, OD-ing just for me, my floor paved with broken hearts. Reckon I'm asking too much?'

'You're utterly ridiculous. I wish Adam thought so too.'

'You mean he doesn't? Disappointed it is I am.'

'There's the little business of picking up the pieces after you leave.'

'So? You and Edie are coming to Paris too, right? When you get back it'll be like nothing happened. Reticence, mortification, secret sorrow.' Frankie picked up the letter and read it over again, humming snatches from the lines as he did so. 'Hey, this bit I like, "The question is how far both of us can believe in it. You, of all people, will appreciate how much can spring from paradox and apparent impossibility." Don't you just adore that? Specially "you of all people". It's obvious what he means.'

'That you're supposed to carry on a relationship with a thousand miles between you.'

Frankie laughed savagely. 'I should have thought a relationship with a thousand miles was easier than one with this particular little Brit.'

'People do, you know,' Daisy persisted, 'quite successfully.'

'Not me, sugarplum. The stuff's got to be there, palpable, fuckable. I'm not interested in doing *La Princesse Lointaine*.'

'Did you ever . . .?' She shrugged, as if the rest was too plain to need articulating.

Frankie sat upright in mock outrage. 'Oh per-*lease*! Does this read like a letter from someone I already fucked with? Where are your powers of deduction, Agatha?' Daisy giggled. 'Don't you like being Agatha? I'm Agatha all the time, so very Miss Christie.'

'It's just something I remember Adam saying.'

'What?'

'Doesn't matter. Anyway you couldn't have, could you?'

'It's that important?'

'Only because it'd seem so uncharacteristic. I don't like to think of your spoiling your image. Or your reputation.'

Frankie winced in alarm. 'Adam'd talk? God, no!'

'A feather in his cap, don't you think? "I scored with leading international choreographer", one of the *Observer*'s "Millennium Makers", along with Jude Law and Alexander McQueen and Daniela bloody Nardini? Irresistible, I should have thought.'

'I don't think that's his style. Adam likes secrets, or hadn't you noticed?'

'I've been noticing things about Adam for at least ten years,' said Daisy smugly. She turned round to wipe Edie's face, covered in an egg-and-breadcrumb impasto. Frankie scanned the letter once more. His evident pleasure at having elicited the thing in the first place was starting ever so slightly to irritate her.

'Will you answer it?' she asked, with a shade more apprehensiveness than intended.

'I don't write letters, you should know that by now.'

'He'll be expecting one.'

'So? If I did, what would I say?'

'That you're not in love with him would be nice. To start with.'

Hastily Daisy turned again to Edie, quietly engaged in the business of squeezing lumps of bread between her fingers.

'Nice for whom? You, me, us? Not for Adam. Can't you see him on Tuesday at the opening, that little sad face, like he's a soufflé somebody left in the oven too long? I want positive vibes, darling, a strict door policy at Aurora's christening, no fucking Carabosse.'

The note reassured her. 'So there we aren't,' she said contentedly. 'We'll just have to pretend you're too busy — which you are — and then if he asks you directly . . .'

'He won't. Guys like that never do. This is part of the scenario. They wait for you to turn. You know what Pessoa says, one of those lines they're putting in the programme, in the "Tobacco Shop" poem, "You who console, who don't exist and so console"? That's me for Adam, that's all the guys he was ever in love with. Or thought he was. I never existed, so he's cool with that.'

Daisy stared at him for a moment, knowing he guessed she'd not understood.

'Adam,' she said, 'has never been cool with anything. Ever.

I'm taking you upstairs, Edie love, away from all these perplexing ambiguities. And then we're going out to buy you something seriously chic for Paris. We can't have you looking a fright when you're being trundled up and down the Luxembourg and getting put down by all those *b.c.b.g.* Frog sprogs.' Bundling Edie into her arms, she turned at the door to look at Frankie, settled comfortably amid the litter of breakfast as if quite agreeable to remaining there for ever. 'Shall I see you tonight?'

'Yeah, maybe, but don't wait for me. And if he calls, you know what to say. But I guess he won't.'

Frankie waited until Daisy was halfway up the stairs before taking the letter to read yet again. Its style had pleased him inordinately, or at least so far as to make him feel that if ever he fell into the letter-writing habit, Adam would be the ideal correspondent, still better unmet, like Tchaikovsky with Madame von Meck. In the weight and balance of its sentences and paragraphs, there was a seriousness underlying the text which continually managed to sidestep pomposity, combined with a not uncongenial air of slightly formal distance, as if after all they did not know each other that well – which was true – and the proposal of a greater intimacy must be offered with a due degree of circumspection. To others perhaps it might have seemed absurdly old-fashioned and the very act of writing a letter, as opposed to uttering the words directly, merely laborious, embarrassing and inept. To Frankie the gesture was admirable in its intrinsic grace. For only the second time in their brief acquaintance Adam had succeeded in surprising him.

The document was, besides, one of apparently effortless reticence, a love letter in which the word itself somehow went unmentioned. He'd had declarations like this before, but none of them as sparely and elegantly phrased, with such an obvious ardour enshrined in the deliberate act of suppression. That Adam should be in love with him seemed the most natural thing in the world, though from her tone rather than her actual words Daisy seemed to suggest that it was a matter of moral choice rather than of instinct or accident. Frankie's experience had taught him otherwise. From his earliest childhood people had been unable to help adoring him, and the sole effort he needed to make in return was that involved in a gracious acceptance of the force of his own enchantments.

Therefore there was no need, in this case, for heartless rejection. Abject insincerity wasn't his style either. 'Look like you mean it, *ciccio*,' said his grandmother to him before he went up, in his crimped white shirt and bow tie, to take his first Communion, and he had done so without difficulty ever since. Lacking conviction in anything but his own talent and vigour, he had inexhaustible gifts for convincing others of his complete faith in the validity of whatever they happened to be doing with him. The ferociously energetic sex in which he and Paul had regularly engaged over the past two months was the better for an element of professionalism in the concentration each brought to the exercise. Frankie wasn't altogether satisfied that Paul's particular intensity was unalloyed by emotion of a kind he himself was incapable, in this respect, of acknowledging, but the maleness here, unlike Adam's, was one which depended on silence for its credibility.

In Frankie's case appetite, from which complications other than purely practical were so gratifying absent, supplied the place of feeling. He had no scruples as to mixing work with dalliance, and Paul was visibly there to be enjoyed. During the weekend in Worcestershire, not in itself disagreeable, he'd found himself lickerishly remembering a physicality which

decorum as much as geography had placed for the time being
out of reach. The rhythm of his breathing, as he lay alone in
bed in the curiously stultified perfection of Jeremy and
Serena's converted farmhouse, reminded him that Paul wasn't
just then sprawled there also, zonked after three hours'
clubbing with maybe a hit of something nice to make it go,
followed by a chill-out somewhere and then the sudden reprise
of forces in a fuck as the full morning broke, pert and
unresponsive. He'd smell that peculiar scent of Greek sweat,
slightly acrid, like certain kinds of dried herb, which experience
had taught him is different from French or Italian or German
sweat, and which, contrary to received wisdom on the subject,
has to do with inheritance rather than diet. He'd feel the
hairiness of Paul's flanks and arsecheeks and the lines of sinew
down his sleep-slackened arms. And always lightly dusting
such moments there'd be a seasoning of transgression, the
sense that as agent and instrument in a serious artistic
enterprise, they had no business to be drifting off to sleep
together behind blinds pulled against a daylight which merely
seemed to aggravate the calculated offence.

There'd been nothing as enjoyably transgressive in his time
with Adam at the ruin, even allowing for Serena's presence as,
presumably, a reluctant witness, about which Frankie of course
had kept silent. The edge of lust that evening had needed
taking off and Adam, considered from certain aspects, might
easily answer the purpose. What he lacked in glamour or
loucheness could be supplied by the moonlight falling so
ingratiatingly on the preposterous Hermitage, in whose tallest
turret a woman sat trapped for as long as Frankie, orchestrating
the occasion, cared not to get dressed. Which was, when he
came to think of it, quite long, since he rather liked the notion
of himself thus naked yet in control of other destinies.

Wanting to retain this position, he had taken the trouble to lie to Daisy, assisted by Adam's careful and apparently deliberate sidestepping of any reference to what had passed between them at the Hermitage. There was something uncomfortably officious in her attempts at directing his response to the letter which instantly put Frankie on his guard. He needed time in which to consider the question of how far she actually disliked the idea for its own sake of Adam seeking a stronger intimacy, and of how much it merely irked her because it upset the arrangements she flattered herself on making. Even the most oblique manoeuvre of possessiveness had not coloured any of her responses until now. Scenting this possibility, Frankie's instinct was to resist, but with subtlety in evasion rather than anything too openly aggressive. If *A Keeper of Flocks* were a success, and even if it weren't, they'd ask him back to London, and the house in Alwyne Villas was as agreeable as anywhere else for hanging out. He just didn't want her getting too heavy, as if expecting something it didn't suit him to offer in return.

Perhaps this was the difference between Daisy and Adam. Whatever the letter's assumptions it did not demand a reply. Rather the opposite in fact, as Frankie had already perceived. So in order to confound the pair of them, Adam wasn't to be put off quite yet. Frankie would break the habit of a lifetime and write a short but entirely courteous answer. Better not to do it here, but at the theatre during one of the breaks in rehearsal. There was a store on Upper Street which sold classy paper and envelopes. Adam'd like that.

XXI

'THERE'S the flower rota to do,' said Serena, 'and I've got to ring the Lampards about tidying up the mess in their field after the barbecue. I thought Gary was going to do it, but he was roofing the barn all last week apparently. And then I'm going over to Fladbury to find a chum for Gaga. The people were really nice, made it sound a perfect match.'

Jeremy looked at her in patient wonder. 'You don't half get attached to things, Sibby.'

'Some things get attached to me. Gaga's so sweet like that, I'm worried I might grow jealous.'

'I very much doubt it.'

'Why?'

'Just do, goosegirl, it's not your *assiette*, as the French say. If I were you, I'd be more worried about Gaga not getting on with the chosen consort, whoever it may be.'

'It's he, not it,' said Serena reprovingly. 'I'm surprised you can find it in you to worry about Gaga. I hope you're not turning soft.'

'Not specially. The fitness training sees to that.'

'I didn't mean it in that way.'

'Only teasing. Did you know there was a review of Baz's book in the paper yesterday? Quite nice, actually. The writer was paying him back for a rave notice last year, so I suppose it doesn't count.'

'I wondered why he was so benign.'

'He's been coming on like a nurse plumping up the pillows in hospital, it's totally uncharacteristic. Last night he asked me whether I was happy. Baz? Can you imagine?'

'And what did you answer?'

Serena's question took Jeremy slightly by surprise.

'Well, yes, I said I was, I hadn't got anything much to ruffle me at present, thanks very much. In fact, I thought it was a bit impertinent.'

'You can hardly expect him to be . . . whatever the opposite of impertinent is, can you?'

'I just didn't think my happiness was any concern of his.'

'You were at school with him, Jay-Jay. And he's a friend of my sister.' Serena uttered both facts with an air of cool logicality which implied that each should have been obvious in the first place. 'So I don't really see why it's not his business. Anyway it's nice that he's concerned.'

Jeremy laughed. 'Sounds like the Princess of Wales! I'm Baz's equivalent of a landmine victim, oh God!'

Serena did not pursue the idea, but picked up her bag and the car keys.

'Be nice to Adam, goosegirl, won't you, if you're dropping in up the road.'

'I've never not been.'

'I know, but say something kind about the ballet. He got seriously into it during rehearsals.'

'Perhaps he'll be able to tell me what it meant. The programme was utterly useless, with all those bits of poetry floating about. And I didn't understand why the man in the waistcoat who kept doing those tiny steps changed into a woman all of a sudden. But that girl doing the muse was brilliant, wasn't she?'

'The guy dancing Pessoa was quite watchable too.'

'I thought he was a bit sinister. He looked like a gangster with that greasy black hair. It seems weird spending your life being four different people. As if you didn't know who you were to start off with.'

'Maybe it was easier for him to write poetry like that,' said Jeremy, not altogether convincingly.

'Don't you have to be sincere to write poetry? If it's any good, I mean. That's what I've always imagined.'

'No, of course not, a lot of the best stuff is just pretending. Or showing off, it's the same thing. If I'd been Pessoa, I'd have wanted to be more than four people. Eight might have been nice. Or sixteen. Or perhaps thirty-two.'

Serena caught the edge of his smile, appealing for her laughter. Not for the first time she felt the wiser of them both. 'Don't be ridiculous. And yes, of course I'll be nice to Adam. He looked so forlorn at that party afterwards, dragging around after Daisy and Frankie. They ought to have been nicer to him, specially Frankie.'

'Why Frankie in particular? Given the circumstances I thought they were both quite attentive. Those sort of occasions are so mwooah-mwooah darling-you-were-marvellous, it's a wonder they noticed poor little Ad at all. Anyway, off you pop, and drive carefully, there's that bend after Marsh Common if you're taking the Croome Road.'

'You're the dangerous driver, not me. And I know the roads

better.' She gave him a little proprietary kiss on the forehead, taking care not to ruffle his hair, something he never liked. Then, with what might have been a sigh of contentment, she went out to the car.

Her lightness of spirit was one she'd felt for several weeks now, ever since that night Frankie and Adam had surprised her in the tower. Or she'd surprised Frankie, she couldn't decide which way round it was. It had been obvious to Serena from the look on Frankie's face that he wasn't going to tell Adam, but she was to be punished for watching by the hanging about which followed. First one, then another cigarette while she was dying for a pee. In any case she hadn't seen absolutely everything, just bits of Adam with Frankie attached to them, or vice versa, and it was all over in minutes. That was the thing about sex, the timing was so completely inappropriate to the degree of expectation.

Whatever her incidental unease she had not been altogether dissatisfied, crouching there on the stair, listening to them talking about Frankie's incomprehensible ballet in the thick, still air before at last getting back into their clothes and sloping off down the track towards Alice and Will's. The moon, supposedly a source of madness, seemed on the contrary an aid to immediate rationality. She'd do nothing, she decided, about Jeremy, because there was nothing to be done, was there? She wasn't into making scenes. Daisy was the one for those when they were little. And their mother, she'd been – still was, indeed – a perfect virtuoso in the genre. The pair of them had spent much time trying to upstage one another in the art of tantrums, flounces and hysterics, while Serena looked on with a regretful air of *si la jeunesse pouvait, si la vieillesse savait*. So she wouldn't advance on Jeremy inquisitorially brandishing a builder's, plumber's and decorator's bill, heavily itemized, for what appeared to be the last phase of work on a flat in Bayswater, which Adam, thinking to be of service, had brought down for him that weekend from the office, to which it had been providently directed. She couldn't absolutely deny the instinct of curiosity which made her open the envelope. It was tiresome, what was more, having not so much to lie to her husband as to conceal the truth from him. She'd never told Jeremy a lie. You just couldn't, could you, not to somebody like that, even if they hid things on so elaborate a scale.

The awareness that he had spent substantial sums of money on the redecoration of a flat she did not even know was his in the first place, while being prepared to lay out equally large amounts on the creation of the *foresteria*, was not as galling to Serena as it should have been. She had returned from the tower that night, after an hour or so more among the owls and what sounded like several nightingales in the copse near the lake, with an extraordinary sense of advantage and self-possession, grounded in her confidence that Jeremy was doing nothing worse, in this instance, than what he did most of the time, which was simply showing off. There was a purpose behind it, no doubt, but she wasn't particularly annoyed at the deceit, since she was certain, with the kind of assurance which by its instinctive nature demands no explanation, that another woman was not involved.

She turned the car neatly into the scrubby little lay-by below Will and Alice's hedge. Jeremy had never mastered the technique of parking unobtrusively. Why on earth had he warned her about the Marsh Common bend? Walking through the house, she found them all with books or the papers in the garden; Alice, Will and Basil under enormous white sunshades on the terrace, and Adam dimly visible amid the clump of fruit trees at the other end.

'I'm off to Fladbury to choose a best friend for Gaga, if anybody wants to come with. Not the most exciting jaunt, I do see, but it might be amusing. And you're all to be there for tea when I get home.'

'At the double,' said Will. 'You're very assertive, Sib, I'm getting a bit antsy, as Frankie would say.'

'Don't mention the "F" word,' whispered Basil. 'Someone's feeling rather nesh.'

'Stop showing off, Baz,' said Serena.

'It's a northern word meaning tender and susceptible.'

'That party, I suppose. But you can hardly blame Frankie for al that huggy-kissy stuff, even though it probably did make Adam jealous.'

'Maybe. A little more attention from that quarter would have helped, no?' Basil put down his book. 'Everything fine with . . .' He gave a flick of his eyes in the direction from which she'd just appeared.

'Jeremy, you mean? I'd soon know if it wasn't. Anything you want me to pick up from Evesham? No? Well, four thirty, teatimeish. I might buy some goodies off the fruit stalls on the way.'

She whisked out almost as swiftly as she had arrived. The three others resumed their reading with an obvious air of waiting to hear her shut the front door. Then Will said, 'I was right. She is.'

'Is what?' asked Alice.

'Assertive.'

'She always was. It's her way of showing it which has altered. I wonder if Jeremy's noticed.'

'Probably not. Anyhow, why should it have changed?'

'Experience?' suggested Basil delphically.

'Even if I knew what you meant I probably wouldn't believe

it. She isn't the sweet indecisive biddy we knew.'

'Nobody's anyone we know, Will, and you aren't either, so stop worrying and eat your bun, as my granny used to say. She's just a bit up today for having to choose a long-time companion for that wretched goose.'

'They're devoted to each other,' said Alice. 'She'd bring her to London if she could, and apparently Gaga goes totally ape when she comes back down.'

'I love the idea of a goose going ape. How will Jeremy cope with two? Will told me about the green bum episode.'

'He'll have to offer it up as a mortification. And when the goslings arrive . . .'

'The shit hits the fan, to coin a phrase. That "goosegirl" he's started calling her will lose its ironic edge.'

'He'll find something else,' said Will, 'he can't live without labels. Shall we ask Adam if he wants to stay put this afternoon? He mightn't be feeling extra sociable.'

'If I were you I'd leave him alone just now,' warned Alice.

Adam knew, without having to move from his deckchair under the apple tree, that they were watching and talking about him. It must, after all, have been fairly obvious why he was here and not in London. He'd seen it in the way Alice's blonde, medieval-looking head was tilted towards him in compassion when she got out of the car at the station, as though she were not so much his cousin as the representative of some host family receiving a refugee. He'd noticed it in the arm Will put round him in the kitchen when they made drinks before supper, and in the solicitude with which he brought out a pile of books for him to take to bed, implying that Adam probably wouldn't sleep much and must require substantial distraction during the hard hours before dawn. Then there was Basil, who, though there ostensibly for the chance it gave him to watch Jeremy and Serena more closely, had somehow at the same time appointed himself Adam's minder and grown more solicitous in the course of a single weekend than he'd shown himself to be in a dozen years.

At times nothing seems more irritating to a gay man than the sympathy, wherever directed, of his straight friends. Adam would not have denied that the visit was by way of being an escape from a situation which threatened less to resolve itself disagreeably than to achieve no outcome at all. What annoyed him, even if he didn't suspect Basil of having primed them all beforehand, was that everyone had clearly guessed the extent of his feelings for Frankie when he'd piqued himself on being careful not to disclose them until the appropriate moment, whenever that should be. It was as though they had made up their minds as to how the scenario ought to conclude, on a basis of what they already knew of him. The sense of their collective heads, not to mention those of Serena and Jeremy, nodding with sage anticipation like a chorus in a Greek play, filled him with silent rage.

He should never have come, yet what would he have done hanging about for the weekend in London with nothing to chew on but a useless sensation of missing Frankie? Who had, hadn't he, remarkable as it must seem, answered his letter. Or rather, sent something which would have to do, but which patently wasn't an answer. In comparison to Adam's two pages, it was disappointingly short. There was no reference, what was more, to anything which could have been identified as an emotion. It seemed merely to imply some sort of blame on Adam's part for not having perceived how totally preoccupied Frankie must be by *A Keeper of Flocks* and for seeking to distract him with matters so personal as this at a time when he couldn't do them justice. Adam's own letter was nevertheless,

Frankie conceded, 'beautiful', a word you could almost hear him say, but which in this case meant so little that he had probably selected it with that in mind. So why didn't Adam wait a while and then come over to Paris, next week maybe, where they could both relax and talk? He'd call Adam before they all left on Monday and they'd fix something one way or the other. Meanwhile, *à bientôt*.

Aw biawnteau, Fernawndeau. The bastard! Yet Adam clung to the letter as if it had been a manuscript beyond price, something dug up at Oxyrhynchus or Nag Hammadi, inscribed with a text whose recovery must alter the face of received wisdom. He had read and reread it with the persistent purpose of seeking to uncover fresh revelations within its crisply phrased lines, written in black ink in a script which, like the writer, managed to be both attractive and impatient while at the same time preserving a studied neutrality. There was a suggestion – or one at least Adam wanted to find – of things carefully put aside until a more acceptable moment, made with a realism entirely characteristic of Frankie, whose idea of appropriateness as somehow a specifically English obsession was hardly supported by his own readiness to cultivate it now. A shade sardonically, Adam thought of the quotation Theo had thrown at him ages ago, the lines about making deliberate difficulties for those you love best, whose pleasure lies in the delay. He was about to prove the truth of the principle, which in any case he already yearned to accept. Frankie, however fretful himself, must think the better of this sober patience and reward his journey to Paris as it deserved. The solution was not quite what Adam originally had in mind, but as somebody accustomed to instant gratification he was prepared, at present, to believe in the value of postponement.

Meanwhile, the weekend seemed to have been designed on

purpose to distract him. Between them on the train from Paddington he and Basil, as far as might be possible in a carriage packed full of potentially inquisitive ears, had pulled the ongoing question of Jeremy as Guy in a variety of directions, none of them yielding a satisfactory answer, if only because, as Adam finally pointed out, the whole affair was up to Theo to deal with as he saw fit. To the extent that it was, in the end, none of their business Basil had been right from the beginning. Adam held firm, on the other hand, against his insistence that Theo should be told. This of all weeks was inauspicious, with the press night of *Troilus and Cressida* looming, and there were vague intimations besides of something in Bayswater having not altogether proceeded according to plan. His instincts towards his lodger had always been broadly protective, never more so than now, at a moment when Theo seemed undefended by anything stronger than his own youthful resilience. Age, Adam was starting to learn, brought its consolations in the way of practicality and the rational perspective induced by the limits attaching to hope and desire.

There was no knowing, besides, what Theo's reaction would be when he learned the truth. Doubtless the fantasy of Jeremy's elaborate deception, in which the flat was clearly a crucial element, had some sort of power which could still captivate him. Looked at purely as a game it wasn't without its advantages, either material or sensual, and the two might choose to go on with the illusion even after truth was substituted for fantasy. The possibility, however, discounted itself almost as soon as Adam considered it. In Theo, as he knew, there lay a positively old-fashioned earnestness, a wish to believe so that things should exist, which must make disenchantment unendurable. Guy could survive, therefore, only as an act of faith. As Jeremy's invention he was doomed.

There was something admirable, nevertheless, if only for being completely unexpected, in the mere fact of Jeremy having invested so much in his own re-creation. It was impossible, Adam and Basil both acknowledged, to accept him any longer as the uncomplicated organism whose innocent vanities they had delighted for so many years to make fun of. The desire to know where Jeremy ended and Guy began was perplexed by the likelihood that Jeremy himself might at various times be on the edge of losing control, feeling Guy coming on irresistibly. Adam longed to know how much, in any case, of the performance, if it were only that, had been shaped by an impulse towards acting up to Theo's wide-eyed expectations, and whether Jeremy had been Guy to anybody else, too cruel a discovery if Theo were ever to make it.

The sole imaginative exercise Adam found genuinely irksome was that of having to conceive of Jeremy as being, in one incarnation at least, a gay man. It was not as if, the truth having been grasped, any attendant mists of doubt had cleared in consequence. You couldn't in that instant summon up a vision of Jeremy with plucked eyebrows and disco tits grinning frenziedly at the camera in the pages of *QX* or *Boyz*, and his peculiar species of preening physicality didn't immediately readjust itself to kick in as that of the homosexual you'd never recognized earlier. Perhaps after all Frankie had been wrong — and there was, wasn't there, a certain luxury in merely being able to entertain that idea — in talking of Jeremy as "the sort you don't want on the team", not because it wasn't true, but because in Jeremy's case, regardless of what any of them now knew, he remained curiously somehow unassigned to either squad, a fact which in itself needed taking seriously.

Serena, for sure, understood how much, but for whatever

reason was waiting on her hour. In the comparatively short space of time which had elapsed since his arrival, Adam had learned to stop feeling sorry for her. Even if being in control mattered less to her than it eternally mattered to Jeremy, she appeared more obviously than ever to have seized command, if not of the realities themselves, then of that overarching spirit of suppression and mendacity which animated them. It seemed to Adam that she knew without having to be told and that the awareness wasn't one which, for the time being, she chose to share even with Alice, who, he imagined, was dying to find out more. She could hardly not have guessed that Serena's new self-possession involved some sort of concealment. He was obscurely reluctant just now to reveal anything to Alice. His role of Frankie's victim was both geniune and convenient, since it distracted her from any suspicion that Adam must be the guardian of secrets more suitable for her possession.

Wary of this aspect, Basil proved a more than competent accomplice, but neither Friday nor Saturday offered him and Adam much in the way of an opportunity for comparing notes at any length. For each of them the pleasure of superior awareness was starting to lose its edge, not so much because of the honourable resolve Basil had forced on Adam not to share the discovery with anyone else, but for the sense they had felt from the outset of a certain uselessness and embarrassment in having gained hold of some, though not all, of the details. What both privately dreaded was a confrontation with Serena. The idea of her as some kind of sphinx, which only a week ago would have seemed ridiculous, now possessed them to the extent that practically nothing she might say or do lacked the potential for some alternative interpretation. Adam's general mistrust of innocence, already strong enough, was fortified still more by what he accepted as her practised deviousness, designed to shield Jeremy from inconvenient curiosity and to cover her own manoeuvres, characteristically gradual and oblique whatever their object. From this it was the easiest of steps to a nervous assumption of her alertness as all-inclusive, a sort of lifted veil beneath which she could peer unobstructed at them as they tried to dodge her.

Hence her disappearance that morning in search of a gander was a matter for some relief, though Basil refused to accept this as a genuine reason for leaving Jeremy on his own. Adam, on the other hand, felt inclined to ponder the apparent serenity which had marked Jeremy's behaviour for the last forty-eight hours. He ought to have seemed restive at not being with Theo or simply at being out of London, yet he had never appeared more affable and relaxed. It was evident, as indeed it had been when they were both at the office during the week, that he had made himself master of a set of circumstances, probably involving Theo, which merely required a certain measure of patience in order to produce a favourable result. Charm, attentiveness, the ideal posture, if not necessarily the actual virtue, of a listener, were all luxuries Jeremy could afford within his general aura of command, and he was lavish now in indulging them.

Only the slightest suggestion of strain was traceable in his features at tea, when a jubilant Serena retailed her profitable morning to the others. Jeremy had never cared for Gaga, yet was prepared to put up with her honking, her mess and her aggressive ubiquity for the sake of domestic tranquillity. There was some mild amusement to be gained, besides, from the mere fact that his wife's most marked eccentricity should be her fondness for a pet goose. It had occurred to Adam more than once, however, to consider whether Gaga would ever be forgiven for the green bottom episode which had sent Jeremy into such a spin a few weeks back. In medieval France pigs and cats had been publicly executed for less. Gaga, through innocently undermining his vanity, must stand condemned already.

Serena, on the other hand, was busy predicting a fresh lease of life with the gander.

'He's lovely!' she exclaimed. 'I was going to say an absolute duck, but wrong bird if yer foller me. No, seriously, one glance and it was undying love.'

'Now *Swan Lake*'s been commandeered by the blokes you can go one better and stage a goose version,' said Adam, at which Jeremy gave a benignly irreverent giggle.

'Don't bitch, Ad, I mean it, he's a work of art.'

'I wasn't bitching, honest, Miss. We're all very happy for you.'

'Insincerity's worse still. It's Gaga you should be happy for. This is a pure-bred Emden, with really subtle bits of grey on the wing feathers, and his bill's a sort of light tangerine colour, whereas hers is more yellow. I thought I'd make them both a kind of goose wedding cake and we could have a little ceremony.'

Jeremy at this moment was the pattern of self-control.

'You'll have to do proper photos,' said Will. 'It'll be like Becks and Posh.'

'They've got to be colour, not black and white,' added Alice.

'I fancy champagne might be bad for them though,' Serena said solemnly, as if already having weighed up the option. 'And then there's a name to choose. That's one we're going to have to think very carefully about.'

'Who's "we" exactly?' muttered Basil, so that only Adam could hear, but Serena, too quick for him, said:

'What?'

'Count me out was all I meant, I'm hopeless at names. Except for characters in books.'

'I'm sure Sibby the goosegirl can come up with something,' said Jeremy. 'She usually does. But just give us time, eh? The male of the species is going to take a bit of getting used to.'

Adam caught Basil's eye and felt a trifle cheap for doing so. 'You realize you're going to have to enlarge the pond,' he said.

'I should go the whole hog and turn it into a lake,' said Will. 'After the *foresteria* there's no saying what you won't be at.'

'Yes, well, we're not made of money,' laughed Jeremy.

'Some of us,' Serena said quietly. 'You like your tea strong, don't you, Ad? Like a workman.'

'He'd always rather have the workman, if forced to choose,' said Basil.

There was a light breeze blowing, making the sun tolerable rather than oppressive as they might have expected. Soon enough they all got up and started to drift about the garden, while Gaga, whose fiefdom this essentially was, padded to and fro along the grass borders as though she were a duchess who had thrown open the grounds for the day and was keeping a condescending eye on *le peuple* enjoying its afternoon out. Adam thought he understood now why Jeremy hadn't made more fuss about the gander's impending arrival. Even though a troop of goslings might be a little too much to stomach, the role of goosegirl for Serena would supply another level of rustic distraction on top of parish council meetings and fundraising for the bells. Sunday departures would thus get a little earlier, and he'd have more time, presumably, for getting himself into character as Guy before Theo showed up. Such a degree of calculation ought to have seemed dastardly, but with the light glistening on the leaves of the pear trees and a gentle susurration among the pleached hornbeam hedges it was somehow easier to think of it as just a mutually satisfying arrangement, enabling each of them to indulge their private diversions without crossing one another.

At the bottom of the hornbeam alley lay the bit of their garden Adam liked best, an open space for rough grass behind a semicircular plantation, from which you could look across a sort of ha-ha into the field beyond and hedgy Worcestershire stretching eastwards, with a couple of church towers and a red farmhouse or two to vary the prospect. He sat down on a bench in the slope of shade and gazed out into the landscape with a vague sense of temporary safety, something almost like contentment, and was not displeased to watch Gaga appearing round the corner of the alley. She paused for a moment, neck bent back, head alert, acknowledging his presence before starting to peck among the long grass. Then he heard Serena's voice calling 'Are you there, Gaga my love? Are you hiding from me?' and winced apprehensively as she came into view.

'We were having a bit of quality time together, as people call it,' Adam said.

'I didn't want to interrupt.' She came and sat down beside him. 'The light's good today, you can see right over to the belvedere on Bricklehampton Court.'

'You're lucky having this. I just look out on a lot of London plane trees and a designated bus route.'

'Yes, we are. I was thinking about that earlier, coming back from Fladbury. Honestly, I thought, I've got nothing to complain about.'

Adam glanced at Serena sidelong, hoping his face conveyed nothing of doubt or incredulity.

'How did you enjoy the ballet the other night?' he asked.

'We never got to talk about it properly.'

Her eyes widened. 'I thought it was so clever, the way they did that shape-changing business. The music was a bit too modern for me. But the lighting was marvellous. Frankie must be pleased. He was anyway, wasn't he, you could see that afterwards. It's had such good notices.'

'I thought you didn't read the papers,' said Adam, marvelling at her charitable insincerity.

'Jay-Jay read out the one in *The Times* and Alice showed me the *Guardian* crit, which was ecstatic.' Looking around for Gaga, who had wandered off up the alley, Serena asked, 'Did you get to see him after the party? Frankie, did he . . .?'

'No. He went off with some people from the cast.'

'And tomorrow he's off to Paris, I suppose,' she said breezily, 'with my sister in tow, God knows why. Keeps him off the streets, presumably.'

'I can't imagine Daisy doing that, can you? She just went along with Edie for the ride.'

'Story of her life. Are you going too?'

Adam, experiencing one sort of surprise, was quick to feign another. 'Why on earth should I?'

'Might be worth a go.' Serena leaned over and took his hand. Her eyes were wider than ever. 'I shouldn't leave it too long if I were you. Now where's that silly bird of mine?'

As they walked back slowly up the garden, Adam still wondering how Serena could have guessed of his intention to take Frankie at his word and meet him in Paris, they saw Will coming across the lawn.

'Jezza's on the phone to someone, and then he's off on his jog, and Gaga's into your guest wing and poor Al is trying to get her out. I don't know how she got in there to start with.'

'I left the door open,' shouted Basil from the house.

'Well, you're a disgrace and we'll never ask you again,' Serena called back.

'Promise?'

'No, seriously, Baz, you mustn't, otherwise she might start thinking of it as home.'

'Everywhere's home to Gaga in a sort of way,' said Adam. Serena smiled at him, a big, melting grin, as if he'd excelled himself in the business of saying the right thing.

'You're a world-class sweetie-pie, Ad. We promise to love you for ever.'

'Who's we?'

'Gaga and me, of course. And the as yet unnamed consort.'

Alice had somehow managed to coax the goose back into the big kitchen yard in front of the garages. The almost completed *foresteria*, with its new roof of Welsh slate and its big windows, the glazing bars freshly whitened, lay on the opposite side and even Basil was constrained to acknowledge that it looked not too shabby, all things considered.

'I don't know what exactly we haven't considered,' said Serena, happy enough with everything not to want to get the bearings of his remark.

'The question is whether you use it as a grace-and-favour residence,' Basil said, 'or a punishment island. Do guests get banished there for snoring?'

'Or something else,' said Alice.

'At any rate there won't be your son and daughter giggling in the corridor,' retorted Basil.

'Oops! Walked into that one.'

'We shall consult your wishes, Baz darling,' said Serena, 'as we always end up doing. Here's Jay, ask him what he thinks, he's always got a plan.'

Jeremy came out on to the steps, kitted up for his early

evening run. The sudden radiance of him silenced them all for a moment, like the apparition of something divine. With a confidence born of accomplishment he stood, hands on hips, the sun catching those waves of reddish-blond curls which made you think of an imperial coin portrait. You could see the veins along his biceps and those down the hollows of his lightly tanned thighs below the line of the red trunks. He looked no different now, Adam thought, from all the gay men you watch at half past six on any fine evening in summer sweating their way earnestly along the tracks around the edge of Clapham Common or past the Nightingale Walk tennis courts. Considered thus, it was possible for the briefest of moments to understand how much Theo must want to believe in him.

'Knock 'em dead, Jez,' said Will good-naturedly.

'I intend to. What am I meant to have a plan for?'

'Everything, according to your wife. Do you ever think of just running up and down the lane, or is the preliminary car journey to a local beauty spot essential?'

'Something like that. You ought to join me, it'd do you good.'

'Have you ever seen Will run?' said Alice. 'His arms go up and down like a windmill.'

'Oh, I expect it's rather decorative,' Serena said, vaguely amiable. 'I'm going over to make sure Gaga hasn't left anything untoward in the *foresteria*. You were naughty to leave that door open, Baz, you know how inquisitive she is.'

'It's a way you women have, I should have remembered.'

Crossing the yard, Serena motioned towards Gaga and then blew her a kiss. Jeremy, pulling down his vest, which had ridden up to show the narrow line of hair running below his navel, announced:

'I'll be off then. And see you all tomorrow morning, I expect. We've got that project to look through, Ad.'

'Don't start coming on like a workaholic because you're in your fitness gear.'

'Who you are is what you wear,' Jeremy flung back over his shoulder as he opened the car. 'Or maybe it's the other way round.'

'More a case of what you don't wear,' murmured Alice as they watched him bending over to move something from the driving seat, so that you saw the scarlet lycra sheer across the contours of his arse. 'Why exactly are we standing here giving the master a send-off? Even Gaga's at it.'

The goose moved with a questing yet always imperious air along the side of the *foresteria*, until a little tuft of something growing at the foot of the wall halted her dowager-like progress.

'I'll never forgive you if you get to look like that,' Alice said to Adam as Jeremy finally swung his legs into the car.

'Nowadays, people with bodies like Jezebel's are the ones who get forgiven most,' rejoined Adam sombrely. Feeling her solicitous stare on him and wishing it would go away, he kept on looking at the spectral shape of Serena moving to and fro inside the *foresteria*.

Jeremy had started the car. To get it between the gatepiers of the yard it was necessary to edge it slightly on one side and then back a bit, so as to avoid the little stone wheel-buffers at the base of each pillar. Now, as he shot forward in a practised manoeuvre, Gaga ambled out behind the vehicle. Its swift, nonchalant reverse caught her unawares, and for a moment she seemed to disappear under the wheels, before Jeremy drove on through the gateway to speed down the drive towards the road. Their sudden shouts were unavailing, and the execution was almost soundless in any case beneath the gravel-scrunching and the noise of the engine. For an instant the four of them standing on the steps remained numb with amazement at the abruptness of it all, at the grey bird lying there between the tyre marks, her neck skewed and bloody, and at Serena, who had seen everything, a horrorstruck spectre behind the upstairs window. Then Alice darted off across the yard, while Will began awkwardly to rearrange Gaga as something better than a bundle of feathers.

'Hit and run,' muttered Basil. 'Stupid cunt.' There was no one to hear him. Adam had slipped into the house and picked up the phone in the kitchen. He needed to make absolutely certain that Theo this time would be there when he got home.

XXII

ONE of these days somebody will write a history of the Stanley knife, one of those little books which became so popular at the end of the 1990s on subjects like cod or the longitude or the making of porcelain. They'll praise its versatility and swiftness of execution in the hands, not merely of artists, leather workers and paper-cutters, but of muggers and murderers and those who purpose is solely that of carving an initial or two on the faces of others as something by which to remember them.

This thought crossed Serena's mind as she began slashing the white leather of the sofa. There was a technique to be acquired with Stanley knives, she realized, and once you'd mastered it they were a blessing in terms of efficiency. The mistake she'd made initially was in starting on the pillows without pulling off the cases first. That way it was easier to get at the feathers and scatter them all over the room before carefully scoring open the mattress. After that the duvet was a breeze, and as for the sheets, it was a simple matter of cutting a hole or two and then ripping them across, taking care to do it in such a way as to prevent any plausible repair. For the clothes piled in the wardrobe you had to use a pair of scissors to begin with, the heavy-duty sort sold by the deserving young unemployed from baskets of chamois leathers, tea cloths and ironing board covers, but the knife worked like a dream when it came to slitting the T-shirts and those great armfuls, as they seemed to her, of white, white underpants, the names – All Star, Zara, Olaf Benz, Nikos, Armani – picked out with such bravado around the waistband.

The bathroom was just as much of a doddle. She had taken the trouble to bring both a claw hammer and a mallet, so in no time the gels, shampoos and liquid soap dispensers had been swept off the shelves, themselves providently smashed with two or three neat little blows. For good measure she knocked the shower head out of true and stuffed the lavatory bowl full of towels, before opening whatever bottles might have survived the first attack and pouring their contents over the snowy mound like sauce on top of ice cream. The kitchen, too, could be dealt with in a matter of minutes. Opening the cupboards, she simply dragged the hammer's end along the ranks of glasses, so that they rumbled to their destiny on the stone worktops below, then dropped the plates on the floor as if to say 'Oops, silly me!' or 'Butterfingers!' Everything in the fridge must then be unstoppered and flung as exuberantly as possible over the staring white surfaces of the living area. With a spoon for better aim, she lobbed pesto at the screen, hurled sundried tomatoes towards the right-hand wall and sprinkled the carpet with a bottleful of preserved gooseberries from a shop in Place Vendome.

Should she pop the champagne? Perhaps just one bottle for luck, shaken up and down, as if at a Formula One victory celebration, to get the fizz. The rest she'd cart downstairs: shame to waste decent stuff like that. Probably better to leave the pots untouched, but rolling them across the floor among the goo on the rug would at least make them look as if they'd fallen victim to the general devastation. Then in the process of deftly smashing the lamps, she remembered something left unattended to in the bedroom. With the hammer's claw end she pulled out the stereo and quickly disabled its speakers. All that was left now was to put a signature to her achievement with the paint-spray she'd bought at the last minute from an art shop on Westbourne Grove.

Taking off her overall, Serena looked around her at the desolation she had made and stood for a moment in slow-breathing triumph at its swiftly effected totality. Then something she realized she'd wanted to ignore earlier caught her eye. Knocked on to the floor beside the bed and half-hidden by a rag of the dismembered pillow lay a framed photograph of a young black man wearing a pale-coloured shirt and glamorously lit to enhance the strong lines of his face and the look of exhilaration, positively childlike, in his eyes. Briefly she pondered on the image and read what was written across it, before slipping it into her toolbag and, picking up the box with the remaining champagne bottles, descended to the front door.

'All finished?' said Alice, waiting, as promised, in the car.

'All finished,' answered Serena. 'Brilliant of you to think of me trying those keys. One of these days I must ask him why he put them in the Michael Cardew. Actually there are several things I thought I'd ask him when we've got a moment.'

Alice drove on for a while in silence towards the Bayswater Road. Then she said:

'Sib?'

'Mm?'

'You're going to divorce him, right? Not just a separation or anything.'

Serena burst into laughter. 'I was brought up a Catholic, so divorce over my dead body, darling. Anyway what'd be the point? And a separation . . . well, he'd probably think that was a bit naff.' She paused to look at Alice, who still didn't seem altogether to understand. 'I don't think we'll have any more trouble, do you?'

Alice frowned at the road.

XXIII

SITTING in the ruin made out of his flat, Jeremy waited for
Theo. If he turned his back to the window, where the blind had
been ripped in such a way as to hang with a crazy air of always
being just about to tumble off its roller on to the floor, he could
avoid looking at the inscription sprayed across one wall, from
which the big abstract had been carefully unscrewed so as to
leave enough room for the words 'Molly Hardacre, her tag' and
a row of enormous Xs. Easier, or less painful at any rate, to
survey the kitchen, with the door of the empty fridge hanging
open, the crumbled remnants of a whole pecorino littering the
mash of shivered glass and crockery, and the slate worktop
lacquered and sticky with libations from a champagne bottle
left standing upright like some hopeless marker placed there by
a passing explorer.

For a mercy the taps hadn't been turned on, either here or in
the bathroom, except one running desultorily over a pile of
shards in the washbasin. A glance into the bedroom made his

blood run cold at the sheer completeness with which everything except the bedstead had been placed beyond any
possibility of redemption. He had knelt down for a moment or
two, browsing in numb, repetitive desperation among the
shredded shirts, the black Schott jacket with its wadding
yanked out of the sleeves, the boots with their sides hacked and
gouged, and the socks so sedulously sliced at the toes.
Something here threatened to demand his admiration for the
professionalism, the regard for detail, by which his entire
apparatus of happiness had been thus extinguished.

He couldn't imagine how he was going to start being Guy
again. Everything else could be replaced tomorrow – the
shower gels, the olive oil, the duvet cover, the lamps – but the
essence of Guy was precisely the fact that his surface was so
immaculately prepared, without the least detectable flaw
running across it. In the bedroom mirror, which from
compunction or superstition had been left untouched like those
around the shower and in the hallway, Jeremy looked forlornly
for that part of himself he most enjoyed because its fashioning
had nothing to do with anybody else, an autonomous creation
to whose energies and perspectives he seemed to have devoted
years of endeavour, even if its reality had only been credible
for the past seven months. The flat was there to be Guy in, but
not like this, corrupted or effaced, and needing resurrection
when the whole point lay in what was perfect being in-
destructible.

Only Theo could help. Jeremy regretted having put him off
last week when, after carefully measured dialogue over the
mobile, they seemed to have arrived at something like a
civilized truce. Then this morning, when he knew Theo was
free and would have liked nothing better than an unscheduled
daytime rendezvous in Bayswater, the voice had been chillingly

matter-of-fact, tinged by no sort of excitement.

'Yeah, OK, I'll be there, just don't bother to hang around if I'm late.'

'Midday, choccy.'

'Yes, you said.'

'I'll make it worth your while, tarbaby.'

'Whatever.'

A spot of attitude maybe? He was like that. Well, they all were, honestly, weren't they, in Jeremy's experience, despite their refinements, and Theo was quite bizarrely refined, to the point where you suspected him of not really liking Nina Simone and wanting Mozart instead. One had to be on one's guard over little surprises of that kind. He simply wasn't like the others, and for this very reason he might be useful now, not just with the tidying up, but in the business of reassembling Guy, without, of course, having to be told that somebody else had invented him.

'It's gone.'

Jeremy, perched on the edge of the wrecked bed, swung round in amazement at hearing his voice.

'Choccy! How the hell did you get in?'

'You left both doors open,' said Theo, as if wearily answering a stupid question. 'My picture, it's gone.'

'Did you think it'd still be here?'

'Everything else is. Who's Molly Hardacre?'

Jeremy had got up and begun to move across the room when the sight of Theo, motionless and cold, halted him in his tracks. In his blue shirt, carefully pressed beige trousers and suede loafers, he was no one immediately recognizable.

'Of course I didn't really want you to find it all like this,' Jeremy said, ignoring Theo's question, 'but since you're here . . .'

'I can help you tidy up, yes?' Theo's lips pursed in evident distaste at the conclusion. 'Is that it?'

'Something like that,' admitted Jeremy, laughing uneasily and irked in any case by the way Theo appeared to be so consistently ready to misunderstand him.

'I don't do tidying up, as a rule. Not for other people anyway, unless I'm feeling guilty. Which at present I'm not. That was something I used to like about you.' Theo's long fingers ran abstractedly up and down the door frame. 'The way you never made me feel guilty. I oughtn't to have liked it, but I did.'

Jeremy leaned back on his hands across what remained of the mattress. Theo had puzzled him before, yet never so much as in this instant.

'What's so virtuous about feeling guilty?'

Theo didn't answer. Instead, gesturing towards the kitchen, he said quietly: 'You know who did this, don't you?'

'It's not really important now.' Jeremy stood up once more, angry at Theo's near-impassivity and wanting to shake him out of it. They'd not seen one another for a fortnight, and he felt entitled, at this of all moments, to a little more enthusiasm.

'What's eating you, tarbabes? Aren't they enjoying your tartuffo ice cream down The Cut? I thought the leather jock was a one-size-fits-all. Even on a big coco pop like yours.'

Theo didn't smile. His eyes, on the contrary, seemed brimming with contempt. Furious at such silent insolence, Jeremy burst out:

'Look, what the fuck are you messing me around for? You can see what's happened, I don't see why I should have to explain. The least you could do is offer to help. I can't exactly do it on my own, can I?'

Theo was still silent. Again Jeremy got up, possessed now

with an insane desire physically to shake him out of his glacial composure.

'We really can't be doing with this!' he cried. 'Chocolate soldiers mustn't . . .'

But before he could go on, Theo, in the deftest of movements, had jerked him forward with one hand while jamming the other over his mouth hard enough to choke him. Disagreeably close to Jeremy's ear he whispered:

'Don't ever say those words again. To anybody. Got that? Or any of those other names you call me.' Pushing against Jeremy's face, he succeeded in flinging him back on to the bed. 'Ever.'

'What's got into you?'

'I've got into me. Probably I wasn't there before. I honestly don't know how I permitted you to do it.'

'To do what, for Christ's sake?'

'All last night I lay awake thinking about it, and the night before that. And I saw what I was.'

'All right then,' said Jeremy sullenly. Theo, absorbed by the truth so long delayed in arriving, no longer bothered to look at him.

'You were always reminding me. You kept on reminding me that I'm black.'

'I thought that was the whole point.'

Theo put his hands up to his face, having grasped at this moment that Jeremy, in addition to his other assets, might be capable of stupidity. 'I suppose I can't really blame you,' he said, still talking to the wall. 'It's something most people do. Black people too, it's quite cringe-making sometimes when they do it. You get made to remember all the time. I just . . .' He turned to look at Jeremy, hunched there in wonder and apprehensiveness. 'I didn't need you to keep on telling me, that's all. I've always known I was. Adam's good like that. He just lets it mean whatever I want. Or at least he's tactful enough to give me that impression.'

That name, by slipping out a little earlier than Theo had intended, startled them both.

'Which Adam are we talking about?'

'Adam Killigrew. Your friend. Who told me your wife took the photo. She's called Serena, right? And your name's really Jeremy.'

Listening to Theo's voice going up instead of down at the end of each phrase, Jeremy recalled his own remark on the subject to Will at the christening party. Anything was better than having to listen to Theo saying:

'There isn't a place called Chillingbourne in Kent, where you were supposed to live with somebody named Mark in an oast house. There's Sittingbourne and there's Chilham, but no Chillingbourne. I looked it up in the atlas. That was after Adam told me. I wouldn't have done it before.'

'That little bastard,' muttered Jeremy.

'Yes, maybe. But then so are you, for lying to me.'

'Why not? You enjoyed it.'

'Like "we had some good times, didn't we?" Come on, Jeremy!'

'I wish you wouldn't call me that. Some fucking revenge this is.'

'I don't want revenge.'

'Are you angry with me then? Expect me to say sorry?'

'Angry, no, not specially. And I don't expect you to apologize, because you're temperamentally incapable of that sort of thing.'

Jeremy stayed silent for a moment, then asked: 'When did Adam tell you?'

'On Monday night, after I came back from the theatre. It wasn't the best of times, but he was still anxious not to hurt me.'

'I suppose he didn't think about me. His best friend.'

Theo laughed. 'Bollocks, Jeremy, you're not his best friend, I am. It doesn't matter either way. He's gone to Paris for a couple of days, but you probably knew that.'

'I can't believe he did this.'

'Tough.'

'So why are you here?'

'Because telling you over the phone would have been too easy. And I somehow feel you wouldn't have taken a letter seriously, if I'd sat down and written one. You'd have thought I was letting you off.'

'As if I'd done something wrong in the first place. It was only a different name, choc . . . Theo.'

'Just a bit more than that.' Theo took an audible breath and looked at his watch. 'Got to go now, Jeremy. And I haven't said half the things I wanted to, which is probably just as well. You can always get Adam to tell you. I said most of them to him the other night.'

Jeremy stared at Theo in impenetrable disbelief. 'Are you walking out on me?'

Theo nodded. 'Like I walked in.'

'No you didn't,' Jeremy objected peevishly. 'I found you, remember? When you were feeling blue after that dodgy audition.'

'What's the matter, can't you cope with metaphor all of a sudden? Or are you going to tell me it was actually a simile?'

'Oh, for God's sake, stop wrong-footing me all the time! I can't handle it just now, I should have thought that was obvious.'

Theo leaned back against the door frame, his face trans-fused with the relief which comes from successful deduction. 'You hate me knowing, that's what it is. I don't mean about you pretending to be someone else, though no doubt that pisses you off a bit. I mean knowing things, anything, and always trying to know a bit more. Because you want me to be just another dumbo nigger boy you fished out of the steam-room in a gay tub where your sort goes to fool around. The kind of guy you did it with before.' Jeremy winced. 'I'm not the first, I realize that. Though I'll bet you were careful to check them out for knives and things when you brought them back here. We didn't want blood on the carpet, did we, and Duwayne doing a runner all the way down to Railton Road with your platinum plastic.'

'You're the only one I ever brought here, supposing that matters.'

'Yeah, I forgot, I was intended for the fucking fairy on the top of the designer Christmas tree.'

'It's true, I promise.' Anyone other than Theo might have been moved by Jeremy's pathetic insistence.

'I'm simply not interested in being some grinning Sambo on an old tin of boot polish, that's all.'

'It never bothered you earlier. When you used to ask me about the Ruinart and those artists in the Saatchi catalogue and whether I'd ever met Isabella Blow,' Jeremy remonstrated, in a final effort at recovering his authority. 'And now, just because you think you've found me out, I'm suddenly transformed into the biggest cheapskate in London.'

'No, not cheap exactly,' Theo began.

'Thanks a bundle.'

'Merely not very original. Don't get me wrong, Jeremy, I'm not ungrateful. You're probably right about all this happening because Adam blew your cover. But I'm not having you blaming him, OK?'

'Oh, God, we're so protective of little Master Killigrew!'

'Like he is of me. That's something else I've only just started to appreciate.' Theo paused, then, as if catching an idea never properly pursued before, asked: 'Have you ever heard of Diedrich Becker?'

Jeremy looked puzzled. 'You don't mean David Beckham, do you?'

'Forget it.' He had turned to leave when Jeremy said:

'May I ask you something?'

'That's the first time you've ever done that. Said "may I" instead of just pushing ahead. It's rather nice. What exactly?'

'Are you . . . Do you still love me?'

'Since you mention it, and I wasn't supposed to . . .' Theo halted, smiling to himself in amazement at the question. 'Quite a lot, actually. Which is why I never want to see you again. Probably I won't be able to stop myself asking Adam now and then how you're doing, but I'll try. And you're not going to give him the push, are you? That'd be just spiteful. Guy would never do a thing like that.'

Jeremy shook his head. 'You just dropped in so as to drop me. I'm not hearing this!'

'From me you are. "Pardon's the word to all". Write that down, look it up, it'll help take your mind off missing me. Oh, and we never talked about your wife, did we? Adam says she's rather nice, if that's any consolation.'

Theo ran downstairs and out of the front door, left open as he found it, then steadied himself for a moment against the area railing in a sort of tremulous exhaustion, a reactive aftershock, as it were, of his earlier self-control. The effort involved in being magnanimous was greater than expected, but in this at least he had satisfied himself. 'He too is an Alexander.' It was easier for Alexander, only having to tell a bunch of Persian princesses that they could have their jewels back. To forgive an elaborate construction of falsehood which he had accepted as truth was far, far harder, yet he had done so at the cost of perpetual embarrassment. It wasn't his fault if Jeremy learned nothing from the experience. For a moment, however, Theo toyed with the idea of going back inside and helping him clear up the mess, but as he stood there irresolutely, a man he hadn't bothered to notice approaching along the pavement, in black jeans too short for him and a denim jacket, turned in over the step towards the house.

'Is Jeremy up there?' he asked, looking directly at Theo, his eyes full of assumption. Nice-looking in that thoughtless, unmoisturized way straight men have. Theo, nodding him onwards, couldn't help observing as he pushed open the door and called 'Jezza?' into the hall, that in one of his socks there was a large hole.

XXIV

AT some time during his late twenties, when he'd gathered enough experience to make an informed judgement, Adam grasped the simple truth that a love affair possesses more than one scenario. What actually takes place, influenced maybe by the encouragement or censure of friends and the intervention of possible rivals, is not necessarily what either of the central pair tells himself he wishes would happen. Added to which there often exists another kind of script altogether, truculent and subversive as some Jacobean antimasque peopled with hodge-puddings, jack-o'-lanterns, flibbertigibbets, gypsies, bedlams, comic Welshmen and Virginian selvages, a plot outline designed by one of the lovers to place him beyond the tyrannous reach of his own feelings. More than one liaison had started thus, with Adam in the position of an arriving guest whose first precaution is to check the timetable in order to make absolutely certain of the trains available for his departure.

Not that this was quite yet a fully fledged affair, whatever his determination that it should become one. He had nothing to throw in Frankie's face as proof except that neatly turned little letter of a week or so back, by now somewhat crumpled through overenthusiastic reading, and in any case he was unlikely to need the support of such hard evidence. Searching his conscience thoroughly enough, he saw no need for clocking any train times beyond those which were to send him back to London the day after tomorrow. He could afford a certain smugness with himself over the possibility that Frankie might press him to stay longer, assisted no doubt by Daisy, who'd need company for shopping trips and help in wheeling Edie up and down the 7ième, among all the little Aymérics, Gonzagues and Constances in their tartan knickerbockers and navy gabardines. To disappoint them both was something of a moral luxury. Having successfully made his pitch, Adam would return to England with virtuous abruptness, secure in the necessary sense of being wanted and missed.

This element of absence, created from the outset, was essential to the relationship as he now conceived it. There was no question as to its being of the kind which involved settling down, buying a dog, appearing inseparable in public or playing the ungrateful role of that other half for whom provision is grudgingly made at dinner parties and weekends in unofficial exchange for the hosts' right to bitch about him afterwards. Hankering, vacancy, gaps in time, reasoned Adam to himself, must produce those delicious billows of intensity riding on which the pair of them would meet for a handful of hours and days in the various alien cities where Frankie was programmed to triumph. Adam would drop out of the clouds like one of those Baroque deities they'd fantasized about in the ruin, there'd be rapturous squeezes and smotherings in the hugger-mugger of airports and railway stations, carnal, gourmandizing midnights in lofts, entresols and hotels of that artistic sort under which late trams rattle and the rhythmic blink of illuminated advertising whitens the darkness behind the grey window nets. At the post-show bash or the jubilant progress to some restaurant behind the theatre he wouldn't need to worry about feeling as he had the other night after *A Keeper of Flocks* was premièred, a creepy little adjunct to the proceedings, embarrassed by his own presence less because nobody knew who he was than because none of them needed to care. They would love him at once, those dancers and balletomanes and rich hangers-on wrapped in the purity of austerely insouciant chic, for his unexpectedness, his elemental differences from Frankie, for that shrewdly centred calm which, even if he didn't exactly possess it now, he was determined to master out of a growing conviction that his lover would need it more than anything else he had to give.

And after a few years of this pattern of backing and advancing, there'd arrive a moment, perhaps as they sat together in some café or other after a rehearsal or rustled the heavy drifts of leaves off the path winding through some public garden full of statues (somehow there'd have to be statues, with plenty of moss on them), Frankie would say that he was tired of a life of hotel rooms and theatre flats for guest artists or of staying with friends, and that there was nothing left for him in New York that wasn't his family (most of whom were in Boston anyway) so why didn't they buy a place together in London? Get a dog maybe. He'd always wanted a pooch. And they'd both laugh at the idea, because they knew how much it would annoy Daisy.

It seemed to irk her in any case that Adam was here now. His own presence was more rationally accounted for than hers, a fact which probably made her the more crabby. She was always at her edgiest when she had least to complain about. Paris at the beginning of July was still as emphatically self-conscious, peopled and fretfully luminescent as she could have wanted, the warmth in the streets was ingratiating rather than dusty, and the friend's apartment in rue Bonaparte which she had borrowed for the occasion, complete with a Portuguese maid and, for Edie, an immense baldacchino'd cradle supposed to have belonged to the wife of a Napoleonic field marshal, was the perfect *mise en scène* for a week or so of indolent amusement. She ought at least to have seemed grateful for it all, though an impulse towards gratitude was hardly her most instinctive quality. 'Assume a virtue if you have it not.' Instead Adam found her alternating between glum and tetchy, and distinctly unwilling to be cajoled into any more cheerful frame of mind by his offer to cook supper.

'No, that's ridiculous,' she'd said at first. 'We're in Paris, for goodness' sake.'

'So what do you plan to do? Edie's not quite at the Véfour stage, though I expect her menu-reading skills will be finely honed by the time she goes to nursery school.'

Daisy peered at him crossly over the bar of sunlight sloping so seductively into the room.

'We'll manage, I expect.'

Baffled by her hostility and unreason, he was nevertheless determined to remain upbeat.

'I suppose we could go somewhere child-friendly. It might be amusing, late nights for the little princess and all that.'

'Not my idea of amusement,' she muttered, turning back again as if suddenly absorbed by the roofscape opposite. Adam had thought of something flippant to say, but realized almost as soon how inappropriateness triggers catastrophe. They sat, then, in silence. He couldn't remember when it had been like this between the two of them.

At length, for embarrassment's sake as much as anything, he said: 'So have you seen much of Frankie?'

'He's busy, isn't he?'

'He was quite busy when he was staying at Alwyne Villas from what I recall, but that didn't prevent him from seeing people.'

Daisy snorted cynically. 'Oh, he's seeing people all right. Not us, of course, but people.'

Such as, Adam longed to ask. 'But you've met once or twice.'

'Yeah, we did lunch.'

'Frankie likes his lunch.'

'Mm.'

'And then?'

'I don't have to give you my whole bloody social calendar,' she snapped.

'Sorry, I didn't mean . . .'

'You're so fucking well brought-up, aren't you, with your nice manners. I suppose that's what Godalming does to a person.'

'It wasn't Godalming, it was Haslemere,' said Adam, thinking it best to tough out the squall.

'Surrey, Sussex, whatever. I need a glass of wine. You'll find some open in the kitchen.'

Without another word he slipped out across the book-lined passage to rummage about for a glass. The idea that Daisy might already be drunk, in the savage, self-gnawing fashion of baffled attention-seekers, ignobly suggested itself, as did the possibility that he might have to spend the evening looking after Edie, having put her lachrymose, incoherent mother to bed. Nothing in the kitchen, however, hinted that other bottles before this one had recently been swigged.

Neither thanking Adam nor encouraging him to take a drink for himself, which he'd prudently avoided doing on his own initiative, Daisy gulped down the wine with a grimace, as if he had administered it to her on the end of a spoon. Then, with something almost like a charitable impulse, she pulled herself together enough to smile at him, saying:

'Look, you honestly don't need to stick around, Ad, I'll be all right. I've got Edie to see to, she'll wake up in a bit.'

'I just thought it'd be . . .'

'Nice, yeah? Well, tomorrow maybe, unless you've got other plans. I'm simply not on for a comfortable coze tonight.'

'And I was all set to give you a Kate Adie number on the Gaga affair.'

Daisy gave another bleak laugh. 'That? Alice rang this morning and told me all about it. And what Sibby did afterwards, bless her.'

'Sorry?'

'Oh, you'll find out, I can't be fished with all that sort of thing just now. Imagine having a sister who's in mourning for a goose! One better than being in mourning for her husband, I suppose. Do you think she's a dyke?'

'No. Anyway what did she do afterwards?'

'Run along, Ad, there's a poppet.'

Obediently he did so, even while wondering whether Daisy would despise him the more. At an opportune moment he would chide Frankie for neglecting her, yet he still wondered why she was there in the first place, unless, like himself, allured beyond common sense by such ineffable glamour. It ought to have been disheartening, this turning away when he had envisaged an uncomplicated evening with her listening gleefully to his tale of what had happened when Jeremy came back from his jog and found Basil and Will waiting for him like a pair of detective inspectors and what remained of Gaga decently placed inside a sack for interment at the bottom of the garden. Buoyant anticipations of tomorrow, however, made Adam philosophical. He'd go and find somewhere modest and retired near his hotel behind rue de Rennes, where he could sit with a book over the kind of dinner which wouldn't look as if it needed taking too seriously, before going to bed early in a spirit of virtuous abstinence from late-night pleasures he'd automatically have sought out on any other occasion. And before tucking himself up he'd ring Frankie.

The number had been folded neatly into the letter's final phrases. He was glad not to have had to ask Daisy for it. In her current mood she'd either have been unbearably resentful or else withheld it from him completely. There was the agreeable feeling besides of that old complicity between him and Frankie which must enhance the delight of their meeting again. If she suspected anything it wasn't enough, at this juncture, to make her start probing him as she might otherwise have done. Her sudden access of misanthropic peevishness tonight was probably of some use after all. Tomorrow, with everything clarified and aligned, Adam wouldn't specially care if she succeeded in extracting what sooner or later she must have to discover anyway.

Trembling slightly, he tapped out the cipher. It was answered almost at once, and with no hint of surprise, by Frankie himself.

'So we're finally across the little pond.' The voice packed a breathy warmth around its habitual knowingness.

'You make it sound as if we haven't seen each other for ages.'

'A week is a year in the life of a dancer, honey. Tell me you're alone.'

'OK, I'm alone.'

'I'm not sure about the "OK" bit. Can we press the edit button on that?'

'If you like.' Adam cleared his throat, wondering whether he had anything to take should palpitations inconveniently set in. 'What happens if I ask you the same question?'

Frankie had the ghost of a pause. 'You get the same answer. But hey, you should have guessed that.'

'Because I know you well enough by now?'

'Exactly.'

The agreeable sensation started to dawn on Adam of being kept talking for the pleasure of it.

'And how did we find Madame la Marquise *ce soir*?' asked Frankie. 'A little *boudeuse*?'

'Rather too much so.'

'That, my precious, is this season's fucking understatement. I didn't ask her to come.'

'You didn't ask me for that matter.'

Frankie laughed. 'Yeah, right, but you don't sulk like she does.' Adam thought ruefully of the party the other night and of how, without then feeling particularly guilty, he had done little else but sulk. 'We don't pay her to do that, it's not in her contract.'

'Is this how you see us all?'

'Sure. Do you have a problem with that? Friends are there to behave the way you expect. I can't handle interpolations in the score.'

'So you just run away.'

'I guess so. And don't get British all of a sudden and tell me I'm a coward.'

'It's a bit rough on Daisy.'

'So?' There was a little non-specific noise at the end of the phone. Adam wasn't surprised to find himself wondering what, if anything, Frankie had on. 'When am I seeing you, Addy?'

'Tomorrow, I expect,' he answered as nonchalantly as he could manage.

'Tomorrow is perfecto. We have rehearsal scheduled *jusqu'à midi*, and I'm a little busy after that, but why don't you drop by at, like, five o'clock and fix me a *thé anglais*. There's no concierge, just a bell with the name Toledano, can you remember that? It's kind of nice here off Counterscarp Square, we have a roof terrace, *les toits de Paris*, you know the shtik.'

'Yeah, why not?' said Adam, more tremulous than ever.

'I guess you can wait that long. I can't.' And something that it was desirable to suppose a kiss fulsomely blown came down the receiver before Frankie abruptly rang off.

Sleep thereafter was useless and the alternative of reading impossible. In the knowledge that by the time they met tomorrow afternoon he would be too tired to make sense, Adam propped the pillows against his bedhead and sat up, hearing rather than listening to occasional voices rising through the open window from the street, with the murmur of traffic along the boulevard beyond. Such sounds seemed only to sharpen his present loneliness, bring home the realization of how far beyond any rescue he was now in love. It had been stupid pretending he didn't mind the endurance of another seventeen hours. 'Why not now?' he should have said. Before charging wildly across midnight pavements towards Saint-Sulpice and the Panthéon, looming guardians of a logical consummation awaiting him somewhere on the slopes beyond.

For this affair, however, he'd wanted a different style, one whose measured, respect-inducing process would serve to convince him of what he didn't altogether believe, that passion, like taste or judgement, reaches its maturity at last. So for the present he condemned himself to an interval of carefully tempered frustration, in which it seemed only natural to prepare as meticulously as possible his words, not to speak of his whole script, for tomorrow. Even for the sake of humouring Frankie's most cherished Yankee notions of English gaucherie Adam wasn't going to descend to the full Hugh Grant number, blurting it out as a spontaneous confession while the blue gaze dwelt on such awkwardness with a luminous, half-smiling indulgence.

Besides, what was there to confess? That he'd fallen in love must have been obvious from the sedulously crafted reticences of his own letter, by which, as days passed, he grew less and less embarrassed. Hadn't Frankie something to acknowledge in return? Via those peculiarly precise sequences of emotional archaeology through which lovers refresh the truth of experience, Adam found himself assembling a little vivid collection of finds and evidences from the previous three months, which should serve to bolster his confidence when he at least found the courage to speak. The moonlit ramble to the Hermitage he was now tempted to see as the clincher of a whole series of events which, however casually occurring in themselves, had combined to form an inescapable momentum. He remembered Frankie's coquetry after the rehearsal in Farringdon when they'd first met, the curious amalgam of lust and anger in his eyes that afternoon of the grand walk-out from Maschera, the night at Daisy's when his propositioning had seemed too easy for simple acceptance, and all those other instants, on the telephone, in the theatre, a giggling, self-parodic shopping trawl beginning in Knightsbridge and ending in Soho, slumming at a tapas bar in Shoreditch after a gallery opening when the pair of them had pronounced a shade too loudly on the installations for the comfort of the artists present, moments when it had seemed that the merest nudge or tap, should Adam choose to offer it, must compel Frankie to a confession. For it was only bravado, wasn't it, which kept him silent, a mixture of his homosexual horror of getting serious with something of that real-men-don't-kiss impulse by which backroom tricks preserve themselves against the insidious menaces of unsafe affection or that girly thing called tenderness. Hating banality as much as he did, Frankie must see this reaction at last as nothing more than a vulgar commonplace and move as swiftly and elegantly as possible beyond it.

Adam did not dream of him when, eventually, with the earliest light of dawn through the hotel curtains, he fell asleep. The Parisian day thereafter was a kind of occupational therapy programme designed, not to take his mind off the meeting ahead – that was impossible – but to afford him, as he soon realized, a means of offering the impression that there hadn't been a moment to spare for overmuch hankering and expectation. He did not ring Daisy. By tomorrow, he sensed, she would have stewed long enough in her unspecified disappointment with Frankie, and by then, if he needed a shoulder to cry on, her cynicism and asperity would prove sovran against self-pity. After an exceedingly slow lunch, he dawdled back to the hotel and lay on his bed, periodically looking at his watch, feeling like an officer in the trenches waiting for the signal to dash across no-man's-land in a raid to collar a Boche. Then he undressed, went into the shower and soaped himself laboriously all over. Because you never knew, and Americans – though not necessarily always Frankie – were awfully particular about that sort of thing. It was one of the many reasons why they made such lousy travellers. With his clothes on and his hair brushed and a little spritz of Eau d'Issey behind the ears, Adam looked at himself in the glass. Not for the first time did he wish he were taller, less tubby and plump-cheeked. The total effect, as always, was of someone not quite grown up, an impression which however at odds with his anxiety over being thirty-five, did nothing at all to mitigate it.

The walk would do him good, but he needed to time it carefully. Too soon would look clamorous, puppyish, positively amateur. On the other hand he didn't want to overemphasize the casual aspect, in case it gave Frankie the wrong ideas. So he zigzagged somewhat, round the back of the Luxembourg, past the Ecole Nationale, into the bottom of Boul Mich and along rue Soufflot, pausing here and there for breath in the patches of afternoon shade. When at length he reached the edge of Place de la Contrescarpe and turned into the street behind it where the apartment was, he realized there was still an unseasonable five minutes in hand. Going back towards a bar on the corner, he lurked there with a coffee, the last thing in the world to steady his nerves, hoping not to be visible, through some malign coincidence, from the roof terrrace. Then it was time. Positioning himself once more in front of the house he pressed 'Toledano' and the door clicked open almost at once with an apocalyptic loudness. Up the narrow staircase, smelling so nicely of beeswax, he heard another door being opened. And there, on the next landing to which he rose, stood Frankie, looking ever so faintly grotesque in cropped orange trousers, a pair of blue Birkenstocks and an Albanian waistcoat with frogging across the front.

'All you need are dreadlocks, an Alice band, some pink shades and a pencil moustache, and you could go to the party as Galliano at his next collection,' said Adam.

'Hey!' was all Frankie's response, accompanied by a we're-going-to-have-fun smile and an embrace which might have been described as abstractedly fraternal. Do I get a kiss, thought Adam, do I bollocks.

'We've had ourselves a coffee, no?'

'A *grand crème*, to be precise.'

'I should have guessed no less. Only big cream for the English mister.' Frankie stood, hands on hips, planted firmly in the doorway. 'We've missed you, mister.'

'So much that you're not going to ask me in?'

For a second he turned to look over his shoulder, as if making quite certain it was safe.

'*Prego, si accommodi, signore.*'

Something distant and mocking in his air made Adam nervous again. Nothing had prepared him, in any case, for the apparent vastness of the apartment. Having walked down one corridor lined with gilt mirrors, marble-topped tables and halfway decent portraits of men in wigs, they walked up another full of Tibetan scrolls and porcelain camels till they came to a door behind whose leaves it might have been expected that a pair of footmen was waiting to fling them open. The room beyond had busts in the corners, a Pompeiian freize, black curule chairs with curved backs and a sofa resting on couchant sphinxes. It was absolutely the last place in the world where Adam could have imagined himself making a declaration, let alone a commitment.

'Doesn't suit you, Frankie,' he said.

'Maybe that's the reason I like it,' said Frankie, kicking his clogs off and stretching catlike across the sofa. 'Culturally confusing, no? Did you think it was going to be Muji meets Philippe Starck? Uh-huh, baby, not this one. Ari does interiors for the ladies in the big chateaux.' Sha-Toze. 'He's in Venice right now with Roger.' Ro-Zhay. 'So when he offered, who was

I to refuse? And it's kind of fun playing palaces for a while.'

He pulled his knees up under his chin, cosying his back against the cylindrical cushion, his smile laden with discomfiting suggestions of a willingness to be entertained.

'So what did we do today, while poor me was trying to get this dumb-ass French bitch they've got for the Muse to count correctly? It's not my fault she flunked math in grade school, but if she can't do simple steps . . .' Frankie paused, beaming indulgently as if suddenly realizing he had somebody else there. 'Addy, you've got to forgive me, rehearsal was a real mess. Now tell me what you did, run it past me.'

Again he stretched out full-length, placing his hands behind his head, so that the embroidered waistcoat fell back to reveal the black fuzz in his armpits. Adam couldn't help noticing, was quick indeed to notice, that a couple of the metal studs on the fly of his trousers had come undone. Nicer to think they were unfastened already.

'After breakfast,' Adam rather reluctantly began, 'I went across the river to the Place des Vosges and just wandered about a bit . . .'

'And called on Madame de Sévigné?'

'She went out.'

Frankie giggled at the ceiling. '*Je suis désolé*. Darling, everyone's out in the Marais. It's in to be out on rue Sainte-Croix.' He giggled once more. 'De la Bretonnerie, whatever that may be. And then?'

'I went for a drink at Charbon.'

'Oberkampff! *Que tu es câblé*!'

'And then it was time for lunch.'

The blue eyes swivelled towards him, wide with expertly simulated astonishment. 'You mean you didn't find time to seduce a nice preppy young *étudiant* doing *sciences po*, whose mommy has horses and a *manoir en Normandie* and at least sixty-four quarterings of nobility? Addy, you're a disgrace.' Frankie sat up once more. 'So how was lunch? Or rather, where was it?'

Adam could bear it no longer. 'Do you very much mind,' he asked, 'if we don't talk about lunch just now?'

'OK.' Frankie beamed anew. 'Some things are best forgotten, some Parisian lunches best of all.'

'There's something else, something . . .'

But the other was too quick for him, springing up from the sofa in a parade of agony.

'Shit! I promised, how could I be such a selfish bastard?'

'What?'

'*Le thé anglais*, of course. Addy precious, hold it there, don't fly away, read a magazine, I'll be right back,' and in a moment he had slipped out of the room.'

The delaying tactic was evident, but to cover what? It could only be embarrassment. Adam needed simply to keep his nerve and play by these new rules. He wasn't going to let Frankie chicane his way out of things just for the sake of some emotional face-saving. So he sat there with a copy of *Elle Décoration* on his knee, quiet yet primed to spring, like one of the ebony sofa sphinxes, until after what seemed like an age Frankie returned bearing a laden tea tray.

'I asked Marcel to bring us the madeleines, but he got careless — it's some book he's writing — so we'll have to eat these foofy little nut cookies instead. Not exactly an *aide-mémoire*, but I guess we'll manage. This is where I do my Martha Stewart. Sugar?'

'Yes?'

Frankie laughed apologetically. 'I mean, do you want sugar? Like in your tea? And cream? Oh yes, of course, I forgot, you like *lots* of cream.'

'Frankie, I . . .'

'There!' he cried, clapping the saucer on to the table beside Adam with an air of satanic beatitude. 'Nobody can say I don't look after my guest artistes.'

'I've got something I want to tell you,' persisted Adam bluntly.

'Try the nut waffles, be my official food-taster, and if they're poisoned I promise you we'll stage a funeral at Père Lachaise no less.'

'I've thought about it for a long time,' continued Adam, pointedly ignoring the hazelnut wafers. 'And I tried to let you know in that letter I sent you.'

'Mm, gorgeous, or what's that English word, "scrumptious"?' Frankie lay back against the sofa, kicking his feet in the air, and repeated 'Skerumpshissss! Nuts, they're just so sexy they're to eat! I should have been in TV commercials, I'm wasted on fucking dance.'

'I honestly didn't think you'd answer.'

'Maybe that's what I need to get me back to the States for good. Like a vocational crisis or something. Did you know I have a brother who's a priest? In Cambridge, can you imagine? That's Cambridge, Mass. They call him the Professors' Confessor. His real name is Salvatore.'

'Then when I got your letter it rather changed things.'

'We call him Sal, only that's kind of nelly, like Sal Mineo in *East of Eden*, who got himself a premature end to a promising career, from a hustler down some mean street.'

Adam, feeling his gorge rise, wondered whether he might actually be sick and what it would look like on Ari Toledano's beautiful Aubusson carpet. In any case, he realized, he was close to tears. He held silent for an instant, purely in order to trip up Frankie's intolerably deliberate logorrhoea.

'It made it easier,' he said at length.

'What made it easier?' asked Frankie reluctantly, keeping his eyes on the Pompeiian garlands.

'The letter. I mean your letter.'

'That was not exactly my intention. If you make life easy for people, they get lazy and start to assume things.'

'Hadn't I a right to assume something?' said Adam, his voice starting to shake.

'Nope.' Frankie sat up, resting on one arm. 'I guess you better tell me,' he said with a certain weariness, 'though maybe I already know.'

'Then you wrote that letter already knowing I was in love with you.'

'Sure I did.' He glanced fiercely at Adam. 'That doesn't mean I believed you.'

Adam's voice had sunk to a whisper. 'If I tell you now . . . that I love you . . . will you still not believe me?'

'Yeah,' was all Frankie muttered, in a kind of amazement, as though it were something which should have been instinctively understood. 'I wouldn't believe you, not in a million years. And nothing you could do would convince me.'

'But if you knew . . .'

'Oh I did, Adam.' He hugged his knees defensively under his chin. 'From day one. It happens all the time, and I don't mind, it feels kinda nice. But its name isn't love, that's for sure.'

'You're going to throw that old sophistry at me, aren't you, the one about the difference between loving and being in love.'

'No doubt.'

'And I'm going to chuck it back in your face, together with most of the furniture. Because I . . . Oh Jesus, Frankie, you don't know.' Adam heard himself squeak as the tears began, 'how can you, you're so fucking in control all the time.'

'God, how I wish,' murmured Frankie.

'And just because I'm not doesn't give you the right to . . .'

'To what? It's like I'm hurting you by telling you this?'

Adam's face crumpled into disbelief. 'How dare you say that, when you know it's true? I . . . I just can't . . .'

What had tipped him over the edge was the mere fact of Frankie seated there, poised and rigid, waiting for him to finish. Doubling up with wretchedness, Adam leaned against the chair-back's hard, black-lacquered curve as if it had been a ship's side and hurled himself into abject, choking sobs. For a long time Frankie offered no hint of consolation. Then apparently judging that matters had gone far enough, he got up, and coming towards Adam, knelt down deftly behind the chair, took his face between both hands and whispered:

'Hey, Addy, you don't love me. OK?'

'Stop telling me what I feel.'

'It's what you don't feel,' persisted Frankie, tyrannically sagacious and calming. 'You do not love me.'

'I do!' Adam wailed, at which Frankie snorted with indulgent laughter.

'I don't think so. Oh, Addy, what do you need so you can understand? You're not even in love with who you think I am. Which is probably more real than who I actually am. God, are we getting philosophical here?' With a tenderness which seemed nothing short of outrageous, he continued to cradle Adam's head in his hands. 'No, it's been something else completely, from the moment you saw me in – what's the name of that square?'

'Canonbury,' sniffed Adam instinctively.

'Yeah, right. I know because I read it in your face. You didn't want me.'

'Don't be ridiculous.'

Frankie cast his eyes heavenwards. 'You didn't want me. You wanted to change places. You wanted what I've got, my arms, my legs, my nose, my ass, my dick maybe, though for some reason it wasn't on display just then. Because you know what? You're one little jealous queen.'

'No!' Adam recoiled furiously.

'Yes, fucking yes, a thousand times, admit it, my envious baby! And you're not the first and you won't be last. Something deep inside wants to hang me in your closet like this season's Prada and put me on. *Le tout ensemble*, the lover *prêt à porter*. And you know I'm not going to let anybody do that number. I've been there, I've mixed the wannabe cocktail with ice and tabasco and angostura bitters.'

'You? You never wanted to be anyone else.'

'Jesus, quit the adoration bit for a second, can't you? Get a hold of who I am. Somebody perfectly imperfect, if that doesn't sound too glib.'

Frankie stood up, put on his shoes and paced across the room to stare out of the window or else to take a breath of needed air. Then, with an unexpected briskness, he announced:

'Adam, I want you to leave.'

Dazed, Adam felt himself straightening up all of a sudden.

'And then I want you to tell yourself you'll never come back. And that you'll never feel ashamed of what you just told me.'

'As you'd probably say, I'm too British not to do that. Being American is all about trying not to feel guilty for anything.'

Frankie laughed ruefully. 'Maybe. It's why everyone except me does therapy. Therapy means never having to say you're sorry. God, that's embarrassing!' he spread wide his arms, magnanimous. 'I envy you, Addy, can you imagine that?'

'Don't patronize me, Frankie, that's not fair.'

Frankie drew himself upright, defensive yet more completely engaged than he'd ever seemed to Adam in the past. 'Possibly you'll never understand why, but I'm not going to explain, because I'm not your teacher. Just remember that I envy you, that's all. For ever, I guess. So that makes me one jealous queen too.'

His radiant, comprehending smile appeared to affirm some sort of new compact between them, as if, against the emotional odds, they could begin again as friends. He put out his hand to clasp that of the uncertain Adam, who would never know whether the gesture was one of acknowledgement or merely of farewell. For as Frankie did so, the door opened quietly and Paul walked into the room.

'Have you nicked my fags again?' he muttered sleepily 'They were on the table by the bed.' He stood there for a moment, blinking towards their shared silence and scratching the crotch of a pair of floppy blue-and-white-striped boxer shorts, out of which the end of his cock hung down against his thigh. In anger and incredulity more intense for the vagueness of their origin, Adam stared at Frankie, whose scowl all too easily implied that the intrusion had been unscheduled.

'They're on the bookshelf,' he said. 'Adam is . . .'

'Just leaving, as it happens,' said Adam, and raced towards the door. Blundering down the alley of Tibetan prayer wheels and Tang horses, he quickened his pace almost to a run as he heard Frankie come hurtling after him, crying:

'Addy, wait, for Christ's sakes, you can't just . . .'

Adam spun round, almost dancing in the exuberance of his rage as Frankie came towards him among the periwigs and ormolu.

'It's like before, do you remember? At the restaurant?

Lavender custard and beef teriyaki with plum chutney? I wish you'd choked on them, you fucking tosser!'

Frankie held up both palms in a desperate gesture of negotiation towards an incandescent Adam.

'And for goodness' sake button your fly, Francesco, you look ridiculous like that!'

'Come on, Addy, don't get mad at me just because of Paul.'

Wrenching open the apartment door, Adam got out on to the staircase with Frankie still following.

'Get some new trousers, orange doesn't suit you,' he flung up the stairwell, 'and those Birkenstocks are totally last year!'

The street door banged with a sumptuous European heaviness of bolts and hinges as he tottered, still dizzy with indignation, on to the pavement.

The late afternoon spread a smug varnish over the city. It was a time which ordinarily Adam loved best, *le cinq à sept*, when the air becomes charged with lubricious possibilities and a vague yet potent sense of something expectant and available transfigures the faces on the café terraces, in shops or along the platforms of the Metro. He contemplated these hours now with a kind of satanic exultation sharpened by the uselessness of any sort of rage at Frankie's prodigal arrogance. Let them destroy one another, let Paul's imbecile beauty wither in his embarrassing attempts to hang on to it, let Frankie turn to ashes in the acrid consciousness of what he had lost for the sake of a hairy six-pack, a flat stomach, a flunkey's calves and an arse like a fives court. As for his own sense of overflowing absurdity, that must endure a little while yet, but within a few minutes Adam had begun to recognize the approach of that deliverance from the tyranny of self, that renewal of a connection with the world, whereby the defeated lover clambers back towards something like dignity.

He made towards his hotel along the way he had come, but this time wandered into the Luxembourg, as if the gardens, with their early evening strollers, might act as a medicine for the raw consciousness of his injury. For a while he walked slowly along the neat alleys, glancing furtively at those around him with the sort of envy which foolishly assumes the presence of an unsensitized contentment in everybody but oneself, and remembering what he had once told Theo about his father's account of going back to school on the train.

'Ad?'

He turned round, not seeing at first who it was.

'Adam? We're over here.'

Daisy sat on one of the benches along the avenue, with Edie in a yellow smock placed commandingly in her buggy, being gently trundled to and fro by a sad-looking woman with heavy eyebrows and a chignon.

'This is Maria. They're always called Maria in Portugal. She's actually Maria das Dores, which means Mary of the Sorrows, and she comes with the flat.'

'I was going to call you,' lied Adam.

'Then I suppose Frankie got in the way.'

'A bit. But he isn't any longer. We had tea.'

'I know. He's just phoned me on the mobile.' Daisy's countenance had adopted an air of virtuous reproach. 'You've upset him, Ad.'

'Yessss! I meant to. Perhaps it doesn't occur to you that he might have upset me. Or are you going to tell me I don't matter?'

'You wouldn't let him explain.'

'Paul did everything that was necessary.' Adam's stare disconcerted her, as he intended. 'How long have you known?'

Daisy shrugged. 'Your cousin Al told me, but I'd guessed before that.'

'You're lying.'

'No I'm not.'

'Yes you are, you just can't bear not to seem wised-up about everything that's going on between your friends. Presumably you discussed it with Frankie.'

'Presumably.'

Adam felt a hollowness within him, followed almost at once by a spurt of righteous fury at Frankie's betrayal of confidence.

'You wanted me to fail,' he said with lethal softness.

She laughed a shade uneasily. 'Why on earth should I? You know I can't stand losers?'

'It's true, only you'll never admit it. Or anything else. The pair of you are as bad as each other.' He scuffed the gravel with the toe of his shoe. 'Do you know who I feel like just now?'

'Surprise me.'

'I feel like the soldier in Baz's story about the shark, when the jaws get hold of him. "And in that moment he knew who he was." Why didn't you like that story?'

'I never said I didn't.' Daisy leaned back wearily against the bench. 'All right, I hated it. I'm glad it didn't get published. Satisfied?'

'More than you'll ever be. Ring me at my hotel if you feel like it. And you can tell Frankie I'm sorry I called him a tosser. I should have thought of something more original, but you know how it is in situations like that, your inspiration just flies out of the window. Bye-bye, Edie darling, look after mum, there's a poppet.'

Pleased with himself, he returned to the hotel, took a luxurious shower and read for an hour or two before setting out to dine in solitary state, with the money he had been preparing to spend on Frankie, at a restaurant off avenue Wagram. Afterwards he repaired to a poky little art cinema and sat through an idiotic German film in which people sang bits of the statue scene from *Don Giovanni* and occasionally turned into pigs. He might have gone to a club, Depot or La Luna perhaps, but scorned the idea of capitalizing on his disappointment via recreational sex. It was so unfair to the partner, anonymous or otherwise, to use him merely as a vessel for the see-if-I-care process by which a damaged ego was to be put back together. Thus morally satisfied but still bruised from that day's events, Adam went to bed alone. As he expected, no message had come from Daisy.

He could not quite bring himself to ring her before he left at lunchtime for Gare du Nord. Punishment had always seemed to him a contemptible business, however it was managed. Nevertheless, there was the faintest possibility that she might wonder why he had abandoned her there in the gardens and realize it was because she had no business letting him know of her tête-à-têtes with Frankie. It was entirely typical of Daisy that she should fail to appreciate how much, in all this, Adam had been hurt, preferring instead to cherish the image of Frankie as a martyr to wounded sensibility.

Calmer now, and sobered besides by wisdom after the event, Adam, scudding across the dull, sunlit plain into the tunnel, grew puzzled with the recollected image of Frankie running towards him down that corridor full of marble and periwigs. The bitterness of failure and self-deception was softened by the realization that in that brief instant when he turned to face those vainly pacifying hands, he was the one who fixed the terms, leaving Frankie pleading and confused. Having been ordered to leave, he was being begged to stay, apparently because Paul had fluffed his entrance cue and the scenario had somehow wrenched itself out of sequence. It was just possible to imagine that for this unprofessional solecism the Greek would never be forgiven, yet even more desirable to think of Frankie being merciless with himself for having allowed so gross an interruption.

This then was to be his perpetual sentence. Otherwise Adam had had enough of even a notional justice. Punishing Jeremy for Gaga's death was foolishly vindictive insofar as it was the result of a horrified impulse. A certain crude sense of fairness in the wish to put Theo right had been rapidly succeeded, for Adam, by a shameful vision of himself as the wrecker of that painstakingly constructed armature of happiness and desire around which almost the whole of his friend's existence had shaped itself for the past six months. He remembered now, as self-absorption had hitherto prevented him from remembering, Theo's pole-axed acknowledgement of the identity of the figure in the photograph, following an initial flourish of heroic disbelief. With what had thereafter seemed an amazing single-mindedness he had left for the theatre and somehow dragged himself through that night's performance, before returning to sit up alone, almost till morning, with that image of his lover who was also unaccountably a fantasist, or else, less politely, the most thumping liar.

Separating Guy from Jeremy, a process not without its imaginative complications, Adam understood how lying, more than anything else, must rank as the principal offence. That largeness of gesture and engagement so enviable in Theo, the assumption that others would always match him in frankness, trust and integrity, had been cynically rejected by Jeremy in favour of a selfish projection of amusement achieved through an elaborate imposture, more attractive, no doubt, for being so expensive. Embarrassed by the thought of how much Theo's expectations had built on this very contrivance, as well as by his own part in engineering its collapse, Adam had avoided him as far as possible the next day, slipping out early with his bag to Waterloo after leaving a hastily scribbled note indicating that he'd be back on Wednesday afternoon. It was bad enough now to be returning with nothing but a bleak sense of having snatched a scrap or two of self-respect from his débâcle with Frankie, but to have to face Theo as the instrument of his unhappiness was not something to which Adam felt equal in his current rawness to the touch.

Nesh, wasn't that what Basil always called it? Thinking of the Cave of Spleen as a useful refuge for the next few hours until Theo had left for the theatre, he considered ringing Basil from the station, but then recalled that Betsy had made one of her lightning descents earlier in the week, en route to Jakarta, and that a metaphorical 'Don't Disturb' hung outside till she was gone. The sense of others pottering on with the ordinary demands of existence made Adam sigh audibly as he lifted down his bag. There was Alice to be called, largely in order to find out about Serena, though she'd almost certainly require edited highlights from Paris in exchange. And there was Jeremy – oh God, yes, Jeremy – to be neutralized or pacified in the wake of everything that had happened.

His heart sank as he descended to the platform. For a time he was half afraid to budge from where he stood, as if taking up a fixed abode within this enclave of the transitory and the impermanent must guarantee him a safety from any further involvement with his kind. Gloomily he started to move through the barriers and out on to the concourse, below the inexorable glare of daylight through the glass panels above it. How hot and thick the air suddenly felt! He should have been wearing shorts, like the man standing directly in front of him, little black shorts like those, and a black vest. The man smiling so broadly at him, who only reminded him of Theo because he couldn't have been anybody else.

'What the . . . I don't . . .'

'Aren't you going to give me a hug, Adsy? It's what you're meant to do.'

'You are such a jammy bastard, Theo Lestrange. How ever did you know?'

Theo grinned. 'Took a gamble, didn't I? But I'd have waited for the next one anyway. I know it isn't an airport, and "I as your friend, not as your lover speak", but it's still someone here to meet you like you wanted, remember?'

Adam shook his head. 'You're the one who remembered, The.'

'And do you know what, Aubrey gave me his car, the blue BMW convertible, while they're in Italy staying with some poncey QC at a villa with a swimming pool and its own olive oil. The law's pulled me over three times already, "Excuse me, sir, are you the owner of this car?" They have to call me sir after the Lawrence case, but they still think I've got a stash somewhere in the boot.' Theo picked up Adam's bag. 'So, my little Adipose, we can go home in style.'

With lingering amazement Adam followed Theo to the car. When they'd settled themselves and Theo was about to start, he suddenly turned and said:

'It's not all right, is it? You haven't been Agatha.'

'How do you know?' said Adam, biting his lip.

'Because in the first few seconds you'd have told me if you had. It's the way you are. And you haven't.' He ruffled Adam's hair. 'I'm ever so sorry, Ads.'

Adam laughed. '*You* are?'

'Anything wrong with that?'

'In the script it should have been me, except it was sorry grovelling rather than sorry compassionate.'

'I don't understand.'

'About the business with Jeremy and the photograph. I suppose you must have forgiven me or else you wouldn't be doing all this.'

'Only creeps never forgive,' said Theo grandly. 'I told him he'd got to do the same. He wanted to murder you, but I said it was unworthy, so he'll settle for just a spot of resentment.'

'Did you meet him at the flat?'

'What remains of it. Somebody completely trashed the place, sort of brilliantly, if you see what I mean. I think it's someone he knows. But come on, we'd better be off lickety-split, 'cos I've got a show to do and we've had ace notices, except one critic said it was too homo-friendly, too much getting our tits out for the lads.'

Theo's driving had the sort of panache which brings the passenger's heart into the mouth. As they neared the Elephant and he slowed down a little, Adam said:

'Mind if I come to the show tonight, The? I mean, do you think you can get me a seat? Otherwise I'll queue for returns.'

'You don't need to go on feeling guilty, sweetheart.'

'I'd love to see it, honestly. I don't think you can legitimately put me off any more.'

They had swung round into Kennington when Theo chose unexpectedly to turn off along a side street between ware-houses and brought the car to a halt.

'What's happened?' asked Adam.

'Nothing,' said Theo, unfastening his seat belt, then, laughing, 'I suppose that's the point really, isn't it? I just thought it was time we kissed, that's all?' and leaning over so that Adam caught the delicious wood-ash musk of his sweat, he took him in his arms.

'I'd really like it if you saw the show tonight. If I knew you were out there. And then afterwards we can go to a club and be Agatha.'

'Somewhere where there aren't loads of boys drinking Jack Daniel's and Coke and mugging to Steps with bent straws behind their ears.'

'Then tomorrow I can play you this Rosenmüller disc I got, and maybe we can do the Fort, if we still feel up for it.'

'We're little gay boys, we're always up for it. Rosenmüller, wickeeed!'

'Do you think he's handbag or hardbag?'

'Definitely handbag. He was one of us, dontcherknow. Got done for sex with a choirboy in Stuttgart, I fancy it was, and had to run away to Venice. Lickety-split.'

'He's the new obsession, I prefer him to Diedrich Becker.'

'Well, you would, wouldn't you?'

'Don't look so glum,' said Theo, and putting his large thumbs on either side of Adam's mouth he pulled them upwards. 'That's your facial exercise for the next few weeks,' he said. 'It's not quite a smile, but it'll do to be going on with.'

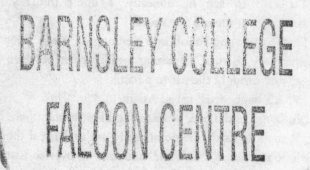